SHANGHAI DREAMS

A WWII DRAMA TRILOGY BOOK TWO

ALEXA KANG

✿ Created with Vellum

ACKNOWLEDGMENTS

Shanghai Dreams has been a monumental project, and I would like say a special thank you to those who had helped me along the way. This book wouldn't have been possible without them.

Thank you to my editor Kristen Tate, for making sure I stay grounded and keeping me in the right head space when, after working on my manuscript for months, I could no longer view my work in an objective light. Thank you, too, to my other editor (and U.S. veteran) Aaron Sikes, for his insights and advice on my action scenes.

Thank you also to Keri Knutson of Alchemy Book Covers and Design for creating such beautiful covers for this series. So often while I was writing, I would look at the covers to imagine what Clark and Eden were like in various scenes.

Thank you to my friend Mylius Fox, author of the thriller novel *Bandit*, who has been on my author journey with me since my first book, *Rose of Anzio - Moonlight*. His input and advice on writing and publishing, as well as moral support, have been wonderful and invaluable.

Lastly, thanks to my husband, Dan, for being the most

understanding, the most patient, and the most supportive person to me all summer as I buried myself in the bat cave writing this book.

On October 30, 2018, one of my all-time favorite authors, Jin Yong (aka Louis Cha), had passed away. To say Jin Yong is a titan in Chinese literature is an understatement. It would be rare for a Chinese person or anyone of Chinese heritage to not know him or be familiar with his work. Jin Yong is known for his Chinese historical martial arts novels (*wuxia*). He began writing serialized stories in 1950 for the Hong Kong daily paper *Ming Pao*. All of his work has been made into TV series and movies. Numerous remakes had been produced over the years because the Chinese audience couldn't get enough of them.

I grew up watching those TV series. But as an adult, I have read all of his books. When I was a freshman in college, I even skipped classes for three days reading one of his series. I couldn't put the books down.

The closest work in English I can compare his stories to is *The Lord of the Rings*. I am a huge fan of *LOTR*, but based on my utmost objective opinion, Jin Yong's stories are even better than *LOTR*. Jin Yong's plots are riveting. His characters are complex. Through them, he conveyed his insights on human flaws, desires, and behaviors. He used his stories and characters as a way to illustrate his views and observations on politics; in particular, the hypocrisy of politicians, corruption stemming from the hunger for power, and criticisms against Mao Zedong's communist regime. His books were banned in mainland China until after

Mao's death. They were also banned in Taiwan, ironically for being deemed supportive of Mao's Communist Party.

Most people who can't read Chinese have never heard of Jin Yong because few of his work has been translated. In my opinion, his books are not translatable. For one thing, he wrote them in classical Chinese language. Even Chinese today no longer write this way. His prose is poetic, creative, and exquisite. His writing is witty and full of cultural connotations. His mastery of the Chinese language is unimaginable. His skills were a gift and a curse. He could manipulate the Chinese language so well, it is impossible for any non-Chinese readers to fully see the elegance of his writing by reading a translated version. All the subtlety and cultural concepts would be lost too.

This year, MacLehose Press produced a translation of one of his stories, *Legend of the Condor Heroes*. I understand that the translator had put a lot of efforts into the book. Nonetheless, I'm afraid the translated versions will never be even half as excellent as the original. Some of the proper names in the translated version make me cringe. To me, they sound kitschy and too oriental exotic. I honestly believe that, in foreign languages, a TV production or movies would be the better medium to showcase Jing Yong's stories to a foreign audience.

That said, some literary establishments in foreign countries are aware of his contributions. Jin Yong had been awarded honorary fellowship at both Universities of Cambridge and Oxford. He was also the recipient of the Order of the British Empire by the British government, and the *Chevalier de la Légion d'Honneur*, and a *Commandeur de l'Ordre des Arts et des Lettres* by the French government. Unfortunately, the powers that be had declined to offer him the Nobel Prize in literature. This, I think, is a travesty!

As a writer, I can only dream of ever achieving anything remotely as good as Jin Yong's creations. He is, still, in a class of his own. However, he will always be my inspiration. I like writing epic tales. Through his works, I learned that there are no boundaries as to how big and epic a story can be. His books taught me how to create characters that readers would want to read about. I'm very fortunate to have a chance here to pay him a small tribute. At some point, maybe I'll give it a shot to unofficially translate one of his stories myself.

And now, I join the chorus of his fans who would say to him: Master Cha, I wish you a peaceful journey.

CONTENTS

PREFACE

AUTHOR'S NOTE ON LANGUAGE

The following information on Chinese language had already been given in Book One of the *Shanghai Story* trilogy. Minor details have been added in Book Two, *Shanghai Dreams*, and are indicated below. I hope these explanations will help readers who are not familiar with the Chinese language, and ensure they have a fully immersive read and a good reading experience.

(i) Dialogues between Chinese characters have been written as closely as possible to how Chinese people actually speak, with inclusions of Chinese colloquialism to add authenticity. In some parts, the dialogues of Chinese characters may defy an English reader's expectation of how something would be said. Some parts might also come across a little bit odd. However, I can assure you these are not errors. I made a sincere effort to ensure that the dialogues would read smoothly and naturally to English readers, and also be true to how these dialogues would be spoken in Chinese.

(ii) To adhere to authenticity, the use of honorifics was unavoidable. Chinese people often address others by honorifics instead of names. Simple salutation would not be enough, and depending on the person being addressed, salutation as used in English would also be wrong. My editorial team and I considered adding footnotes, but ultimately decided it would disrupt your reading experience. Therefore, I have decided instead to provide below a list of honorifics used in this book and their explanations.

(iii) [_Added_: There are some parts of the Chinese dialogues in this book that sound like contemporary colloquial English. These were not oversights nor anachronism. In these instances, the statement would actually be spoken in Chinese the same way as it would be spoken in English. I found this very interesting, and it shows that people have similar ways of expressing themselves, even if their languages are different and they live continents apart.]

(iv) Finally, except for references to certain locations in Shanghai, I have chosen to apply _pinyin_ for Romanization of Chinese names and words used in this story. For those who are not familiar with the pronunciation of _pinyin_, I hope this will help:

"q" is pronounced "ch"
"g" is pronounced like "g" in "gas"
"x" is pronounced "sh"
"c" is pronounced "ts", as in "bits"
"zh" is pronounced like the Polish "cz"

Honorifics:

- _Ge_: means older brother.
- _Jie_: means older sister.
- _xiao jie_: means Miss.
- _Da xiao jie_: means "first Miss." Before and up to the pre-war era, servants addressed the daughters of the family they work for as "Miss." When the family has more

than one daughters, the servants would address the daughters by their birth order. *"Da"* means "biggest." *Da xiao jie* means "first Miss."

- *Shifu*: means driver.
- *Amah*: means "a mother" and was used to address a female servant, often one whose work involved childcare.
- Uncle, Aunt, Auntie: the honorifics are often used to address someone who is a friend of one's parents, as well as siblings of parents.
- [*Added*: *Xiong*, meaning older brother, but when used for addressing someone, it would only come up when the speaker is speaking to someone who is not a blood relative or in his own family. It is used more commonly between two men in a conversation, as a polite way to address each other.]

Note also that *Ge* and *Jie* are often used to address someone who is not a blood relative, but who the speaker holds in higher regards. In such cases, *"Ge"* or *"Jie"* is always added to the first name (and occasionally the last name) of the person being addressed.

I hope the above guide will enhance your reading experience. You can read more about the process of how *Shanghai Story* was created in the Afterword at the end of this book. And now, let's begin this story and step back in time to the glamorous and treacherous world of Old Shanghai in 1936.

List of Main Asian Characters

Note: Surnames of Chinese and Japanese characters are placed first except when shown last and separated by comma.

The Yuan Family

Clark Yuan (Yuan Guo-Hui) - Son of a prominent Chinese family in Shanghai. He recently returned from America after studying abroad and graduating college. He is addressed as **Young Master Yuan** by Chinese servants and in public. He is also addressed in honorific as *Guo-Hui Ge* by his younger sisters, with *Ge* (pronounced "guh") meaning "older brother", and **Yuan Xiong** by non-blood relatives sometimes, with *xiong* also meaning "older brother".

Wen-Ying, Yuan - Younger sister of Clark. Her family servants address her in the honorific as **Daxiaojie**, meaning "Eldest Miss".

Mei Mei/Wen-Li, Yuan - Youngest sister of Clark. **Mei Mei** is her nickname. Her family servants address her in the honorific as **Erxiaojie**, meaning "Second Miss".

Master Yuan Ren-Qiu - Clark's father. He is addressed as Master Yuan by Chinese servants and in public.

Madam Yuan - Clark's Mother.

Other Main Characters in Alphabetical Order
(Minor characters excluded)

Chiang Kai-Shek, Generalissimo - President of the Republic of China and leader of *Kuomintang* (KMT), the Chinese Nationalist Party.

Dai Li - Head of *Juntong*, the Chinese Secret Police.

Gao Zhen, Director - Family friend of the Yuans. Director of the Shanghai Commercial and Savings Bank.

Huang Shifu - Yuan family chauffeur. *Shifu* is not a name but a way of addressing drivers.

Konoe Kenji, Captain - Member of Japanese *Kizoku* (Japanese equivalent to nobility), of the family Konoe, who ares descendants of the Fujiwara clan. Military attaché to the Japanese consul.

Liu Kun - Owner of tobacco manufacturing business. He holds a grudge against Clark for being forced out of his seat on the Shanghai Municipal Council (SMC) by First Lady Soong Mei Ling. The SMC is the local government of the British and American controlled sector of Shanghai known as the International Settlement.

Liu Zi-Hong - Boyfriend of Mei Mei (Yuan Wen-Li), Clark's youngest sister. Communist sympathizer.

Mao Ze Dong - Leader of the Chinese Communist Party.

Peng Amah - Longtime servant of the Yuan family. Amah is not a name but a way of addressing female family servants.

Peng Ji-Rong - Grandson of Peng Amah who escaped the Massacre in Nanking during the Japanese invasion.

Shen Yi - Clark's ex-fiancée by arranged marriage.

Sītu Yong-Jian, Deputy Secretary - Clark's boss at the Chinese Foreign Affairs Bureau in Shanghai.

Soong Mei-Ling - First Lady of the Republic of China; wife of Chiang Kai-Shek.

Sun Xiu-Qing - Girlfriend of Xu Hong-Lie. Xu is Clark's right hand at the Yuan Enterprises.

Tang Wei - Clark's friend and former schoolmate who recruited Clark to join and work for the KMT.

Xiaochun, Liang - Maidservant of the Yuan Family.

Xu - a rickshaw coolie.

Xu Hong-Lie - Clark's right hand at the Yuan Enterprises.

Cross-over Characters from the spinoff novella
The Moon Chaser

Fan Yong-Hao - Member of the underground resistance group Tian Di Hui (the Heaven and Earth Society).

Masao Takeda - Member of the underground resistance group Tian Di Hui (the Heaven and Earth Society).

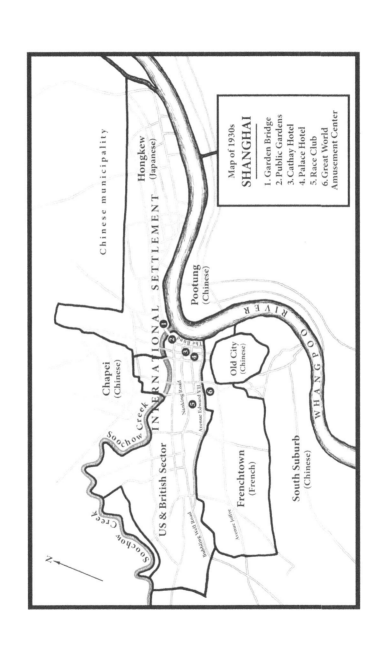

Map of 1930s
SHANGHAI

1. Garden Bridge
2. Public Gardens
3. Cathay Hotel
4. Palace Hotel
5. Race Club
6. Great World
   Amusement Center

Chinese municipality

Hongkew
(Japanese)

INTERNATIONAL SETTLEMENT

Pootung
(Chinese)

Chapei
(Chinese)

Soochow Creek

Soochow Creek

US & British Sector

Nanking Road

Avenue Edward VII

Bubbling Well Road

Avenue Joffre

Frenchtown
(French)

Old City
(Chinese)

South Suburb
(Chinese)

WHANGPOO RIVER

The Bund

N

SHANGHAI DREAMS

A MAN'S DILEMMA

WHAT SHOULD a man do when the survival of his country is at stake?

On the pier stretching out to the Whangpoo River, Clark ruminated on this question as he watched the sampans and boats crisscross each other in the water. A large ship pulled into dock, reminding him of his own return to this city last year. Back then, he had never thought it would be his duty to confront a question this big.

The fishermen steering downstream looked so small from where he stood. For a moment, Clark almost envied them. Their only worry was the day's catch. As long as they returned with a bountiful supply of fish to feed the city, they would have done their part. In the evening, they would return home, ending their day's work with a hearty meal with their wives and children, oblivious to the greater forces controlling the world—forces which could completely destroy life as they knew it.

And it was up to him to do his part so that these men and their families could continue living this way, and for the country to move ahead in the direction of peace and greater prosperity. At least that was what Sītu, his direct superior, wanted him to believe.

Just an hour ago, before he left his office at the Foreign Affairs Bureau, Deputy Secretary Sītu proposed an assignment for him that would set him on a course to become someone he had never wanted to be.

"Her name is Ekaterina Brasova," Sītu said when he first showed Clark the photo of the stunning blonde. Tang Wei, Clark's own friend and the Kuomintang's prized propaganda specialist in Shanghai, beamed with a half-jealous smile. "Princess Ekaterina Brasova, daughter of Grand Duke Michael Alexandrovich. The Grand Duke was Tsar Nicholas II's younger brother."

"Fallen royalty." Tang Wei's eyes lingered on the photo. In all the years Clark had known him, he could not recall ever seeing the upright and proper Tang openly admire any woman. Then again, the beauty of the woman in the photo could move any man's heart.

Any man, perhaps, except his. His own heart was already taken, and there was no room left for anyone else.

Only the Party's plans had no room for his heart. The KMT wanted him to make room for another woman in his life.

"The kidnapping of Generalissimo Chiang was an unacceptable insult." Sītu flicked his hand, a cigarette held between his fingers. "Nothing like this can ever happen again. Going forward, we need to make sure the Generalissimo will never be betrayed or put in this humiliating situation. Not by his own people, not by anyone, friend or foe. We can't risk him looking weak in public." Sītu huffed out a stern cloud of smoke. "Mao Ze Dong, that nail in the eye. He's telling people he would defer to Chiang Kai-shek for the sake of protecting our ancestral country against the Japanese. Only his band of ignorant followers would be gullible enough to believe him. Those uneducated peasants." He snorted. "We all know he has no choice because

Stalin pressures him. But regardless, the Generalissimo would like to keep up that pressure."

Clark studied Sītu's face, then glanced at Tang. The kidnapping of Chiang Kai-shek two months ago had shaken the KMT to the very top. Publicly, the Party was putting up a unified front. It was a peaceful negotiation, according to the official story from all sides. A temporary conflict among all those in power to determine the best way forward to support Chiang to defend China against Japan.

In truth, Chiang's hold on power had suffered a great blow. Within the KMT, Chiang's rivals no longer felt restrained from voicing their criticisms and raising their doubts. Chief among the critics was his political nemesis Wang Jing-Wei. A game of power was being played, and Wang was maneuvering to take Chiang's place.

And then, there was Mao, the ominous leader of the Communist Party hovering in the background. An ever-present threat that would never go away. He had his own hope to take over the country, except he couldn't do it without Stalin's support. Stalin couldn't care less who ran China, as long as it wasn't Japan. He had enough troubles tangoing with the Germans without the Japanese pushing into Soviet land. At the moment, his bet was on Chiang and the KMT to keep the Japanese out and away. But all that could change if he thought Chiang could not hold onto power. For the KMT, it was imperative to know which way Stalin leaned.

Tang picked up the photo of the princess. "Sokolov has a weak spot for women." Constantine Sokolov, the Soviet consul, was their primary liaison to the Kremlin. "As hard as I've tried to gain his trust, the old fox still keeps his guard against me. If I get him drunk enough, he'll let loose a bit of new information now and then. Given time, I can probably work my way through to him. But we can no longer afford delays." He put the photo in front of Clark. "We have to change tactics. She can help us."

"Ekaterina Brasova is a spy for hire," Sītu said. "The existence of White Russian royalists outside of Russia undermines the Bolshevik government's legitimacy. The Kremlin wants to know everything these royalists are doing in Shanghai. Brasova has information they want. All we need is to find a way to connect her with them. If we can do that, she will do her part to get close to Sokolov and gain his trust. In turn, she will gather for us information we need from the Kremlin. We just have to pay her the right price."

"And this is where you come in." Tang smiled at Clark. "We need you to give her a cover. If she can pose as your lover, we can create a chance encounter to introduce you and her to Sokolov. You can work with her to gain influence over Sokolov from a different angle."

"Why me?" Clark opened his hands. "We have other agents. I don't know what it takes to be a spy. Certainly, you can find others more suitable than me. Why not ask someone who works in intelligence?" He tossed his head at Tang Wei. "Why don't you pose as her lover? You've already established a rapport with Sokolov."

"I wish." Tang Wei snickered. "Who would ever believe a Russian princess is my lover? I'm nothing more than a nameless, insignificant chess piece. You, now, make perfect sense. You're Young Master Yuan. A beautiful young woman with no fortune to her name but who still carries the luster of royal lineage would attach herself to someone like you. Besides, didn't you break off your engagement to the Shen family's daughter last month? The timing couldn't be better. You wanting to show off a foreign princess on your arm would surprise nobody. People will easily believe you now want to play around and join the rank of Shanghai's wealthy sons."

And be known as just another lascivious *gonzi ge-er* who took advantage of his wealth and position? "That's preposterous." Clark shook his head. "I'm not that kind of person."

4

"No one is saying you are," Sītu said. "This will all be a pretense. The reality is, we need to know what kind of support Stalin is giving the communists behind our back. If he switches sides, we have to know."

Clark crossed his arms. Beyond his gut resistance, he had so many questions. "Are you certain she's a Russian princess?"

"We have no reason to doubt her," Sītu said. "We've done a thorough investigation into her background. We didn't find anything that would discredit her identity. The Russian community in Shanghai acknowledges her as Grand Duke Michael's daughter."

"But if she's from the royal family, why would she want to associate herself with the Bolsheviks to help us?"

"About that," Tang said. "Brasova's mother was a commoner. Worse, she was a divorcée. The Grand Duke renounced his right to succession to marry her mother in defiance of the Tsar, and the Tsar never formally acknowledged her mother or their children. Ekaterina Brasova has every reason to hold a grudge. I don't think that's her motive though. She's too smart to risk herself for a grudge. What she wants is money. She knows the novelty of a royal title can only go so far unless she has the cash to back it up. Money is something we can offer." He gave Clark a sly glance. "Wait until you meet her. She's quite exceptional. She can warm her way into anyone. She'll cast a spell over Sokolov at a snap of her finger."

Clark lowered his eyes and gazed at the photo. The girl's coaxing smile beckoned him, as though inviting him to agree. Still, his heart said no. He didn't break off his engagement, defy his parents, and raise a storm at home, only to make himself available to the Party's agenda.

"I know our request is a bit over the line." Sītu softened his voice. He spoke now more like someone seeking a favor rather than a superior. "If you would consent to do this, the Party will not forget to reward you. Mao Ze Dong isn't the only thing that makes this matter so pressing. If war breaks out with Japan, fuel will be one of our top concerns. We need all the details we can get on whether the Soviets can be a possible source of our oil supply. We need a closer link to Sokolov. Brasova could be that link."

Frowning, Clark shifted in his seat. "Is that all there is? This Ekaterina and I pretend to be lovers. We introduce her to Sokolov. Will my part be over then?" He didn't want to compromise himself any further.

"Actually . . ." Sītu brushed his nose. "We want Sokolov to think you're smitten with Brasova. Aside from getting confidential information from Sokolov, Brasova can help us supply information to him. We can feed him information that would steer Soviet decisions in ways that would best serve our interests. Brasova's job will be to make Sokolov think she got intelligence information about the KMT from you."

Clark balked. "How long do you want me to do this for?"

"For as long as necessary," Sītu said. "If you would agree to this, we will arrange to introduce Brasova to Sokolov at the American Chamber of Commerce Ball. You will escort her to the event that evening."

"The American Chamber of Commerce Ball?" Clark sat up. This couldn't be. He had already invited Eden to attend the Ball with him.

An office clerk knocked and opened the door. "Secretary Sītu, Mr. Keswick is here. He's waiting in the conference room."

Sītu nodded. "Tell him I'll be right there." The clerk bowed and closed the door.

After the clerk left, Sītu said to Clark, "We won't compel you to accept this task if you don't want to, but we hope you will. A lot is at stake." He stubbed out his cigarette. "By the way, Madam Chiang will be in Shanghai again in two days. She wants to see you."

Clark kept his face straight. He was no longer the naive pawn he once was. A meeting with the venerable Madam Chiang had its price.

"She's quite taken to you." Sītu took a sip of his tea.

Yes, Clark thought with a cynical smile, of course she was. All these months, he'd been pressuring and extorting others to fill up the Chiangs' coffer with "donations" and money from sales of government bonds.

"Perhaps she'll be able to explain to you the critical need for your help better than I can."

Perhaps. Clark's smile deepened. Only this time, he would be in a better position to bargain, and he was prepared to say no. Even to her.

"I'll leave you to think this over." Sītu stood up and left for his meeting with Tony Keswick, taipan of the British firm Jardine Matheson & Co.

Left with Tang Wei, Clark sank into his seat and propped his chin on his fist. Tang Wei smirked. "What more do you need to think about? It's not as if you're a girl being asked to sell your body." He gazed at the photo again. "Look at her. This woman's looks can light a fire. This time, the fortune of ravishing beauty is really flying your way. How about you make the ruse into a reality this once?" He grinned.

Clark scowled and glared at him. Tang Wei could joke about this, but he could not.

"All right, I won't make fun of you anymore." Tang Wei stopped smiling. A grim look darkened his face. "Our situation is precarious. When I was up in Peking last week, I could feel the tension simmering. People are restless. They're at a tipping point. I'm afraid we can't contain the hostility between them and the Japanese anymore. Of all the foreign powers, the Soviet Union is the only one with as much interest as we have in keeping the Japanese down. You and I both know Chiang can't hold off Japan alone. One wrong move, and the entire KMT could topple. Everything we do now will carry grave consequences." He narrowed his eyes at Clark. "You won't really say no, will you?"

Without answering, Clark picked up the photo and walked out to return to his office. He tossed down the photo onto his desk and tried to review the reports his secretary had typed for him. His eyes, though, kept sliding back to the photo. Frustrated, he got up and grabbed his coat, then took off to try to clear his head.

Walking along the streets with no destination in mind, he ended up here on the Bund, watching the junks and the boats as he tried to decide what he should do.

He could turn down the assignment. Sītu gave him the choice. But could he really? Could he ignore all the forces that were threatening his country's fragile regime to pursue his own happiness?

Would it be selfish of him to do so?

What should a man do when the survival of his country is at stake?

Guo-Hui. Glory of the country. That was the meaning of his name. Could he live up to his own name?

He stared at the sky and watched the sun glide across the horizon. Dusk was settling in. The oncoming twilight reminded him of the evening last summer when he brought Eden here to the Bund to watch the sunset after he saved her from a false charge of endangering a child. His heartbeat quickened at the very thought of her.

They had barely begun. What kind of future lay ahead of them?

If they had a future, they would chart their own paths. There was so much unknown, and so much to explore. Of course, there would be obstacles. They would have to overcome society's disapproving eyes. But for a moment, he was finally convinced that they could try.

How could he let go of a future of happiness so close within his grasp?

His grasp. His happiness. And hers too?

He thought of her soft hair blowing in the wind. Her deep, brown eyes that captured his heart the moment he met her. Those eyes with a soul. He realized now, she was what he'd been searching for his whole life, even though he didn't know it before.

Could he tell her the truth and go through with what Sītu asked?

Of course not. He couldn't divulge a government secret, even to someone he felt he could trust. And even if he told her the truth and she understood, what then? Would they see each other in secret? For how long would they have to pretend? What right did he have to ask her to wait indefinitely for him? It would be hard enough dealing with his parents' disapproval and the social prejudices she would face. Could he ask her to bear this burden too above everything else?

At the top of the buildings lining the Bund's waterfront, the flags of the nations fluttered in the cold, winter wind. The wind carried with it the echo of Eden's voice.

I dream of a day when all nations' flags would fly in the unity of peace.

Would that day ever arrive if he walked away from the call to protect his country to pursue the woman of his dreams?

Between a possible future with him and a future of peace, what would Eden choose?

The threat of Japan was growing every day. So was the resentment of the people against them. What would happen to Eden if war broke out? What future could they have if the country descended into chaos?

Hadn't he promised her, China would be her refuge? A place where she would no longer have to live in fear?

What was more important if he truly cared for her?

Being a man, he should make sure she was safe. Being a man, he should protect women and children. He should not indulge in matters of the heart.

He clenched his fists in his coat pockets. His heart was still unwilling, but the force of something bigger was pulling him away. In front of him, the path he knew he should take began to unfold. The only thing left was for him to take the first step.

Should he follow the path or remain still?

2

FRIENDS COME AND GO

AT THE CHINESE tea house in the heart of the Old City, Eden scanned the guests, searching for Miriam Stein.

There, over at a table in the back, her friend was already seated and reading the menu.

Friend. Did Miriam still think of her as a friend? Eden wondered as she made her way over.

She supposed she was about to find out.

At least Miriam called her and invited her to tea. That was a surprise. She sounded amicable on the phone too.

"Hello." Eden pulled out a chair when she reached the table.

"Eden!" Miriam raised her head. A quick, sheepish smile flashed past her face. "I'm so happy to see you."

Eden smiled back and sat down. It wasn't lost on her that Miriam had chosen for them to meet at a Chinese tea house. Few foreigners frequented this place, unlike the White Horse Cafe where they used to gather with their group of friends.

Miriam's group of friends. To them, Eden was a race traitor. They probably all wished she was burning in hell.

The waitress came and poured tea into Eden's cup. Miriam ordered several sweet dishes in Chinese.

11

"Eden." Miriam folded the menu when the waitress walked away. "I want to apologize for everything. I want you to know, I believe you. I think you're right. Roland Vaughn was the one who murdered Lillian."

Eden hadn't expected this. Even on her way here just now, she had been mulling in her head how to justify herself to Miriam for defending Johann Hauser, the Nazi soldier accused of raping and murdering their friend, Lillian Berman. Relieved, Eden loosened her shoulders.

But wait, why did it matter what Miriam thought? They were the ones who were wrong. And if Miriam believed her, why didn't she say so earlier? "You had doubts before. What changed your mind?"

"I don't know that I ever really doubted you," Miriam said. "You're a good reporter. We both loved Lillian dearly, and Lillian's infatuation with Roland Vaughn wasn't exactly a secret. You were so convinced that the killer was someone else and not the Nazi, I thought you must've had good reasons. But I couldn't bring myself to agree with you. I really, really wanted to believe the Nazi did it, so much so that I wished he had done it. Everyone else felt that way too. I know it was wrong, but I wanted to think the worst of him. I wanted some form of vindication. I wanted it on record in public that we're the victims and the Nazis ought to be punished for being who they are. I wanted justice, but I lost sight of justice for Lillian."

Eden turned the little Chinese teacup on the saucer. What more could she say? Miriam looked so sorry, and she already apologized. What use would it be to give her a hard time?

"But that wasn't all," Miriam said. "I was afraid to say anything the others didn't want to hear. I should've spoken up for you. At least, I should've given you the benefit of a doubt. When the news of Roland Vaughn's suicide note came out, my gut told me he was the perpetrator. A vain man like Vaughn wouldn't have killed himself in regret. Someone must have found him out. Since he died, there had been so many rumors about him hurting women back when he lived in Manchester. Anyway, I should have defended you, but I didn't. I was a coward. I'm a lousy friend. I hope you'll forgive me."

"Miriam." Eden grabbed her hand. "It's okay. It's all over now anyway. Vaughn got what he deserved." She drew back her hand and took a sip of tea. "How's everybody? How are Yuri and Igor?"

Miriam relaxed. "Igor's fine. He's the same. And Yuri . . . You know Yuri. He's stubborn. He's still convinced the Nazi killed Lillian. The authorities have planted enough suspicions around Vaughn's suicide to make it look like the Germans staged it. Right now, a lot of people still want to believe the Nazi got away with murder."

Eden put down her cup. All that was to say, the Jewish community still hadn't forgiven her. It didn't look like she and Miriam would be visiting the White Horse Cafe together any time soon, even now that they'd made up. "You know what the worst part of this is? My parents can't go to the synagogue anymore. If they show up, people won't talk to them. The ladies won't invite my mother to join them when they meet. My father lost a lot of his foreign patients. Some have returned, but many haven't. And Joshua. Children can be mean. They make fun of him at school. I feel like it's all my fault they have to go through this."

Miriam sighed. "Give it time. People will come around. They feel strongly about what they believe right now, but things will pass. They always do."

Eden nodded. Less because she believed what Miriam said, but more because there wasn't anything she could do about it.

The waitress brought the snacks Miriam ordered. A small plate of gooey round-shaped dumplings rolled in dried red bean flour with red bean paste inside, plus a plate of little squares of red dates and goji berry jelly cakes. Miriam thanked the waitress and served a piece of jelly cake to Eden. "What have you been doing with yourself lately? Anything new or interesting at work?"

"Well, my old boss, Mr. Zelik, is no longer there," Eden said, not without some regret. "I don't have my special column anymore either. I'm not very popular with Jewish readers these days. No one wants to read what I have to say about life in Shanghai for a Jewish transplant from Europe. On the other hand, Charlie, our new editor-in-chief, gave me a raise." She thought of her next assignment. "And guess what? I'll be going to the American Chamber of Commerce Ball. Charlie asked me to write an article about that."

"So you'll be going to the Ball as a reporter?"

"Not exactly." Eden bit her lip, trying to restrain her excitement. "My friend, Clark, invited me. I've told you about him before, haven't I? He's a foreign affairs official for the Chinese government."

Miriam scratched her temple. "Yes, I think I remember." She gave Eden a side glance. "Did he invite you as his date?"

"I think so," Eden said. A date. The thought made her feel giddy. She spooned a piece of jelly cake into her mouth to hide it. Miriam was still staring at her, looking curious but amazed.

She bit her lip to stop herself from looking too excited. If Miriam was surprised, how would people react if she were to openly appear in public with Clark as her beau? Would people constantly stare at her the way Miriam did now? "I'm going to the tailor's to pick up my dress after we finish our tea," she said in the most casual tone of voice she could manage. "Would you like to come?"

"Why yes," Miriam said. "I'd love to."

Eden beamed. She watched Miriam struggle to accept the news. Oddly, she found herself unaffected. From that moment, she knew that no matter how people might judge her choice, she could find it in herself to hold her head high. Clark had asked her to accompany him to the Ball. She was thrilled. Why should she hide it if it made her happy?

Besides, people already thought of her as a race traitor. The fact that she was seeing a Chinese man could hardly make things worse.

———

Two hours later, Eden returned home, humming to the tune of "The Way You Look Tonight" as she brought her evening gown back to her apartment. "I'm back," she called out as she closed the door.

No one answered. She laid her gown on the sofa and checked the rooms to see who was home. Isaac, in his room with his back toward the door, was packing his belongings on his bed.

"Isaac?" She knocked.

"Eden." Isaac turned around. "I didn't hear you come in."

"Where's everyone?"

"They're not back yet." He walked over to his closet.

Eden glanced at his open suitcase. "You're really moving out?"

He stood with a hanger in his hands. "My lease starts the day after tomorrow."

She leaned against the door frame. Last week, Isaac announced to her family he'd decided to move into his own flat. The news took everyone by surprise. He assured them it was not because he was unhappy living with them. He said he felt he should depend on himself now that he had found a job. He also thought he should prepare a new home for when his father and mother arrived.

Her parents had tried vehemently to convince him to stay. Her mother was especially concerned. "Who's going to look out for you if you're all alone?"

"I'll be fine," he told Mrs. Levine. "I want to stand on my own two feet."

There was no changing his mind, even though Eden was sure his new home wouldn't be nearly as comfortable for him. There was nothing wrong with the flat itself, although it was older and less spacious than the one she and her family were living in. The flat Isaac had picked had two bedrooms, a functioning kitchen, and a bathroom with a Western-style toilet. The problem was, Isaac was moving to a building occupied by local Chinese. Coming to a country this foreign had been hard on him. He'd done his best to adapt, but she could see his frustrations every day. From his inability to read and speak Chinese, the disorderly ways of the people, the constant noises and the crowds. Everything was a struggle for him. He never quite got used to the local food either. Here with the Levines, in a building occupied mainly by foreigners, he could at least feel less alone.

But he insisted on moving out, and a flat in a building with local residents was all he could afford.

"You really are welcome to stay." Eden crossed her arms. "You're as good as family to us. You know that."

Isaac tossed a shirt onto his bed. A moment of silence hung between them, and he looked up. "I'll stay if you want me to."

The seriousness of his voice took her aback. His directness surprised her. They had never spoken about his feelings for her. She wasn't ready to confront this. She didn't want to either.

She shifted her eyes away from his deep, hopeful gaze. The evening dress she'd brought back, still in its bag, lay waiting on the sofa.

No. She couldn't give him any false hope. She didn't want him to mistake her intention to be kind as something else. And would it be a kind act anyway? How would he feel when he saw her all dressed up and leaving the apartment for a date with another man?

Maybe it was best to spare him from all that. Away from her, maybe he could move on. Without her family to rely on, maybe he could even find ways to adapt better on his own.

"You shouldn't make your decision to please us," she said, sidestepping the intensity of his gaze and remark with a light smile. "We all just want you to be happy."

He slumped and returned to packing his clothes. Before he looked away, she caught a glimpse of the hurt in his eyes. Silently, she sighed and uncrossed her arms. "I'll put my things away and make us some tea." She returned to the living room, picked up her dress, and brought it back to her own room. This was for the best, she thought as she hung her dress in the closet. Straightening the skirt, she exhaled a guilty gush of relief. Without Isaac here, she could enjoy herself without restraint when she prepared for the night of the Ball.

What would it be like that night?

She closed the closet and fell back onto her bed. She couldn't hold back her joy. In Munich, she had never gone to a fancy gala attended by international businessmen and diplomats, escorted by someone as worldly as Clark.

Closing her eyes, she imagined what it would be like when Clark took her hand and led her out to a future filled with possibilities, to a world so much bigger than the one she had known.

3

NO SELF, HIS WAY

THE TEN DAYS of Chinese New Year celebration had barely passed. In most households, the joyful mood of the holiday would still linger, and leftover sugar *nian gaos*, turnip cakes, and New Year sweets would find their way into each meal. For the Yuan residence, however, all the pots of mandarins adorned with red money envelopes, and all the gold and red scrolls welcoming the new spring, could not mask the heavy discontent brewing underneath. Clark could feel it every time he entered the house. Everyone, it seemed, was waiting for a resolution to his decision to break off his engagement. No one, except Mei Mei, his youngest sister, actually believed his decision was final. All were waiting for the wandering son to come back.

Come back was out of the question. Eden or no Eden, he would not marry Shen Yi. On that matter, Clark had made up his mind.

But being the one from the younger generation, he had to take the first step and mend what was broken with his parents. His long walk on the Bund had prompted him to decide on his next path. It wasn't what he had envisioned. The last few weeks, he had only two concerns. How to persuade his parents to accept the idea that his choice of a wife was his own, and whether he could break through social constraints and pursue the woman he really loved.

Sītu's proposal changed everything.

"Young Master." A maidservant approached him as he walked through the front door. "This delivery came for you today. It's a gift from a Japanese military captain, Kenji Konoe." She handed him a long, thin box. Clark passed her his briefcase and opened the box. Inside, he found a paper scroll with the word "Wu" handwritten in calligraphic script.

"Wu." No self. Was this a coincidence? A sign? A bitter smile crossed his lips as he stared at the word.

To commit his next course of action, he would have to leave his own self behind.

He rolled up the scroll and put it back into the box. "Is Old Master home?"

"Yes. He's in the study."

Clark handed her the scroll and instructed her to bring it to his room, then went to look for his father. When he entered the study, his father glanced up from his desk. Without acknowledging Clark, Master Yuan turned his attention back to his work. Clark gathered his nerves and sat down across from him. "I know I've disappointed you."

Master Yuan paused his pen.

"It's not my intent to defy you and Ma. But if I marry Shen Yi, I will never care for her the way a husband should. Of course, she will be well taken care of. She will never lack any material things money can buy. But I cannot give her happiness. Maybe many would say that doesn't matter. Men have always married women they didn't care about. But doesn't she deserve more than what I can give her? Considering our long friendship with her family, shouldn't we care about her happiness?"

His father let out a long sigh. "You humiliated her. She's a good girl with a clean reputation. How will she recover from this?

You made Old Shen lose face. How will I ever make it up to him? Decades of friendship, all destroyed by you."

"I bear sole responsibility for any harm to her name. I will let it be known publicly I'm a womanizing scoundrel not worthy for her. When I'm done, she will preserve her good name."

"What?" Master Yuan dropped his pen. "Have you gone insane?"

"It's the best solution," Clark said. "I'm a man. A reputation as a philanderer won't harm me nearly as much as it would harm her to be a jilted fiancée." He turned his clasped hands over. If he accepted Sītu's assignment, a skirt chaser would be his new persona anyway. If it could save Shen Yi's name and reputation, then it would be one thing he could do for her. "It won't be hard to convince people. I've returned from overseas. They'll just think I've been spoiled by Western ways of free thoughts and loose mores." Furthermore, if his father believed him, he would have a good excuse at home too for why he was cavorting with the Russian princess Ekaterina Brasova.

Master Yuan scrunched his face. "You're going to upset your mother to death."

"I'm sorry. In the future, if I marry, she and everybody will see me settle down and be a good husband and father." Clark shifted his eyes to the side. He only said this to appease his father. His own marriage was the farthest thing from his mind. "I have a solution on how to make it up to Shen da ye too, as well as many of our family friends who contributed money to the KMT on my account."

"How?"

"I will get you a seat on the Shanghai Municipal Council."

"The SMC?"

"Yes," Clark said. The SMC was the governing body of the Shanghai International Settlement. Its members consisted of a select group of major property owners representing their nationalities. Of the fourteen seats on the SMC, five represented the British, and five represented the Chinese. The Americans and Japanese each held two seats. "Voting for the next slate of Council members is coming up. Foreign investments and commerce are the reasons why Shanghai prospered. If you're on the Council, we can drive businesses to our friends. We'll be the first to know about any policy changes that might affect the people we want to protect. We can influence decisions. You're a member of the Chinese Ratepayers Association already. You're entitled to vote. Why not take a step further and hold a seat of power yourself?"

Master Yuan crossed his arms. "I've never cared much for that kind of power."

"I know. But it'll be a way to give an advantage to everyone we know who had given money to the Party because of me. As for Shen da ye . . . the bid is open now for the repair of the Garden Bridge. The British will be lighting up the bridge again for King George's coronation in May, just like they did when King Edward was coronated last year. If Shen da ye gets the bid, they'll invite him to the celebration as a special guest of honor. His name and photo will be all over the news, along with reports about the King. He'll be pleased. Trust me, Ba. Take the seat."

Master Yuan uncrossed his arms and dropped his fists to the desk. "I'll have to take it even if you don't ask. These debts of human relations have to be repaid in the end. You think I can just swing my sleeves and don't care?"

In shame, Clark hung his head.

Master Yuan sighed. "You believe you can get me voted into the Council?"

"I'm nine parts out of ten certain. I'll know for sure in two days." In two days, he planned to demand the seat from Madam Chiang herself.

His father took off his glasses. "You've made some powerful connections in the Party, haven't you?"

Clark smiled. Yes, he had, but not without a price.

"What about coming back to work for me? How much longer do you want to stall before you give me an answer?"

"This question . . ." Steeling himself, Clark said, "Give me one year. After Chiang Kai-shek's abduction, the Party's badly shaken. I can't simply walk away. There is still work that I must do. One year. Whatever happens then, I can at least answer my own conscience."

"One year? You're sure?" His father looked him in the eye.

"Yes," Clark said, forcing himself to hold his father's gaze.

His mouth didn't reflect his heart. How could he foresee what would happen a year from now? He brushed his forehead. When did he learn to deceive this way? Had the KMT changed him?

Walk a step when you see a step, he told himself. As for things that would happen in the future, he'd figure it out when the time came.

"You're not a child anymore," Master Yuan said. "You have your own ideas. What can I do?"

Clark looked apologetically away.

"Don't forget what you promised me." His father pointed at him.

"I wouldn't dare," Clark said, mustering as much earnestness as he could to allay his father's doubts.

Master Yuan put his glasses back on and returned to his accounting books.

Relief washed over Clark. He withdrew from the study and closed the door. The anchor of family responsibility had rolled off his back.

But his father was only one hurdle. The next one was no less daunting.

In the sitting room on the second floor where his father kept their family's antique and art collections, Clark found his mother on the sofa, directing a maidservant how to massage her neck. She gave Clark a cold glance when he walked in, then stared away. Clark drew in a breath and approached her. He knew the drill. His mother had been waiting for this moment. He could see it on her face despite the feigned cold glance. When a parent was angry, they expected the children to apologize, no matter who was right or wrong. The only difference for him this time was that he had never defied his parents to such a great extent.

In an odd way, his mother's act touched him. It was a blessing, too, to have his mother healthy and alive, angry at him over something that affected only them and didn't shake the world.

"Ma." He bowed his head in respect but raised his eyes to gauge her mood.

"You still know your mother?" Madam Yuan snapped.

Clark dropped his head lower. The maidservant darted her eyes awkwardly to the side of the room. Madam Yuan huffed out a self-righteous breath and waved her away. The servant ducked her head and shoulders and scampered out.

"Ma, it wasn't my intention to make you angry," Clark said after the servant closed the door.

Madam Yuan turned to face him. "What's not good about the girl Shen Yi? I watched her grow up. All these years you were in America, she remained faithful to you. How will you ever make it up to her? How is she not better than that foreign girl?"

"There's no foreign girl. If you're talking about Eden, she has nothing to do with this. That was a misunderstanding. Please don't blame her anymore. No matter what, I won't marry Shen Yi. I'll do anything else you ask. Please, Ma. I've been away from home for so long. When I was in a foreign country, I always thought about home. Don't let this matter create a conflict between us mother and son." Clark sat down next to her. Madam Yuan's furious exterior softened.

24

"If you want, I'll kneel before you," Clark said and pretended to move to the floor.

His mother pressed his shoulder for him to sit back down. "Be serious!"

Clark hid his chuckle. "I know you want to see me set up my own home and family. If the world were at peace from heaven to earth, I would be able to help Ba grow our business with my full heart and full attention. I would think about doing what's good for me and our family. But I have other important things I need to do outside. Right now, I fundamentally have no time to think about private affairs and feelings between men and women. Keeping Shen Yi around would be akin to wasting her youth and future." As it would be too if he had Eden with him, Clark thought to himself.

Madam Yuan's face changed from anger to despair. "You won't be coming back to work with your father then?"

"Not yet," Clark admitted. "I spoke to Ba already. I asked him to give me one year." He leaned closer to her. "I'm asking you for the same."

"And your father agreed?" Madam Yuan frowned.

"Yes. Things are very chaotic outside right now. There are some things that I must do. He understands that."

Looking confused, Madam Yuan shook her head. "Your father is too lax. I don't understand your way of thinking. What's outside that's more important than your own family?" She sighed. "All these business matters, I won't care anymore. You two father and son can sort it out."

Seeing his mother easing up, Clark pressed on. "Come on, Ma. Don't be angry anymore. You're going to stay mad at your only son forever?"

Madam Yuan scowled, but soon lost her will. "Of course not." She touched him lightly on his face. "But losing such a nice girl like Shen Yi . . ."

"Like they say, Ma, an upstanding man doesn't have to worry

about not having a wife. These matters, we'll leave them to the future."

"Your casual attitude. How long will I have to wait to have grandchildren?"

"Besides me, you have Wen-Ying and Wen-Li. In the future, you're sure to have a reception hall full of children and grandchildren."

"Wen-Ying, Wen-Li. Grandchildren with different last names, how can that be the same?"

Clark laughed and stood up. "You'll love them when you see them. I'll go get changed for dinner."

"Tell Xiaochun to bring me a cup of ginseng tea," Madam Yuan said as he walked out.

"Yes," Clark said. A gush of warmth comforted his heart. Ginseng tea, grandchildren's last names. If these small domestic matters were all that his mother ever had to worry about, then this too would be a great blessing.

Quietly, he left the room.

There were more ways to be a good son than being straightforward and honest with one's parent.

He thought of the scroll Konoe had sent to him today. No self. The Japanese captain wanted him to explore the idea of transcending himself.

Konoe would be disappointed if he knew how Clark had chosen to interpret "no self." For Clark, "no self" meant leaving behind his own wishes and desires, if doing so would keep the Japanese and war at bay. What happened to him didn't matter. If what he was about to do would taint his name and corrupt his soul, then so be it. Let nothing interrupt the lives and peace of the people he cherished and loved.

If deference was the way to appease his parents, dealing with Madam Chiang Kai-shek would require a diametrically different tack. Not that she didn't expect deference. The first lady of China received plenty of deference. No one in China would dare to treat her with anything less.

But since the last time they met, Clark had learned that with Soong Mei-Ling, pure deference would only put him in a position of compromise. In any encounter with her, he had to be prepared to claim what he wanted, and never let down his guard.

The first lady greeted him in delight. "Yuan Guo-Hui, so glad to see you. Take a seat." She signaled her assistant to pour Clark a cup of tea. "How've you been?"

"Fairly well, thanks to good fortune." Clark acknowledged the assistant with a nod and sat down across from Soong. The view of the sky above the Bund through the windows in the hotel suite looked glorious behind her.

"I was just telling my husband on the phone I'd be meeting with you today. He's so pleased with your work. Next time he visits Shanghai, he'd like to commend you personally."

"You mean my work improving our relationship with the Americans?" Clark casually picked up his cup. "I'm only doing my job. Just a minor contribution on my part. Not worthy of mentioning."

Soong gave him a quick once over. She didn't change her demeanor, but Clark knew the game was on. For the other, less mentionable work he was doing for her, mere praise would not be enough. Not even from the Generalissimo himself.

"Yes. The Americans." Soong tossed back her head. "Of course, you know I haven't invited you here today to talk about the Americans. Secretary Sītu said you haven't accepted your new assignment yet."

Clark took a sip of his tea and placed the cup back down on the coffee table. "It puts me in a difficult spot. My father and mother have only me as their son. If they hear I'm attached to a foreign girl outside, how will I explain this situation to them? It would hurt their hearts."

"You're a good son." Soong studied his face.

"I try to be," Clark said in a cheerful voice. "Then again, if you asked for my help, I'd certainly make my best effort and do what I can. The problem is, I need to show my parents I can do things to make them proud too. My father, especially. Maybe then, they'll forgive me for a few private indiscretions."

Soong looked at him intently. Her expression gave no sign of her thoughts.

"The vote for the Shanghai Municipal Council is coming up. My father would make an excellent candidate."

"The Council?" Soong drew back. "I didn't think your father was interested in government and politics."

"He isn't. That makes him an even better candidate, don't you think? With him as a Council member, you won't have to worry about him acting in any way that might damage the Party's carefully cultivated friendships with the British and the Americans, or the delicate relationship with the Japanese."

Holding her cup, Soong lowered her eyes to her tea. Clark decided to press on. "My father's an expert businessman. From his position on the Council, he'll know how to take advantage of any profitable opportunities when they come up. He can do that not just for himself, but for a lot of his friends who would know how to seize chances and generate cash. Our friends, in turn, would want to show their gratitude. They might decide to expend a little effort for the country and make further contributions to the Party. The arrangement will be good for everybody. Wouldn't you say?"

Soong sat up. He could see she was surprised, but also impressed, that he dared to make a demand.

Still confident, Clark relaxed and crossed his legs. In the end, money was what the Chiangs needed most. With the money he had brought in for them, she couldn't simply threaten him into doing what she asked like she did last time. If he refused to play along with their scheme with the Russian princess, they couldn't simply dismiss him either. But what she probably didn't expect was that an inexperienced beginner like Clark would bargain with her, trading this for that. She probably thought she could charm and persuade him to fall into her fold.

"You know I'm only thinking of the overall good for the Party," Clark added with an innocent smile.

"A seat on the Council, huh?" Soong asked, hiding her lips behind the rim of her cup.

Clark opened his hands. "It would help me steer more funding to the right causes."

"The five seats representing the Chinese are already taken. All of the candidates have close ties to the Party. Who would you have me push aside at this late hour?"

"I'm not in the position to make any suggestion about that. I'll defer to the Party to decide which five people would best serve our interests," he said. Let her be the one to choose the unlucky loser. He had no need to make an enemy of anyone.

Soong cocked her head and stared at him, as though observing him anew. Clark waited until she broke into a deep, meaningful smile. "Very good. A worthy young person can be taught," she said, surprising him with the old adage to openly acknowledge that she saw through what he was trying to do. "I know I'm a good judge of people. I told Sītu, Yuan Guo-Hui can do great things in the future. We can trust you to do our work better than anyone else." She sat up, reclaiming her dominant air. "You're right. Your father would make an excellent Council member. Now. Let's talk about your next assignment. Are you ready to meet the Russian princess?"

"Yes?" Clark straightened up in his seat. He hadn't expected her to acquiesce so quickly.

"Good. I'm not one to waste time. You'll get what you want, and I expect you to get on with what we need you to do. I'll arrange for you to meet the princess tomorrow night. Seven o'clock at the Chez Rovere. It'll be good for you two to get acquainted before you bring her to meet Sokolov at the American Chamber of Commerce Ball."

Tomorrow night? So fast? He didn't even get a chance to ask questions.

"This assignment is serious," Soong said, her voice solemn. A hint of honesty broke through her face for the first time since he arrived. "The threat of Japan has grown. We need the Soviets' support. We have no hope for help in Europe. Hitler's power is growing. Britain and France are preoccupied with their own defenses. The United States doesn't want to get involved anywhere. We'll see how long that lasts. Roosevelt's a fool if he thinks he can remain on the sideline when the whole world begins to burn." She swirled her tea. "Germany, I don't trust. They say they're our ally, but they would absolutely welcome it if Japan starts a war in China. It would divert Stalin's attention and resources away from the Soviet border in Europe. They'll like it even more if Japan can draw all the other European countries and America away to a conflict in Asia. The Soviet Union is the only country with anything at stake in the East. Stalin doesn't want to fight a war on two fronts. If Japan pushes their way in, he'll want us to fight the war for them. We can use their need to our advantage, as long as he believes our Party is the best equipped to defeat the Japanese."

Clark's body sunk. When Soong described everything this way, their reality sounded so bleak.

"We're on our own. I have people observing Stalin's moves in every corner. Each corner is vital. We didn't choose you for this assignment in haste. Your personal background will make a good cover. But more importantly, I want someone competent. I need someone who can adapt quickly and seamlessly when the situation changes or opportunity arises. I believe you can do that."

"I understand," Clark said. He was sure now. He had no more reservations or doubts. The Chiangs and the KMT were imperfect, but letting them fail would lead to doom.

In the grand scheme of things, his own self mattered so little. If he could help prevent a great calamity by doing what was best for the country instead of what was best for him, how could he refuse?

But what would he tell Eden?

This was the only question left. The answer could leave him drowning in regret.

THE HOUSE IN HONGKEW

"GOOD MORNING," Eden greeted everyone as she entered the conference room. With her notebook and pen ready, she took a seat next to her fellow reporter Emmet Lai. At the head of the table, Charlie Keaton, her boss and editor-in-chief of the *China Press*, scowled at the papers before him, groaning as he crossed off one thing after the next.

"What's bothering him today?" Eden whispered to Emmet.

"Don't know." Emmet shrugged.

The rest of the staff quietly waited. Charlie slashed his pen across the paper, scratching off whatever else he found so displeasing. Eden couldn't understand why he had become so grumpy and irritated all the time. He had worked his whole life to become an editor-in-chief. But since he took over the job from Zelik, he'd been nothing but miserable.

Finally, Charlie began to speak. "I asked you all to give me proposed topics for our weekly features. I've gone through all your suggestions here." He waved the papers he was reviewing to make the point. "They aren't bad ideas, but circumstances have changed. None of your ideas are going to work."

Eden and Emmet exchanged a look.

Charlie tossed the papers onto the table. "Up till now, we haven't reported much on what the Japanese are doing in Shanghai or in China. We've always focused more on what's happening in Europe, given that our readers are more concerned with what's happening in their home countries. Starting today, we're taking a new direction. I want stories. Stories pertaining to Japanese transgressions. I want you to find stories that might shine a spotlight on Japan if they're doing anything out of line with international law and order."

"Wouldn't that make us biased?" Eden asked. Why were they singling out Japan to look for dirt?

"I'm not asking you to slant your story or lose your objectivity. All I'm asking is, if there is something to report, I want you to find it."

Eden raised an eyebrow.

Charlie flashed her a stern look. "You don't think we should be worried?" he asked. "Japan signing the Anti-Comintern Pact with Germany should've sent off all kinds of alarms. If Chiang Kai-shek wasn't abducted, that would've been our biggest story back in December."

Everyone shifted in their seats. A few staff members muttered beneath their breaths and a sense of indignation overtook the room. This always happened when anyone directly or indirectly mentioned Hitler.

"So." Charlie flicked his pen. "If you all agree, I would like each and every one of you to go out and find out anything you can. Talk to your sources. Call anyone and everyone who might be able to give you tips."

The staff mumbled a series of yeses. Eden couldn't think of anyone who could give her tips relating to Japan. Aside from her neighbor Keiko, who was a housewife married to a French man, she didn't know any Japanese. In the months since she'd come to Shanghai, she had rarely gone into the Japanese sector.

Maybe it was time to venture back there then. She doubted

she would find anything useful to bring back to Charlie. But since Charlie had asked, she couldn't ignore his direction and do nothing. Why not make a trip to the Japanese sector in Hongkew and take a closer look? It would be a good excuse to get out of the office.

The same afternoon, after a quick lunch at a cafe near her office, Eden set out for an afternoon trip to Hongkew, the place everyone called Little Tokyo. Why hadn't she visited this part of the city more often? she asked herself. She had only been here twice. Once when Ava wanted to buy a kimono to send to a friend back in Boston, and another time when her neighbor, Keiko, brought her and her mother here for a sushi dinner. Both times, Eden didn't linger long.

As she arrived at the Garden Bridge separating the International Settlement and the Japanese sector north of Soochow Creek, she realized why she had subconsciously avoided this place. It was the presence of the armed guards. On her end of the bridge, there were men on patrol from the Shanghai Volunteer Corp, the International Settlement's own little band of armed forces. Some of the Corp's members were British, Americans, and other Europeans who had chosen to volunteer their time. The rest were Russians and Chinese who were paid to serve. On the other end of the bridge were the Japanese. Real Japanese soldiers standing ready to scrutinize everyone who crossed over into their zone.

It had been months since Eden last visited. When she entered Hongkew off the bridge, she could feel the intensity of the Japanese guards' watchful eyes had increased. There was something else too. Along the border of their sector, the guards had put up high piles of sandbags. The Japanese had barricaded themselves. Against what? Shanghai's other sectors had no such barricades. At the borders between the International Settlement, Frenchtown, and the Old City controlled by the Chinese, people spilled in and out every day. There was never a need for armed guards or sandbags between the territories controlled by the different countries, except Japan.

Anxious to get away from the Japanese guards, Eden quickened her steps. At the first shop displaying kimonos, she stopped. Yes, she was just a silly white woman who had come to shop. She pretended she was admiring the silk patterns until she felt they were no longer watching her.

Was she being overly sensitive? Why did she feel like she had to pretend? She had nothing to hide.

Silly, she chided herself and continued walking.

Where should she begin? She checked the street signs. The signs were of no help. All the street signs were written in Japanese, as were the store banners and advertisements displayed on the windows. She could only tell what the stores were selling by looking at their goods, be they home decor, dried goods, and other ordinary household items. Some restaurants had signs with drawings of sushi and noodle bowls. But without more, she would certainly get lost wandering around.

There were rickshaw coolies clustered at various spots. If she couldn't find her way back, she could hire one of them to take her back.

Aha! A cinema. She could remember a landmark like that. She made a mental note to remember the posters plastered on the cinema's walls. They showed only Japanese movies. This place truly felt foreign to her, and not entirely welcoming either. Not like the areas where the Chinese lived.

Was she imagining it? No, she didn't think so. The Shanghai she had come to know was an exuberant place. Lively, reckless, full of rancor and fun. That blissful atmosphere pervaded the city, whether the areas were inhabited by Westerners or the Chinese. Here, the streets were too quiet. The air felt oppressed.

Everyone's behavior felt restrained. A brooding, militant discord brewed underneath. Where had she felt this before?

Munich.

Eden gulped and tensed her body.

A Japanese man nearly walked into her when she suddenly stopped on the narrow sidewalk. "*Sumimasen*," he said and walked around her. His female companion followed, keeping a steady two or three steps behind, always slowing down to never walk ahead of him.

"*Uttei!*" Someone barked from the public park. Eden turned to the direction of the voice. In the park, a troop of Japanese soldiers charged to their positions and raised their rifles, as though they were ready to shoot.

Eden walked closer. The soldiers' faces looked so serious. So focused. All for a training exercise?

She held her breath and watched. Their brown uniforms sent a shiver up her back.

No, she told herself. These men were not the Brownshirts. They were Japanese soldiers performing regular military drills.

Regular? The British and American soldiers didn't train in public parks. Even the German soldiers in Shanghai trained in the suburbs away from civilian eyes. If they even trained. In Shanghai, one would more often find foreign soldiers from the West in bars and clubs. They earned their battle scars mainly from drunken brawls on the streets. None of them looked ready for war like the Japanese soldiers training here in the park.

Her heart pounding, she turned around and walked away.

But there was no getting away. A unit of four soldiers was approaching. The Chinese men near her stopped talking and changed directions. A Chinese amah walking a child grabbed the kid's hand and pulled him into a store. "*Na bian, na bian*," she told the child, dragging him away so fast, the child had to run to keep pace.

As the soldiers came closer, the remaining pedestrians veered to the side. When the soldiers passed, they bowed and averted their eyes. Eden turned to pretend to look at the ceramic sake cups displayed in a store window. Out of the corner of her eye, she saw the white armbands with red letters the soldiers wore around their sleeves. She had seen those armbands in newspapers before. They were the mark of the *Kempeitai*, the Japanese military police.

The Nazis wore special armbands too.

What was happening here?

She took one more discreet side glance at the *Kempeitai* as they walked away.

Should she leave? This whole environment reminded her too much of Munich. She didn't like how conspicuous she looked here either. There weren't many Westerners on these streets. Her white face stood out. How could a foreign woman like her find any story to uncover and report?

She halted her steps, ready to give up, except for the unusual sight of the Japanese marines ordering a group of girls off a military truck across the street.

How odd. Why were the Japanese marines transporting girls?

Her curiosity piqued, Eden pretended to stroll. Taking a languid, slow pace, she turned her face just enough to watch what was happening.

Those girls sure looked young. If she had to guess, she would say they looked fifteen or sixteen.

She could be wrong. Asian people often appeared younger than their ages. The girls could be older. They could be adults, transported here to perform clerical or secretarial work for the Japanese navy.

No. A voice inside her shot down that thought. The Japanese army and navy didn't employ women, and women did not serve in the Japanese military.

The girls huddled beside the truck, looking apprehensive and lost. One of them, a girl with wide cheeks and hair cut to a bob, stared in Eden's direction. For a brief second, their eyes met. Eden's breath stopped when she saw the fear and confusion on the girl's face.

A marine toting a rifle shouted an order at the girls and led them into a colonial-style building three stories high. Soon, they disappeared behind the large red wooden door. When the door closed, two soldiers remained outside, standing guard.

Unable to stall any longer without inviting attention, Eden had no choice but to walk away. She hastened her steps and returned the same way from which she had come. But what had she just witnessed? Something sinister was happening. She was sure of it. Her reporter's instinct told her so.

She needed time to think. She needed more information to piece it all together. Whatever was happening, she intended to do everything she could to find out.

5

THE PRINCESS OF RUSSIA

AT THE RESTAURANT CHEZ ROVERE, Clark sat hidden at a corner table. The restaurant host had wanted to seat him at a coveted space by the window, but Clark opted for a less visible spot. More romantic, he explained to the host. More discreet, he thought to himself. The Russian princess he had come to meet was a mystery, and he had many questions for which he didn't want the answers to be overheard.

While waiting, he scanned the wine list, then signaled the sommelier and ordered the most expensive bottle of Bordeaux. From this moment on, every detail about him and the princess would become the subject of society gossip. To feed the prying ears, they would have to look and act their parts.

The idea of it made him wince. He'd come so close to having a chance with Eden. All his hopes were dashed now before they even had a chance.

He would have to withdraw his invitation to her to the Ball. How he would do that? He still didn't know.

He picked up the menu and stared at the courses. Nothing registered. If they served him dragon meat now, he would still think it was tasteless.

A shadow moved into the flickering light of the candle on the table.

"Monsieur?" asked the host.

Clark looked up. In front of him stood a slender young woman. She couldn't have been more than twenty-two or twenty-three. Nonetheless, her light, ash blonde hair, pulled back into a chignon, gave her an elegant air of maturity. Her lips, painted with a bright coat of red, further masked the youthful freshness of her face.

But even without these superficial efforts, she struck him as someone older. It was her eyes. They looked like eyes that had seen too much. A gleam of sadness with no end hid behind them.

The host pulled out the chair across the table and the woman sat down.

"Ekaterina?" Clark asked after the host walked away. Did he just commit a faux pas addressing her by her first name? Should he have called her Princess? Or was it "Her Royal Highness"? No one told him this small detail and he hadn't thought to ask.

The princess smiled. A reserved smile. "Pleasure to meet you, Clark," she said in accented English.

"The pleasure's all mine." He put the menu aside. What should he say to her? This setup felt utterly awkward.

"I'm looking forward to working with you," she said, her tone of voice all businesslike. "I see I'm lucky. I was worried they might pair me with a lecherous old man." She smiled again, more warmly this time, and immediately put him at ease.

Clark relaxed. "I'm sure I'm the lucky one." He meant it too. She knew how to handle this matter much better than him.

He poured the wine into her glass. "Madam Chiang wants us to get acquainted. Do you mind me asking you some questions upfront?"

"Sure. Ask me," the princess said. "What would you like to know?"

"Are you really a princess?"

"You doubt me?" She twirled her earring.

He didn't say it out loud, but yes. He doubted her even after Sītu and Soong Mei-Ling had both reassured him she was a descendant of the Romanovs. If he believed every person calling themselves count, countess, prince, and princess in Shanghai, he would have to believe the whole city was occupied by royalty.

The princess took a sip of her wine. "I am the daughter of Grand Duke Michael Alexandrovich," she said, her demeanor now entirely serious. "He was the youngest brother of Tsar Nicholas and second in line for the throne. He was anyway, before the Bolshevik revolution. After the Bolsheviks took power, they placed him under house arrest. He disappeared soon after that. I still don't know what happened to him, although I believe he's dead. My mother had him declared dead back in 1924."

"I'm sorry," Clark said, to be polite. Holding on to the stem of his wine glass, he continued to observe her.

"My mother, Natalia, got me and my siblings out of Russia before my father disappeared. We escaped to London. A few years after that, we moved to Paris, except for my stepsister. She got married and remained in England. My brother, unfortunately, passed away in a car accident six years ago."

Clark swirled the base of his wine glass on the table. Could he believe her? The KMT had verified her story. The Grand Duke's wife, Natalia Sergeyevna Sheremetyevskaya, did escape Moscow with her children with the help of the Germans. Reports confirmed that the Grand Duke's son had a propensity for motorcycles and sports vehicles, and he died in a car crash. Information about the daughters was harder to come by. The daughters weren't prospective heirs to retake the throne in the event the royal regime returned.

"Why did you come to China?" Clark asked. "This is such an unlikely place for you to live. Didn't you like living in London or Paris? It seems to me those would be easier places for you to live."

"Easier?" Ekaterina laughed. "My mother's a commoner. Everybody shunned us. Even my uncle, the Tsar, never recognized her marriage to my father. The only reason my uncle granted her the last name Brasova was to give my brother a proper surname to make him legitimate. After my brother died, an old friend of my father wrote to my mother and asked us to come to Shanghai. He told us about the contingent of royalists here. He thought it would boost their morale if a member of the royal family would come and visit. My mother declined. She's content to live the rest of her life in peace. I was lured by the excitement. I asked him if he would bring me here on the *Félix Roussel* in first class. He said yes. That was how I got here, and I haven't left since."

"Okay," Clark said. "You're the royalists' figurehead. Why are you helping us? Why do you want to risk yourself for us?" He lowered his voice. "Are you trying to use us to help the royalists? Are you using us to get close to Sokolov to harm Soviet interests?"

Ekaterina stared back at him. "For someone who's supposed to work with me, you doubt me too much." She reached out her arms and showed him her hands on the table. "Look at these."

Clark glanced down. The jeweled rings on her fingers and gold gemstone bracelet around her wrist sparkled in the candlelight.

"Aren't they beautiful?" Ekaterina turned her hands. "They have sentimental value too. My jewelry is all that I have left from my father."

He still didn't understand.

"A girl's got to eat, even if she's a princess," Ekaterina said. "My father's bank accounts in London had ninety-five pounds left when my mother finally got his inheritance in England. Her luck in Poland was even worse. The Polish government confiscated all of the Russian imperial assets. Since then, my mother's been selling everything we own just to feed us. I won't follow in her footsteps." She pulled back her hands and stroked her rings. "I'm rather fond of these pieces. I won't have to sell them now. The

Chinese government is paying me handsomely for what I'm offering to do."

"And you have no plans to get close to Sokolov to help the royalist groups?" Clark asked.

Ekaterina dropped her arms. "Your government questioned me about this already. Don't you trust them? Even if you don't trust me?" She picked up her glass of wine and took a hearty sip. "No. I do not have plans to help the White Russian royalists. Especially not the ones in Shanghai. Do you know what I discovered after I arrived here? The royalists in this city are nothing but a group of loud drunks. I'm a realist. They'll never drive the Bolsheviks out of power. Anyway, it doesn't matter. I don't have any grand dream of returning to a palace or holding aristocratic reign over my motherland. I'm just a woman trying to survive. I came to Shanghai on a whim to seek excitement. I find this city a better place to live. I can make a living trading and selling information." She gazed at Clark. In that instant, Clark finally believed her. Not because of what she said, but because of the raw sadness he saw behind her eyes.

"Forgive me." He eased his voice. "I hope you're not offended if I've crossed the line asking you so many questions. I'm trying to understand how you came to the decision to work with us."

"It's all right." Ekaterina's playful tone returned.

"What do we do now?" Clark sat back. "How do you plan to get close to Sokolov? If you're a descendant of the Romanovs, wouldn't he be naturally suspicious of you?"

"I'm sure he would be. But he's also desperate, and I know secrets that can save him. Do you know about the political purge going on now in Russia?"

"Only what I've read in the news."

"It's a lot worse than what's being reported. Stalin is eliminating all the old-guard Bolsheviks. Sokolov's on the hit list. If he wants to live, he'll have to find something to show Stalin his loyalty. Do you know about the Russian Emigrants' Committee?"

Clark shook his head. "No."

"This group is headed by former imperial Russian consular officials. They operate out of Shanghai. They work to dispute the legitimacy of the Bolshevik regime. I'm close to the Committee's leader. Anatoly Borodin's been collaborating with the Japanese. When Sokolov finds out I can give him information about Borodin and his people, he'll want to get to know me."

"And why would he think you would want to betray the royalists who support you?"

"Because I'm a woman." She tilted her head and peered coyly at him with half-opened eyes.

"What?"

"Men. They always grossly underestimate the intelligence of women. That's one of men's greatest weaknesses. The men running the Kremlin are no different. I'll use that to my advantage. Have your colleagues told you? Sokolov likes women too. He fancies himself a womanizer. So I'll let him chase me. If everything we know about him is true, then my guess is, he won't be able to resist the conquest of a Romanov princess with close ties to the royalists. And then, I'll let him think he's tricking me into divulging their secrets and activities. If he can feed information about Borodin back to the Kremlin, it might be enough to keep him alive."

Clark watched her finished her drink and shook his head. "You make it sound so easy."

"It's not the first time I've gone undercover. I'll admit, I've never targeted someone as high up as Sokolov. But I think I can handle him. Having access to you will help."

"Me?"

"We're lovers, right? I'll let him think he can get information about the KMT through me."

Clark laughed. This woman had thought of everything.

The waiter came by to take their orders. Clark waited as Ekaterina select her courses of duck and foie gras, then randomly selected a steak dish for himself. Before the waiter walked away, she grabbed Clark's hand on the table. Clark flinched, but she held on, refusing to let him pull back.

"Thank you." She looked at the waiter as she caressed Clark's hand.

"You're welcome, mademoiselle." The waiter smile discreetly and walked away.

Bewildered, Clark widened his eyes at her. "What are you doing?"

"We're supposed to be lovers," Ekaterina whispered. "We need to start acting like it."

Not exactly comfortable, Clark nonetheless stopped himself from squirming. "Right. Princess . . ."

"Don't call me that. Call me by my name."

"Ekaterina—"

"Katia."

"Katia?"

"Yes. That's what you should call me. It's short for Ekaterina. It's a term of endearment."

Clark frowned and nodded. A term of endearment. For a woman he just met.

"I'm looking forward to the American Chamber of Commerce Ball."

The Ball. Like he needed the reminder.

"What's wrong?" Ekaterina asked. "You look ill suddenly."

"I'm fine." He shifted in his seat. "About the Ball, I invited someone before Sītu told me about this assignment. I guess I'll have to disinvite her."

Ekaterina studied his face. "Is she special to you?"

"She could've been." Clark watched the fire flicker on the candle. "Now, it's a good thing she hasn't become that."

"I'm sorry." Ekaterina loosened her hand, then gripped him again. "You don't have to disinvite her."

"What do you mean?"

47

"You have ties with the American consulate, right? Why don't you see if you can get an additional invitation or two? Invite your friend to come as our guest."

"Our guest?" Clark asked. "I don't know . . ."

"It'll save you from having to withdraw your invitation. Come to think of it, you should invite more guests. Maybe a whole table if you can." She threw him a conspiratorial smile. "We might as well present ourselves as a couple to everyone you know and make it official." She winked.

"I don't think that's a good idea," he said. How could he relegate Eden to being a table guest while he escorted another woman to the Ball?

Ekaterina shrugged. "It's just a thought." She let go of his hand. "I'm not here to interfere with your private relationships. If you want to pursue someone else in secret, I'll stay out of your way. But publicly, we'll have to convince everyone you and I are lovers. Our plan depends on it. If Sokolov thinks I'm deceiving him, you'll put my life at risk."

Clark pulled back his hand. Her reminder shook him, and she was right. Ekaterina was putting herself in the center of a very dangerous game. He couldn't do anything to put her at any more risk. "You don't have to stay out of my way. I won't be pursuing anyone until this is over."

"That's your choice," she said.

The first course arrived. Ekaterina unfolded her napkin onto her lap, and spread the butter on her bread.

Clark picked up his glass and took a slow sip. It dawned on him then, it wasn't enough for him to refrain from putting Ekaterina at risk. He had to protect her. Even if no one demanded that of him, it was the only right thing to do. If he didn't, no one else would. Whatever were the reasons that had led them to cross each other's paths, she was now his partner, and she was all alone. If any harm should befall her, he would never forgive himself.

6

YUAN FEN

BACK IN THE HONGKEW DISTRICT, Eden retraced her steps to the street across from the three-story house where she had seen the Japanese marine bring the group of girls the day before. Nonchalantly, she pretended to view the trinkets and ornaments in a store window. Yesterday when she left, she was overwhelmed and confused. But her curiosity grew as she thought more and more about what she had seen. Today, she had decided to come back to take another look.

Maybe she was insane to have returned. If only she hadn't seen the girl with the wide face and short bob. She was almost sure, the look in the girl's eyes was a cry for help. She couldn't ignore it.

No harm in returning one more time.

Outside the house, Japanese soldiers were lining up in a queue. Whenever one exited the door, the next one in line would go in. Something in the smiles of the soldiers exiting the place repulsed her, but she couldn't grasp what it was.

She paced up and down the block. How could she remain here longer without looking conspicuous? There had to be a way for her to stay longer and observe what was going on, but where could she go?

The ramen noodle house. Of course! It even had a long table facing the window out to the front street. She could sit there as a customer. It was almost noon anyway. No one would suspect her presence if she was coming here to eat.

She pushed the restaurant door open.

"*Irasshaimase*," the servers and the cooks behind the open counter shouted in unison as soon as she entered.

Startled, Eden took a step back.

A chubby waitress in a dark blue kimono came up to her. Holding a menu, she began to lead Eden toward one of the small tables against the wall.

"No," Eden said. Puzzled, the waitress turned around. Eden pointed to an empty seat at the long table against the front window.

"Ah!" The waitress exclaimed and held out her arm, inviting Eden to take the seat.

At the long table, Eden took off her coat. The view here was perfect.

The waitress laid down the menu. Right away, Eden could see that everything was written in Chinese and Japanese. Rather than struggling to order, she pointed at the bowl a man was eating in front of the open counter. She had given up on a strict kosher diet, especially in restaurants serving non-Western cuisines. Eating out was impossible otherwise.

The waitress bowed, then took the menu and returned to the back.

Another waitress came and served her a cup of tea. Eden wrapped her cold hands around the cup and let the warmth soothe her as she watched again what was happening through the window. Across the street, the queue had grown even longer. More soldiers kept arriving to join the line even in this cold.

In the back of the restaurant, the chubby waitress shouted her order to a cook behind the counter. Eden recognized her words. "*Mien tiao*" and "*yi wan*." Noodle and one bowl. Eden herself had heard these words hundreds of times in restaurants since coming to Shanghai.

The cook spoke back to the waitress. Somewhere in his speech, he said several times, "*laowai*." Old Foreigners. It was what the Chinese called Westerners.

Were they talking about her? She turned and looked over her shoulder.

"*Yi wan. Kaui dian*," the cook said to the boy draining noodles in a huge metal pot. Eden let slip a half smile. The cooks and the server weren't Japanese. They were Chinese.

This really didn't surprise her. Chinese locals worked at French, German, Italian, and other restaurants too. Someone had to do all the menial hard work. The kind of work that foreign elites in the city didn't want to do.

She put the thought behind her and looked out the window again. That building she had come to watch stood like a prison. All the windows were closed, and all the curtains were drawn. Why would a military building use curtains instead of blinds, and why would they keep them drawn in broad daylight?

The waitress returned with a bowl of noodles on a tray and set it down in front of Eden. Instantly, the aroma of the noodles filled her nose. She picked up her chopsticks and began to eat. Her mind wasn't on food when she first came in, but the noodles tasted delicious and she took another hungry bite.

A new thought occurred to her. Why not come back tomorrow? And the day after? She could keep coming back as a regular patron of this restaurant. Everyone would think she was coming for the food. In time, no one would question her presence here.

She pushed the tender slices of roast pork to the side, then changed her mind and took a bite.

Anyhow, she had graver concerns on her mind. God might

forgive her for eating a few slices of pork if she could uncover what was going on across the street.

Coming up the steps leading to the statue of the Angel of Peace on the Bund, Clark scanned the area for Eden to see if she had arrived. No, she wasn't among the scattering of winter tourists and the vagrants braving the cold to beg for cash.

Reaching the platform, he slowed his pace and rehearsed in his head what he had planned to say. There was no good way around it. He had come to tell her he would be escorting someone else to the American Chamber of Commerce Ball. Whatever he said, it would surely disappoint her.

Or maybe it wouldn't matter much to her. Maybe she accepted his invitation because the Ball was the most exciting event in town this month and tickets were hard to come by. After all, who was he but a Chinese man she might not have given a second look had she not come to live in Shanghai by a twist of fate?

But Mei Mei thought Eden had feelings for him too.

Oh, what did little Mei Mei know? Her idea of love included that little imp Liu Zi-Hong. In the West, they would call that "puppy love." He shouldn't put too much weight on what she said. Eden had accepted his invitation to attend the gala with him, nothing more. One evening didn't mean she had deep feelings for him the way he had for her.

He circled around the statue and dropped his head. What he had come to do would probably break his own heart ten times more than it would Eden's.

But it was the right thing to do, was it not? If men like himself didn't step up to protect their own country, what hope would their people have?

Standing there, he read the names engraved at the base of the statue. Frank Buckley, Archibald Swain, Clarence Comstock. These were among the two hundred names of the fallen soldiers who had lived in Shanghai before they went to fight in the Great War and died. The Western Allies erected this monument in their honor.

Was it worth it? Clarke wanted to ask these men whose names their countrymen deemed worthy of memorializing here. They had given their lives to bring forth a better world. Today, the world was once again at the brink of war. What would they say if they knew that their sacrifices weren't enough to stop men's incurable desire to expand their powers and inflict harm onto others?

Down the road, when he, too, had given his all to save his country from failing, would he be looking back, satisfied in knowing that his own sacrifices had indeed made a difference? Or would the world turn to ashes and he'd be left with nothing except regret? Would his own fellow countrymen deem his sacrifices worthy of remembering for the future generations to come?

As he pondered these questions, Eden approached him on the sidewalk. Her appearance was such a beautiful sight to his eyes.

"Hello," she greeted him. Her smile ever so bright.

"Hi." He wanted to walk toward her, but his better senses held him back and made him stay in place.

She came up next to him and waited for him to speak. He started to talk, but the words he had planned to say escaped him.

"Is something wrong?" she asked.

He closed his mouth and shook his head.

Her tone changed to one of concern. "You asked me to come here. What is it?"

Go on, he said to himself. Tell her. Do what you came here to do.

He curled his fingers in his pockets and took a deep breath.

"On Chinese New Year's Eve, I asked you to come with me to the American Chamber of Commerce Ball."

"Yes," she said. Her smile returned. Her eyes full of anticipation.

"I hope you'll forgive me. I can't take you anymore." He lowered his gaze to the ground. There. He told her. And now he hated himself.

"Oh?" Her face dropped. "Why's that?"

He could hardly look her in the eye, but he forced his guilt and shame aside and raised his head. If what he was doing did upset her, then at least, he should face her and take the consequences. "I need to take someone else. Someone who will become a very important part of my life."

Eden fell speechless. Clark's own heart fell too. The hurt look on her face cut him like a knife. He'd almost convinced himself that her interest in him was nothing more than cursory, something that only he had hoped would turn into more. Her crestfallen face showed him otherwise. Even worse, he could see now he was letting go of something more than wishful thinking on his part. The chance of happiness with the woman he loved was slipping away, all by his own doing.

"I'm sorry," he said through the web of his own heartache. "When I invited you, I didn't know this would happen."

"I see." Eden lowered her head.

"This is all my fault. I didn't mean to disappoint you." I never meant to hurt you, he wanted to say. If he could bear both of their pain, he would.

"Does she mean that much to you?" Eden asked, her voice trembling.

"Yes." If by working with the princess, they could ensure the Soviets' support for the KMT, that would mean everything to him.

Everything, except the one thing his own heart wanted.

"She must be an extraordinary woman," Eden said with a shaky laugh.

"Maybe," he answered. His throat felt so tight. He hated seeing her hurt. It tore him up to know he was the one who was hurting her. "I wish I hadn't told Charlie I was going to the Ball." She tossed her head. "He was all set on me writing an article about that evening."

"You can still come," Clark said. The words came out of his mouth before he realized what he was saying. "I'm reserving a full table. I'm inviting some of the most important clients of my father to attend."

Eden wrinkled her forehead. "Well, I . . ."

"I can't escort you, but you can attend as one of my table guests," he offered. Anything he could do to make it up to her. Even if it meant he had to beg Joseph Whitman for extra seats, or pay an outrageous sum to buy seats off someone else.

"I suppose." A blast of wind swept by and blew her hair. She looked away and pushed the strands back behind her ear.

"I mean, if you'd still like to come." Clark lowered his voice. What a dumb idea. Why would she accept a lesser invitation like that? He shouldn't have mentioned it. He wished Ekaterina had never suggested it and put it into his head.

To his surprise, Eden said, "Why not? I accept. Everyone I know wishes they had an invitation to this ball. How could I possibly pass on the chance? I'd love to see in person all the men who wield the power behind this city." She smiled. A proud smile that made him feel even guiltier than before.

"Okay." He nodded. Such a travesty this was turning out to be. The woman he wanted to escort to the ball would now be watching him escort another woman all evening instead. "I'll make the arrangements. Would you like to bring a guest?"

"Bring a guest?" she hesitated.

"Yes," he said, silently laughing to himself at the irony of it all. He would spend the evening watching her with another man too.

"No." She lifted her chin. "I shall attend the gala on my own. I appreciate your inviting me. I'll be going as a reporter. This way I'll be able to observe the scene without distractions."

She would attend the gala on her own. This was horrible. Even worse than if she would come with another man. How could he let her or any woman arrive without an escort? "In that case, at least let me pick you up. Please?"

Eden blinked and looked away. For a moment, he thought she would say no. "Sure." She shrugged, then checked her watch. "I have to go. Would you please send the invitation to my office?"

"Yes, of course." Clark watched her turn around. He didn't want her to leave.

"Clark." She looked back at him.

"Yes?" His heart still yearned. His arm almost reached out. His dream was slipping out of his grasp.

"I'm happy for you. Finding someone you love, it's something we all should celebrate." She smiled again, this time with genuine warmth, even though her eyes still looked hurt.

He watched her walk away. Alone now, he held his fist up against the monument. Only he knew the reason why he had picked this spot today. The Angel of Peace could remind him, the price of peace was worthy of the cost.

Coming off the steps of the monument of the Angel of Peace, Eden tightened her scarf and wrapped her arms around herself. The wind blowing in from the river was so cold. She wanted to run away. Run away to somewhere warm, somewhere inviting, somewhere that could take away the sting of wanting someone who didn't want her at all.

What happened? What went wrong? On Chinese New Year's

Eve, she'd felt something between them. She was sure he'd felt it too. It wasn't only that night. She dared to say, that feeling had been there all along. How could he come to her and tell her he now had another woman in his life? It hadn't even been two weeks since he invited her to the Ball.

She must have misread him. That could be the only explanation. Her own fantasies had clouded her head, and she thought what he felt for her was as much as what she felt for him. If that was the case, then it was her own fault for thinking something more existed when it didn't.

Who was this woman? Was she more beautiful? Was she Chinese? Did she have something no other woman had? What made her so important to him that he had to change his plans so suddenly?

No. Eden straightened her back and squared her shoulders. She was not going to fall into the trap of being jealous. Whoever this woman was, she had her own pride to protect. She would not allow herself to feel jealous of a woman Clark fancied, especially when he obviously thought more highly of that woman than herself.

Wasn't it rude of him to withdraw his invitation though? Since he'd invited her first, he could've taken her to the ball anyway.

She stomped on ahead. Angry. Yes, she was angry. Who wouldn't be? How insulting of him to disinvite her? She never thought he could be so callous.

Would she have wanted that though? She slowed her steps. If, ultimately, his heart belonged to someone else, what good would it have done for her if he had taken her? In the end, she would still be disappointed. She would still feel the heartache, maybe even more than she felt now.

She never wanted to talk to him again. Oh, why did she agree to go to the ball as his table guest? To show up and make herself a pariah? What was she thinking? But when he brought up the suggestion, she felt she had to say yes. Her pride wouldn't let her to scurry away and hide like a wounded animal. If she had said no, she'd be admitting that she wanted to go to the ball only because of him. At that moment, holding her head high was all she could do to keep her dignity.

She wished she hadn't blurted out Charlie's request for her to write about the ball. She wished Charlie had never made that request. Why did she ever mention to Charlie that she was going in the first place? Couldn't she take everything back?

She stopped in front of a wharf. She could take it back. Tell Clark she changed her mind and decided not to go. After all, he changed his mind, so why couldn't she?

Sure, she relaxed her arms and laughed at herself. Why not make it obvious how upset she was to have been disinvited? It would only make herself look like a jealous woman.

She could tell him she changed her mind about not inviting her own guest. She didn't have to go alone. But who would she invite? All her old friends, like Yuri, weren't talking to her anymore, and all the men at her office who could make an appropriate escort for such an occasion were either married or already had a girlfriend. There was Isaac, but . . . She sighed. She didn't want to give Isaac any wrong ideas or false hope.

Who was this new woman who had stolen Clark's heart?

He'd helped her so much since she came to Shanghai. And now, he was telling her he had found someone he loved. Could she not be gracious and wish the best for him? Would she disregard all his kindness toward her and her family for no other reason than the fact that his heart didn't beat for her? If he loved someone else, it wasn't something he could help.

Before she left him, she'd told him she was happy for him. She should be a good friend then and wish him well. She did mean what she said. Love should be celebrated. This world suffered enough cruelty already.

She blew out a white cloud of air. Well, she still had her dress.

At least now, it wouldn't be wasted. She laughed quietly at her own thought.

Slowly, she turned around and continued alone on her way. She walked into the crowd, joining the hundreds of pedestrians coming and going every day on these busy streets who were no one special. In this city full of people, she was just another woman, easily lost and forgotten.

7

NIGHT AT THE BALL

THE CONCIERGE'S call came at six-thirty to inform Eden that Clark had arrived to pick her up for the American Chamber of Commerce Ball. Eden had prepared for this moment. All dressed, no fuss. In her champagne satin evening gown, she looked fashionable and presentable. She could hold a candle to anyone, even if she wasn't Cinderella going to the ball to meet her prince.

Stop. She swatted away her thoughts. She wasn't in competition with anybody. She didn't need to be. Surely, Clark would have eyes only for his girlfriend.

Jealous? No! Of course she wasn't jealous. Why should she be? The thought never even crossed her mind.

She picked up her scarf and her purse, and left her room. She had told the concierge she would come downstairs herself. No need for Clark to come up for her.

Who said she needed an escort? She had a job to do. She was going to the gala to observe the event as a reporter.

"Look at you," Mrs. Levine said when she saw Eden on her way out. "You look lovely. I still don't understand why you want to go to the ball alone. There have to be plenty of young men who would be delighted to escort a beautiful girl like you."

"I told you, Mother, I'm attending as a reporter," Eden said. "I don't need an escort, and if I had one, I wouldn't have time to keep him company. Anyhow, I have to go. Goodnight. Don't wait up for me." She hurried out of the apartment to avoid any more questions.

On her way downstairs, Eden put on a smile. Yes. She would keep her smile and stand proud for the rest of the evening.

The elevator reached the ground floor and the door opened. In the lobby, Clark waited. Beside him, a stunning blonde woman looked her way.

She's gorgeous, Eden thought. She clutched her purse against herself.

Such a magnificent gown the woman was wearing too. The burgundy floor-length gown, held together by a golden embroidered waistband, looked majestic on her.

What a beautiful woman. No wonder Clark fell for her. What man wouldn't?

Well, then. She ought to be happy for him.

Gathering her composure, Eden inhaled a deep breath and walked toward them. "Clark?"

"Eden." He turned around at the sound of her voice. For a moment, his eyes lit up. The light, though, quickly disappeared and he looked away.

"Hello, you're Eden," said the blonde woman who had come with him.

"I'm sorry," Clark interjected. "Allow me to introduce. Eden, this is Ekaterina Brasova."

"A pleasure to meet you." Ekaterina offered to shake her hand. "Clark told me all about you. You're a reporter with the *China Press?*"

"Yes." Eden shook her hand. "How do you do?" She widened her smile, suddenly wishing she did have an escort.

Clark kept his head down. Was that hurt in his eyes? Why?

Never mind. Whatever she thought she saw, she was probably

wrong, as she had been every time when it came to him. There must be some Chinese cultural cue she was missing.

Ekaterina turned to Clark. "Shall we?"

Clark nodded, ready to take her arm. Instead, Ekaterina came beside Eden and linked her arm around Eden's. Surprised, Eden tensed, but Ekaterina's warmth dispelled her unease.

What a gracious girl. Eden couldn't dislike her even if she wanted.

She thought of Shen Yi, Clark's former fiancée. Ekaterina was more than a clear cut above. Clark definitely made the right choice.

Did his family approve of this? What about everything Clark's sister Wen-Ying had told her about his family's expectations? How did they feel about Clark seeing a foreign woman?

Eden stole a look at him. She couldn't tell what he was thinking.

Outside, Clark's limousine pulled up from the waiting area. Clark invited Eden to enter first. Ekaterina took a seat next to her and he followed into the front passenger seat. Once the driver steered the car onto the road, Ekaterina turned to Eden and smiled. "Clark told me you came from Germany."

Eden smiled back. "Yes. From Munich."

"It's horrible. That Hitler. I'm glad you're here now." Ekaterina touched her lightly on the arm.

Eden couldn't help noticing Ekaterina's distinct accent. "Did you come from another country too?"

"Yes. I'm from Russia. My surname was given to my mother by my Uncle Nicholas the Tsar."

"Your Uncle the Tsar?"

"Yes. My father was Grand Duke Michael Alexandrovich, his younger brother."

Eden glanced at Clark in the front seat. Ekaterina came from a royal family? "Pardon me. Clark didn't tell me you're a member of the royal family. How shall I address you?"

Ekaterina smiled again. "People address me as Serene Highness, but between us, you can address me by my name. You're Clark's friend, which means you're my friend too."

Eden pulled her scarf closer over her arms. That might explain it. Clark's girlfriend was not just any foreign woman. She was a princess by birth. Perhaps his family might find it an honor to see his name publicly connected to a royal descendant.

Whether that was the case or not, she had no way to know. Clark himself was gazing out the window, seemingly not listening to their conversation while Ekaterina continued to try to engage her in small talk. Something was bothering him. She almost wanted to reach out and ask him why he looked so troubled. Only it wasn't her place to do so.

Leave him alone, she told herself. From now on, it would be best for her to keep her distance.

Arriving at the entrance of the Cathay Hotel, Eden forgot for a moment the disappointing circumstances that had brought her to the gala tonight. Watching the men in tuxedoes and women in glittering evening gowns entering the lobby, a rush of excitement overtook her. This was her chance to glimpse at the exclusive world of the men and women who shaped and ran Shanghai.

The hotel's staff led the guests to the elevators to the eighth floor. Upstairs, they followed the orchestra's music to the grand ballroom, where the lights of chandeliers glistened from above. The brightness and glamour of the scene took her breath away. For one night, the elite of the Western world in Shanghai had gathered. Taipans, diplomats, politicians, even movie stars. All of them legends in their own right.

Two weeks ago, Eden had dreamt about this night. She had fantasies of herself as the star of a memorable evening in which she might discover love in the most elegant ballroom in this spectacular city.

That dream was not meant to be. That dream belonged to Ekaterina, who Clark, looking so well in his black tux, had on his arm. He and Ekaterina made such a handsome couple together. She even made him look regal. Like an extra piece of a puzzle that fit nowhere, Eden followed, slowing down and trailing back further with each step.

"Clark! How are you? Great to see you." A short, balding, middle-aged man greeted Clark and slapped his arm.

"Mr. Huddleston." Clark shook his hand. "Great to see you too. Ah, let me introduce you—this is Her Serene Highness Ekaterina Brasova of Russia."

"Of Russia!" Huddleston exclaimed. "My honor!"

Ekaterina held out her arm. Eden watched her shine an alluring smile on Huddleston as she graciously accepted his kiss on the back of her hand.

"And this is Miss Eden Levine," Clark introduced Eden next. "She's a reporter for the *China Press*."

"How do you do?" Huddleston threw her a quick glance, then turned his attention back to Ekaterina.

"How do you do?" Eden said. Huddleston didn't even hear her.

"I've never been to Russia," Huddleston said. "I'm from Oakland, California. My business is lumber importing . . ."

Eden took a step back. A waiter came by with a tray of cocktails and she picked one up. Quietly, she sipped her drink while Clark, Ekaterina, and Huddleston talked.

A Chinese man came and greeted Clark and Eden. "Sorry, Mr. Huddleston. If you don't mind, there's someone I'd like Clark and the Princess to meet."

"Of course, Secretary Sītu." Huddleston raised his wine glass to signal he understood. Sītu, perhaps mistaking Eden as Huddleston's guest, flashed her a quick, businesslike smile, then led Clark and Ekaterina away. Eden thought Clark would invite her along, but all he did was give her an apologetic glance before he disappeared into the crowd.

"I'm a self-made man." Huddleston continued talking, as if he had been conversing with Eden all along. "You can't get ahead unless you can sniff out opportunities before everybody else. I have a keen eye for opportunities. And not only that. You can't be afraid to seize opportunities. The problem with people today is they're afraid to seize opportunities. Don't you think?" he asked, not waiting for Eden to answer. "I for one am not afraid of jumping on opportunities. That's why I'm here. The economy back home goes down, onto a ship I jump. Look at me. I haven't lost a penny since the Great Depression started—"

Unable to bear his talk any longer, Eden interrupted. "Excuse me. I need to go to the powder room."

"Oh." Huddleston twitched his mustache. "Of course."

Eden raised her near-empty glass at him, then slipped away. Weaving through the crowd of guests, she came upon a standing cocktail table beyond the seafood bar and put down her drink. Now what should she do?

From here, she had a full view of the people in the room. There was Cornell Franklin, the lawyer from Mississippi rumored to be the next chairman of the Shanghai Municipal Council. He was talking to tonight's keynote speaker, Wendell Wilkie, president of the Commonwealth and Southern Corporation, one of the largest utility companies in America. He'd traveled all the way from abroad to attend this event. Rumors had it, he wanted to run for President of the United States in the future. Behind them was Cornelius Vanderbilt Starr, founder of the American International Assurance Company who had first introduced insurance to the Chinese, and Baron Lawrence Kadoorie, son of the rubber magnate Elly Kadoorie.

Eden took her pencil and a small notepad out of her purse. All of Shanghai's upper echelon was here. She did say she was coming as a reporter, didn't she? Maybe she should go near these men and eavesdrop on what they were saying. Maybe she could approach one of them, charm them, and persuade them to give her an exclusive interview.

A plump Chinese woman in a brown floral silk qipao walked past. She plopped her empty champagne glass on the cocktail table without as much as a look at Eden or even saying "excuse me."

How rude. Eden threw her an indignant look, until she recognized the woman as the late Silas Hardoon's widow, Liza Hardoon. Silas Hardoon was a Sephardi Jew who had made his fortune in real estate in Shanghai. When he died in 1931, he left his entire estate to his wife. Six hundred fifty million dollars! She was now the wealthiest woman in Shanghai, and still fighting her late husband's relatives who were contesting the will in the Iraqi court.

Eden tapped her pencil on the table. Why not add a disparaging remark or two about the haughty widow's rudeness? She twisted her lips with a mischievous smile.

At the next table, a man was staring at her with playful eyes. When she noticed him, he didn't turn his gaze away. He looked quite harmless. In fact, he carried a gentle air of refinement distinct from even the men in this room.

His friends offered him a cigarette. He held up his hand and declined. Cocking his head, he raised his wine glass at Eden. His playful smile never left his face.

Unsure how to respond, Eden looked away. Thankfully, the dinner bell rang. She put her notepad and pencil back into her purse, and left for her own designated table.

Leaving Eden behind with the insufferable Huddleston was the last thing Clark wanted, but when Sītu came to bring him and

Ekaterina to meet Sokolov, all he could do was to glance back at her to show his regret. He wouldn't have left Eden by herself tonight but for this.

Sītu played his own part surprisingly well. Casually, he led them toward Tang Wei and the Soviet Commander, all the while pretending to be in conversation with Clark. At just the right moment, he cried out, "Commissar Sokolov! Very good to see you tonight."

Clark exchanged a look with Tang Wei, then shifted his eyes to the Soviet Commander. From what Tang and the others had said about Sokolov's love for alcohol and women, Clark had imagined the Soviet to be a slow, lecherous, and possibly overweight political operative who was past his prime. In person, Sokolov was nothing like that. Although in his forties, he still maintained a strong, athletic physique. His chiseled face showed he must have been even more handsome in his younger days. But his face was one that repelled rather than attracted. His eyes reflected a coldness rare even for a man from the Slavic North.

No wonder Soong Mei-Ling replaced Sītu with Tang Wei to woo this man. While Sītu was closer to Sokolov in age, she needed someone with sharper energy to keep up with this Siberian wolf.

Could Ekaterina really deceive someone like Sokolov? Clark shuddered to think of her being alone with the man.

"Secretary Sītu." Sokolov raised his glass. He stopped short when he laid his eyes on Ekaterina. Eyes that stalked like a predator's. Instinctively, Clark pulled Ekaterina closer.

"What a surprise to see you," Sokolov said to Sītu. "I thought you were still in Nanking. Does your return mean everything is back to normal with the KMT? How is the Generalissimo?"

"He is well, thank you. We had quite an ordeal last month," Sītu said, referring to Chiang Kai-shek's kidnapping in December. "We're forever grateful for General Secretary Stalin for giving us his moral support. By the way, have you met Clark Yuan? He works for my office. He's our foreign affairs officer working with the American consulate."

"No, I haven't. How do you do?" Sokolov held out his hand, his voice distant and uninterested.

"Clark, this is Commissar Constantine Sokolov," Sītu said, continuing their charade. "He's a special friend of China. Our forces have benefited greatly from his help and advice on border security—"

Ignoring Sītu's praise, Sokolov cut him off and asked, "And who might this lovely lady be?"

Without missing a beat, Clark said, "Allow me to introduce Her Serene Highness, Princess Ekaterina Brasova, daughter of Russian Grand Duke Michael Alexandrovich." He paused to make sure Sokolov heard him. "She's my companion for this evening, and beyond tonight, if I should be so honored." He threw her a loving gaze for good measure.

"Daughter of Grand Duke Michael?" Sokolov's face stiffened.

Warily, Ekaterina drew back from him, but Clark knew this was an act. The witty boldness in her eyes had vanished, replaced by a doe-like innocence that could have fooled him too had he not met her before.

"Anatoly Borodin warned me about you," she said, sidling closer to Clark. "You're part of the disease he's trying to eradicate."

Her insult did not deter Sokolov. The corner of his lips raised into a half smile as he studied the princess. "You know Anatoly Borodin?"

"Know him? He treats me like I'm his own daughter." Ekaterina held up her chin, then turned to Clark. "I would like to move on."

"Katia . . ." Clark frowned, as though she had put him in a difficult position. Just then, the dinner bell rang. He pulled Ekaterina closer to his side and said to Sokolov, "Perhaps we shall continue our conversation later."

Sokolov raised his glass. His eyes remained on Ekaterina, like a hunter watching his prey. Clark excused himself and led Ekaterina away. Behind him, he could hear Sītu apologizing, "Please forgive us, Commissar. I had no idea one of my men would be bringing someone related to Tsar Nicholas tonight . . ."

When they were far enough away, Clark asked his partner, "Do you think he took the bait?"

"He did." Ekaterina linked her arm closer around his. Audacity once again shone in her eyes. "He absolutely did."

"What do you think he'll do now?"

"I know his kind," she said. "To him, I'm just a dumb girl. Someone he'd like to toy with and destroy. We'll let him think that. He won't pass up a chance to wreck one of the last imperial descendants, but not before he tries to convince me to tell him everything he wants to know about Anatoly Borodin."

The casual way she spoke worried Clark. He thought of Sokolov's cold, ruthless face. "You are aware he's a dangerous man."

"Where would the adventure be if he wasn't?" Ekaterina tossed her hair. The daring smile never left her face. Clark still worried, but they had come to their table and the guests were already seated, including Eden.

Seeing Eden sitting by herself with the Chinese guests, most of whom spoke little or no English, Clark moved to take the seat next to her, but Ekaterina pulled him back and stopped him. Subtly, she shook her head and placed herself in the seat Clark had meant to take.

He sighed and sat down on the other side of her, one seat away from Eden. Throughout dinner, Ekaterina kept Eden engaged in small talk. With the princess and Eden conversing between themselves out of his earshot, Clark spent the rest of dinner talking business with his Chinese guests and their wives. Inviting them to this ball had been a good move. An invitation to an exclusive event hosted by Western foreigners went a long way to make them feel important and respected.

When Wendell Wilkie, the keynote speaker, finished his speech, the orchestra music began once again. As the guests took to the dance floor, Ekaterina turned to him. "Well?"

"Sure." Clark forced out a smile and held out his hand to invite her for a dance. What he really wanted was to remain at the table until the evening ended so Eden wouldn't be left alone. He had no interest in dancing tonight anyhow.

"We'll be back in a little while." Ekaterina patted Eden on the back.

"Enjoy yourselves. Don't worry about me," Eden said, averting her eyes from Clark. He wished he could change everything. If only he had the power.

On the dance floor, Ekaterina pulled him closer so he could hear her under the music. "Remember, you can't give any hint that you're anything but smitten with me. At least not in public. If you look like you're more interested in another woman, you'll blow our cover."

"Did I look like I was more interested in somebody else?"

"Not yet," Ekaterina whispered. "But we'll have to work on this."

Suddenly, he felt exhausted. "I'm not a professional spy. I'm not an information broker like you."

Ekaterina darted her eyes over to Eden. "You have feelings for her?"

"Who?"

"Eden."

Clark tensed. He didn't trust Ekaterina enough to share with her his own private thoughts. "I feel responsible, that's all. I invited her to come. I don't like leaving her alone all night."

Ekaterina touched him gently on the shoulder. "Life pushes us in unexpected directions. Sometimes not in the directions where we want to go."

Her consoling words did little to make him feel better.

Just then, Sokolov appeared behind him. "Counselor, would you kindly allow me to interrupt and ask Her Serene Highness for a dance?"

Quickly, Ekaterina assumed an indignant air and turned her head the other way.

"Commissar," Clark said, "I'm afraid she is not interested."

"Please, Your Serene Highness." Sokolov bowed his head. His icy stare sent a chill up Clark's spine. "One dance? At least give me a chance to say I'm sorry for all the grievances your family has suffered. You are still a daughter of Russia. Your opinions matter to me. All the honors ever bestowed upon me would be hollow if Your Serene Highness would not grant me at least one dance."

Ekaterina lowered her eyes, as if she were thinking, then took one step back from Clark. "One dance," she said, her voice a perfect mix of resentment and vulnerability. She touched Clark on the arm. "Do you mind?"

Doing his best to play his part, Clark caressed her hand. "I don't want to, but anything your precious heart desires, my dear Katia." He put on a glum face and let go of her. Before he walked away, he cast a suspicious look at Sokolov, who ignored him and swept Ekaterina away. Clark hoped his act was adequate. This plan was much harder than he'd thought, and he couldn't believe he had delivered Ekaterina into the hands of that cold-blooded man.

He made his way back to his table. By now, his Chinese guests were gone. Only Eden still remained, all alone. His heart quickened and he hastened his steps. He could take this chance to tell her how sorry he felt. He owed her at least that.

"Yuan Guo-Hui!" The harsh voice calling his name stopped him. Clark turned to see who was speaking. The stern eyes of a middle-aged man with bronze-tone skin bore down on him.

"Liu Kun," Clark said. He didn't know Liu well. Liu ran a

business manufacturing tobacco. Their families rarely crossed paths.

Liu came closer. His shoulders hunched and the corners of his mouth tight.

Clark looked around himself. Was Liu Kun coming at him, or someone else?

Liu stopped within inches of him. "You're good. Fiercely good," he sneered. "Twenty plus years I've worked to get to where I am today. Five years I've served on the SMC. You came back to Shanghai for no more than a year. Having spent not even the strength of blowing away dust, and you could already break open all the doors to take what you want. I admire you. I really do."

"What are you talking about?" Clark asked. "I don't understand."

"They said you bartered with the KMT for a seat on the SMC."

Instantly, Clark pressed his lips shut. He wasn't about to disclose to Liu anything he discussed with Madam Chiang. Especially not his bargain with her for a seat on the SMC for his father.

"If someone goes on stage, naturally somebody else will have to come off the stage. Don't say I didn't warn you though. I, Liu Kun, can't be chased away so easily. Watch slowly how I'll make you pay for this debt." He twitched his face and turned around.

"I never asked anyone to take away your seat," Clark said. It was true, too. He had demanded Soong Mei-Ling to put his father on the Council, but he did not ask her to remove Liu or anyone else.

Of course, that was a poor excuse. Only five Chinese representatives could sit on the Council. Obviously, someone had to be removed to make room for his father.

Liu Kun wasn't fooled either. He sneered again and left in a huff.

Clark shook his head. When he started to walk back to his

table again, a dashing young man with a winsome smile had joined Eden. Whatever he was saying to her delighted her. Clark stood. His heart dropping as she leaned her ear closer to the man and joy returned to her face.

Let them be. He slid his hand into his pocket and walked away. It was because of him that she had to endure this wretched evening. And now, someone had come to her rescue, and she seemed to be enjoying herself. Why ruin that for her too?

When Clark left with Ekaterina for the dance floor, Eden couldn't help thinking back to the time when Clark and his sisters took her to the Paramount Dance Hall. That night, in the mesmerizing realm of the Orient, she and Clark had danced in a world away from all the threats and harshness she had known. The spellbinding sounds of the music enveloped them. In this city, where the party seemed to never end, she could almost convince herself such rapture could last forever.

Was the magic of the Orient all but an illusion? Tonight, Clark was dancing with somebody else.

One by one, the Chinese guests got up and left the table. They were all older. Distinguished businessmen closer to her father's age and their wives. The married ones brought their spouses to the dance floor. The two who had come alone left the ball when the dancing began. They nodded politely to her before they departed, leaving her to wonder if she, too, should quietly withdraw herself from this scene.

"May I join you?" A man pulled out the chair next to her. Surprised, she looked up. It was the same man who was staring at her before the ball began. The one with the playful smile. Before she could answer, he took the liberty and sat down. "Why is the most beautiful girl of the evening sitting all alone by herself?"

"That's very flattering, thank you," Eden said. "But I'm certainly not the most beautiful girl of the evening."

"Oh no? Pardon me then, but I have to disagree." He put his glass of wine on the table. When he smiled, his eyes crinkled like cheerful half-moons. "I'm Neil Sassoon. May I ask your name?"

"Sassoon?" She raised her brows. "You mean, the Sassoons?" Who in Shanghai hadn't heard of the Sassoons? They had dominated the city for three generations. Their business empire extended beyond Shanghai to India, Japan, Thailand, Southeast Asia, and the Middle East. Even the Hardoons and the Kadoories had their start as employees for the Sassoon enterprises. The Sassoons owned the grandest properties in all of Shanghai, including the Cathay Hotel where this ball was being held. People called them the Rothschilds of the East.

"Yes," Neil admitted. She liked the humble way he spoke. "Victor Sassoon is my uncle."

Sir Victor Sassoon. Third Baronet in the Order of the British Empire. Patriarch of the Sassoon family in Shanghai. The most revered member of the city's Jewish community. Arguably the most powerful man in the city's international community.

"It's an honor to meet you," Eden said. She couldn't believe she was talking to one of the Sassoons.

"No. It's my honor." Neil rested his arm on the table. "You still haven't told me your name."

"I haven't?" Eden laughed. "I'm sorry. My name's Eden. Eden Levine."

"Eden Levine?" he asked. "The star of the *China Press*? The truth-seeker who single-handedly riled the entire foreign community as no one has ever done?"

Eden slumped in her seat. "Don't remind me." She rolled her eyes. "I'm no star. All the Jews in Shanghai have practically disowned me for defending a Nazi. Now that you know who I am, maybe you should stay far, far away from me. People might scorn you too for associating with me. You probably think I'm a race traitor too."

"Do I?" He took a sip of his wine. "You'd be surprised. May I invite you for a dance?"

"Really?" Eden couldn't believe he asked.

"Really." Neil finished his drink and stood up.

Eden glanced at his open hand. "All right." She placed her own hand in his and let him lead her to the dance floor. As they made their way through the room, people around them whispered and stared. People she didn't know smiled at her. Everyone seemed to be stepping aside for them. Confused, she glanced at Neil. The attention of the guests didn't bother him. Holding her hand, he walked on until they reached the center of the splendid white maple dance floor. When they began dancing, the curious looks of the guests only intensified. Female guests began flinging envious glares her way.

Was this what Cinderella felt like when the prince picked her out at the ball?

"What's the matter?" Neil asked.

"I . . ." She glided her feet to feel the bouncy softness beneath her shoes. She felt like she was walking on clouds. Literally.

"It's the floor, isn't it?" Neil swung her around so her skirt twirled. "There are springs built under it. Look at everyone dancing. The springs give their movements a gentle flow."

She let him lead her as they weaved through the people dancing around them. How amazing. Everyone was moving so softly, like they were dancing in the air.

"My uncle thinks highly of you," Neil said as they swayed to the music.

"You're talking about Sir Victor?" She didn't think someone like Victor Sassoon was aware she existed.

"He thinks the SMP is run by buffoons. He didn't believe their trumped-up charges against the Nazi at all. He thought it was brilliant how you called out the Municipal Council for their lapses and failures. Every week, he'd read the morning paper just to look for your articles."

Eden didn't know if what he said was true, but it sure felt good to think that an important man like Sir Victor was her fan.

And she had to admit, it felt good to be dancing here with Neil. Tried as she might to hide it, the truth was, she did feel the sting of rejection. She was disappointed that Clark had escorted Ekaterina tonight instead of her.

Finally, she could admit it. And Neil's attention made her feel worthy.

"Neil?" she asked.

"Yes?"

"If your uncle didn't think Johann Hauser was guilty, why didn't he say something in public? Your uncle is the most respected man in this city. They would have listened if he spoke."

"Well," Neil muttered and slowed down, "for one thing, he detests politics. They've asked him to join the Municipal Council five times. Each time, he declined. He'd rather be tending to his stable of racehorses. Besides, like you said, his words carry a lot of weight. He had his beliefs, but he didn't have solid proof. He didn't want to jeopardize an ongoing investigation in case he was wrong."

"I see."

"But he did think you presented a good case for what really happened."

"Thank you," she said, grateful for the compliment. She looked over his shoulder at the crowd. "Is he here tonight?"

"I'm afraid not." Neil picked up their pace to match the music. "This is an American event. He thought his attendance might upstage the host and the British would get all the attention again. I'm here on his behalf."

"That's too bad." Eden laughed. She would have liked to see the man in person.

"Eden, pardon me for asking. Do you not have an escort tonight?" He peered into her face.

"No." She put on a proud smile. "I came alone. I'm here as a reporter. My boss, Charlie, wants me to do a write up about this event."

Neil gazed at her, his eyes softening. "Must be my lucky night."

"What about you? Where's your companion for the evening?"

"She had to return to London. Her great-grandmother passed away suddenly. She had to cancel and go back to England with her family."

Eden dropped her shoulders. "I'm sorry to hear that."

"Don't be. She and her parents haven't seen her great-grandmother for more than fifteen years. I'm sure they're more interested in attending the reading of the will than the funeral."

"Oh."

"Anyhow, she's only an acquaintance," Neil said. "Besides, I'm now with someone I'd much rather spend time with."

Eden blushed.

"Listen." Neil drew her closer. "Can I escort you home tonight?"

Tonight? What about Clark and Ekaterina?

She laughed at herself then. Surely, they wouldn't miss her if she chose to ride home with somebody else. "I would like that," she said to Neil. "Thank you."

"What about after tonight?" Neil pulled her hand to his chest.

"What about it?"

"Could I see you again? I have tickets to a wonderful show at the Lyceum Theater next week. It's Noël Coward's *Private Lives*. Have you heard of Noël Coward?"

"No."

"He's an English playwright. He wrote the play a few years ago when he was staying at this very hotel with a bad case of flu. He said the Cathay Hotel was the inspiration for the play."

"Really? How interesting."

"Come with me. You can see for yourself whether his work is any good or not."

Eden hesitated. They had only just met. This was all happening a little too fast. But on second thought, why not? Why shouldn't she accept an invitation from someone who clearly admired her? It would be a good diversion. She didn't want to live only in dreams and fantasies anymore. "Okay. I'll come."

Neil gave her hand a light squeeze. A playful glimmer sprung to his eyes.

Yes, Eden thought. It was time she explored possibilities with someone who wouldn't leave her guessing and wondering.

Not just any someone either. The invitation came from Neil Sassoon. When her parents heard about this, they would be so surprised.

8

THE ASPIRING HEIR

AT THE ICHIBAN RAMEN HOUSE, Eden sat at the long table against the front window with her half-eaten bowl of noodles. She had been coming every other day for lunch for the last two weeks. By now, the restaurant staff had grown used to her. She was the white woman who liked to come to eat while she read.

Reading was part of her guise. With a book in hand, she could stay for hours, pretending she was immersed in the story. The restaurant staff didn't mind. She always made sure to come after the lunch rush to avoid interfering with their business. Coming later also helped to ensure her table would be empty.

Today, she'd brought something else besides her book. A handheld camera. It wasn't enough to just observe the building across the street where the Japanese marines queued up anymore. She wanted pictures.

Taking photos could be risky. What if someone saw her? What if they questioned her and asked why she was photographing the Japanese military?

This had to be discreet.

The line of soldiers today was unusually long. The line was long last Saturday too. The number of soldiers who came on weekends more than doubled compared to the number who came on weekdays, and the weekend was when they were officially off duty. What did that mean? Was this building a place for leisure, or a place of military business?

Something else was different today. On each side of the entrance, the marines had hung a banner written in kanji. Kanji was Chinese written characters that the Japanese had adopted into their language. If she could take a photo of the banners, she could show it to her Chinese colleagues back at the office and find out what they said.

Slowly, she pulled the camera from her purse. Her heart was beating so fast. Holding the camera on her lap, she checked her left and right to make sure no one was looking. Casually, she turned to look over her shoulder. At the counter, the chubby waitress was laughing and swinging a wet towel at one of the cooks. The other cooks joined in the laughter. By the wall, a woman was trying to calm the crying baby in her arms while she urged her older boy to finish his bowl. An older man sat at the table behind her, reading the newspaper while he ate.

Eden opened her book and stood it vertically on the table. Keeping it open and upright, she raised the camera and placed it behind the book. Using her body as a cover to shield the camera from the sight of the restaurant staff and guests behind her, she peeked into the lens and snapped, then slid the camera back into her purse.

No one noticed.

Trembling, she gulped her tea and wiped the sweat off her palms with the napkin, then signaled the waitress for the bill.

After she put on her coat, she checked her watch. She still had more than an hour to get home and get ready before Neil Sassoon came to pick her up. After their evening at the show at the Lyceum Theater, he had asked to see her again. This time, he wanted to take her for a ride in the Sassoons' private rickshaw.

Flattered by his ardent attention, and curious to see what his rickshaw was like, she had told him yes.

———————

At five o'clock, Neil Sassoon arrived at Eden's home. As soon as she came downstairs, he walked up to her, took her hand, and planted a light kiss on its back. "I'm so happy to see you."

"Thank you for inviting me," she said. In his long coat and hat, he looked absolutely dandy.

His rickshaw looked even more impressive. "How beautiful!" She stepped down the curb and walked around it to examine its gold trim and red hood. Its black surface was so clean and smooth, she could see her own reflection shining through. "I had no idea rickshaws could be this luxurious."

Neil's eyes gleamed. The coolie, his hair combed and his uniform spiffy, opened up the tarpaulin. "Good afternoon, Miss, welcome."

"Hello," Eden replied. The coolie could speak English!

"Shall we?" Neil held out his arm to help her in.

"Yes." Holding on to his hand for support, Eden climbed up onto the spotless white upholstered seat. "This is so comfortable." She patted the cushion.

"A little tight for two people, but I hope you don't mind."

"No, not at all."

"Good." Neil climbed in after her. Before sitting down, he picked up the folded blanket on his side. Once seated, he unfolded the blanket and spread it over their laps. "Warm enough?"

"Yes." The blanket was just what one needed to keep warm against the February chill.

The coolie picked up the bar and pulled them down the street. Eden ran her fingers down the top of her side of the panel. This felt unreal. She was riding in the Sassoons' private rickshaw.

"I thought we could ride around the neighborhood," Neil said. "After that, we can have dinner at the British Club. How does that sound?"

"The British Club?" That exclusive premier men's club in Shanghai? "Sure. I've never been there. I didn't know women were allowed in." And even if they were, she didn't know anyone else who could bring her.

"It's time you grace it with your presence then. The dining room is opened for us to bring guests, even ladies, on Saturday nights. My uncle has the number one spot at the Long Bar. From there, you can look out and see the Bund. We can have a drink there before we eat if you like."

"What do you mean your uncle has the number one spot?"

"You don't know?" Neil asked. "The Long Bar is reserved for a select group of Club members. The members who are allowed to use it are each given a spot. The spots are assigned according to the member's status, from the one nearest the window to the one farthest away."

"I see." Eden touched the skirt of her wool dress under the blanket. "Am I dressed properly?" She looked at her suit jacket and her scarf. "I'm sorry. You must think I'm such a rube."

"Not at all." He smiled. That playful smile that had drawn her to him the first time they met. "It is I who should be mindful that my family enjoys a lot of privileges wherever we go, and we ought not to take it for granted."

How humble of him to say that. He looked like he meant it too.

"And the way you're dressed is fine. There's no requirement for ladies to be in evening wear."

Relieved, Eden sat back and watched the pedestrians on the sidewalk. When she looked up, she found Neil gazing at her.

Was this the real future waiting for her?

She lowered her eyes and bent her head. Neil wasn't a prince, but he was the nephew of a baron. A baron who was the most powerful man in Shanghai.

Clark wasn't the only one who could step out with an aristocrat.

What kind of thinking was that? she chastised herself. She shouldn't compare their situations that way. Neil had been so earnest, he deserved better. And why was she thinking about another man? She was out with Neil. She should be giving him her undivided attention. She decided to ask Neil about himself instead. "Neil, may I ask, what exactly do you do for your uncle's company?"

Neil stopped smiling. He glanced away from her to the road ahead. "Right now, I'm on the board of his charitable foundation. He'll be bringing me into the real estate business though. That's where I should be." He smiled. Not the playful smile she'd seen up till now, but a more calculating one that she found hard to read. "Anyway, he'll have to let me in sooner or later. He's fifty-six years old. He still doesn't have an heir. He's got no children. Someone will have to look after his business one day."

"Will that someone be you?" Eden asked, not because she cared about his wealth, but because the shifty tone in Neil's voice made her wonder if he wasn't telling her the whole story.

"It's not official yet," he said under his breath. "I came to Shanghai only three years ago. Uncle Victor and my father are brothers. My grandparents disowned my father for marrying my mother. She's an Anglo-Catholic."

"Disowned?"

"Yes. Disowned and disinherited."

"How awful." Why couldn't their world be simpler? Why did love between two people have to be so complicated when entangled with the issues of culture and race?

"Moneywise, it didn't affect my parents," Neil continued. "My mother came from a very wealthy family herself. She has a very sizable income of her own. But naturally, the assets on her side of the family would go to her brothers and their sons. Right now, I'm the one best suited to succeed Uncle Victor and his title. It would make perfect sense for him to let bygones be bygones, accept me back into the family, and designate me his heir."

"I hope so, if that's what you want," Eden said. "It must have been hard for you growing up." All the money aside, how sad it must have been for him to know that his father's side of the family had disowned all of them. It wasn't even his fault. "You know, everyone in the Jewish community still blames me for writing all those articles that favored the Nazi soldier in Lillian Berman's murder case. My brother's bar mitzvah is coming up in April. My mother doesn't know what to do. If she throws Joshua a party, no one will come, and this is all my fault."

Neil peered into her face. "Maybe I can help."

"Help? How?"

"Let me and my uncle host your brother's bar mitzvah. We can have the ceremony at the Ohel Rachel."

"The Ohel Rachel? The synagogue on Seymour Road?"

"Yes."

Eden covered her heart. "Those Greek columns in the front are magnificent."

"Uncle Victor's father, Jacob, built it," Neil said with a proud smile. "He named it after his mother."

"That's what I heard."

"I'll talk to Rabbi Hirsch. He can arrange with Cantor Warschaur to take over preparations for your brother. After the ceremony, we'll have the celebration at the Sassoon villa outside of the city. We can have a party in the garden. The weather should be warm enough by then."

"Are you sure about that?" Eden asked. "Your uncle doesn't even know my family. I don't want to impose."

"Yes, I'm sure." Neil laughed. "Like I told you, my uncle has no children. How often does he get to host a party to celebrate a bar mitzvah? He'll love it. Besides, if there's anything I'm sure of about my uncle, it's horses and parties. He never passes up a chance to host a good party. So, how about it?"

Stunned, Eden stared at him. She and Neil had only met three times. This was a huge favor and a serious undertaking. "I don't know what to say. I'm speechless."

"Say yes then," Neil said. "When people hear that we're hosting the party, they'll all want to come. No one would turn down an invitation from the Sassoons, and definitely not if they are given a chance to visit our private villa."

Eden curled her hands under the blanket. She had no doubt about that. Imagine the reactions of all the people who had stopped calling on her mother and father when they heard this. And how wonderful this would be for Joshua! He'd been having such a hard time in school. All the kids were still picking on him and ostracizing him because of her. If the Sassoons would throw their support behind them, her entire family would be forgiven.

Her parents would be over the moon too. They already were when she told them Neil had invited her out. To have the Sassoons host their son's bar mitzvah would be an honor beyond their dreams.

But if they accepted Neil's offer, would that mean she was officially seeing him? Surely, he wouldn't offer to do such a huge favor for just anyone.

Was she ready for this? She needed time to think. "Neil. This is such a generous offer. Would you mind if I pass the idea to my father and mother first? It would be their decision."

"Of course," Neil said. "You just say the word and let me know."

"Thank you." She adjusted herself in her seat. There was no question,her parents would say yes. The hesitation was entirely on her part.

The traffic policeman at the crosswalk whistled a warning at the traffic to let pedestrians pass. The vehicles coming from their direction stopped and their coolie halted the rickshaw. A woman crossing the street stared at their direction and tapped her friend's arm. She pointed at the Sassoon family emblem engraved on the rickshaw's side, then looked up at the passengers' seat. When she saw Neil, her eyes widened in awe and she whispered excitedly to her friend. Her friend turned around and gave Eden a second look.

Was that envy she just saw on the woman's face? It certainly looked like it. Eden could see why. What girl wouldn't wish to be in her place right now, next to Neil Sassoon in his private rickshaw? Who would have to think twice, if given a chance to be Neil Sassoon's girlfriend?

She turned her head and looked at Neil. He wasn't handsome exactly, but no one would say he was unattractive. His jawline might be a little too soft for a man, but his manners were always so refined. And his playful smile and good humor easily endeared him to others.

Noticing her staring at him, Neil smiled. "Are you warm enough?"

"Yes. Just my hands are a little cold, that's all."

He reached out and took her hand. The sudden gesture took her by surprise and she froze in her seat.

"We'll stop at the next block then. We can get a taxi."

"No," she said. He was being so thoughtful, she didn't want to cause a fuss. "I'm all right. Let's finish the ride."

A new tenderness filled his eyes. He sat back, but held on to her hand. He'd misunderstood her intent, but she didn't pull her hand back.

What more did she want? The most eligible Jewish bachelor in the whole country was courting her. And he was so kind and gentle. He was doing and saying everything to make her feel special. If she were smart, she would go on with him. For a girl of her age and background, it would be the right thing to do.

The traffic police waved and the coolie began pulling again.

The seat bounced over a pothole and Neil jostled against her side. When Eden didn't shift, he remained settled in closer to her.

The sky dimmed and the streetlight came on. In her seat, Eden stayed still.

When dinner ended tonight, would she leave it as a social call with no further significance? Or would she open herself to something more?

Do the right thing, her mind told her.

But why did the right thing feel wrong?

Something stronger was pulling behind her. What it was, she didn't know. All the same, leaving it behind left her feeling hollow and a bit sad. She felt like she was walking into something tiresome and all too predictable. Something lacking in adventure and inspiration. Something that would smother the fire within her and snuff out its spark.

A force that would energize her life was out there, calling for her. But as the rickshaw pulled further and further ahead, she was leaving it further and further behind.

9

A CLANDESTINE AFFAIR

IT MIGHT BE JUST his imagination, but Clark swore that each time he stepped into the Metropole Hotel, the concierge would give him a sideways glance coupled with a snicker. Of course, if the concierge was looking at him askance, it would mean his plan succeeded. Ekaterina lived in a deluxe suite here, and he had come to visit her. Each time he came, he would bring a bouquet. He would also make sure to ask the concierge to telephone her suite. This way, the concierge would know that he had arrived, and there was now something for people to gossip about.

Still, knowing it was a ruse didn't make him feel any less uncomfortable. How annoying it was to be grouped with all the Shanghai princelings with too much money who lusted after beautiful women.

Whatever the concierge was imagining to be happening upstairs when he came to see the princess, the man had it all wrong.

"Young Master Yuan, Her Serene Highness said you may come up." The concierge hung up the phone.

"Thank you." Clark slipped him a tip. A generous one of ten

dollars. He did this each time he came. The tip was understood to be a reward for the hotel front desk to keep their mouths shut. In effect, what it really did was to further affirm there was indeed something salacious worth gossiping about. It would ensure the word would spread from the hotel staff to the rest of the town and beyond. The young master of the reputable, upright Yuan family was chasing a foreign woman. A Russian princess! He came to her room every week for their trysts.

"Thank you." The concierge accepted with both hands. "Thank you, Young Master Yuan."

Clark left him and headed for the elevator without a second look. The more he flaunted his money and the more arrogantly he behaved, the more convincing he would be.

The elevator took him to the tenth floor. With the bouquet of pink roses in hand, he knocked. Ekaterina opened the door, grabbed his hand, and pulled him inside.

"If you don't mind me saying so, you still look too stiff." She dropped his arm and closed the door. "And you can look a little more excited to see me." She tilted her head at the flowers. "Is that for me?"

"Yeah." He handed her the bouquet.

"Thank you." Ekaterina took it and set it into a vase on the table. "The flowers are nice, but don't you have something more precious to give me? Diamond earrings maybe? Jewelry from J. Ullmann?" A coy smile crossed her lips.

"No, I'm afraid I didn't think of all that. But I did bring this." He pulled a bank note from Sītu out of his inner pocket.

Ekaterina took it and checked the amount. "Even better. Have a seat. Let me pour you a drink. That might loosen you up." She went over to the bar and poured them each a glass of whiskey over ice.

Clark took the drink and sat down on the couch. "How did it go with Sokolov last night?"

"Better than you'd ever expect." She sat down across from him. "Your people are right. The Soviets aren't working exclusively with the KMT. They're hedging their bets. The Kremlin's still selling arms to Mao and the communists. The sales never stopped. Not even when Chiang Kai-shek promised to make peace with the CCP and bring them into the fold to fight the Japanese together with them."

Clark searched Ekaterina's face. "Sokolov told you this? He only had dinner with you once."

"I don't think he meant to, but I made him feel relaxed enough around me." She sat back and held up her drink. "At least enough for him to think I'm nothing but a dumb girl down on her luck."

"How were you able to do that?"

"It's very basic," she said. "People like to be right. They form an opinion about someone they meet, and they like it when that person turns out to be exactly what they thought. I gave Sokolov the impression I'm a simple-minded girl with little cash who is desperate to hold on the last vestiges of my fallen family's fame. I did what I could to convince him I'm exactly who he believes me to be."

"All right."

"Once I convinced him I was dumb and harmless, it was his turn to convince me he was my friend. He has uses for someone like me." She leaned forward and lowered her voice. "Do you remember the purge I told you about? There's a huge shake-up happening within the Kremlin. A Bolshevik leader, Sergei Kirov, was shot and killed in 1934. Since then, Stalin's been searching for dissidents who might have committed the murder. Do you know about the trial against Grigory Zinoviev and Lev Kamenev last August?"

"I've heard," Clark said. The trial was reported all over the news worldwide. Zinoviev and Kamenev were both former party leaders and close allies of Vladimir Lenin. They were also Stalin's strongest political opponents. Both were found guilty of the assassination of Kirov and sentenced to death.

"Supposedly, they confessed," Ekaterina said. "Last month, seventeen more people were tried and found guilty of plotting against Stalin and conspiring with the Germans. All of them were old-guard Bolsheviks. All of them longtime supporters of the revolution. Stalin's removing everyone and rebuilding the Kremlin with a clean slate."

Clark took a sip of his whiskey. It wasn't unheard of for authoritarian leaders to rid their regimes of those who had won the power for them. Without the people who fought along his side, the leader would not be beholden to anyone, and no one would feel entitled to criticize the leader.

"Sokolov's been with the Bolshevik regime for twenty years," Ekaterina said. "If I were him, I'd be nervous too."

"You figured he wants to use Borodin and his people as his bargaining chip," Clark said.

"Yes. He's desperate for evidence to show his loyalty. He needs information about saboteurs to feed back to Moscow."

"And he thinks you can provide him that."

"I already made a deal with him."

"So fast?" Clark dropped his hand. Drops of whiskey bounced out of his glass.

A wry smile spread across her face.

Such a lonely, distant face. Clark worried for her. "You're putting yourself between Sokolov and the White Russian royalists. It's a dangerous place to be." He warned her again.

Ekaterina turned her head and stared into space. An old weariness filled her eyes. Eyes that carried the sadness of someone who had seen too much.

"Anyway," she said and broke her trance. "He was talking big, trying to impress me. At the end of the night, he invited me back to his flat. He has a flat that he keeps private away from his family. A bottle of Beluga later, his mouth slipped and he told me about the arms sale. He made me swear I wouldn't tell you, but he told me the Soviets are still supplying arms to the CCP. You can pass this on to your Party."

Clark frowned. "Sītu's not going to like it when he hears about this."

"Sokolov said people like you in the KMT are fools," Ekaterina said. "He said the Soviets have you all under their thumbs." She brushed her chin with the back of her fingers. "I think he's a little jealous. I don't think he likes it too much I'm sleeping with you. Or so he thinks, anyway."

Clark looked away and shifted uncomfortably in his seat. "Can you find out what they're selling to Mao and his people?" he asked. The KMT would want the Soviets to sell at least the same amount to them.

"Maybe." Ekaterina twirled a lock of her hair. "I might be able to if I lure him into an affair with me. I know he finds me attractive. Men need confidants. They usually can't resist disclosing secrets when they're in bed with a woman."

"Be serious," Clark said. "I won't ask you to do that."

"Why not?" Ekaterina crinkled her eyes. "Are you jealous?"

"No!" Clark drew back. "An affair with Sokolov. Don't disgrace yourself. You don't have to go that far for us."

Ekaterina giggled. "Look at you." She took a sip of her drink. "I'm just joking."

This woman. Clark shook his head.

"There's something else." Ekaterina's face reverted back to seriousness. "He told me Tang Wei's been negotiating private arm deals with him."

"Say that again?"

"Tang Wei's working as a middleman for Sokolov to sell arms to Chinese resistance groups. He takes a cut of the revenue for himself."

"No," Clark said. "Tang Wei wouldn't do that."

ALEXA KANG

"Yes, he would. This was the deal he made with Sokolov. He gets ten percent of the proceeds when he brokers a sale to local resistance groups. If the resistance groups use the weapons to pick fights with the Japanese, he gets another ten percent."

"That's outrageous! Tang Wei colluding with Sokolov? He's doing Sokolov's bidding? I don't believe it."

"What reason would I have to lie to you? What Stalin wants is for China and Japan to go to war. As long as the Japanese are tied down here, they won't be giving him troubles up north. Surely you, too, can see that." Ekaterina looked him in the eye, then reclined into her seat. "Sokolov would do whatever he can to please Stalin. He's found a perfect pawn to help him in that regards."

Clark gripped his glass. Tang Wei? Not possible. Either Sokolov or Ekaterina was lying. Probably Sokolov. "I've known Tang Wei for years. He's faithful to the Party. He's one of the most trustworthy people I know. Sokolov's lying. He's slandering the KMT to fool you."

Ekaterina tossed up an open hand. "Fine. It's up to you whether or not to believe me. You realize my telling you about his activities isn't part of what the KMT is paying me for. I'm telling you this as a favor, because we're partners. I like giving gifts to my partners. It helps to build trust." Her lips lifted into a quick smile. "There'll be another delivery next Tuesday at the Xinyi Warehouse in Pootung to a gang called Yin Ying. You can check it out yourself."

Clark studied her face, then dropped his eyes to his glass. Yin Ying. The Silver Shadow. He'd never heard of them. But if this group existed, he knew someone who would.

Time to pay a visit to Mauricio Perez at Blood Alley.

In one shot, he downed the rest of his drink. The burning sensation of the whiskey streaming down his throat to his chest steadied his thoughts. Ekaterina was wrong about Tang Wei. He wouldn't doubt Tang Wei based on hearsay from a woman no one could trust. Mauricio would find proof to clear his friend.

If the Princess's information was unreliable, this would be a good test to find out.

10

COMMUNISTS UNDERGROUND

ON THE INFAMOUS strip of Blood Alley, the Sambuca lounge hardly stood out among the bars and casinos where foreign sailors and pleasure seekers came to explore vices of every kind. The lounge's lights paled compared to those beaming from the entrance of the Royal Casino. Its line never stretched around the block like the one in front of the Frisco cabaret. It didn't even have a reputation of having the prettiest hostesses like Fat's Bar.

Clark knew well why Sambuca kept such a low profile in this playground for miscreants. Sambuca was a place that sold more than alcohol, sex, and other opiates of escape. Mauricio Perez, Sambuca's Eurasian owner, was a keeper of information. His contacts began at Blood Alley, where the shadiest visitors from every corner of the world always passed through when they made their stops in Shanghai. From here, his network spread to the rest of the globe. One discreet phone call by him, and a buyer could purchase almost any information on anyone. Especially on those with something to hide.

Word on the streets was, Mauricio sold more information. Rumor had it, Mauricio could make things happen too for the right price.

But Clark wouldn't know about that. For a KMT foreign-affairs agent with a clean reputation, some things were better left unknown.

Information, though, was fair trade. Mauricio kept a finger on the pulse of everything going on in the city's underground. During daytime, as it was now, Sambuca operated as his private office, where the commodity of secrets changed hands every day.

"I wouldn't call the Silver Shadow a resistance force. They're more like troublemakers," Mauricio said as he served Clark a glass of rum. "There are real underground resistance groups in Shanghai. The most lethal one would be Tian Di Hui. I know a number of its members."

"I've heard of that group," Clark said. The name Tian Di Hui meant the Heaven and Earth Society. This band had existed for hundreds of years. It began as a group of vigilantes out to protect the poor and the weak, and to deliver justice as they saw fit. Later on, it morphed into rebels with a mission to overthrow the Qing Dynasty.

"Resistance groups with any substance like Tian Di Hui are all operating under Dai Li," Mauricio said.

"Dai Li? The head of *Juntong*?" Clark asked. He had crossed paths with Dai Li twice before. Once at a banquet held for General Zhang of the Fifth Army. Another time when Dai Li indirectly forced his hand to suppress Shen da ye's protesting factory workers.

"That's him," Mauricio said.

"Interesting. You're saying the Chinese secret police is now working with the resistance forces?"

"Yes. And I know for a fact Silver Shadow is not working with Dai Li. Dai Li's very strict with his underlings. He would have no use for a gang of unruly children like the Silver Shadow. The leader of this gang, Lei Bao, is the second son of Lei Yong-Feng."

"Lei Yong-Feng, the Fifth Army major general?"

"That's him. The father and son had a falling out. Lei Yong-

Feng had both of his sons in the army. Bao accused his father of favoring his older brother. He broke off from the unit and brought a group of army defectors with him to form the Silver Shadow. Since then, they've been riling up people to protest and drive out the Japanese dogs. I wouldn't mistake him for a patriot though. Everything he does is to stir up trouble for his old man. He gets away with it. Everyone gives young Bao an inch because they're afraid of old Lei, and old Lei wouldn't clamp down on his own son."

"Is Lei Bao behind all the recent skirmishes with the Japanese over at Soochow Creek?" Clark asked.

"Yes. The fool's playing with fire. One day, he's going to more than irritate the Japanese troops and pull all of us into a war."

And whoever provided him arms was the one setting off the fuse. Ekaterina alleged it was Tang Wei. Clark didn't believe it. His friend's hands were clean. He had come here today to prove it. "You'll let me know then if you find out who's behind the arms sale to them next Tuesday?"

"No problem." Mauricio scribbled a dollar amount on a piece of paper and handed it to Clark. Clark took a quick glance, then folded it into his pocket.

"Always a pleasure doing business with you." Mauricio raised his glass. Clark clinked it with his own. An early toast to clearing his friend's name.

———

Back at his office, Clark had just settled at his desk when his phone rang. On the line was Officer Zhou from the Shanghai Public Safety Bureau. Clark hadn't spoken to him in months, not since they had colluded to deliver the Nazi soldier Johann Hauser back to the Germans.

"You better come to our bureau," Zhou said. "We raided an illegal gathering of subversive elements."

"What subversive elements?" Clark asked.

"We suspect one of the radicals we arrested has close association with your family."

"Who?" Clark pressed the phone closer to his ear.

Zhou still wouldn't say. He lowered his voice. "It might be best if you come in person and clear things up."

Clark glanced at his watch. Zhou wouldn't call him like this unless it was important. "All right. I'll come right away." He hung up the phone and grabbed his coat.

What could Zhou be talking about?

He exited his office to the elevator.

Subversive elements? Someone associated with his family? He couldn't think of who it could be.

An hour later, he arrived at the police bureau. Immediately, Zhou took him aside to the bureau's guest room.

"What's this all about?" Clark asked after Zhou closed the door.

Zhou invited him to take a seat. "We've arrested someone by the name of Liu Zi-Hong. Do you know him?"

Just hearing the name brought on a headache. "What happened?" Clark asked instead of answering Zhou.

"We raided an unauthorized Communist Party meeting at a rice shop earlier. A student named Liu Zi-Hong was among the people in attendance. When we rounded up the group, one of his cohorts flaunted your father's name. He dared us to touch a hair of Yuan Ren-Qiu's future son-in-law."

"He what?" These idiots. Dragging his family's name into this mess. How often had these ignorant fools hurled insults and scorn against the wealthy? The minute their own safety was on the line, they trotted out his father's name to use as a shield. That bunch of cowards.

And Liu Zi-Hong. Had he lost his mind? Clark had warned him before to stop mixing with the communists.

"Xiao Zhou," Clark said, addressing the policeman as "little

Zhou" as one would when speaking with a good friend, "you know my family has no relations to any communist group."

"Of course not." Zhou waved the idea away. "The Yuan family are communists? No one would believe that."

Clark calmed down a little. "As for Liu Zi-Hong, he's nothing more than an acquaintance of my little sister. She's still a school student herself. She has many classmates. To say Liu is my father's future son-in-law? Really, that's a big joke. Maybe they mentioned my father's name because they got caught and were afraid."

Zhou's face eased. "That could be. This band of mixed eggs. They shouldn't have tried to drag your father into this. This Liu Zi-Hong . . . the best solution would be to quietly let this matter rest. The higher-ups don't want to draw public attention to communist activities. There's no need to fan rumors and gossips by having the Yuan family's name linked to the arrest. Since Liu Zi-Hong is your sister's classmate, why don't you to give him a few words of advice and warn him to stay away from the rotten elements."

Clark understood the message. Zhou was doing him a favor to help his family to save face.

"Come with me." Zhou got up and opened the door. "I put Liu Zi-Hong in a separate cell from the others we arrested. I'll bring him to an interrogation room. You can talk to him there."

"Thanks for your trouble." Clark followed him out.

Zhou. What a reliable friend.

In the interrogation room, Clark stood and waited for Zhou and Liu Zi-Hong. What tone should he take with that little imbecile? Of all the boys in the world, Mei Mei had to pick him for a boyfriend.

The door opened. Zi-Hong took a step back when he saw Clark, then stiffened his face and puffed up his chest.

"Sit." Zhou pointed him to one of the two chairs at the table.

Hanging his head, Zi-Hong pulled out the chair and sat down. Zhou gave Clark a friendly glance and left the room.

Clark gave Zi-Hong a once over. The boy didn't dare to look at him. Clark opened his mouth, ready to chastise him, then gave up. The pathetic little fool. So rash and eager to show off his naive worldview. When the forces of the real world hit, all he could do was sit there, wide-eyed and terrified.

"Do you know you're very lucky this time?" Clark asked, still standing with his hand on his waist.

Zi-Hong dropped his eyes to the floor.

"Good thing I know Officer Zhou. I don't know what will happen to the other people he arrested, but he'll let you off on account of your connection with my family."

"I didn't ask you to help me," Zi-Hong grunted. "I didn't ask for special treatment."

Ungrateful little prick. "Then what? You want to go to jail?"

Zi-Hong shrank in his seat.

"If you go to jail, how upset would Wen-Li be? How worried would your parents be? As if getting yourself into trouble wasn't enough, you brought my father into this too?"

"That wasn't me!" Zi-Hong vigorously shook his head. "I never said anything about Uncle Yuan to the police. I had no intention to cause him any trouble. I'm truly sorry."

Clark sighed. At least, Zi-Hong seemed genuine about that. "Do you understand? Whether you intend it or not, a person's actions always impact those around him. It's a simple fact of life."

Shamefaced, Zi-Hong shifted his legs.

"Why not focus your attention on school?" Clark asked. "Do well in your studies, build a career. What's wrong with that? Why get mixed up with political activities?"

"You're mixed up with politics." Zi-Hong lifted his head.

"I work for the good of the people. I do what I do to protect and improve our society."

"That's what I'm doing too!"

Clark frowned. This idiot. He pulled out the other chair and sat down. "If you want to make society better, joining the Communist Party is not the right way to go about it."

"You're wrong." Zi-Hong clenched his fists on the table. "Too many rich people use their wealth and power to oppress the poor. Look at how hard the poor have to work. Look at their horrible living conditions. It's not fair. It's not right."

"Rich people oppress the poor. Is that what you think of me and my family too? Is that what you think of Wen-Li?"

Zi-Hong averted his gaze. "I didn't say your family." He tightened his lips. "Our system is the problem. We need a better government that would give the workers and farmers their due rights and protections."

"Mao's communist bandits will not bring you that."

"Why not?"

"Open your mind!" Clark threw up his hands. "Look at what's happening outside of your little utopian world. How many millions of people did the Red Army kill for Vladimir Lenin to impose his authoritarian regime in Russia? Look who Mao's allying with now? Josef Stalin is a thug. A brutal, murderous thug. The communists' way to achieve their goals is to crush every dissent, even if they have to commit mass murder. That is not the way to bring about a better society."

Zi-Hong pouted. Clark could see the wheels churning in his head, but the wheels were going nowhere. Zi-Hong showed little emotion at the mention of the atrocities outside of China.

There were people like that. Their sympathies for those who suffered didn't go beyond the boundaries of their own country.

"It's too bad if what you said about Lenin and Stalin is true," Zi-Hong said.

"If it's true?" Clark asked. "Do you even read international news? You're a waste of a university education."

"We won't be like that," Zi-Hong argued. "The Soviets will have to take it into their own hands if they aren't satisfied with how things are run. Here, in China, oppressed workers and farmers now have a chance to rise up." He sat up. Excitement gleamed in his eyes. "Mao Ze Dong can help them. He'll create a system for everyone to contribute to the best of their abilities, and everyone will share in the output according to each of their needs. This will be the way of the future. A revolution is happening. I can't stand by on the side."

Clark bit his lip, ready to refute him, but instead, he sighed. The silly boy. His heart full of ideals. Sheltered in his world of theories at school, he couldn't see the fallacies of communist ideologies. He couldn't understand that people were motivated by self-interest. A society would never succeed if it tried to suppress human nature's desire to compete and surpass others. A country built on the idealism of an egalitarian commune the way Zi-Hong described would fail from the tragedy of the commons.

Moreover, he couldn't see that communism would restrain the most important element of an advanced society—freedom.

How could he explain all this to a boy so lacking in real-world experience and make him see? Sitting there, Zi-Hong looked like a baby-faced puppet.

What could he say to sway this boy from pinning his hopes on a false hero like Mao Ze Dong? How could he save him from being caught up in the thrilling promise of a revolution?

If it weren't for Mei Mei, Clark would gladly walk away. Setting Liu Zi-Hong on the right path wasn't his responsibility. But for Mei Mei, he had to at least try. "Zi-Hong, you're still a student. You have no idea what it really takes to improve the lives of people you say you want to help. If you truly want to do something to make a difference, why don't you work for me?"

"Work for you?" Zi-Hong asked, incredulous.

"Yes. At the Foreign Affairs Bureau. You can be my part-time assistant." He paused to let the idea sink in. "Progress can be built by small steps. Spend some time at my office after school. You'll see our government is indeed working to make things better. I'll introduce you to the foreign officials I work with. You can expand your outlook. There's a bigger world out there. If you work for me, you can see how other countries flourish in other ways. You might find there are better choices than to follow Mao and his communist rhetoric."

Zi-Hong locked his fingers on the table.

Holding back his frustrations, Clark pressed him further. "If you follow what I say, I'll get you out of this place now." He glanced at the door. "You can choose to stay here. But prison isn't a joke. You better be ready for being locked up in filth without food or water. And how would you start a revolution in jail?"

Zi-Hong twitched his mouth, then exhaled and slumped in his seat. "I'll do whatever you tell me."

It wasn't the most enthusiastic reply, but Clark would take it for now. Hopefully, once he got Zi-Hong away from the communists, he could steer him toward less dangerous directions.

———

On their way out of the police station, Clark warned Zi-Hong, "Don't tell Wen-Li anything about your arrest. There's no need to make her worry. I won't let you to get her mixed up with anything involving the communists. You understand?"

"I understand," Zi-Hong grudgingly agreed before they parted ways.

Clark watched him head off to the tram. Thanks to Zhou, the Shanghai Public Safety Bureau in the end released Zi-Hong after they questioned him. The official report now said the police had found Liu Zi-Hong was present at the rice shop as a customer and not a part of the underground Communist Party meeting. His classmate who dragged Master Yuan Ren-Qiu's name into the conflict was released too. Both were recorded as unwitting students who had merely gone to buy rice at the wrong place at the wrong time.

Such a misguided puppet, Clark thought as he returned to his car. How many more young people out there were Mao's destructive ideologies leading astray?

Arriving home, Clark found Mei Mei in the living room with her floral arrangement instructor. This was a new hobby his youngest sister had recently picked up. A bright smile came to her face when Clark entered. "Ge!" She set a stem of lily into the vase and showed him her work. "Look. Aren't these beautiful?"

Clark walked over to the table. "Very."

The instructor bowed her head and gathered up the excess stems and leaves into a bucket. "I'll take these away for disposal," she said and took the trimmings out of the room.

Mei Mei wiped the droplets of water from the vase's surface. "If you like it, I'll put this one in your room. I made one for Jie already." She threw a glance at Wen-Ying on the sofa. Wen-Ying looked up from her volume of the *Dream of the Red Mansion*, then returned to her book.

"I'd like that," Clark said to Mei Mei and pinched her cheek. He knew she was too old for that, but he couldn't help himself. To him, Mei Mei would always be his little sister. "Oh, I ran into Zi-Hong today."

"Really?"

"I asked him to come work for me at the Foreign Affairs Bureau. He agreed. He'll be my part-time assistant."

"Ge!" Mei Mei laid down the towel. "You're so nice! With you, he'll definitely learn a lot."

"I hope so," Clark muttered. At least, one could hope. That foolish, arrogant boy. He couldn't even see the blessings around him. He could be a student, free of worries and fears, free to love.

Free to love. A precious gift Liu Zi-Hong took for granted and didn't know to keep hold and cherish. An intangible treasure which kept falling out of Clark's own grasp.

No point in thinking about it. He turned around, ready to go to give his mother a late afternoon greeting. A photo in the newspaper on the table caught his eye.

Neil Sassoon and Eden Levine at gala performance by violinist Ferdinand Adler.

The words hurt him like a stab in the heart.

"Ge?" Mei Mei whispered. Her eyes fell on the newspaper. She stepped closer to him. "I thought you and Eden would be together." She stole a quick glance at Wen-Ying, who looked immersed in her reading. "How did things end up like this?"

What could he say? How would he begin to explain? *"Yuan fen,"* he said, trying to laugh it off. The predestined depth of relationship between him and Eden wasn't enough.

Mei Mei looked at him with sympathy, but didn't ask anymore. For that, he was glad. "I'll take this vase of flowers to your room." She gave him an encouraging smile and went upstairs.

After she left, Clark picked up the newspaper. Neil Sassoon. He was a better match for Eden anyway. Rich, Jewish, British. Sassoon could offer her much more than he himself could, without any of the obstacles of racial and cultural divides. As for his own pain, he could keep that in the deep corner of his heart. As long as Eden was safe and happy, it was all that really mattered.

He tossed the paper back on the table. On the couch, Wen-Ying was watching him. He stared back at her. "If you have something to say, then say it."

Wen-Ying put down her book. "I don't have anything to say." She blinked.

"Never mind." Clark started toward the hallway.

"The Russian princess is a great beauty," Wen-Ying said behind him.

Clark stopped. "You heard?"

"Heard?" she asked, curling her lips. "All of Shanghai has

heard. Everyone's talking about Young Master Yuan chasing a foreign royal."

"No doubt, you don't approve."

"You're wrong about that." She picked up her cup of tea. "You asked me to stay out of your business. I'll respect your wish." She turned her attention back to her book. Her tone was so casual, so non-judgmental, Clark didn't know what to make of it.

No matter. His sister's opinion on who he was seeing was the least of his concerns. He had the KMT and the Russians to deal with. Ekaterina had accused his good friend of self-dealing. And now, he had to take Liu Zi-Hong under his wing. He had enough to worry about. Besides, his "courtship" of Ekaterina would end eventually. Let Wen-Ying and whoever else think whatever they wanted.

11

THE NAZI DOCTOR

"THIS RAMEN IS DELICIOUS," said Emmet Lai, Eden's colleague at the *China Press*. "It's not my imagination." He slurped the noodles into his mouth. "Japanese ramen at places outside of Hongkew simply doesn't taste as good."

"I'm glad you're enjoying your food," Eden said. From their long table by the window, she kept her eye on the building across the street. "But that's not why we're here." She put down her chopsticks. "Look." She nudged him with her elbow. "The line's gotten longer."

Emmet raised his head. "*Ribengui*." Eden understood it to mean Japanese devil. The Chinese referred to all sorts of dominant foreigners as "devils." The slang originated when they first encountered Europeans traveling to China. They thought only ghosts and devils guarding the gate of hell would be blonds and redheads and have blue or green eyes.

"They're up to no good." Emmet pointed his chopsticks at the queue of Japanese soldiers.

"That's obvious," Eden said. "But what kind of no good?"

Emmet finally put down his soup spoon and chopsticks. Last time she came, she had secretly taken a photo of the banners hung on the two sides of the building's door. When she showed Emmet the photo, he told her that the Japanese kanji on banners, if read in Chinese, would say, "Victory for sacred war and a great welcome to courageous warriors," and "Comfort to heart and body."

"Comfort to heart and body. What do you think it means?"

"I'm not sure I want to know," Emmet said with food still in his mouth.

The waitress came to refill their tea. She was the same chubby one who had served Eden every time she came to observe the Japanese.

"Why don't we ask her?" Emmet tossed his head at the waitress.

Ask the waitress? Eden hadn't thought of that. She didn't speak Chinese and the waitress didn't speak English. Also, she didn't want to draw attention to why she kept coming here.

"I can ask," Emmet said. "She has to know something. She's here every day." He waved the waitress over and spoke to her in Chinese.

The waitress's mouth fell agape. Then, baring her teeth with wry lips, she shook her finger at the building across the street. A tumult of words rolled out of her mouth. When she finally stopped, Emmet said to Eden, "She said that building is a whore house."

"A whorehouse? Here? On this street?"

"Yes."

Eden turned her gaze back to the building. She wasn't entirely convinced. Who would operate a whorehouse on a normal street like this one? Also, the men in the queue came at all hours during the day. How did so many get to leave their posts to visit a whorehouse in broad daylight? And why did she only ever see Japanese soldiers come to visit it?

The more she discovered, the more questions she had.

"Emmet." She tugged him on the sleeve. "Can you ask her

why would someone set up a whorehouse in a normal neighborhood like this?"

Emmet posed the question to the waitress. The waitress answered and Emmet said, "She said the Japanese have no shame."

The waitress tugged her apron and walked away with the pot of tea.

Well, that answer was no help.

"She's probably right." Emmet drank his tea, then wiped his mouth. "It doesn't surprise me. The Japanese are perverts. But that isn't much of a story. Japanese marines visiting prostitutes sounds salacious all right, but the news wouldn't shock anyone. Charlie might run a short article about it, but I don't think that's what he's looking for. The KMT's giving him a lot of pressure to find something they can use to smear the Japanese."

"The KMT?" That was news to Eden.

"Okay, not the KMT exactly. I meant the paper's owner. T.V. Soong."

"T.V. Soong? The brother of Chiang Kai-shek's wife?" Eden asked in surprise. "Wait a minute. I thought our paper was bought by an American."

"An American?" Emmet laughed. "I thought you knew. Your friend Clark Yuan brokered the deal. The American was just a nominee on paper. Didn't he tell you when he brought you back to work?"

Clark had gotten her job back for her? No. He never told her. She had no idea Clark was behind all this.

"Oh, no. You really don't know." Emmet slapped his fingers over his mouth.

"How did you find out?" Eden asked.

"From Dottie," he said. Dottie became Charlie's secretary when he took over as editor-in-chief after Zelik left. "She takes all the phone calls from Soong's office for Charlie, and she overheard a few things when the paper was sold."

The news dawned on Eden. It all made sense now why Charlie always looked so stressed. He didn't always have free rein on what the *China Press* could publish.

"You have to keep this to yourself," Emmet whispered. "No one's supposed to know we're a Chinese-owned newspaper."

"Yes. Of course," Eden said. Her own mind was occupied less by the revelation of the *China Press*'s ownership than the news that Clark had personally arranged a deal to give her back her job.

He never even told her he did this for her.

While she tried to sort out her thoughts, Emmet watched the line of soldiers stretching across the building. "Look at them, standing so orderly in line for their turns. There must be some outstanding prostitutes in there." He smirked and finished his tea. "Let's get going. I have a meeting with the new president of the SMC at three. Lunch is on me." He took out his wallet and put several coins on the table.

"Thank you." Eden stood up and put on her coat. Maybe Emmet was right. Maybe there was nothing more to pursue here. But she didn't believe it. Her gut told her otherwise.

There was one more lead she could pursue. Mauricio Perez. That ethically ambiguous owner of the bar Sambuca in Blood Alley who had a pulse on everything that ever happened in the Shanghai underworld. This afternoon would be a good time to pay him a visit. She could show him the photo she took and see what he could find out.

Back in the International Settlement, Eden said goodbye to Emmet and hopped onto a tram to head to Blood Alley. During the ride, she thought back to what Emmet had said. It was Clark all along who had made sure she got her job back.

A sad sweetness ran through her heart. Clark always looked out for her.

Was she nothing more to him than a foreign refugee to whom he extended a helping hand? Or, had he had feelings for her, but lost those feelings when he met the princess Ekaterina?

Was he happy? Did he find love with the new woman in his life?

She sighed and stared out the window. Plastered above the window frame, she noticed a sickening German leaflet.

Inheritance and Race

A conversation with Dr. Otto Neumann, renowned pathologist, to discuss his latest research and discoveries on how inferior hereditary traits perpetuate weaknesses in lesser races.

7:00 p.m., Thursday, February 25 at the Book Mart. 224 Yu Yuen Road (next to Hungaria)

By the Shanghai Reich Chamber of Culture

Lies! she thought in anger. Pseudoscience. Those despicable Nazis were spreading their lies here too.

She reached up and whipped the leaflet down. The urge to crumple it and tear it to pieces flared inside her. Only her reporter's instinct held her back.

Fight words with words. That was what Zelik would have told her. The best way to dispel lies was to fight them with the truth.

She gritted her teeth and shoved the leaflet into her purse. Dear Zelik. She missed her old mentor.

Zelik's voice echoed in her ear. She could almost hear him.

You're a reporter, he would've told her. Find out what this

Neumann does. Question his credibility. Write something to put away the Nazis' nonsense.

Okay! she yelled back to him in her mind. I'll see what I can dig up.

———

The afternoon was already over by the time Eden left Sambuca. Having secured Mauricio's promise to find out more about the mystifying building in Hongkew, Eden abandoned her plans to return to work and headed home. The tram would take forty-five minutes and the office would be closed when she got back anyway.

"Eden!" Mrs. Levine greeted her from the couch when she opened the door. "I was just showing Isaac the bar mitzvah invitations for Joshua."

"Isaac?" Eden slid him a sheepish glance. She hadn't seen him since he moved out.

"How've you been?" he asked her with a warm smile.

Now she felt guilty. "Good. Yourself?"

"We've got good news," said Dr. Levine.

"Oh?" Eden took off her coat and shoes and joined them. "What good news?"

Isaac passed her a letter, his eyes full of hope. "Hans Müller, our neighbor back in Munich, has gotten most of my parents' money safely out of Germany. He deposited it into a Swiss bank account. My parents are making preparations to leave the country. They just need to finalize the legal documents for selling their business and tie up all the loose ends."

"That's wonderful!" Eden scanned the letter from his parents. "How soon do you think they can come? Do you think they can make it in time for Joshua's bar mitzvah in April?"

"Probably not." Isaac laughed with a shade of regret. "They'd have to get tickets on a ship, and it would be a long journey. They said there are long waiting lists for ocean liner tickets out of Germany. A lot of Jews have decided it's not worth the risk to stay anymore. They're leaving, even if they have to give up everything they own. You all made the right decision to get out early."

"That is true." Mrs. Levine said, then put her hand on Isaac's. "I hope your parents will join us soon. Everything will be better for them once they're here." She picked up one of the invitations. "Look at this. Who would've ever thought? Our Joshua's bar mitzvah hosted by the Sassoons?"

"We Jews always come back together in the end." Dr. Levine blew a cloud of smoke from his pipe.

Eden folded her hands. Just as she expected, her parents were overjoyed with Neil's offer to host the bar mitzvah. The invitations hadn't gone out yet, but the news was already spreading through town. People who hadn't spoken to her mother in months started calling on her again. Jewish patients were returning to seek treatments from her father.

"Neil called me himself earlier today," Mrs. Levine said to Eden. "He's sending me the menu from the Cathay Hotel's manager in charge of catering. He told me he's arranging for a photographer and a classical quartet to welcome the guests at the party." She exhaled a deep sigh. "He's so thoughtful. You must thank him again for us."

"I will." Eden gave her a flat smile. She should be happy about this. And she was, except for the tiny voice gnawing at her. How would she ever repay Neil for everything he was doing?

Clark handled things so differently. When he did things for her, she wouldn't even know about it. Neil, in contrast, had no qualms letting it be known when he did her favors.

She dropped her eyes to the stack of invitations on the coffee table. Was that the Yuan family's name on that invitation? She picked it up from the stack. "We're inviting the Yuans?"

"Of course," said Mrs. Levine. "We never did have a chance to return the favor after they invited us to their house for dinner. And they've invited you to join them on special outings more than once. I thought it would only be right for us to include them. Don't you think?"

"Yes, you're right." Eden put down the invitation. "We should invite them." She couldn't think of any excuse why they shouldn't invite the Yuans either.

Maybe Clark wouldn't even come.

Or maybe he would come, with Princess Ekaterina in tow.

And so what if he did? She would be with Neil. At the bar mitzvah, everyone would acknowledge her as Neil's girlfriend.

Everyone.

Was that her new identity? Neil Sassoon's girlfriend?

That was what all the local newspapers were saying. Photos of her and Neil were showing up in gossip columns all the time. At the bar mitzvah, she and Neil would be the real subject of interest, not the ceremony for Joshua, a thirteen-year-old boy.

"Oh, look at the time." Mrs. Levine glanced at the clock. She straightened the stack of invitations and put them back into a box. "I better get dinner ready. Isaac, you'll stay for dinner, won't you?"

"Sure," Isaac said. "I'd like a home-cooked meal. Thank you."

"Darling," she said to Dr. Levine, "would you go next door and tell Joshua it's time to come back?"

"Certainly, dear." He put out his pipe and got up to fetch his son after Mrs. Levine went into the kitchen.

With only Isaac left, Eden tapped her fingers. Could she excuse herself, or should she stay with him so he wouldn't be sitting in the living room alone?

Isaac broke the ice. "You're seeing Neil Sassoon?"

"Neil and I are getting to know each other." She bobbed her head.

Isaac thinned his lips. "He sounds like a fine man." He clasped his hands.

"He's nice." She flashed him a cheerful smile. "And very generous." She didn't know what else to say. Although, something felt odd. She thought Isaac might be disappointed, and a shade of disappointment did show on his face. Beyond that though, he looked worried.

Why worried?

But quickly, his expression changed. Now he looked resigned.

"I could never have given Joshua such a grand celebration." He stared at the invitations. She could hear the hurt in his voice. "I'm happy for you." He smiled. In that smile, she could see he wasn't only sad. He was heartbroken.

In the past, she would've wanted to get away. Now, she felt real sympathy. She knew a thing or two now herself what it was like when one's feelings weren't returned.

She couldn't give him what he wanted, but she could give him compassion. "Why compare yourself this way?" she asked. "You mean so much more to Joshua than a big party."

He raised his head. Perhaps it was the tender tone of her voice. His expression eased.

She moved the box of invitations to the side of the coffee table. Ironically, now that she had Neil to shield herself, she felt easier opening herself up to Isaac. "You know what I saw on the bus today?" She opened her purse and took out the German leaflet to show him. "Isn't this terrible? The Nazis are spreading their lies here."

Isaac read the leaflet. "Otto Neumann?"

"Yes." Eden moved closer. "You know of him?"

"Unfortunately, I do. He's a visiting doctor at the Sainte Marie Hospital where I work."

"You're joking!" Eden took the leaflet back from him and reread it herself. "Your hospital is employing a Nazi?"

"Most of the staff at the hospital are Chinese. They aren't all that familiar with Nazism or what's going on in Europe. Another thing is, the hospitals here are massive. The administration's a mess. One department doesn't know what another department is doing. They employ foreign doctors so they can treat foreign patients, but nothing's coordinated. I don't even know who hired him. Then again, nothing surprises me at the hospitals in this city anymore. Some of the things I've seen happening . . . I never would've thought such things could take place at hospitals."

"What kind of things? I remember you told me once the surgeons expect bribe money in red envelopes before they would operate."

"That's the least of it," Isaac said. "I'm talking about things like this Neumann's animal experiments. He's set up a laboratory at the hospital to experiment on dogs, cats, and chimps. You can hear the animals scream and screech all the way from the other end of the hall."

"That's terrible." Eden raised her hand to her mouth.

"Sorry. I don't mean to frighten you."

"No, go on, please."

"As you can imagine, this is all very distressing to the patients. One time, some of the chimps escaped from their cages. They wandered into the patients' ward! I was there when it happened. Bouchard, the doctor I work for, he had a fit. It's unsanitary having animals running around ill patients, and it's dangerous." He paused. "I shouldn't be telling you these things. I hope I didn't upset you."

"You're not upsetting me," she said. "I'm glad you told me. Can you get me any proof? I can write an article and expose him. If you can give me photos of him experimenting on animals, I can try to get them published. And if you can arrange for me to interview the patients, I can report on how his ghastly work is causing them distress."

"Sure." Isaac's eyes lit up. "I like that idea. Let me see what I can do."

Eden almost wanted to reach out and squeeze his hand. This was the first time in a long time she felt she could talk to Isaac without keeping a distance. She'd always liked him, only not in the way that he wanted.

At the kitchen door, Mrs. Levine popped her head out. "Eden, I almost forgot to tell you. Neil sent you a new bouquet of flowers."

Eden got up and walked over to the console to take a look. A dozen stems of red roses. He'd been sending her flowers every day. Her father joked that if he kept this up, they could open their own flower shop.

"Neil Sassoon's one of the hospital's top donors," Isaac said.

"Is he?" Eden bent one of the roses under her nose and sniffed the fresh fragrance. "I'm not surprised. The Sassoons contribute money to a lot of charitable causes."

"Yes, well . . ." An odd, hesitant look came to Isaac's face. "He has peculiar ties with some of the doctors there."

"Peculiar? What do you mean?"

Isaac bit his lip. He shifted his eyes to the floor, then shook his head. "Nothing. He's well acquainted with some of them, that's all."

A petal fell to the surface of the console. Eden picked it up. If Neil was in fact an important benefactor to the hospital, she would have to talk to him about this Otto Neumann. Maybe Neil could put an end to the so-called "work" of this evil man.

12

TRAITOR IN OUR MIDST

UNDER THE DIM lights in the small back office at the Sambuca lounge, Clark flipped through the photos given to him by Mauricio Perez. There was no way to deny it now. The evidence was right before him. The photos showed Tang Wei at the Xinyi Warehouse shaking hands with Lei Bao, the lout of a son of Fifth Army General Lei. In the photos, Lei Bao, the self-appointed head of the so-called resistance group Silver Shadow, was passing a briefcase of cash to Tang. The Russian hired hands were unloading a delivery of guns and grenades and moving them onto Lei Bao's trucks. They showed Tang Wei stealthily getting away in the dark of the night. Everything that happened was exactly as Ekaterina had told him.

His heart sinking, Clark stuffed the photos back into the brown envelope. "Thank you," he said to Mauricio.

Mauricio raised his hand from the armrest. "I don't usually put my nose into government business, but if you people can do anything to disband the Silver Shadow, I'll sleep much better at night. Those boys are good-for-nothing goons. Last Friday, my shipment of soju arrived, and I sent two of my coolies to my Japanese supplier to pick it up. The Silver Shadow saw them loading the truck and demanded my men boycott Japanese goods. When my men refused, they took my soju by force and threw the bottles at my supplier's store window. Then they looted the place and broke everything they couldn't take. The *Kempeitai* came then and the whole thing blew up into a shootout."

Clark listened, shaking his head. These troublemakers. Intimidating civilians. They called themselves resistance fighters?

Mauricio downed his whiskey and continued, "My coolies tried to get away but those Silver Shadow bastards kidnapped them and demanded a ransom. They said it was a penalty for my patronizing the Japanese dogs. As if that wasn't enough, I got a visit from the *Kempeitai*. They accused me of conspiring with the Silver Shadow to vandalize a Japanese shop and demanded I pay for all the damages. Good thing I don't operate in the Chinese district, or it could've been an all-out war. I told them to go suck an egg. But now I've lost a supplier and I've got to keep looking behind my back."

"I'm sorry to hear that." Clark put the envelope of photos into his briefcase. "Believe me. The KMT doesn't want these loose cannons running around out there either." That said, how would the Party stop these wild rebels? With the Japanese army ramping up patrol over at Soochow Creek, no one at the KMT would want to do anything to upset a general of the Fifth Army, let alone clamp down on his son. Should the Japanese make any move, the Fifth Army would be the ones they would depend on to defend the city.

"One day," said Mauricio, "those reckless fools are going to set off the Japanese to a point of no return and plunge us all into a war."

Yes. Clark knew that.

And of all people, Tang Wei should know this too.

Could Ekaterina be right? Was Tang Wei really doing Sokolov's bidding to instigate a war between China and Japan?

If Clark hadn't seen the photos himself, he would've never

believed his friend would sell arms to Lei Bao and his band of hooligans.

But what if all was not what it seemed? What if Tang Wei had legitimate reasons for transferring arms to the Silver Shadow?

A ruse. That had to be it. Clark wanted to believe that.

Only he couldn't. If this was a ruse, why didn't Tang Wei let him in on the secret?

To cast away his doubts, he would have to hear it from Tang Wei himself.

The night rain drizzled under the gleam of the street lamps along the quiet sidewalk. Following the sheen of the light reflecting off the wet road, Clark walked up to the building where Tang Wei resided. The dreary weather had chased many people inside, leaving behind only a melancholic silence that made him wonder if tonight was a good night to confront his friend.

Did he have the right to come and demand an answer from Tang Wei?

Yes. Of course he had every right. Tang Wei was the one who brought him into the KMT. All this time, he thought they were pursuing the same cause. He'd made decisions—sacrifices—that set him onto paths he never wanted to take. If Tang Wei was contravening their cause, Tang owed him an answer.

He came to Tang Wei's walk-up apartment and knocked on the door.

The sound of shuffling feet approached and the person inside looked through the peephole. The knob turned and Tang Wei opened the door. "Yuan Guo-Hui? So late?"

Past ten at night. "Sorry to bother you at this hour."

"Come on in." Tang opened the door wider and stepped aside. "What's the matter?"

Clark entered and Tang closed the door. The small apartment

didn't even have a couch. Tang invited Clark to take a seat at one of the two chairs at the square wooden table. "Want some tea?"

"Yes. Thank you." Clark took off his trench coat and pulled out a chair. Across the room, a *xuan* paper notebook lay open under the desk lamp. Next to it, a writing brush lay on the open rim of the ink box. "Still working?" he asked when Tang sat down.

"Yes." Tang poured him a hot cup of dragon well tea from the teapot. "There's a new wave of rumors circulating around. Mao's giving land away free to peasants. These lies keep coming back. I'm drafting new leaflets to dispel it." He poured a cup of tea for himself. "People who believe them are so stupid. In this world, nothing is ever free. There's always a price." The cynicism in his voice seeped through. Had Tang always talked with such contempt? Clark couldn't recall, but maybe he had never listened with an objective ear.

He glanced at the four walls. Tang forgot to update the calendar, which was the only thing close to decoration in the apartment. The page beneath the ad for Victoria brand soap featuring two painted girls in qipao attached to the calendar still showed yesterday's date.

"At least now I can work in peace." Tang sat back with a satisfied sigh. "When you live in a house with three bickering old women and two dozen sons and daughters with the same father and different mothers, every day is like a reenactment of the Warring States. And I'm not even counting the band of sisters-in-law and their spawn."

Clark chuckled. During the Warring States period, multiple kingdoms in China fought for power and control over the land for two hundred years. The battles culminated in the founding of Qin, China's first imperial dynasty. Sadly, polygamy was still a widely accepted practice in China. Tang's father had married three wives. Each wife had multiple children. Tang's mother, the third wife, had two sons before Tang and two daughters after him. How Tang's father kept track of everybody, Clark couldn't imagine.

Thankfully, Clark's own father never took another wife besides his mother. As for Clark himself, he wished this antiquated practice would go away. In America, people had done away with polygamy long ago. It was never even a common custom in the West. Its continuation obstructed modernization and progress.

Of course, some men still saw it as a reflection of status and wealth. For him, the idea of parading a group of wives behind him felt nothing short of repugnant. These marriages were found on lust, ego, and pride, not love.

Love. The image of Eden's soulful face flitted through his mind.

If he loved a woman, it would be impossible for him to take another wife.

Tang Wei lit a cigarette. "The biggest joke was, I thought everyone would criticize me for not honoring my parents if I moved out. I stayed home as long as I could bear it. When I finally had enough and left, I realized, some of them didn't even notice. The ones who did notice began using my old room for storage." He blew out the smoke and tapped his finger on the cigarette to shake off his frustrations and the ashes.

Another reason why polygamy should end, Clark thought. What purpose did it serve to expand one's family if family members no longer remembered or cared about each other because there were so many of them? And for someone like Tang, who suffered the dual misfortune of being the son of the third wife and ranking among the youngest of his crowd of siblings, even being a son gave him no particular advantage. One day, when his father died, the inheritance would be long gone before it reached down the line to Tang Wei.

"Never mind." Tang chugged his tea. "Why did you come this late to find me?"

Clark opened his briefcase. How should he begin? "About this . . ." He pulled out the brown envelope Mauricio had given him. "You and I know each other well enough. I hope you'll be honest with me." He took out the photos and showed them to Tang.

Tang stared at the photos. His hand froze in mid-air with the cigarette between his fingers.

"Can you explain this?" Clark asked.

Tang's face fell. A hardness Clark had never seen before washed over his friend's eyes.

"Don't you think you're stepping over the line, coming here asking me for an explanation?" Tang asked.

"I'd considered that. If what appears to be happening in the photos is true, then no. I don't think I am."

"Is that right?" Tang took a deep drag. The corner of his lip rose into a sneering smile. "What are you doing now? Spying on me? Who gave you these pictures?"

"That's irrelevant." Clark swallowed. "All I want to know is, are you brokering arms deals for Sokolov? Is Sokolov paying you to sell arms to the Silver Shadow to provoke the Japanese?"

Instead of answering, Tang narrowed his eyes. "Who tipped you off? Your Russian girlfriend?" He snickered. "Impressive. Truly impressive. In such a short, short time, you've turned her into someone under your hand. While you're at it, don't miss this chance to have a few rounds with her. She's a very attractive woman."

"Nonsense!" Clark sat up. "What about this?" He tapped the photos. "Answer me."

"What if I am?" Tang sprung up from his seat. "Yes. I am selling arms to the Silver Shadow for Sokolov. Not just to the Silver Shadow either. I sell arms to whoever will cause mayhem to the Japanese. That Russian fur pays me well for what I do. Have you heard enough? What more do you want to know?"

His words knocked the wind out of Clark. Up till this very minute, he was hoping Tang would give him a good explanation.

His admission dashed any such hope. "Why? Why would you willingly do Sokolov's bidding and subjugate our own interests?"

"You're asking me? Why don't you ask your biggest backer, Soong Mei-Ling, or better yet, Chiang Kai-shek himself? In the past, I used to believe in him. But now, after what happened in Xian, it's time to wake up. People have lost faith in him because he continues to refuse to confront and fight the Japanese. When they sent me to Peking after the Xian incident to help salvage Chiang's reputation, I met this boy. He's only sixteen. I asked him why he ran off to join the Communist Party. You know what he told me? He said it's because Mao Ze Dong is fighting the Japanese. I asked him what about Chiang. He said Chiang Kai-shek isn't fighting the Japanese at all. Chiang's doing nothing. Up north, no one has faith in Chiang anymore. He's doomed."

"This is how you really think?" Clark asked. "What about all the things you told me? You brought me into the KMT. You said, ignore the flaws of the party officials. Keep our eyes on the big picture. You urged me to team up with Ekaterina."

"I urged you to look out for yourself!" Tang said. "I always have." He looked away, then raised his head again. "The KMT regime might not stand, and yet, I'm still here, working late into the night doing everything my job requires. I'm doing more for the country than most of the fools running this party. But as the saying goes, if a person doesn't look out for himself, Heaven will smite him and Earth will destroy him. I'm just looking out for myself."

Clark stood up. "How is aiding Sokolov looking out for yourself? The Soviets want us to be at war with Japan. You're putting the whole country at risk."

Tang let out an incredulous laugh. "You still don't understand? I want the money. The kind of cash those fur people pay me, it would take me years to earn with the KMT. If the Japanese fight their way into Shanghai, I'll take the money and I'll be long gone before they arrive." His eyes fell on the Vacheron Constantin leather gold watch on Clark's wrist. "Of course, you don't have to concern yourself with mundane matters like money, right? Young Master Yuan?"

Clark gritted his teeth. Those last words hit him like a punch to his face.

"Forget it." Tang waved his hand. "Consider it my fault for not knowing how to be reborn in the right womb. You're well aware the government is filled with officials using their positions to make illicit money on the side. Even your own boss Sītu does it. If you want to single me out for blame, go ahead." He picked up the teapot, went over to his little stove, and refilled it with more hot water.

Watching him, Clark's anger fizzled. When he left this simple little flat tonight, he would return to a luxury mansion. When he entered the door, his maidservants would be handing him tea, water, or whatever he wanted. If the country fell into disaster, his family had the means to take the first train or ship to get away. But for Tang Wei, this place was all he had.

How could he accuse others not blessed with his own fortunes?

Hypocrite. He could afford to keep his hands clean. Tang had to look out for himself.

Tang Wei seemed spent too. The hardness in his eyes faded. A weary look of resignation washed over his face. "If Japan wants to invade us, they will. In the end, whether I sell guns to the Silver Shadow or not won't make a difference. But since now you know, are you planning to report me?"

Clark curled his fingers. Could he do that? Report Tang?

If he did, he would destroy Tang's life and future. Would that end the threat of war? Would that stop the goon Lei Bao and his gang from instigating fights with the Japanese?

"No." Clark turned his head. "I won't report you."

Tang slumped and dropped his shoulders. "You expect me to be grateful?"

"No. I don't expect that."

"At least you still value our friendship." He looked at Clark. Clark stared back. Although Tang Wei didn't say it, they both knew. What he really meant was their past friendship. The trust had been broken. Things would not be the same again.

The cigarette Tang was smoking had long burned out on the ashtray. He picked up his pack and lit another one. "Since you're here, I might as well give you this." He unlocked the top drawer of his desk and pulled out a stack of telegrams and letters. "I was going to give these to you tomorrow anyway. They're correspondence between Fyodor Lukin and Japanese Kwantung Army Lieutenant General Kazuki."

"Fyodor Lukin? The Cossack Ataman?"

"Yes. The correspondence is fake. I wrote the messages. Sītu coordinated with our intelligence department to put them onto letterheads and telegrams."

Clark flipped through the messages. Except for some of the kanji, which he could read, the rest of the messages were written in Russian and Japanese.

"I've been asked to instruct you to give these to the Russian princess and let her pass them on to Sokolov. The Kremlin suspects Japan is recruiting White Russian forces to join the Japanese Imperial Army to attack the Soviet borders. These messages are meant to convince them their suspicions are correct. Tell the Princess to let him know that our intelligence units discovered this information, but we're keeping it from the Kremlin. Let him think we're hoping Japan will follow through with this plan because we're worried the Kremlin is not giving us their one hundred percent support."

"All right." Clark took one more look at the messages, then put them into his briefcase. He marveled at himself and Tang Wei. Both of them so good at pretending. Here they were, going about the next order of business as if nothing had happened. In truth, neither would look at each other as they had before. "I'll be leaving if there's nothing else."

"That's all for now." Tang leaned his back against his desk.

Clark put on his trench coat, picked up his briefcase, and headed toward the door.

Tang crossed his arms. "You forgot your pictures."

The photos Mauricio gave Clark lay spread on the table. Clark glanced at them, then grasped the doorknob. "Do with them whatever you want." He opened the door and walked out.

Tang followed him to the door. For a moment, he watched Clark depart, then called out, "Walk slowly."

As if he was sending Clark off after a genial visit.

The rain outside hadn't stopped. The streets were now emptied. The faint light of the street lamps could not brighten the void. Clark stepped into the darkness. This time, alone.

13

THE COMFORTING TRUTH

THE SAMBUCA LOUNGE at night was a place where time stood still. At least, that was how it seemed to Eden. The merry scene never changed, no matter what happened in the outside world. Here, one could almost believe that if all hell finally broke loose and the world collapsed, exotic drinks inside would continue to flow, romance would continue to thrive, and the party would go on forever.

Well, something did change. Ava Simms was no longer with the handsome Subedar Major Raj Patel. Swinging her on the dance floor tonight was a world-traveling adventurer and writer six years her junior. Ava said he'd come to China to search for inspiration for his next novel. Eden barely caught his name before he arrived and swept Ava out to rumba.

That gave her a chance to talk privately to Mauricio, which was the real reason she had come here tonight.

"You deserve a prize for this one, Eden." Mauricio picked up the decanter and filled her glass. "You uncovered something even I didn't know about in this city. That's quite a feat." He put down the decanter after pouring one for himself. "I rarely run into dead ends when someone comes to me for information. That building in Hongkew you asked me to look into almost stumped me. I would give you a medal for it. Unfortunately, all I have are wines and spirits. So here. This one's on me." He raised his glass, inviting her for a toast.

Smiling, Eden clinked her wineglass against his. "But you did find something, didn't you?"

"Of course, I did," Mauricio said. "I can't let your case ruin my reputation. I'll admit though, it wasn't easy finding someone with access to the inner workings of the Japanese military. Japanese servicemen don't make a habit of carousing in Blood Alley. But here's what I found out from a Chinese waste collector. He's been going by that building every day for four years. The house is on his route." He scanned the people around them, then lowered his voice. "To answer your question, that place indeed is a house where women provide sexual services to Japanese military members. He knows this because most of the trash coming out of that place are condoms and napkins soaked with dried semen."

"Mauricio!" Eden balked. People didn't speak openly of such things.

Mauricio didn't shy away. "Sorry to be crude, but this is information you asked for."

He was right. She needed to hear everything if she wanted to get to the truth. "What else?"

Mauricio flitted his eyes around them, then continued. "Normally, we'd call a place like this a brothel. But brothel doesn't exactly describe it. It seems the women inside enlisted."

"Enlisted?" Eden asked. "You mean enlisted like soldiers?"

Mauricio nodded. "From what I understand, the women were chosen by the Japanese government to become *ianfu*."

"*Ianfu*?"

"Yes. It literally means comfort women."

"Comfort women. My colleague Emmet told me the kanji on the banner outside of the building's door read 'Comfort to heart and body.' What do you think they mean by 'comfort?'"

"That's the interesting question." Mauricio shook his finger. "The Japanese call that house a comfort station. To find out what the comfort station is really about, my source has been gathering discarded leaflets and papers from the station's rubbish. I had the papers translated. From what I read, the women enlisted to sexually relieve Japanese soldiers and sailors serving overseas."

The military enlisted women to sexually relieve their soldiers abroad? "That's outrageous! I've never heard of such a thing. What kind of society would condone this? Why would their women accept this?"

"I don't think they did. You see, among the papers my source gave me, there are notes describing the ports from which the women came and the dates of their arrival. All of them came from Korea."

Korea. The only thing she knew about Korea was that Russia and Japan had gone to war over control of that country at the turn of the century. The Russians lost and Japan made it a colony by force. If she hadn't come to Shanghai and consequently read about these events in journals about affairs in the Pacific, she wouldn't even have known this. History of smaller regions in the Far East wasn't something she got to learn much about back in Munich.

But this didn't make sense. If Korea was forced to become a colony, why would its women enlist to do this? They couldn't possibly feel patriotic toward their occupier. "Mauricio, do you think these women are forced to provide these . . . services?"

Mauricio snickered. "Eden, I've been lolling around Blood Alley for fifteen years. Prostitution is something I see every day. Even after all this time, I can tell you, I know of no woman who would enter into this business unless she's forced in some way. The only difference is the matter of degree. Forced by circumstances of life, or forced by someone else."

The matter of degree. What about the group of girls she saw the first time she came upon the comfort station? When Eden thought of them, her bones chilled. All those men lining up outside every day. She couldn't fathom what those men were doing to them.

"If it helps, I did find anecdotal evidence these women didn't come voluntarily," Mauricio said. "The discarded notes and papers from the comfort station often have references to a Japanese Lieutenant General named Yasuji Okamura. He's the Chief of Staff of the Shanghai Expeditionary Force. If what I think is correct, he's the one in charge of the overseeing all the comfort stations' operations."

"Did you say stations?" Eden furrowed her forehead. "There's more than one comfort station?"

"I believe so. In the papers, there are orders from him on how the comfort stations should be managed. But I don't have any information where the other stations are located. One piece that stood out was his office's instructions on how to properly determine the actuarial durability or perishability of the women procured."

"Procured? Durability and perishability?" Eden asked. "How could anyone use these words to describe people?"

"Exactly. The women sound more like commodities than volunteers enlisted to support their armed forces."

How horrible. The Japanese military was describing these women the way the Nazis described the Jews, like the people they were talking about weren't even human.

Was there no end to this? Would people never stop denying fundamental human dignity to those who were weaker?

She had to expose this. Those girls inside that building were forced. How could they not be? Someone had to give them a voice. Someone needed to help them cry for help. "Thank you, Mauricio. You've been a great help."

Mauricio opened his hands. "Always at your service."

"Can I have the notes and translations you were talking

about? I'm sure once my boss hears about this, he'll be happy to pay you handsomely for them."

"Certainly. I'll have them delivered to your office tomorrow, along with the bank account where he can deposit the payment."

The music stopped and Ava returned to their table with her new paramour. "What are you doing sitting there talking?" she asked Eden. "You're missing the best part of the night!" She sat down and took a gulp from Eden's unfinished glass of wine. "Mauricio, darling!" She gave him a smacking kiss on his cheek. "Your band tonight is fantastic."

"I'm glad to hear that." Mauricio laughed. "Eden and I are having a little chat about French wine." He winked at Eden.

"Dominic." Ava pulled her new boyfriend into the seat next to her. "Come here. Tell them what you told me." She turned to Mauricio and Eden. "Dom has a fabulous new idea for a book. He's going to write a story about how he learned true enlightenment from the Buddhist monk he met at the Putuo Mountain. Isn't that the most ingenious idea?" She tugged Dominic by the sleeve. "Tell them."

"Sure," the fresh-faced young man said with a bit of hesitation. "I made a pilgrimage there last month and I stayed at the Huiji Monastery . . ."

As he was talking, Eden looked over to the couple sitting at the table near the front door. The first time she came to Sambuca, that was where she had sat. That night, her mind was filled with fantasies of a romance with a man different from anyone she had ever known.

But their paths diverged, and her hope would not come to be. Whenever she thought about him, her heart still ached.

Forget him, she told herself. Wasn't it enough that she was now being pursued by someone everyone considered a catch? Every young unmarried Jewish woman in Shanghai would trade places with her if they had a chance. What more did she want?

But there was more. In her heart, she knew there was a whole lot more, lying just out of her reach.

———

Walking behind three white women in Hongkew, Eden tried to appear as part of their group as she watched the comfort station across the street. Now that Mauricio had given her a fuller picture of what was happening in that place, she had decided to come by one more time. She wanted to see if she might notice anything she had previously overlooked before she brought this story to Charlie.

Everything appeared as before. No banners hung at the entrance today. There were only two armed guards standing on each side. A line of soldiers was queuing up outside in orderly fashion. One would enter whenever another exited.

What if she walked around the block to the back of the building? Would she be able to see what was going on inside from the back? Would it be too risky if someone noticed her loitering around?

Her curiosity got the better of her. She continued walking near the women until she had gone three blocks past the comfort station. Then, without seeming too obvious, she walked away from the group, crossed the street, and circled around to the comfort station on the parallel street from the back. To her dismay, all she could find was another building behind it. It had a barber shop on the first level. The second level appeared to be a residential home. There was nothing suspicious about it.

But wait. The other building didn't completely conceal the comfort station. The comfort station's windows on the third floor, though shut, were still visible.

She gazed up to try to get a better view. Nothing. She could see nothing except shabby white curtains.

Oh well, she tried. At least, she hadn't missed anything. She lifted the purse strap further up her shoulder and turned to make her way back to her office. Without thinking, she raised her head and gazed at the windows one more time.

Someone pushed one of the shabby white curtains aside.

Immediately, Eden stopped. The small face of a girl peered out.

She recognized that face and those wide cheeks. They belonged to the girl she'd seen the first time she came to Hongkew.

The girl was still here.

What happened next shocked her to the core. The girl pounded her head against the window. Once. Twice. And again.

Stunned, Eden tensed and looked around. What should she do? The girl would kill herself! Someone needed to help her!

Before she could think of what to do next, someone dragged the girl away from the window. Who? She craned her neck but couldn't see.

Her body shaking from head to toe, Eden clutched her purse strap and hurried away. Her heart racing as her mind latched onto only one thought. Find Charlie. She had to tell Charlie what happened.

Back at the *China Press* headquarters, Eden dropped off her purse. A large brown envelope lay on top of her desk. The envelope did not identify the sender, but had the word *"ianfu"* written on the front. Ignoring all the other letters and messages sent to her attention, she grabbed a pair of scissors and opened it. Inside, she found a stack of notes, discarded official records, as well as translations of the documents Mauricio had promised her. Clutching the envelope, she went straight to Charlie's office. His door was open and she knocked. "Charlie?"

"Yes?" Charlie looked up from his desk. "Eden. Just the person I want to talk to. Come on in."

Eden entered and sat down across from him.

Charlie put down his pen and clasped his hands behind his head. "I want to tell you, the article you wrote on Otto Neumann, the pathologist, was very well received."

"Was it?" she asked. That article came out a week ago.

"Yes. We've gotten a lot of responses. All positive."

"That's good to know." Eden forced a smile. Holding on to the envelope, she sat up.

"Some of the Jewish readers wrote and said they'd always believed you were right even about the Lillian Berman murder." Charlie chuckled.

"Really?" Where were these readers before and why didn't they speak up when it mattered?

Of course, she knew the answer. The exposé on Neumann helped. But mainly, her association with Neil Sassoon had given her back her credibility. Speaking of Neil, he promised her he would make sure the Hospital St. Marie would get rid of Neumann. She should follow up with Neil about that next time she saw him.

"I'm going to pick one of those responses to print in the Letters to the Editor section. How about that?" Charlie put down his cup.

"That would be terrific," Eden said. Vindication always felt good. But right now, she wanted to talk about something else. "Charlie, I've got a story about the Japanese navy. I've been waiting till I have evidence to bring it to you. I think this might be the story you're looking for. Take a look at this." She leaned forward and gave him the envelope. "The Japanese military . . ." She covered her mouth with her hands. "Gosh, this whole subject is so indecent . . . I can't even say the words to explain this to you."

Charlie glanced at her with a puzzled look on his face.

"I've discovered evidence the Japanese military is providing women to their soldiers for—ahem."

He crooked his brows and stared at her with wry lips, then opened the envelope and laid the papers inside on his desk. Eden watched him flip through the notes and papers Mauricio had retrieved from the comfort station rubbish. His eyes ran from the copy of the translation in his right hand to the one on his left. The more he read, the deeper his scowled.

"Let me get this straight. You're telling me this is military-sanctioned sexual services for the soldiers?"

"It's worse than that," Eden said. There was no way around it. If they were to have a productive discussion about this, she'd simply have to ignore decorum and talk about the subject, even if she was a woman. "I think the Japanese navy is forcing Korean girls to provide sex. See this?" She picked up the note with instructions for the comfort station on how to assess the durability and perishability of the *ianfu*. "They talk like the girls aren't even human, like they're some kind of merchandise. How did they 'procure' these girls anyway? Did they kidnap them? Did they buy them? This is the Imperial Japanese Navy engaging in forced prostitution." She glanced at the paper before tossing it back to the pile. "God only knows what they're doing to those girls? Oh, Charlie, you won't believe what I saw. That girl kept hitting her head against the window. They must be doing something terrible to her. They're driving her to madness. What if they're hurting her? What if they kill her?" She hugged her fists to her chest. "Charlie, we have to help her. We have to get her out of there."

"All right, all right, calm down," Charlie said. "This is a good story. Let's schedule a time so we can sit down and go over all this from the beginning. And before we run anything about it, I want to verify our claims. We need to at least give the Japanese a chance to explain." He clasped his hands under his chin and thought for a moment. "I'll tell you what. Let me make a few calls. The Japanese are quite sensitive about how the West sees them. Let me try and get someone at the IJN to talk to us and see what they have to say."

"And give the Imperial Japanese Navy a chance to make excuses?" Eden frowned. "What if they lie?"

"They might. Or maybe they'll slip and we'll find out even more. Even if they do lie, we'll at least be able to explain why we think they're not telling the truth."

He had a point. But that poor girl. "I don't know what to do. Isn't there any way we can help get those girls out of that place?"

Charlie sighed. "I know you want to help. So do I. The problem is, we're civilians. The IJN doesn't have to answer to us. We can't make them do anything. If they're indeed transporting girls to Shanghai and forcing them to provide sex against their will, the best thing we can do is to expose them and make them answer for it to the public. If we make it a big enough scandal, they might stop to avoid more public humiliation."

"You better be right," Eden said and sagged in her chair. That girl and the others with her were trapped in that building, suffering something horrible. The *China Press* was their only hope.

14

RENDEZVOUS AT CAFÉ CIRO

FROM THE COMFORT of the back seat of his Cadillac, Clark waited for his driver to pull past the crowd of guests waiting to enter Café Ciro, Shanghai's newest ballroom on West Nanking Road. At the moment, this spectacular night spot built by the real estate tycoon Victor Sassoon was the best place for one to see and be seen. Since its opening, the Café Ciro had drawn a devoted following beyond even the famous Paramount and Canidrome ballrooms. The secret to its success? It was the first fully air-conditioned nightclub in the city.

Plus its preferential treatment of distinguished guests. Club-goers like Clark himself could cut the line and drive up Café Ciro's wide driveway, designed to show off the city's wealthiest and most powerful when they arrived in their Cadillacs, Bentleys, and Rolls Royce limousines.

"You ready?" Clark asked Ekaterina when the Cadillac stopped in front of the club's entrance.

"All ready." She flicked her hair behind her shoulders to make sure it didn't hide the diamond necklace sparkling on her neck.

The valet opened the car door. Clark exited the vehicle, then held out his hand to help the princess climb out. Before they walked in, he wrapped his arm around her waist and pulled her to his side, knowing all along that the common club-goers waiting in line were watching them, taking note of who they were and gawking with envy.

The club host led them through the garden past the fish pond and fountain. Once inside, another host took over and brought them to one of the conspicuous elevated private boxes that lined the room. Clark stepped back and let Ekaterina sit down first on the plush velvet couch, then sat down next to her.

Discreetly, their dedicated waiter put down the menu and picked up the chilled bottle of Dom Pérignon already waiting at the table. "Would you like me to open this for you, sir?"

"For the lady, please," Clark said. "I'll take a Manhattan."

"Certainly." The waiter proceeded to pop the champagne.

Clark swept his eyes across the ballroom. Enthroned here, they were guaranteed to be seen by thousands. Tomorrow, his appearance with the princess would be passed on from one mouth to the next in the viral cycle of society gossips.

The waiter served them their drinks, then stood back out of view. When the slow music began, Ekaterina fell against him. Taking the cue, he put his arm around her.

She raised her lips to his ear. "Sokolov is sending another shipment of arms to the CCP in Harbin."

Clark's mind jumped to alert. Keeping his face relaxed and his eyes on the crowd, he asked in a low voice under the cloak of noise, "Do you know when?"

"March 13," Ekaterina whispered. "On the Trans-Siberian line. The KMT can intercept them and take the shipment for themselves."

"Thank you." Clark took a sip of his Manhattan. "How did you find out?"

"A woman has her ways." She swirled her glass of champagne. "I went through his desk while he was asleep."

"While he was asleep?" Clark pulled her closer. "What were you doing with him?"

Instead of an answer, she looked seductively into his eyes.

"We never asked you to sleep with him," he said.

"No, but I want to gain his trust, and this is the best way to do it. He is letting his guard down around me." She dropped her head onto his shoulder, giving him an unexpected whiff of the light, sweet scent of her perfume. "He really believes I'm falling in love with him."

"Do you want me to report that to Secretary Sītu? He'd be glad to hear that, but I doubt he'll pay you extra for it."

"I'm not asking for extra pay." She turned toward him and brushed her fingers along his face. "What's the matter? Are you jealous?"

"Quit playing," he mumbled through his teeth.

"Sorry." She giggled. Her satin evening gown revealed the seductive lines of her legs as she shifted in her seat.

If he wanted, he could easily run his hand down her thigh. He could lift her chin and plant a kiss on her alabaster cheek. Another man might have done these things, pretending he was merely playing his role.

Not him. He still considered himself a *junzi*, a man of character. A *junzi* wouldn't succumb to lust.

How many men had taken advantage of her just because they could?

He would not be one of them. The warmth of her back next to his chest reminded him she was a person. A person could get hurt, no matter how strong she pretended to be.

Besides, his heart still belonged elsewhere. It always had.

"We have something we want you to pass on to him," he said.

"What's that?"

"Copies of correspondence between Fyodor Lukin and Japanese Kwantung Army Lieutenant General Kazuki. They're

145

plotting to form a Russian armed force to attack the Soviet front line."

Ekaterina stopped swirling her glass. "Is this true?"

"You only need to know the correspondence exists." He lowered his lips to the top of her head so only she could hear. "I'll bring them to you tomorrow and you can pass them on to Sokolov. Tell him you stole them from me and made copies."

Ekaterina arched her brow, then snickered. "If you wanted dirt on Lukin, why didn't you just ask?"

"You know him?"

"We're acquainted." She eased back into his embrace. "He's active in the Russian Emigrants' Committee. He's paranoid about appearing in public. I don't blame him. The Kremlin wants his head," she muttered under her breath, then sat up. "I have an idea. Why don't I approach him and ask him if he'd like to meet you? I can tell him you have inside information about the Kremlin. I can suggest to him that he can recruit you to join his cause. If we can convince him you're on his side, you'll be able to find out everything you want about what he's doing with the Japanese."

Clark dropped his arm and pulled away from her.

"What?" she asked.

He scrutinized her face. "Whose side are you really on anyway?"

"The side that pays me, of course. Yours."

So she said. The fact that he wouldn't take advantage of her didn't mean he trusted her. It was always at the forefront of his mind that Ekaterina could be playing every side.

"Well?" she asked. "Lukin? How about it?"

"Let me think about it." Having access to Lukin and his underground activities could give them another edge. It certainly wouldn't hurt to have one more chip in their arsenal to bargain with the Kremlin. "You think he'll fall for it?"

"You question my abilities?" She gave him a playful slap.

"All right." He grabbed her hand. "Let's see you deliver." He pulled her back into his arm and said into her ear. "And your offer will cost us extra, I presume?"

"Always, darling." She gave him her sweetest smile. "You always know exactly what a girl wants." She gazed up at him. That look could have tempted any man, but all it did was make him think of what he'd seen the first time he met her. Her blue eyes looked too old to be the eyes of someone no more than twenty-two years old. They were dull, lifeless eyes, darkened by the shadow of someone who had seen too much.

Whatever her motive, love and passion had no place in her thoughts.

THE JEWISH TAIPAN

IN THE SOLARIUM of the Sassoon villa in Shanghai's western suburbs, Eden joined her new girlfriends as they lounged and waited for the men to return from their game of paper chase. Earlier in the morning, the staff had laid a trail of colored paper through the countryside. When the game began, the riders and their horses would follow the trail and race each other through ditches, fences, and creeks.

The dragon junipers, cedars, and camphor trees, along with the grass in the garden, were showing their first signs of green. Inside, a large stove heated the hall, sheltering them from the last of the cold air as spring arrived.

Eden raised her teacup and soaked in the sweet fragrance of the rose tea before she took a sip. Unbelievable. It smelled even better than perfume.

This whole place was like a paradise.

"Eden, why don't you come with us?" asked Ruth Kadoorie, a distant cousin of the Baron Lawrence Kadoorie. Lawrence Kadoorie began his career working for Victor Sassoon, but he now had his own business empire in Shanghai.

"Come with you?" Eden asked. Her mind had wandered from their conversation.

"Yes. To Bong Street."

Bong Street? That boutique where Shanghai socialites frequented to buy their dresses? Eden never dared to set foot in there. She could never afford anything they sold.

"Of course, one simply can't wear a Bong Street dress without the right matching jewelry," said Celine Bloom, whose father owned the J. Ullmann & Co. on Nanking Road. J. Ullman not only sold the most fashionable jewelry and purses imported from Paris, its own brand of watches was known to be exceptional. "If you come to our store, I'll make sure you get a thirty percent discount." She winked at Eden.

Eden smiled and lowered her tea to the table. Neil's friends had all been so warm and inviting since he first introduced her to them. The problem was, she couldn't keep up with their lifestyle. She could join them maybe once or twice at a fancy restaurant. Beyond that, unless she was with Neil, she couldn't possibly indulge this way.

"So how about it, Eden?" Ruth picked up the floral china teapot and refilled her cup. "Want to join us? I heard the spring collection from Paris is coming in this week. Celine, Dorothea, and I are going there to take a look next Saturday."

Dorothea Meyer nodded enthusiastically. Dorothea was the new bride of Osvald Meyer. Osvald's father was the founder of Andersen, Meyer, which was the General Electric Company's exclusive agent in China. "We can have lunch at Fiaker afterward."

Eden cupped her hand around her tea. What would be the best way for her to decline without sounding standoffish? She didn't mind going along, but how would it look if she went with them from store to store and bought nothing? And lunch at the Fiaker? That would be her entire week's pay.

Celine reached out and patted Eden's wrist. "Just so you

know, the Sassoons have an open credit line at our store. If I were you, I would pick out my favorite pieces and put them under Neil's account. A girl has to test her man's sincerity." She winked and broke into laughter with Ruth. Eden tried to laugh along. Was Celine joking, or was she subtly hinting at a way for Eden to buy things at Neil's expense?

"Celine's right," Ruth said and popped a mini macaroon into her mouth. "You should buy whatever your heart desires and let Neil pay for it. The Sassoons have a credit line with every shop, restaurant, and club worth their money. You can pick whatever you like and put it under their account. I doubt they'll even notice."

Shop to her heart's content and let the Sassoons pay for it? Eden couldn't imagine.

"Thank you for inviting me." She put on her cheeriest face. "I wish I could go, but I'm afraid I can't. I have to work next Saturday."

"You work on Saturdays?" Dorothea asked.

"Yes . . . Sometimes."

The women fell into an awkward silence.

"Look!" Ruth jumped up from her seat. "The boys are back."

Eden followed her gaze to the window. Outside, the figure of Neil galloping on horseback emerged from the tree line, leading the rest of the riders behind him. He had won the game.

"Come on! Let's go greet them!" Ruth made her way to the door. Eden got up with Celine and Dorothea and followed behind her.

In front of the villa, the men gathered to congratulate Neil. When Neil spotted Eden, he brought his horse over toward her.

She left the women to meet him halfway. "You won."

"I did." He took off his hat. "Credit goes to this one." He gave the horse a light slap. "He's a stallion. He lives up to his name. Excalibur."

"I'll take your word for it. I don't know anything about

horses." If she hadn't met him, she wouldn't even have known about the game paper chase. It was a game for people who owned horses, and she didn't know anyone who did. Neil's uncle, Victor, owned an entire stable of thoroughbreds.

"Come on." He offered her his arm as the stable boy came to take the horse away. "Let's go to the buffet. I'm so hungry, I could eat a horse."

Eden laughed and linked her arm around his.

"What do you think of this place?"

"It's beautiful." She looked ahead at the villa's steep roof hanging over the building's outer walls. "It's so grand."

"For Joshua's bar mitzvah, we'll have the party out here." He swept his arm over the garden. "Do you think he'll like that?"

"Like it? He'll be thrilled." Joshua was now a star at school. The invitations had gone out only two weeks ago. Already, the RSVPs were flooding in. Some guests went further and called her home to thank her parents for the invitation. She suspected they did that to make sure their RSVPs were received and their places at the party were guaranteed. Acquaintances who weren't on the guest list were calling too, under the pretense that they hadn't seen her family for a while and hinting that they would love to attend.

To think that only recently, people didn't want to talk to them or be seen with them.

She couldn't deny it. It crossed her mind many times that as long as she had Neil Sassoon by her side, her parents and Joshua would benefit in ways they could never achieve for themselves. And if she ever became one of the Sassoons, how much more she could do for them!

Before she met Neil, she never had to take such things into consideration. She always thought that when she married, it would be to someone she loved. Someone whose presence could make her heart race with anticipation. Someone whose voice would fill her with hope. Someone with whom she could share her dreams. A man who would step with her into the future into a life where adventures and surprises awaited.

With Neil, the prospect of a secured life circled in her mind at every turn. The advantages were so clear, they were impossible to ignore. What girl of marriageable age would forego such an opportunity? What a stupid girl she would be if she gave it up? She could be the wife of the heir of the most powerful man in Shanghai. And they were Jewish too. How could she do any better?

If she were smart, if she had any common sense, if she took life responsibly at all, she should seize this chance.

Did her heart beat for Neil? It hadn't yet. She kept hoping it would.

What about dreams? Neil dreamt of becoming his Uncle Victor's rightful heir. He wanted to take over the Sassoon business empire in Shanghai one day. It was why he'd come to Shanghai, and he was dedicating his life to making it happen.

And her dream? Every time she thought of her dreams, the vision of flags of different nations fluttering in the wind on the Bund would appear. In that vision, a man, one who did make her heart beat faster when he ran his finger lightly down her arm, had asked to share her dreams. He said that if they shared their dreams together, it might double the chance for the dreams to come true.

Silently, she laughed at herself. Her dreams were nothing but a shadow of the wind. Neil's dream was grounded. Solid. It was the kind of dream that a man with aspirations should pursue, and the possibility of it coming true was real and within reach.

By any logic, she should let go of her fantasies and put her efforts into helping him achieve his dreams.

And what kind of life would she be in for if she proceeded down the path with Neil? Looking at Dorothea, she could already guess. Fall and winter in Shanghai, summer in the English countryside. Parties and travels with those within their circle in the spring. All she would have to do would be to look pretty, be sociable, and if she wanted, support a worthy charitable cause or two.

And then what?

So many questions. So impossible for her to answer.

Good thing they'd reached the steps of the south entrance. The buffet had begun and she could put everything to the back of her mind until later. The riders were now coming in, as were her new friends Ruth, Dorothea, and Celine, and the other guests who had gone for a stroll in the nearby countryside.

The hearty laugh of a man bellowed from the veranda before they reached the doorway. Eden looked toward that direction to see who it was. Her eyes met those of a tall man standing in the center of the room. He had such vitality in his eyes. He enlivened everything which attracted his gaze. His thinning white hair and his walking cane did nothing to take away from his robust physique.

"Uncle Victor!" Neil led her over to the man. "I thought you couldn't come today."

"I thought I couldn't either," Victor Sassoon said. "I was supposed to have a telephone appointment with Bette Davis, but she had to cancel last minute." His eyes glinted at Eden. "It looks like I might have better company though."

"Yes!" Neil looked over to her. "Allow me to introduce Eden Levine."

"Ah! Miss Levine." Victor softened his voice. "A pleasure."

"The pleasure's all mine, Sir Victor," Eden said. So this was the man who would invite awe and reverence at the mere mention of his name. He definitely deserved it. Not because he had immense wealth and power, but because of his person. He charisma alone could fill the entire room.

"I've been looking forward to meeting you. Neil's been talking nonstop about you. I wanted to see for myself who is this girl who has my nephew under her spell." His smile beneath his whitish mustache was friendly, but she could feel his sharp, perceptive eyes assessing her.

Why should she be judged and not the other way around? She didn't need his approval. She had no design on the Sassoon fortune. Smiling back, she lifted her chin. "I've been wanting to meet you too. I wanted to see for myself who has all of Shanghai bowing at his feet."

Her defiant tone took him aback. But rather than seeming offended, his smile widened. "Good." He nodded in approval. "Very good. Please, Miss Levine, help yourself to whatever you like." He excused himself and limped away to greet another friend.

Watching him move with the help of his walking stick, Eden felt a tinge of regret. Couldn't she have shown him a bit of deference? The man was crippled. His biggest weakness was on display wherever he went.

"Don't mind him," Neil said after his uncle left. "I didn't know he would be coming. I'd meant to properly introduce you."

"It's all right." She touched him lightly on the arm. "I'm honored to meet him under any circumstance."

Neil brought her to the buffet table, where the servants had laid out an endless spread of main courses and side dishes. Salads, salmon, chicken, fruits, foie gras, cheeses, and all the varieties of bread. There was even a carving station for lamb chops and roast beef. Such an astounding amount of food for a day of fun and games for no more than thirty people.

After they filled their plates, Neil brought her to a table to join his friends. All the while, Victor Sassoon wandered around the room, greeting the guests. As she smiled and answered the mindless chatter of the others sitting with her, Eden couldn't help watching him. This whole time, he'd been on his feet. Ever a good host, he would not sit down until he had spoken to everyone and welcomed them. Not even his disabled leg would deter him.

Clearly, Sir Victor was not a man who would let any obstacle stand in his way.

She glanced at Neil sitting beside her. Would Neil ever grow to match his uncle in strength and stature?

When everyone had had their fill, the party scattered again for desserts. At the long buffet table, half the food still hadn't been eaten. Of course, the Sassoons could afford the excess, but such luxury was hard to get used to.

"Shall I get you something sweet?" Neil asked her.

"No, thank you," Eden shook her head. "I can't eat another bite."

"You'll be missing out on the best chocolate torte in the world."

"I'm sure." She touched him on the arm. "But I really can't. I think I'll get myself another drink instead."

"All right. I'll be right back. Ask the bartender for the vintage port." He winked and left for the dessert table.

Eden put down her napkin and went to the bar. Vintage port? Maybe another time. Right now, a refreshing glass of lemon water was what she needed.

While Eden waited for the bartender to fill her glass, Victor Sassoon came up to her. "Are you enjoying yourself?"

Mindful not to be rash this time, Eden took her water and turned to the Baron with a warm smile. "I am, thank you. Everything this morning has been delightful."

"Have you had a chance to see the rest of the house yet?"

"No. Neil had to get ready for the game as soon as we arrived. I sat with the ladies and had tea while we waited for the riders to come back."

"How about I take you on a tour?"

"Are you serious?" A personal tour by Sir Victor?

"Of course I'm serious. We'll be hosting your brother's bar mitzvah here. Don't you want to see if this place is suitable and to his liking?"

"I'm sure it is," Eden said. To think that a private Sassoon property would not be good enough for anything! "Neil already made plans to bring my family here for a visit next week. They'll decide on the details how they want to arrange the party then. But a private tour by you? How can I possibly refuse?"

Sir Victor laughed. "Well then. Shall we?"

"Gladly." She put down her glass. Together, the walked through the corridor to the large reception parlor.

"See those doors and windows?" He pointed with his cane. "All of them are made with woods with knots. I imported the wood from London to build this house. And over here. My ivory collection." He brought her over to an enclosed glass case displaying Chinese ivory sculptures, figurines, and vases.

"They're exquisite!" Eden exclaimed. These weren't ordinary imitation ivory pieces sold on streets and in shops. Even in museums, she hadn't seen figurines with the smoothness of the surface like that Buddha, or the delicate but intricate carving of the carps. And the ancient brush pot on the second shelf. What a treasure. "Where did you find these?"

"All over China. I have a broker who travels the country to find and procure antiques for me. These are only representative samples. My full collection is held in private under the care of a trust. I have about five hundred pieces in total. Some of them date as far back as the second millennium B.C. I want to preserve history, that's why I do this."

She came closer to the case and put her hands on the glass. Preserve history? She liked that. In the past, her concept of wealth hadn't extended beyond one's own comfort and luxury. The Sassoons' wealth enabled them to think beyond material things. It broke down boundaries and opened up worlds. Given the same magnitude of wealth, she, too, could do so much.

Sir Victor came closer behind her. "I started collecting these in 1915, a year before I got my injuries." He tapped his shin with the end of his cane.

"What happened?" Eden turned around.

"I was in a plane crash." He started toward the door at the other end of the room. "I served in the Royal Flying Corps during the Great War."

"Goodness." Eden put her hand over her heart and continued walking behind him.

"It's nothing." He plodded on with his cane and limped along. "I survived. That's all that matters. To be alive in any form is good. I just hope all the buffoons running the world can figure a way to avoid another one. It's a shame if we keep sending able-bodied men out to be maimed and killed. I'm not counting on it though. Those fools in offices always make a mess of things. It's why I never got involved with politics. I have no patience for fools. My time is better spent with my horses."

Eden smiled. Neil had told her about Sir Victor's love of horses. "Neil said you have the largest stable in Shanghai."

"Yes! That I won't deny. My horses are the real reason everyone knows me and listens to me around here. If anyone tells you differently, they're lying."

Eden dipped her chin and chuckled.

"I'll let you in on a secret." He stopped in the hallway.

"What's that?"

He eyed the room to make sure no one else was present, then sidled back to her. "The only race greater than the Jewish race is the Derby."

Looking at his deadpan face, Eden burst out laughing.

They came to his office and he invited her in. "Would you mind taking a seat?" He pointed his cane at the sofa.

Puzzled, Eden hesitated, but sat down nonetheless. So far, Sir Victor had been nothing but friendly. Was this tour actually an excuse to get her alone for a round of questions?

Sir Victor closed the door. Eden clasped her hands and braced herself. If he began to interrogate her as if she weren't good enough for Neil, she was ready to get up and walk out.

"I can see you like this place." He sat down across from her. "To be honest, I don't come out here much. You probably think it's wasteful of me to build this big villa only to neglect it, but I'm too busy to drive out here very often. We use it mostly for parties and banquets. The reason I really came out here today, Miss Levine," he paused, "Do you mind if I call you Eden? Miss Levine sounds so formal."

"Please do," Eden said.

The Baron opened his hand. "As I said, the reason I really came out here today, Eden, was because I heard you would be here."

"Is that so?" Eden crossed her legs. It was just as she'd thought. The all-powerful patriarch of the great house of Sassoon had cornered her to examine her. "I didn't realize I was that important."

"But you are." Sir Victor leaned forward. "You're a perceptive young lady. I could tell from the moment we met. I know you haven't known my nephew for very long, but I'm sure you can see, he is a long way from being able to manage the family business here."

His comment took her by surprise. And he was wrong. If Neil was lacking in any way as a businessman and a financier, she'd never noticed it. Or correctly speaking, she had never paid much attention. She had no scheme when it came to Neil, and he wasn't so important to her—yet. "I really am not in a position to judge that."

He gave her a look of doubt, but let it slide. "Let's talk frankly then. My nephew came to China with one goal in mind. To get into my good graces so I would appoint him my heir."

Eden shifted in her seat but said nothing. It wasn't her place to give an opinion about their family's internal affairs.

"The problem is, making him my heir was never in my plans," Sir Victor explained.

Why was he telling her this? To let her know she should forget about marrying Neil for his inheritance? If so, he was wrong about her on that too. But still, she ought to answer with tact. "I can understand that." She clasped her hands over her knee. "Who's to say you won't marry and have your own children in the future?"

"Nah." The Baron waved the suggestion away. "That's not the reason. Even if I do have children of my own someday, someone needs to be in line to uphold the family legacy as long as I don't have any sons and daughters of my own. Life is too unpredictable." He gazed at his bad leg.

"What's the reason then?" she asked. "Is it because his mother is not Jewish?" Neil had told her his paternal grandparents had disowned his father for marrying a Catholic.

"That would be my late father's reason," Sir Victor said. "It's less important to me who my brother married, although if theoretically speaking I do make Neil my heir, it would please me if he marries a nice, Jewish girl." His eyes glinted at her. The obvious hint made her blush. "The problem with Neil is his lack of conviction."

"Lack of conviction?"

"Yes. He's smart. He's eager to learn all the ins and outs of how to run a business. Too eager, I would say, to the point where he would be willing to take shortcuts any chance he gets."

This was strange. Why was the Baron criticizing Neil to her? "Sir Victor, I want to make one thing clear. If you're telling me all this to dissuade me from continuing my friendship with Neil, or because you think I'm hoping to somehow benefit from Neil becoming your heir, I can guarantee you, this is not the case. In fact, I shouldn't even be having this conversation with you at all. Neil and I aren't close enough for you to have any worries."

"Eden, you misunderstand me." He cleared his throat. "What

I want you to know is, I considered Neil unsuitable until he met you."

"Excuse me?" She didn't understand.

"I believe a man's success cannot last unless he has strong, moral convictions. Without convictions, a man can too easily succumb to temptations. And temptations can only lead to bad choices." He glanced around the room. "I'm not a greedy man. I'm simply blessed. And I continue to ensure my businesses prosper not because I need any more money. If I live to a hundred, I can't spend everything I own in the bank." He said this as a matter of fact and not in the manner of a boast. "I take great care of how my business is run because everything I own doesn't belong only to me. It belongs to everyone before me, and all those who will come after me. What you see here is my family legacy. As long as I'm alive, I will make sure none of it will be squandered. Not under my watch."

Eden tilted her head. The passion and pride in his voice rendered her momentarily speechless.

"I've been following your writing in the *China Press* since you caused a maelstrom with your articles defending that Nazi."

"Oh, about him . . ." Eden rolled her eyes, ready to explain her case.

"Wait!" Sir Victor held up his finger. "I thought all along you were indeed onto something. It was too bad the powers that be had their own agenda. Anyway, it doesn't take much to convince me those bootlickers had got the wrong person. I have my own experience dealing with them to know they're a lousy bunch of morons."

At that, Eden tried to stifle a chuckle.

"It takes a lot of strength and conviction to stand up for what you believe when the whole world is against you," he said. "I admire you for that."

Taken utterly in surprise, Eden loosened her arms. "Thank you."

"I know Charlie Keaton too. And Saul Zelik."

"Saul Zelik? My old boss?"

"Zelik and I go way back. In fact, I just saw him a month ago on a business trip to Hong Kong."

"How is he? I hope he's well. I don't know if he knows it, but the reason he lost his job at the *China Press* was because of me."

"He's doing fine. Don't worry. He and Charlie both speak very highly of you."

That made her feel worse. She could never make it up to Zelik for losing his position in Shanghai.

"Let bygones be bygones," Sir Victor said. "Believe me. Zelik's enjoying his semi-retirement."

She sure hoped so.

"As for my nephew . . ." Sir Victor sighed. "It is my hope that his relationship with you will finally give him the moral grounding he needs."

Quickly, Eden held up her hand. "You overestimate me. Neil and I, we enjoy each other's company, but I don't think I wield that much influence over him."

"Then you should try. If you can be his source of conviction to pull him back from making mistakes, then my mind will rest at ease and I'll feel a lot better about appointing him as my heir."

Overwhelmed, Eden stared at her hands. How could she take on being the center of Neil's source of conviction? She couldn't even be sure how deep her own feelings were about him.

Across from her, the Baron peered at her. "I don't want you to feel obligated," he said. "And I promise I won't intervene no matter what choices you make in the future. But I want you to know, nothing would make me happier than if we could have you as a permanent part of our family."

Eden's mouth fell agape. Coming from Sir Victor, this was completely unexpected.

"So." He fell back into his seat. "You think your family will be satisfied with this place as a venue for the bar mitzvah?"

"Most definitely," she eagerly answered, relieved he was changing the subject, even though he'd asked her this question earlier already.

"Everybody calls this place the Sassoon Villa. Did Neil tell you what this place is really called?"

"No." She shook her head.

"The Garden of Eden. It's the name I gave the place when it was first built in 1932."

The Garden of Eden? "How lovely." She shifted her eyes away.

"Perhaps one day, it will have a mistress who can make it worthy of its name."

Eden raised her hand to the side of her face. This entire session felt surreal. Could it be true? The world of the Sassoons was open right before her, and all she needed to do was say yes? Such fortune shouldn't befall anyone without some kind of price.

What would the price be?

"Let's go back and join the others." Sir Victor picked up his cane and rose to his feet. "I don't want Neil to think I've abducted you."

She let out a deep breath with a laugh and followed him back to the dining room. Along the way, he spoke no more of the topics they had privately discussed. Instead, he told her about all the paintings of the Sassoon ancestors on the walls, and recounted stories he remembered about each of them.

Back in the dining room, the Baron left her to join another guest. Neil left his friends to greet her the moment she reentered. "Where did you go? I was about to send a team of police to go look for you."

Eden returned to his side. "Your uncle took me on a tour of the house, that's all."

"Oh?" Neil gazed over at Sir Victor, who was now deep in conversation and laughing. "My uncle can be quite a character. I hope he didn't say anything to put you off."

"He didn't." She smiled and swung her dress. "He's a very nice man. I quite enjoyed learning about his ivory collection."

Neil sighed in relief. "Good thing you say that, because in a few weeks, you're going to meet my mother."

"Meet your mother."

"Yes. She sent me a telegram this morning and told me she was coming. It took me by surprise. I was waiting for the right moment to tell you. She'll arrive two days before Joshua's bar mitzvah."

"Oh? Will that be a problem? I didn't want you to be preoccupied with making plans for Joshua if that would take your time away from her."

"Not at all. I just wish I could properly introduce you to her. But with so little time, that won't be possible. She always needs at least two days of rest to recover from a long journey by sea, and I have to invite her to your brother's party, so I'm afraid the bar mitzvah will have to be where you'll both meet."

"Will she be coming to the synagogue for the ceremony too?"

"Probably not. Anyway, if you can handle my uncle, I'm sure you'll handle her just fine too."

"You sound like your family is nothing but problems." She laughed.

"If only that's all they were."

As they talked, Sir Victor made his way back to them. "I apologize but you'll all have to carry on without me. I'm heading back into the city."

"So soon, Uncle? You weren't even here for the game this morning."

"I'm afraid so." He looked over at Eden. "It was a pleasure to meet you. By the way, I didn't mention earlier. My foundation runs a number of soup kitchens. We serve the Jewish refugees coming into Shanghai from Germany. Perhaps you can talk my nephew into going there for a round of visits." He pointed the top of his cane at Neil. "It wouldn't hurt for him to see there are people out there who need help."

"I'll go, Uncle. I want to help. Seriously, I do. I'll go as soon as I find some time."

"Find time. Why don't you have time?"

"Because I've got my hands full with my real estate development projects. And I'm starting a new venture. I'm in talks with an American company. Sam Foster. They're making a new kind of sunglasses that protect your eyes from UV rays. Their glasses are very fashionable too." He glanced at Eden. Pride shone in his eyes. "I'm going to be their exclusive distributor for the Chinese market."

Sir Victor stared at him. He had skepticism written all over his face.

Trying to smooth things over, Eden said, "I think what your uncle mean is, he'd like to see you do more charitable work."

"Yeah, well." Neil tossed back his head. "I do plenty for charity work. I'm a patron of the Hospital St. Marie."

Sir Victor flicked his eyes. "All right. I'll be off. Eden, I hope to see you again soon. Keep up the good work at the *China Press*. The first thing I read in the morning these days are your articles. Do you have any shocking new exposé coming up?"

As a matter of fact, she did. Before she left work last Friday, Charlie told her he had managed to convince the Japanese General Yasuji Okamura to come to their office for an official interview with her. The interview would be through a translator, but still, it was a coup.

But she wasn't about to reveal this to anyone yet. "If I do, I'm sure you'll be reading all about it." She hooked her arm around Neil's. "Thank you, Sir Victor. You've been the most delightful host."

Sir Victor raised his cane goodbye, then slowly limped his way to his servant and bodyguard.

"Just wait and see," Neil said to her as they watched the baron depart. "I'm going to show him I can run a successful business on my own. I know what he's thinking. He doesn't want to leave his businesses to me until I can prove I have what it takes to make it without him. The real estate projects will take some time, but these sunglasses?" He patted her hand on his elbow. "These sunglasses are going to make a fortune. And then, he'll know he can trust my business acumen."

Eden smiled, if only to be agreeable. Neil didn't understand his uncle at all. If she were to help him like Sir Victor asked, it would take a lot of work, and this was neither the right place or time to try.

Did she even want to try?

"Come." Neil nudged her. "Let's go see what our friends are up to."

"Okay," Eden said. Before she followed him away, she turned and looked at the door. Sir Victor had left, but their earlier conversation still resounded vividly in her head. His words led her to a crossroad. Once she chose a path, she might not be able to go back.

Maybe that was why, when it came to Neil, she could do nothing but to stand still.

16

RISING RESISTANCE

On the tennis court, Clark hit another winner to get to 40-30. Not giving up, Joseph Whitman hit a backhand slice and spun the ball across the net. Following its direction, Clark charged forward and volleyed the ball back to the other side, landing it on the line out of Whitman's reach.

"Nice shot." Whitman tapped the strings of his racquet on his palm.

"Thank you." Clark walked up to meet him at the net.

"Come on. I'll buy you a drink."

They strolled to one of the outside tables at the back of the Columbia Country Club. Tucked away on Shanghai's outskirts on Great Western Road, this private American club felt like a sanctuary. Surrounded by the sounds of children and women laughing by the pool, Clark thought back to the times when he played tennis on the Wesleyan campus in Connecticut. Everything here felt so peaceful as the late afternoon sunlight gleamed on the clubhouse's window panes.

Whitman signaled the waiter and ordered each of them a Carlsberg. It had been weeks since Clark had last caught up with the American foreign service officer. More and more, he felt like he was an American liaison for the KMT only in name.

"I wish I could do more." Whitman took a gulp of his beer. "It's difficult for the folks back in the States to feel the urgency for what's happening half the world away. You might not believe me, but it frustrates me as much as you. Every time I send a report back to the State Department, I wonder if it's sitting on a pile, gathering dust."

Clark believed him. He had known Whitman for almost a year now. Stalling might be the policy of Roosevelt and the U.S. Congress, but Whitman? Clark didn't doubt him. "I know you want to help. We appreciate it."

"It's not just that I see what's happening here. I understand where you're coming from," Whitman said. His eyes took on a look of someone reminiscing about the old days. "I had a chance to be a businessman myself once. When I was growing up, my father was a big-time industrialist. He had high hopes for me to join him back when I first started my career. I had other ideas. I wanted to do something more worthwhile. I thought, the business would always be there. I was young. I wanted to travel the world. Maybe even do some good along the way. Congress had just passed a law to bring the consulate and diplomatic services under the State Department. They were taking applicants for a new foreign service exam. I applied on a whim and passed. Uncle Sam gave me my first assignment and sent me to Singapore. Before I knew it, I'd been in service for over a decade."

"You must like it. You're still doing it."

"I don't dislike it," Whitman said and rested his elbows on the armrests. "But I don't have anything else to go to at this point."

"What about your father's business?"

"That's long gone. He lost everything when the stock market crashed."

Clark gave himself a mental knock on the head. The Wall

Street crash of 1929. He should've known. "I'm sorry. That must have been tough for your father and your family."

"It was," Whitman admitted. "My father couldn't face it. He took his own life."

"That's terrible," Clark said. This he couldn't have known. What a sad tragedy.

"After that, I remained in foreign services. I don't know if I ever wanted to make so much money that I would want to kill myself if one day I lose it all. Anyhow, all that's in the past."

"Do you have any regrets?" Clark asked. Lately, he'd been asking himself this same question.

Whitman thought for a moment. "I don't know that I feel regret, exactly. I would say, twelve years with the government has turned me into a cynic. I wish I could be more effective in what I do. But there are a lot of changing agendas, egos, and conflicting interests to manage."

"I know," Clark said. He rubbed the condensation off the surface of his glass. "It's the same way for me too, a lot of times."

Whitman waited for him to explain. When he didn't elaborate further, Whitman let him be and stared out into the green field. "I've learned over the years that doing good doesn't always have to be something earth shattering. In my role, I'll never be the one to make the most important decisions or form policies that impact millions. I'll never be someone who can change the world. When history books are written, I won't even show up as a footnote. But my job gives me certain powers. Sometimes, I can lend a helping hand to an individual in need. Whenever a chance comes up, I try to make a difference that way."

Small differences. Clark gazed at the ground and considered this point.

"What I'm trying to say to you is, it might not be in my power to get your government what it wants. But if you yourself ever need anything, you can call on me anytime. As long as it's within my power, I'll try to help in whatever way I can."

"Joseph . . ." Clark looked up. How unexpected. "Thank you. That's very kind of you to offer."

"I mean it too." Whitman gave him a reassuring nod. "That's how people like you and I really work together. We help each other. We pass on small favors. We don't change the world, but we tow it forward by building a chain, one link at a time. When a real disaster hits, we can use that chain of connections to rescue those who are caught in the tide."

Not too different than the Chinese concept of *guanxi*, except *guanxi* was how people exchanged benefits and gave advantages to one another. What Whitman was talking about was something less self-serving.

"You're part of that chain," Whitman said. "Don't lose hope yet." He signaled the waiter for the bill.

Was he? Clark wondered. Part of that chain? A link to the chain of hope?

"By the way, I have the letter from Ambassador Johnson to Secretary Sītu," Whitman said as he signed the bill. "Let me give it to you before you go."

"Of course." Clark stood up. He could drop it off for Sītu at his desk on his way home.

───────

When Clark returned to the Foreign Affairs Bureau after his game of tennis with Joseph Whitman, it was already past six o'clock. If he didn't have a breakfast meeting scheduled with Edward Nathan, the chairman of the Kailan Mining Company, he would've waited until tomorrow to pass on Ambassador Johnson's letter to Sītu. But Nathan had traveled all the way back to Shanghai from Peking for the meeting. The breakfast could go on all morning. He'd rather not make Sītu wait.

The elevator opened to a dark, quiet floor. Clark hurried past the janitor and the rows of empty desks toward Sītu's office. In a haste, he almost missed the shadow of movement slipping by the corner of his eye. Who was in his own office? Not the janitor. The janitor was out front.

He changed direction. In his office, Liu Zi-Hong was riffling through the folders in his file cabinet. He entered the room. "What are you doing?"

Zi-Hong jumped at the sound of his voice, then turned around with a file in his hands.

Clark strode toward him. Without asking, he snatched the file from Zi-Hong's hands. He opened it to find the photo of Princess Ekaterina Brasova and her confidential records.

"Why are you looking at this?" he demanded to know.

"I . . . I . . ." Zi-Hong stuttered. Unable to come up with an answer, he took a step backward.

Clark looked at the folder and back at Zi-Hong. Realization dawned on him. This ungrateful little rat. "You're still with the Communist Party, aren't you?"

Zi-Hong's mouth dropped open.

"You're stealing information for them. I brought you here to give you a chance to walk a straight path. This is what you do instead?"

The weasel hung his head, then looked up. "The KMT is for cowards." He twitched his lip. "Chiang Kai-shek doesn't have the gall to fight the Japanese. You're all a bunch of cowards. It's time for someone else's turn."

"Nonsense! The KMT isn't afraid."

"Oh yeah? Then why doesn't your own sister trust in you? Why is she running east and west for Dai Li, doing his bidding?"

"My sister?"

Zi-Hong sneered. "You don't even know, do you? The Communist Party got wind of it two months ago. All you Kuomintang people are like this. Incompetent. Wrapped in a drum about everything."

"Tell me what you're talking about!" Clark grabbed his shoulder.

"Wen-Ying." Zi-Hong shook him off. "She's a key member of Tian Di Hui in Shanghai."

Tian Di Hui. The Heaven and Earth Society. The deadliest underground resistance group in Shanghai.

"That's right." Zi-Hong lifted his smug face. "Even Wen-Ying Jie is working with subversive groups behind your back. So why are you faulting me?"

For once, Clark couldn't answer this brat. Wen-Ying? A member of the resistance working with Dai Li? What was she doing getting herself involved with something this dangerous?

He had to get home at once and get an answer. And he had to get this treacherous little spy out of here. What a colossal lapse of judgment to bring him to the KMT.

And Ekaterina. If word ever got to the Kremlin she was an agent for the Chinese government, she could be killed!

"Leave now." He tossed Ekaterina's file to the side and yanked Zi-Hong by the sleeve. Ignoring all else, he dragged him from his floor down the elevator to the front entrance of the building. Before he let go, he pulled Zi-Hong closer by the collar. "I warn you. Whatever you saw in my office, don't you dare leak it to anyone," he said to his face. What threat could he give to make sure this rascal would not put the princess at risk?

He tightened his grip. "Ekaterina Brasova is my lover. If you so much as harm a strand of her hair, I will take your life."

At the mention of the word "lover," Zi-Hong's defiant eyes wavered. Clark thrust him forward off the steps in front of the building. "Don't ever let me see your face again."

Zi-Hong stumbled and crawled back up. His chest heaving, he watched Clark glare at him. In fury, Clark stood his ground. The little imp needed to know he meant every word of his threat.

Taking several steps backward, Zi-Hong swung his body

around and scampered away. Clark hoped he'd done enough to stop the damage.

And now, he had to get home and find Wen-Ying.

———

"Good evening, Young Master." The maid bowed when Clark entered the house.

Paying no attention to the small tray with a wet towel and a glass of water she was trying to serve him, he asked, "Where's Da Xiao Jie?"

"Da Xiao Jie? I think she's in her room."

Without another word, Clark hurried upstairs to find Wen-Ying. Her bedroom door was open and he found her seated on her couch reading a book.

"I need to talk to you." He came inside and closed the door.

"About what?" She flipped the page.

"Is it true? You're a sworn member of Tian Di Hui?"

Wen-Ying stared back at him. Calmly, she set her book aside and stood up. "Yes. I am."

"For how long?"

"Since two years ago."

"Before I came back home. Why? Aren't you afraid of danger?"

"Danger? Ge, the real danger is if we let Japan bring on a full-fledged attack. These past three years, they've been encroaching further and further into our land. Sooner or later, there will be war. My Tian Di Hui brothers and sisters are ready to sacrifice our lives to fight them."

"If you're worried about Japan waging an attack, why didn't you talk to me? You don't have to be part of the resistance. I work with the highest level of Chiang Kai-shek's regime. You could've left it up to me."

"Why should I leave it up to you? Our country's in danger.

Why should you bear all the burden? Why shouldn't I stand up and protect it?"

"You're a young woman. You shouldn't get involved with matters of war and resistance. It's too much risk."

"That's strange. Aren't you the one who's always telling me I should be more forward-looking? You always said my views of a woman's role are outdated, and now you think I shouldn't take the same risk as you when Japan is about to take over our country?"

Clark bit the inside of his lip. "You work for Dai Li. He's a dangerous man. I don't want you near him. Why do you have to join the resistance fighters anyway? They're unstable." He came closer to her. "Join me. You can work with the KMT instead."

Wen-Ying shook her head. "You're already there. Having both of us in the government would be redundant. Besides, the government has too many constraints. In Tian Di Hui, we get things done quicker."

"What kind of things?" He dreaded to ask.

"I'm not at liberty to say," Wen-Ying said, her face firm and determined as he had never seen it before. "Don't worry about me. My role isn't as dangerous as some of the others. Mainly, what I do is gather information on British intelligence and help analyze political developments in Europe that might affect us."

"Is that your true reason for working at the British consulate? Is steering businesses to Chinese companies just a cover?"

"Yes."

Clark dropped his shoulders. When did Wen-Ying become someone so remarkable? All this time, she'd been part of a terrifying organization, silently carrying out her plans, revealing not a trace of who she really was even to those in her own family.

"One more thing," she said. "I don't work for Dai Li. Tian Di Hui collaborates with him, that's true. But we're an independent group. We don't answer to him. He can't make me do anything I don't want to do."

"You may think that, but Dai Li is not a person anyone can say no to."

"I'm not 'anyone.'"

Clark could see that. He could also see that nothing he said could stop her from doing what she wanted.

"Ba and Ma would be worried to death if they found out." He appealed to her guilty conscience.

"You don't tell, I don't tell, how will they know?"

Just like that, she'd turned it around and imposed it on him to keep her secret.

Liu Zi-Hong. Wen-Ying. Tang Wei. Everybody had their own agenda. All of them were taking diverging paths that complicated his own life.

"We're both doing what we have to do," Wen-Ying said. "If you don't interfere with me, I won't interfere with your phony love affair with the Russian woman."

Clark's breath nearly stopped. How did she know? Did outsiders in the resistance movement know about his secret plot with Ekaterina too? "How much do you know?"

"Don't worry," Wen-Ying told him. "It's just a hunch on my part. I don't believe you're a lust-driven playboy who takes pleasure in showing off a foreign beauty around his arm."

He let out a sigh of relief. He was starting to wonder if Liu Zi-Hong was right about the KMT being incompetent.

A knock on the door cut short their conversation. "Ge, Jie." It was Mei Mei.

Wen-Ying glanced at Clark, then said, "Come in."

Mei Mei opened the door. "Ma asks you both to come down. It's time for dinner."

"Sure," Wen-Ying said and shifted her eyes back to Clark.

But Clark wasn't thinking about their discussion anymore. He was thinking about Mei Mei. What would he tell her about him terminating Liu Zi-Hong? What could he say to convince her to stop seeing that little rat?

Oblivious, Mei Mei showed them an invitation. "Today truly is two times the joy at the door. The Levines invited our family to a 'bar mitzvah' celebration. I think it's some kind of birthday party."

"A bar mitzvah is a Jewish ceremony for boys when they turn thirteen. It's a rite of passage," Clark explained.

"Oh." Mei Mei flipped the invitation, then handed it to Clark.

Clark opened it and read the details. His thoughts invariably flowed to Eden. Mei Mei smiled at him. His urge to demand her to cut off his relationship with Liu Zi-Hong dropped. He knew the pain of having to stop seeing someone he loved. How could he ask Mei Mei to bear the same?

"This is a tricky matter." Wen-Ying threw Clark a mischievous smile. "Ma won't go. She knows now Eden Levine didn't make you break your engagement with Shen Yi, but you know Ma. She won't lose face and admit she was wrong. And Ba wouldn't want to cross her by going without her."

Refusing to take the bait, Clark looked away. The temptation of a chance to see Eden again could spell bad news for him.

"I want to go," Mei Mei said. "I like Joshua. He's a good kid. And I very much want to see what a bar mitzvah celebration is like."

"What's the other happy occasion?" Clark asked, wanting to divert their attention.

"That one . . ." Mei Mei turtled her head and squeezed her arms behind her back. "Shen Yi's getting married."

So soon? "To whom?"

"Liu Kun, the president of the Yao Xin Tobacco Company. Madam Li and Madam Wan told Ma today when they came to play mahjong."

The news didn't sit well with Clark. Liu Kun was the man the KMT had forced out to enable his father to take a seat on the Shanghai Municipal Council. At the American Chamber of

Commerce Ball, Liu Kun had tried to threaten him. That man marrying Shen Yi felt too much of a coincidence.

"Isn't Liu Kun in his forties?" Wen-Ying asked. "He's more than twice her age."

Mei Mei shrugged. She stole a curious glance at Clark.

Clark couldn't help feeling this was partly his fault. Shen Yi. Why did she have to act in such haste? She didn't need to marry someone so much older.

"The madams think they make a good pair," Mei Mei said. "He's very wealthy. Their marriage qualifies as a good match between two comparable families."

"Didn't his wife pass away last year?" Wen-Ying crossed her arms. "Then Shen Yi is marrying to be his *tianfang*?" *Tianfang* meant the wife of a widowed man. Usually a younger woman. It literally meant a replacement in the bedroom.

"It looks like it," Mei Mei said.

Wen-Ying tossed her head at Clark. "Ge, what do you think?"

Clark didn't want to think. The day had gone by with enough troubles without him taking up a pile of guilt for Shen Yi marrying an older man as a second wife. "I think I'll go to the gold and jewelry shop tomorrow and buy them both an extra-grand gift."

17

EVIL AMONG US

THE FIRST THING that struck Eden when the Lieutenant General Yasuji Okamura came to the *China Press* office for his interview was how oversized his army cap looked on his head. It was a silly irrelevant thought, she knew, but it was true. Despite his impressive military title, the little man didn't have the physique of a warrior. His scrawny shoulders couldn't hold up his decorated uniform. Paired with the thin-rimmed glasses he wore, his entire appearance seemed like a parody of the Japanese's samurai tradition of *bushido*.

But that was often the case when it came to men who would inflict the worst sufferings on others, wasn't it? They didn't always have a face that shouted devil. They needn't appear in a body worthy of Hercules or Goliath. They came in forms that drew no notice. Or, they came in comical forms that in no possible way could project the vigor and ideals they inspired. They took everyone by surprise. By the time people realized the magnitude of harm they could do, it was too late.

Back in Germany, she had already seen such men. Adolph Hitler. Henrich Himmler. Homely little men who, by a series of

179

mechanisms of fate, came into positions of power. With their power, they held in their hands the ability to unleash hell.

Keeping her expression blank, Eden stood and let Okamura and his translator take their seats in the conference room before she and Emmet sat down across the table.

Don't judge until you have all the facts. She could hear Zelik reminding her.

She didn't need Emmet here, really, but Charlie insisted on it. "They would never talk if I send in only a woman," Charlie told her.

The prejudice against her gender annoyed her, but Charlie was right, and their priority was to get the story.

At least, she could count on Emmet being on her side.

Okamura sat with his shoulders open and his hands on the armrests. His naturally dour lips and wrinkled nose reminded Eden of a prune. He barely acknowledged her and Emmet, as though they were beneath him.

She let Emmet begin with their introductions. When Emmet told them her name, the translator stared at her. He then said to Emmet, as though she wasn't present, "The subject matter might be uncomfortable for Miss Levine."

Annoyed, Eden opened her mouth to object, but Emmet put his hand lightly on her forearm on the table. "We believe it will help to enlighten our readers if we include both the male and female points of view."

The translator explained this to Okamura, who barely gave Eden another glance. He gestured for them to proceed.

Immediately, Eden jumped in to fire her first questions. "What is that building on Yuhano Road used for? Is it a military-occupied building?"

To her surprise, Okamura answered yes. "The building is a service station for our soldiers," he said through his translator.

"What kind of service?"

Okamura waved his hand and spoke. When he finished, the

translator threw an awkward glance at Eden and cleared his throat. "Our soldiers and sailors are far away from home. Many are here for a long period of time. They have certain biological needs. Our navy has therefore established a system to address those needs."

"A system?" Eden asked. Now they were getting to the heart of it. "What kind of system? Can you elaborate?"

At her belligerent tone of voice, the translator creased his forehead, but proceeded to translate and facilitate the conversation. "A system where women volunteer to provide sexual release to our men," he said, without attempting to couch the subject in sensitive language for her sake this time.

"You say these women are volunteers. Pardon me, but, what kind of women would volunteer for such a thing?" She stared directly at them.

"Japanese women, of course." The lieutenant general turned up his nose.

"Really?" Eden would not let up. "They're not Korean women?"

Okamura snorted. "There are no such things as Koreans anymore. They're Japanese women."

Japanese? Eden looked at him askance. She was prepared for this. She'd done her homework before this interview. Since Japan annexed Korea as its colony in 1910, it had been systematically taking Korea's cultural identity away. It had forced Koreans to speak Japanese and take on Japanese names. Even surnames. Those who did not comply were deprived of jobs, school, food, sometimes even punished.

"So they were not forced?" she asked.

"No. Never."

He was lying. Eden was sure. She wanted to call him out on it, but Emmet kicked her under the table.

"Being a comfort woman is an honor," Okamura said. "The women are not prostitutes. They're virgins serving at the command of our Emperor. They're a gift from our emperor to our imperial forces for their loyalty and their military services to our country."

What nonsense! Eden opened her mouth, ready to give him a piece of her mind, but Emmet spoke first. "Lieutenant General, I'm curious, how did the Imperial Japanese Navy first come up with this idea of providing sexual services to its soldiers? My understanding of the military from around the world is that they want their soldiers to be disciplined and to exercise self-control. For the navy to be in the business of supplying women, it seems a little . . . dishonorable, doesn't it?"

"Ah! That's where you got it wrong." Okamura waved his finger. "But I'm glad you asked. I can tell you as the person who initiated the comfort women project, our system is all about honor and discipline."

Eden held her pen. Did he just say he initiated the project?

"Allow me to explain," Okamura continued through his translator. "In 1932, when I first implemented the system, there were a total of 223 rapes reportedly committed by Japanese troops in Shanghai. I was very unhappy that our men were assaulting local civilians that way. To solve this problem, I made a request to our government to send women to our soldiers and sailors. After the comfort houses were established, rape crimes by Japanese troops in Shanghai completely disappeared. Our soldiers are once again men of honor, and that made me very happy," he said with an emphatic nod.

So this was for the safety of local women? Eden eyed Emmet to show her disbelief. Could there be a more twisted justification?

Emmet, however, continued to speak to the Japanese in a cordial tone. "Yes. We Shanghainese thank you very much for that. Can you please tell us how do these comfort houses operate? Are they managed like a bar? A club? Do the women dance with your servicemen like taxi girls? Do they sing and listen to music when they socialize? Are there performances to create an atmosphere of entertainment? Do you serve food and drinks as well?"

"No, no, no." Okamura adamantly waved his hands. "Our troops don't engage in frivolous recreations the way soldiers from Western countries do. And this is the part where you can see our men exhibit a much higher degree of discipline. In a comfort station, the soldiers are required to abide by a strict set of rules. When they come in, they have to register and pay to obtain an entry voucher and a condom. Two yen for regular non-commissioned personnel, five yen for military officers. Each soldier will then be assigned a room. He is allotted thirty minutes. Everything is done in a straight, orderly fashion."

Eden watched him talk. The man was actually proud of what he'd done. What was more, he was eager to tell them about it.

She looked back at Emmet. She understood now what he was doing. He'd coaxed Okamura into volunteering more information than they could've ever gotten by demanding answers.

Holding back her outrage, she changed to a more empathetic tone. "Lieutenant General, it certainly sounds like you have a very well-managed operation under your watch."

"That's correct." He jutted out his chin. "The way we operate, we keep drugs and alcohol out of our soldiers' hands. You'll never see a Japanese sailor stumble around drunk or mentally impaired by heroin or opium at Blood Alley like the Western soldiers. Our soldiers' minds are never impeded by addictive substances. We also keep them healthy and uninfected by venereal diseases, because they don't ever have to visit prostitutes."

Eden stared down at the table, resisting the urge to roll her eyes.

"Our comfort women receive regular gynecological checkups to make sure they're disease free," Okamura added.

Gynecological checkups, Eden wrote in her notes. How thoughtful. The women must be grateful so for that. At least they were kept disease free for the men's sake. "Sir, you mentioned earlier the soldiers were allotted thirty minutes for each visit. That's an awfully short time. How many men does each woman have to service each day?"

On this question, Okamura demurred. "The comfort stations have standard working hours. Non-commissioned servicemen are allowed to visit from ten in the morning to five in the afternoon. Officers can visit from one in the afternoon to nine at night."

Not giving away her reaction, Eden jotted the information down. He didn't directly answer her question. She noted that before she turned the page. "You said the soldiers pay to receive a voucher. Do their payments go to the women?"

"No! Of course not." His mouth drooped and his nose wrinkled. "We're not running brothels. The payments are for upkeep of the stations. Anyway, the women don't need money. They're well-provided for with food, clothing, and housing."

So were prisoners, Eden thought. But she let it slide. The more freely she let him speak, the more readily he gave away the details.

"One more thing, sir." She shuffled her notes. "You told me the women aren't forced. We have an eyewitness who said there was a girl in that building who tried to break through the window. She looked like she was trapped. Perhaps she was trying to break out. Our witness actually thought she might have been trying to jump out the window to kill herself. Do you have any explanation as to why she might have done that?"

A look of shock registered on the Japanese men's faces. Okamura pressed his lips into a line, then said, "Maybe your witness saw wrong."

Saw wrong? Eden wasn't about to let him off that easily. "No. We're sure our witness is reliable."

Okamura crossed his arms and tightened them around his chest. "If that's the case, then the girl must have been upset because she was jilted by a soldier."

"Jilted?"

"Yes. She must have been heartbroken because she fell for one of our soldiers, and he is no longer interested in her."

This was his answer? A jilted lover? What kind of monster was this man? Either he was suppressing reality in his mind so he wouldn't have to acknowledge the shame, or he had no sympathy whatsoever for the women who had become his victims.

"This kind of thing happens." He swayed his body slightly from left and right. "It is not our Navy's job to tend to the private relationships that might grow between the soldiers and the women as byproducts of the system."

Such cold words. As much as she tried, Eden couldn't continue to pretend to be nice and respectful anymore. She put down her pen and sat still. If she opened her mouth, she would have something very unpleasant to say.

The Japanese didn't notice her silent protest. Turning back to Emmet, Okamura said, "As you can see, we've developed a system that is the best solution to build our troops' morale and keep our soldiers healthy and clean. Ultimately, this will make our military stronger than any others." He paused, then looked at Eden. "Armies that let their men run wild will eventually fail. The West could do themselves a favor by seeing how to do things our way."

Eden drew back. Why did he look at her when he said that? Did he think she was the ear of the West? What a dunce.

The translator switched his eyes from Okumura to Emmet and Eden. "That's all the time we have. Thank you, Mr. Lai, Miss Levine. We're grateful for your giving us a chance to share our views with your Western readers."

Eden returned a fake smile.

"Thank you. We appreciate your time." Emmet stood up and thanked both men on their behalf.

When they were gone, Eden and Emmet returned to the

room. "It was a good thing you were in the room with me," Eden said. "I almost made a blunder. Thank you."

"Don't mention it." Emmet picked up his pen and notebook. "I don't blame you for feeling outraged."

"Can you believe the man? He really believes he's doing something commendable."

"He's going to have a major shock when he reads your article." Emmet winked.

Eden glanced at her notes. "He has to be lying, don't you think? When he said the women weren't forced?"

"He was never going to admit they were forced."

"I wish I had some way to prove it."

"You saw the girl trying to break out. That's proof. Only an egomaniac could think that the girl was suffering a heartbreak. If this is the kind of madman running the Japanese military, I'm afraid to think what they would do if we ever go to war with them."

So was she. Until she ventured into Hongkew, Eden had felt secure and comfortable in Shanghai. Since then, she no longer felt completely safe. Too many things about the Japanese felt wrong. An angry, dark force was mounting on the horizon. She could not explain it, but she could feel it. Evil resided here among them.

"I'm glad you picked up this story," Emmet said. "Now we can expose their hideous act."

"I'll get started right now." She gathered her notes. Back at her desk, she began to type.

Military-Sanctioned Sexual Servitude

Shanghai may be a city of sexual sins and indulgence, but the systematic coercion of women to provide sexual services to men in the military would shock the conscience of even Shanghailanders who think they've seen it all. Every day in the open streets of Hongkew, soldiers line up to take advantage of girls and women shipped from Korea to Shanghai for the specific purpose of providing Japanese servicemen sexual release. Lieutenant General Yasuji Okamura, the mastermind behind the Japanese navy's "comfort women" project, claimed the women are volunteers. Are they? What are "comfort women"? The way Okamura explained it . . .

18

THE BAR MITZVAH

ON THE DAY of the bar mitzvah, Eden couldn't have been more proud watching Joshua recite passages from the Torah and get his aliyah at the bimah in front of all the guests who had come to the Ohel Rachel to attend the service. When the Cantor presented him the kiddush cup, she almost choked up with tears. After months of being shunned by his friends, all because of her, her little brother still kept his head high. He didn't hold a grudge against her or the children who had picked on him. Graciously, he forgave them and invited all his friends from school to come to attend his party. How extraordinary for a boy who was only turning thirteen.

"He's going to grow up to be a fine man," Miriam whispered next to her.

Eden had no doubt about that.

Of course, Joshua's moment to shine couldn't have happened without a little help on Neil's part. Okay, more than a little. Overnight after Neil offered to host the bar mitzvah, her parents went from worrying whether anyone would come to the event, to who might be miffed for not being included.

What an honor it was, too, that Sir Victor Sassoon himself

was present here. When she and her family arrived, he heartily greeted them and invited them all to seder later that month at his private residence at the Cathay Mansions.

Since the last time they met, Eden's admiration for the Baron had only grown. Sir Victor was a visionary with no parallel. When she walked through the streets of Shanghai today, she could see his touch all over the city. From the architecture of the buildings in the skyline, to the commerce and activities that served as the driving forces behind the economy. Few men could claim to have had as much a hand in shaping this city as Victor Sassoon could.

She also hadn't forgotten his private chat with her. Regarding her relationship with Neil, Sir Victor had given her his firm seal of approval.

Harder to grasp was Neil's mother, Ann Marie. Ann Marie Wycroft had arrived shortly before the ceremony, and Neil had introduced them before they sat down. She seemed friendly enough, but Eden could tell the matriarch was sizing her up.

She could be wrong, but Eden had the feeling Ann Marie wasn't ready to fully accept her yet.

Was it always like this with these rich people? Anyone who was seeing one of their offspring had to pass a test?

Up front, the ceremony was coming to an end. Eden brushed aside these trivial concerns, and watched her brother return to his seat.

The extravagance of a party hosted by the Sassoons was everything it was reputed to be. At Sir Victor's summer villa, the festivities were well underway even before the guests had arrived. Along the gardens paths extending out to Hongqiao Road, the staff had hung up red, blue, and green paper lanterns to help everyone find their way. The colorful bright lights declared that a celebration was about to begin.

Following the lanterns, Eden, Neil, and her parents brought Joshua to the main garden, where a string quartet offered their first welcome with the pleasant tunes of Chopin. As the rest of the guests arrived, waiters in white tuxedo coats appeared, carrying silver trays of drinks and hors d'oeuvres to everyone's delight.

"Joshua! Joshua!" Two of his friends ran up to him. "Did you see the peacocks?" One of them pointed at the flock roaming the grounds. "Come take a look."

"Wow!" Joshua yelled. Together, they ran off to see the birds.

Dr. Levine gazed at the quartet and the bar, where the bartender was opening a bottle of wine. "This is quite unorthodox."

"What can I say?" Neil tossed up his hand. "My uncle likes to throw a good party."

"This is too much. Joshua's only a boy," Mrs. Levine said to him. Nonetheless, her face glowed and she couldn't stop her smile.

"Nothing's too much for Eden and her little brother," Neil winked at Eden. She could've taken the liberty to tease him and say she wanted more, the way a girl could with an ardent suitor. Instead, she stiffened. "Joshua will never forget this."

"Would you like me to show you the new additions to my uncle's ivory collection? The one that Eden told you about?" Neil asked her parents.

"That would be lovely!" Mrs. Levine pulled her husband closer. "What do you think?"

"Yes. I would love to take a look," Dr. Levine said.

Just then, Eden spotted Miriam coming into the garden with Ava Simms. "Neil." She touched him lightly on the arm. "I want to go over and say hello to my friends. Do you mind taking my parents without me?"

"Not at all." He stopped a waiter and offered her parents each a cocktail before taking one for himself. "Go on. I'll take good care of them."

"Thank you. I'll meet up with you all in a bit," she said to them and headed over to join Miriam and Ava at a table by the bar.

As soon as she came near them, Ava stood up and shouted, "Eden! What a gorgeous place this is!"

"Hello, Ava." Eden kissed her on the cheek. "You make this place even more gorgeous." She looked over her friend. Ava looked radiant in her hat with a red and white striped brim and lipstick with a matching shade of red.

"That was a wonderful ceremony, Eden." Miriam gave her a hug.

"Thank you." Eden took a seat. A waiter came by with a tray of drinks and she picked out a Bellini.

Miriam opened her lace fan. "I have to say, Eden, Neil Sassoon is quite a catch."

Eden blushed. "I'm not trying to catch him. We're enjoying each other's company, that's all."

"That's all? I think not. Seriously, you're smart to attach yourself to a Sassoon. With all the talk about an imminent war between China and Japan these days, I'd hold on to him for my dear life if I were you."

Eden kept her lips against the rim of her glass. She hadn't thought of this. Or rather, she had actively avoided thinking about it. She didn't want to take advantage of Neil. "That's not why I'm seeing him."

"Maybe not." Miriam fanned herself. "But as a friend, I'm telling you, it's something you should think about." She put her hand on Eden's wrist. "The Sassoons aren't like the rest of us. If anything happens here, they can pick up and move somewhere safe in the world." She paused, noticing Ava giving her an eye. "And Ava. Ava can go anywhere she wants whenever she wants too."

"Thank you." Ava grinned.

Miriam turned back to Eden. "Your family left everything behind in Munich, for what, if not to find a safe place to live? Neil Sassoon looks smitten. If I were you, I'd latch onto him. Nothing wrong with a girl being practical. It'd help me sleep better at night, that's for sure." She closed her fan. "I don't trust those Japanese or the Italians. Anyone who'd sign a pact with Hitler is evil in my book."

Eden put down her glass. She felt the same way. Especially after her interview with Okamura and what she'd found out about the comfort house. And having seen the growing presence of Japanese soldiers in the city and their military exercises, which frequency had increased each time she visited Hongkew, her apprehension about Japan had only worsened. Moreover, everyone was talking about it. China and Japan would go to war. They all said, it was only a matter of when.

The strange thing was, no one in the international community seemed seriously concerned. The media articles talked about the risks of war, but mostly in terms of how it might affect the foreign expats' commercial activities and financial interests. Perhaps everybody was right. Japan wouldn't dare to wage war in the international districts, no matter what else it did with China. But if war did break out, who would want to stay in an area surrounded by bombings and gunfights?

She hated thinking she was with Neil because of what he could do for her family.

Joshua and his friends ran by, bubbling with laughter.

She watched her brother play. Her will began to shake. What if she could secure a safe passage for her brother and her parents, no matter what happened?

Across the field, Isaac had arrived. He joined Joshua and the kids chasing the peacocks. To her annoyance, after meeting Neil at the synagogue, Isaac insisted on coming separately to the party.

Isaac's parents were still back in Germany.

The thought made her shudder.

What price would she pay to make sure her family was safe?

"Yes. I'd definitely latch onto him if I were you," Miriam said. "A guy like Neil has a horde of girls wanting to marry him if you won't. You should watch out for them, too, or someone might steal him."

"That comes with the territory," Ava said and took out a cigarette. "You can latch on all you want, but if you're going with a guy like Neil Sassoon, you'd be naive not to expect a few sideshows."

"What do you mean?" Eden looked at her, puzzled.

"It's a given. Every man with that much money will always stray. I have no advice for you whether you should or shouldn't be with him. I'm an advocate of free love. I would never encourage anyone to marry someone they don't love, especially after I made that same mistake myself." She blew out a cloud of smoke. "What I would advise you, darling, is if you decide to marry him, you go into the marriage with your eyes wide open. I've been in high society all my life. There's a rule to this game. You turn a blind eye. Don't stoop to the level of the hussies. They'll never stop swarming around your man. Just know that as long as you play your cards right, the man will always come back."

"That sounds terrible," Miriam said.

"I'm speaking the truth," Ava said. "That's how things work when you're in the market for a husband of Neil's caliber. If you're going to advise Eden to marry him, I ought to warn her what she's getting herself into."

Eden frowned and shook her head. "Neil's not like that. He's a good man."

"Is he?" Ava held up her drink. "Darling, a good man is a myth. In reality, what you're looking for is 'good enough.'"

Was that right? Was 'good enough' the standard by which she should make her choice?

"Either way," Ava continued, "the way to approach all this is to never take anything too seriously. Everyone should marry at least once anyway, if just to say you've done it. The great thing about marrying a man like Neil is, if he strays and you can't live with it, you can always divorce him and take him to the cleaners as a punishment. You win either way."

Miriam laughed. Eden fiddled her fingers around the stem of her glass. If only she could live life so casually like Ava.

She turned her head. Over by the flowerbed, Ann Marie, Neil's mother, was watching her. She didn't look away either when her eyes met Eden's. Out of courtesy, Eden smiled to acknowledge her. Ann Marie smiled back.

Was that an invitation? She couldn't expect Neil's mother to come over to her. She would have to go over to show her respect.

Eden excused herself from Miriam and Ava, then got up and made her way to the flowerbed.

By the newly planted daffodils, Ann Marie stood waiting.

"Hello," Eden greeted her. "We didn't get a chance to talk earlier."

"No. And I've been looking forward to talking to you. Walk with me?" Ann Marie tilted her head. The garden surrounding the villa had a long path ideal for an afternoon stroll.

Eden nodded and followed Ann Marie away from the main garden toward the blossoming marigolds. "How was your journey on the ship?"

"Oh," Ann Marie huffed. "I'll be honest, I don't take well to the sea. Long trips tire me out. But my son's here. He's tied up with business, so what's a mother to do? I have to see him some time."

She took a step toward the small lily pond up ahead. "Look at that. Is that new? That wasn't here last time when I came to visit. Victor really knows how to pick the right help. I would steal his landscaper and bring him back to England with me if I could, but his landscaper is Chinese and I can't speak Chinese. What a shame."

A warm breeze blew and Eden brushed her hair away from her face. "You have a beautiful garden back home too then?"

"Of course! In Cheshire where my family's from. It's every bit as grand as this one here." Ann Marie threw her silk scarf over her arm.

"That sounds wonderful," Eden said. "I'd love to visit and see it."

"You would, wouldn't you?" Ann Marie glanced at her sideways. Her smile remained, but her voice rose in alert.

Eden stiffened. "What I mean is, I love gardens. There's a beautiful one here in Shanghai. It's called the Yu Garden. It's one of my favorite places in the city." She didn't know why, but the Yu Garden and the night she spent there with Clark on New Year's Eve jumped to her mind.

"One of your favorite places? You like it more than this garden?"

Eden never thought of comparing the two. She answered as she felt. "Yes."

Ann Marie looked at her in surprise. "I see."

They continued their stroll. Eden stared at the path. Memories of Chinese New Year's Eve came flooding back, warming her heart and bringing a smile to her face.

"I know everyone here thinks Victor is equivalent to God," said Ann Marie, her voice now warmer and less guarded, "but my family, the Wycrofts, can stand head to head with him. When Neil's father and I got married and the Sassoons disinherited him, he didn't have to worry for a day how he would give me a comfortable life. It's unfortunate my family already has male heirs in line to inherit our businesses. I'm proud of Neil for being ambitious and wanting to get back into his uncle's good graces to become his heir. But on the issue of money, the Wycrofts can take care of their own, including Neil. Neil will never want for anything."

Why did the subject of money keep coming up with these people? Irritated, Eden tried to steer the conversation another way. "You and Neil's father married for love then. It was a brave thing to do to defy traditions and family expectations for love. I admire that." She sincerely meant it. Neil's father gave up his inheritance, and Ann Marie, a Catholic from a distinguished family, chose to marry a Jewish man. Whatever else Ann Marie might be, she was a romantic. And she didn't look down on the Jews the way many people did.

Ann Marie slowed her pace and smiled at Eden. This time, her smile felt genuine.

Eden's heart softened. She shouldn't blame Ann Marie for doubting her. With so much wealth, there had to be many women out there scheming to get close to her son. But she wanted to make it clear she was not one of those women. Not to impress Ann Marie, but for her own pride and dignity. She stopped walking. "If I ever get married, I would only do so for love too."

"I believe you," Ann Marie said. She stepped toward a magnolia tree and smelled one of the flowers. "Of course, when you marry for love, you'd do everything in the best interest of the other person."

What did she mean? Eden couldn't tell.

"You're a reporter?" Ann Marie abruptly turned around.

"Yes."

"I've read some of your articles."

Eden relaxed. Her articles were something she felt confident about. "Do you like them?"

"For the most part, yes."

Not a full praise or endorsement. "What didn't you like? I always want to know what readers think."

"It's not so much what I don't like. There are just some subjects about which you've written that might be . . . shall I say, inappropriate?"

That again? "If you mean my articles disputing the guilt of that Nazi—"

"No," Ann Marie stopped her. "You were trying to get to the bottom of the matter. On that subject, for once, Victor and I are in total agreement."

Now Eden was puzzled. "Then what is it?"

Ann Marie came closer to her. "We're good women. Our reputation is something we need to protect. When we speak too publicly about subjects like sex and prostitution, people might get the wrong impressions about us."

Sex? Prostitution? Was she talking about her article on the comfort women? "I don't understand. Why would people get the wrong impression?"

"An unmarried young woman writing extensively about these things?" Ann Marie touched her on the back. "People would wonder where has she been to pick up all that knowledge."

Eden thought back to what she'd written in her article. She was proud of it. Not once did it occur to her that exposing the Japanese military's exploitation of women would raise questions about herself. "All I did was try to bring attention to the girls who might need help."

"I'm sure your intentions are good, but . . ." Ann Marie scowled and shook her head. "Such a distasteful subject."

"So I should not try to help because the subject is distasteful?" Eden asked. "I don't think I can do that."

"I didn't say you shouldn't try to help. But look at it this way. Does writing these articles really help? Do you think the Japanese navy will stop what they're doing because some English newspaper published a few articles about it? They're a military organization of a sovereign nation. They don't have to answer to you."

Eden squeezed her hands. At the *China Press*, Zelik, Charlie, everyone always talked about words being a powerful weapon. Here, Ann Marie was making her feel her words were useless.

"I can see you're a good person," Ann Marie said. "You have no idea how deviant people's minds can be. Take it from someone older like me. When you write articles like that, a lot of people who read it aren't thinking they should help those girls." She leaned in and whispered in Eden's ear, "They read it only to get some perverse thrill from something salacious."

Eden frowned. Was that true? People would read an article about girls being exploited, but instead of sympathizing and wanting to help, they were getting pleasure from it? The idea made her ill.

"And you probably hadn't thought of this, but you're Neil's girlfriend now. Like it or not, that draws a lot of attention, here and back in England. You're no longer a nameless reporter of no consequence. People are watching what you do and what you say. The attention will only get worse if you and Neil ever decide to get married. People love to gossip."

"Ann Marie." Eden laughed. "Your worries are premature. Neil and I have never talked about marriage."

"All right. Then let's make sure we understand each other, because I'm not in Shanghai for long and this might be the only chance I'll get to say what's on my mind before it's too late. How you manage your reputation is your business. But when it comes to my son, that's my business. If he were to choose a wife, she can't be someone who'd bring embarrassment to my family. Some things are just too indecent to be discussed publicly." She covered her mouth. "This is nothing against you. Please understand, I need to protect my son. I need to protect my family's good name. If you don't agree with me, then I ask that you don't take things any further with Neil. If you care about him, then at least consider the kind of damage it can do if people think his girlfriend or his wife is the kind of woman who has knowledge of filthy, abominable places where men engage in all sorts of obscene depravities. In their minds, they'll associate you with all the things you write about."

Shaken, Eden tried to reply. It would've been better if Ann Marie was hard and mean, but the woman before her looked helpless. Once she started talking about Neil, her guarded exterior fell apart. She was only a mother who wanted to protect her son.

But Neil wasn't the one most in need of protection. The girls at the comfort station were.

Would she end her relationship with Neil to pursue this matter? Ann Marie had a point too. Her English articles might upset the Japanese, but she couldn't exert the same amount of pressure on them as she did to the SMP. She untensed her body and loosened her fist. "I want to help those girls."

"Find another way," Ann Marie said. "You don't always have to help by making a lot of noise. That's how we, the Wycrofts, do things. We give a hand to people when they're in need, but we don't do it publicly. We don't draw attention. You're a smart girl. I know you'll find another way. A better way."

What other way? What else could she do?

"Or find another cause. We can't save everyone in the world. There are a lot of other causes you can advocate for and write about. Find something more suitable for a woman in your position to fight for. Let other people with less to lose handle those things that could compromise your name." She patted Eden on the back, then stared out at the field toward the crowd of guests. "We should head back. Neil might be wondering where you are." She turned around and started walking, leaving Eden to try and follow through a maze of confusion.

Back in the main garden, a guest came up and greeted Ann Marie. Eden took the opportunity and excused herself. Their conversation had left her bewildered and torn. She wanted a moment to herself to gather her thoughts. She had barely escaped a few steps when Clark and his youngest sister Wen-Li arrived. In the midst of the crowd of guests, Clark gazed at her. And she felt it. Even before she saw him, she felt his gaze.

She knew he would be coming, so why was she feeling so nervous in his presence? She wanted to go near him, and also to stay away from him.

"Eden!" Wen-Li called out to her and waved.

Whatever she was feeling, she couldn't ignore them. Putting on a friendly face, Eden walked over to them. "Clark, Wen-Li, welcome. It's so good to see you both." She quickly glanced away from Clark and talked directly instead to Wen-Li. Why did her voice have to quiver?

"What a beautiful place this is." Wen-Li looked around in awe, shading her eyes from the sun with her hand. "Thank you for inviting us. Our parents sent their regards. We came on their behalf."

"We're glad you're here." Eden swayed her body sideways away from Clark. He was still staring at her and she didn't want to do or say something stupid under the force of his gaze.

"Wen-Li! Clark!" Joshua ran up from the field.

"Hello, Joshua," Wen-Li greeted him. "Happy birthday."

"This place has peacocks. Want to come see?"

"Peacocks! Yes."

Before Eden could stop him, Joshua grabbed hold of Wen-Li's hand and led her away.

Now what? She glanced back at Clark, trying not to appear awkward. "Princess Ekaterina didn't come with you?"

As soon as the question slipped out of her mouth, she wanted to knock herself on the head. Of all the things she could've asked him, why did she have to sound like a jealous woman?

Clark almost looked hurt, although she couldn't immediately make out if that was the case. She couldn't look him in the eye.

"No. She didn't," he answered. He didn't explain further why he didn't bring the princess along.

"How is she?" Eden swung around, mentally knocking herself on the head again. Stop acting so pathetically curious, she told herself.

"She's doing very well. Thank you for asking," Clark said. His soft, gentle voice calmed her somewhat. "How've you been?"

"Good." She plastered on a grin. "Joshua's doing well at school, and now we have this wonderful party. My father's Jewish patients have returned and my mother's little business with children's clothing is growing." She pulled away from him and lifted her chin. "I'm doing well at work, although you'd know that, wouldn't you?" She stopped. She didn't mean for her question to come out like she was holding a grudge. Why did she even bring this up?

He looked surprised. Well, she might as well bring this into the open. "I know you were the one who arranged to get rid of Zelik and bring me back to the *China Press*."

"So you found out after all," he said. "You never should've been let go. I hope you aren't upset with me for meddling." He gazed down. She always liked the way he lowered his eyes when he was deep in thought.

She moved back closer to him. "How could I be upset? You're always looking out for me. I appreciate that." Yes. She was grateful. And it wasn't right for her to speak to him as if he owed her an apology.

Why not just admit to herself? She held a grudge that he fell in love with someone else. She couldn't get angry at him for that, so her heartache manifested itself through an entirely unrelated subject matter altogether.

Now that she saw him again and they were speaking alone, she could finally be honest with her own feelings. She wished she was the woman he loved. And she had every right to feel angry about it.

As she stepped closer, he raised his head. "I'll always look out for you." He said this so quietly, she almost wasn't sure if she really heard it. And then, he hardened his lips. "But I guess that really isn't necessary anymore, is it?"

Was that a grudge in his voice? She could've sworn she sensed something wrong in him. Bitterness? Self-pity? But his expression changed so quickly. He gazed warmly at her. The kind of warmth that initially drew her to him and made her feel as though they could be something more. "Neil Sassoon's a lucky man. I'm sure he's smart enough to know not to lose a good thing when he finds it."

"Clark . . ." A rush of thoughts ran through her head. Whatever hard feelings she felt dissipated. She wanted to ask him, if he meant she was a good thing, then why didn't he come after her? If he had, Neil wouldn't even be in her life. So many things felt unsaid between them, she didn't know where to begin. And how could she begin? How could she openly say any of these things when he'd never given her any convincing reason to believe he had real feelings for her?

"There you are!" Neil came up from behind her. "I've been looking all over for you."

Eden gave him an uneasy smile. Before she had a chance to respond, he held out his hand toward Clark. "Hello, I'm Neil Sassoon."

"Clark Yuan. Pleased to meet you." Clark shook his hand.

"Where are my parents?" Eden asked Neil, diverting his attention to something else lest he could read her thoughts.

"They've gone inside to the dining room. Seating's about to start. Shall we go in?" he glanced at both Eden and Clark.

"Sure," Clark said, his voice tight but friendly "I'll see you both inside. I'd like to go find my sister first." He rested his eyes on Eden for another moment, then walked away.

Did he look hurt just now? Eden tried to catch a glimpse of his face as he left.

"Come on." Neil offered her his arm. She took it and followed him. With each step, she felt she was walking further away from where true happiness would be.

On their way inside, a large beady-eyed man came up and greeted Neil. Neil welcomed him like an old friend. "Dr. Green, this is Miss Eden Levine. She's the sister of the boy whose bar mitzvah we're celebrating today."

"Miss Levine, how do you do?" Dr. Green bowed.

"Dr. Green is a specialist in urology at the Hospital St. Marie."

"The Hospital St. Marie?" Eden asked. "That's where a good friend of mine works. His name is Isaac Weissman. He's here today too. He's an assistant to Dr. Brouchard."

"Yes, yes. Of course. I know Dr. Brouchard."

"Dr. Green has been with that hospital for fifteen years," Neil said. "He's indispensable."

"You're too kind, Neil. Too kind. If you ask me, I'd say you are the one who's indispensable." He turned to Eden. "The amount of money Neil has contributed to St. Marie is unbelievable. If only more people would take charity as seriously as he does."

"It's the least I can do." Neil put his arm around Eden and said to her, "Uncle Victor wants me to do more charity work, remember? He just doesn't know all that I'm doing."

"Anyway," said Dr. Green, "Miss Levine, it's a pleasure to meet you. My table is over there. I'll talk to you both later?" He excused himself.

After he left, Neil led her toward the host's table. "You didn't tell me Isaac works at the Hospital St. Marie. He's close to your parents, isn't he?"

"Yes," she said. "He's practically family." And no, she hadn't told him where Isaac worked. Isaac wasn't something she wanted to discuss with Neil. Besides, Isaac himself hadn't shown much interest in Neil either. Whenever the topic of Neil came up with her family, Isaac would just stay quiet. "Isaac's father and mine are best friends. There isn't much to talk about. He always wanted to be a doctor, but right now, he doesn't have enough money to go to medical school. His parents are still in Munich and they've been having trouble getting their money out of Germany. He said their neighbor is helping them get their savings into Switzerland. When that happens, his parents will come to Shanghai. He'll be able to go back to school and pursue a medical career then."

"I don't see why he has to wait."

"What do you mean?"

"The only issue is money, right? I can help with that. I can set up a scholarship fund."

"You'd do that?"

"Of course! Why wouldn't I do whatever I can to help your friend?"

"Neil! That's such a kind offer. I feel like it's too much to ask."

"Not at all." He squeezed her arm. "Supporting education is always a good cause. Let's arrange a time for him to come by my office so we can talk more about it. By the way, I have another piece of good news to tell you. The hospital got rid of Otto Neumann."

"Did they? I'm so glad to hear that!" Such a despicable person should never have been allowed to operate in a hospital in the first place.

But even as she was thrilled, Clark's voice came back to her. *I'll always look out for you,* he'd told her. *But I guess that really isn't necessary anymore, is it?*

With the Sassoons behind her, she didn't need him, right?

Why did the thought make her sad?

They came to their table. Sir Victor and her parents already took their seats. Sir Victor was delighting her parents with the wild tales of his travels around the world.

Also with them at their table was Ann Marie Wycroft. The

matriarch blinked at Eden with a meaningful smile as Eden sat down.

Eden gave her a courteous nod back. Come to think of it, Neil couldn't help her with everything. There were certain things that people of a certain class deemed "inappropriate" for a young lady like her to even discuss. She smiled sarcastically to herself as she unfolded her napkin.

But could she still go to Clark when she was in need? She gazed over at the table far on the opposite side of the room where he was taking a seat.

———

Leaving Eden behind with her new beau, Clark made his way toward Mei Mei, who was now admiring the blossoming azaleas with several ladies attending the party.

He couldn't deny it. Seeing Eden with another man hurt. It hurt him more than he imagined.

But he made the right decision, didn't he? By letting go of his own chance with her, she had found herself someone much more suitable. Someone better. Her happiness was all that mattered, he reminded himself.

They certainly made a good match too. And with Neil Sassoon, she would never have to face any family or societal constraint and prejudice.

He tapped his sister to get her attention. "Mei Mei, it's time to go inside."

"Ge." Mei Mei greeted him and introduced him to the other ladies, then followed him to the veranda where the guests were taking their seats at the white linen tables. "What's that?" She pointed to an easel propping up a large poster board next to the reception table. A small group had gathered in front of it. They stopped to take a look.

Mei Mei read the poster board and tugged his sleeve. "It looks like a riddle."

"It is." An old lady who was studying the riddle turned around. "It's a contest. If you can solve it correctly, you'll be entered into a drawing. That's the award." She pointed at the antique jade hairpin displayed in a glass case on the reception table. "Sir Victor always has a surprise in store when he gives a party."

The old lady's companion, a short man with a full white mustache, pulled his glasses up the bridge of his nose and bent closer to the sign displayed in front of the hairpin. "It says here the hairpin was made during the Tang Dynasty."

Mei Mei read the sign. "What a beautiful hair ornament. Ge, this hairpin has a name. It's called 'Dreams of Liang and Zhu.'"

The name piqued Clark's interest. The hairpin was actually a long stick, the kind that women used to hold their hair up in a bun before they changed the way they wore their hair during the Qing dynasty. At its decorative end, it had a delicately carved design of two butterflies representing the love of Liang Shan-Bo and Zhu Ying-Tai.

"What does it mean, Dreams of Liang and Zhu?" the old lady asked.

"It's an old folk tale," Mei Mei told her. "Have you heard of *The Butterfly Lovers*? That's what the story is called in English."

The old lady returned a blank face. "No, I don't think I've heard of it." She turned to her husband. "Marvin, have you heard of the story?"

"No." Marvin shook his head and stroked his mustache.

"It's a very famous love story," Mei Mei said. "It's about Zhu Ying-Tai, a daughter of a wealthy family. She convinced her father to allow her to leave home and go to school disguised as a young man back in the days when girls didn't go to school. At school, she met a poor student, Liang Shan-Bo. The two became close friends, and Liang Shan-Bo suggested they take an oath of fraternity. All the while, Zhu Ying-Tai had fallen in love with him."

"How lovely!" the old lady slapped her hands on her cheeks.

"It didn't turn out so well for them though. Three years later, Zhu Ying-Tai got a letter from home. Her parents told her she had to come home because her father was very sick. But they were lying. The real reason they wanted her to come home was because they'd arranged for her to marry the son of the powerful Ma family."

"Oh dear." The old lady gasped. "Poor girl. Then what happened?" Her husband too, was now drawn in and listening. Without looking at them, Clark rested his fingers on the edge of the display table and listened on the side.

"Well, Zhu Ying-Tai didn't know it was a scheme. Before she left the school, she invited Liang to come visit her home. She told him she had a twin sister, and she promised him she would act as a matchmaker for him and his twin sister. A few months later, when Liang came to visit Zhu at her home. She revealed to him he she was actually a girl, and he fell in love with her too. Unfortunately, her parents had already arranged for her to marry someone else. Liang Shan-Bo was heartbroken and went home."

"Oh no, that's terrible."

"Yes." Mei Mei nodded. "At home, he became lovesick. He got so sick, he passed away. When Zhu Ying-Tai found out, she asked her entourage to stop at Liang Shan-Bo's grave during her wedding procession on her way to the Ma family home so she could pay her respect one more time. When she came to the tombstone, the wind swept up a sandstorm and the grave opened. Zhu Ying-Tai jumped into the grave. When the storm ended, her spirit and Liang Shan-Bo's became a pair of butterflies and they flew away together."

"Oh! That's so sad." The old lady covered her heart with her hands. She moved to look at the hairpin again. Clark stepped back to give her space.

He knew well the story of Liang and Zhu. Every Chinese person had heard of it.

When love became hopeless, Liang went home and died of a broken heart.

What would he have done if he were in Liang's place?

The old lady turned to her husband. "Marvin, can you try to solve the riddle? I'd love to have this hairpin now that I know the story."

"Aww." Her husband rolled his head. "I'm no good with these things. I can never solve these brain teasers."

"It doesn't hurt to try. You never know. Maybe you'll get it this time. You're so good with your crossword puzzles."

"That's not the same thing."

Clark chuckled. He watched Mei Mei admire the prize and asked, "Do you like the hairpin? I can try to solve the riddle and win it for you."

"I do like it," Mei Mei said, "but I don't want it. Liang Shan-Bo and Zhu Ying-Tai both died in the end. It's bad omen."

"You shouldn't be superstitious like Ma."

Mei Mei stuck out her tongue.

The man named Marvin squinted at the poster board and said to Clark. "I can't figure this out, can you?"

Clark glanced at the riddle.

You have me today
Tomorrow you'll have more.
As your time passes,
I'm not easy to store.
I don't take up space,
But I am only in one place.
I am what you saw,
But not what you see.
What am I?

Could he solve it?

Yes. He could.

He picked up a pencil and wrote the answer along with his name, then dropped the little piece of paper into the drawing box.

At least the riddle gave him a temporary distraction. Throughout dinner, he couldn't help looking over at Eden at the host's table. Silently, he laughed at himself. He could understand how Liang Shan-Bo died in despair.

After the last course, Sir Victor took to the microphone before the roomful of guests. "Thank you all for joining us today for this delightful afternoon."

The room fell quiet and everyone turned their chairs to listen to him speak.

"Joshua, we wish you a happy birthday. I hope you'll enjoy all the gifts. I tell you, when I think back to my own bar mitzvah, the money gifts are all I remember." Laughter broke out from the floor as Joshua sucked in his cheeks and flitted his eyes left to right. "But we still have one more gift to give away." He lowered the microphone. A waiter rolled out the jade hairpin in the glass display and a drawing box. "An antique broker brought this piece to me recently. I thought about keeping it for myself, but as you can all see, my hair's getting a little thin and my barber couldn't quite figure out how to keep it on my head."

This time, even Clark cracked a smile.

Sir Victor walked to the drawing box. "So, I've decided to offer it up today to someone who can make better use of it. But only if the recipient is worthy." He glanced at a second waiter, who brought out the easel and the poster board. "The answer to this riddle is memories."

The guests groaned. A man at Clark's table whispered to his wife, "Damn! I should've thought of it."

"My staff had gathered all the entries with the correct

answer." Sir Victor stuffed his hand into the drawing box. He picked one out and read the name. "The winner is . . . Mr. Clark Yuan."

The guests applauded. Clark sat back, stunned.

Mei Mei's mouth dropped open. "Ge! You won!"

"Mr. Yuan, would you please come up?" Sir Victor searched the room for the winner.

Clark got up and tugged his suit. He knew he'd solved the riddle when he threw the answer into the box, but winning the prize was an afterthought.

"Congratulations." Sir Victor shook his hand and presented him the gift. "I hope you have a very special lady who can make good use of this."

Clark thanked him and accepted the hairpin lying in its case. A sudden urge overcame him. At the host table, Neil Sassoon had his arm resting on the back of Eden's chair. Clark gazed at the delicately carved butterflies. Eden might never be his, but he would not go away and mourn in despair like Liang Shan-Bo. He would love, his own way.

He spoke into the microphone. "There's a special lady in this room who I have always admired. For her courage, conviction, and her sense of justice." He turned to the direction of Eden's table and held up the gift. "Eden, no one deserves a gift more than you for the way you stand up for the truth." He walked toward her. Under the sound of applause, Eden stood up, her face overflowing with shock as he handed her the gift.

"To our eternal friendship," Clark said, holding her gaze. "Between us. Between our families. And between China and all the Jewish people in the world."

Cheers broke out from among the guests. Their voices, however, faded into something in the distance. In that moment, Eden was all he cared about. No one else mattered.

"Thank you." She gripped the box that held the gift. Her eyes sparkled with tears she was holding back. Clark wondered if she,

ALEXA KANG

too, felt all the unspoken pain behind the unyielding barriers that always stood between them.

Finally, when the applause subsided, he broke their gaze and nodded at Neil. He acknowledged her parents, then returned to his seat.

The waiters began serving desserts. Clark stole one look at Eden. What he did was a bold move, but he didn't regret it. It was probably the only chance he would ever have to give her something that embodied how he felt about her. Maybe one day, years from now when she was married and whatever she could recall of him had become distant memories, she would even learn of the story behind the butterflies and understand the meaning of his gift.

On his way home in the car after the party was over, Mei Mei asked him, "You still love her, don't you?"

Clark didn't answer. He kept his gaze out the window.

"Why don't you pursue her then?"

He pulled his gaze back and looked at her. "You're too young. A lot of things, you won't understand."

Mei Mei puckered her lips and didn't ask anymore. He gave her a light pat on the hand. Maybe some feelings were meant to be buried, never to be revealed.

19

RINGS OF MU

Eternal friendship.

Since the day of Joshua's bar mitzvah, Eden had thought so many times about what this phrase meant. If she couldn't have a chance at love with the man she wanted, could she accept his offer of eternal friendship?

And if love, as she fantasized it to be in her dreams, full of romance, beauty, and the desire to satisfy one's heart—if it could not be realized, could she settle for love in the practical form of security, safety, and the wellbeing of her own family?

When she first began dating Neil, all she wanted was a little distraction. Neil's appearance patched the wound she'd felt when she learned that Clark had fallen in love with a Russian princess. It gave her a shield to protect her pride, however much she wanted to deny that she needed it.

Now, she had come to a crossroad. If she didn't intend to have a possible future with Neil, she should not allow him to pursue her any further. She could not in good conscience continue to let him invest so much of himself in her. Especially when everyone was so happy she and Neil were together. Her parents, Sir Victor. Joshua too after his wonderful bar mitzvah. The longer she remained with Neil, the more she would let everyone down if their romance didn't come to the happy end they all wanted to see.

Being with Neil, though, came with certain expectations. His mother, Ann Marie, had made this very clear.

Could she live with those expectations?

Neil could do so much for her, and his pursuit of her had been so sincere. Why the hesitation? How ungrateful of her to have doubts when life had dealt her this winning card? Other girls would do anything to be in her place. Couldn't she accept a few demands for the sake of her family?

If she became Mrs. Neil Sassoon, she would no longer be stateless. All the advantages that came with being a Sassoon would become hers. And if war broke out anywhere in the world, Neil could take her and her family to a safe place.

Would she be compromising her principles in exchange? Would she refrain from speaking out about the atrocity of the comfort house, as Ann Marie wanted?

But Ann Marie was right, wasn't she? Exposing the Japanese wasn't enough to stop them. The *China Press* had run her article. Yes, there had been public outrage and criticism from the international community. The Japanese navy was outraged too. They'd responded with a scathing letter against the Western press for exploiting their good will. The article humiliated them, but didn't stop them.

Words were powerful, but the power of words was also limited.

Find another way, Ann Marie had told her.

So here she was, walking down the side of the Bund, coming once again to seek help from the only person who might be able to find a way. Up ahead at the wharf by the Whangpoo River, Clark stood waiting. He cut a handsome figure under the sunlight. Deep in thought, he hadn't noticed her approach.

Quietly, she walked up to him. "Hello."

"Eden." Clark turned around. A spark of tenderness brightened his eyes. It soothed her and tormented her.

"Thank you for coming to meet me."

"I was glad to hear from you."

Trying to find the right words and strike the right tone, Eden shifted her weight to the side away from him and wrung her hands behind her. "Thank you for the hairpin. It's exquisite."

He softened his gaze. "I'm glad you like it."

"You should've given it to Ekaterina. It would've looked beautiful on her."

"It suits you more."

Eden bit her lip. What did he mean? That the hairpin looked better on her than the princess? Or that she would appreciate Chinese antique more than Ekaterina?

"Did you ask me to come out to thank me?" Clark asked.

"No." Eden chuckled. "Actually, I wonder if you can help me with something." She pulled a brown envelope out of her bag. "I've been researching an operation by the Japanese navy. They've been shipping young girls and women from Korea to Shanghai to provide services to their soldiers and sailors. It's the same kind of services prostitutes provide. I believe the women are coerced. These are my notes." She took a manila folder out of the envelope and handed it to him.

Clark opened it and looked at the notes and the photo inside.

"I even interviewed the Japanese Lieutenant General who initiated the program," Eden said. "It's surreal. He really believes he's doing a good thing. The *China Press* ran an article I wrote about this. You'll find a clip of the article in there. Unfortunately, this is about all I can do."

Clark frowned and closed the folder. "What would you like me to do?"

"I don't know. I'm not sure if there's anything you can do. But you're the only person I know who has contact with the different governments. You probably can't do anything officially to stop it.

But if you can think of any other way, I hope you can try and save these women." She looked him firmly in the eye. In China, there were always other ways. It was only a matter of having the right connections and paying the right price.

He stared at the folder. "I'll see what I can do."

She gave him the brown envelope as well. The closeness she always felt toward him lingered between them. Why? How did they never try to explore this before other people came into their lives, setting them off onto different paths?

She sighed and gazed out to the river.

He joined her. Silently, they watched the boats, junks, and sampans sail down the river. "Are you happy?" he asked. His gaze remained fixed on the water.

What an odd question to bring up.

"Yes," she said. Looking at the peaceful scene, it felt wrong to say otherwise.

What else could she say? That she would be happier if he had loved her and not the princess Ekaterina? "I'm very happy."

If he had questioned her further, she might have taken back what she said. If he'd pressed her, she might've broken down and told him everything about how she really felt.

But he didn't. Without even looking at her, he slid his hand into his pocket. She adjusted the strap of her bag, and accepted her fate. Between them, there would only be eternal friendship. Her future lay with Neil.

"Are you happy?" she asked him.

He pulled his gaze back from the river toward her, then looked behind her to the flags of the nations flying in the wind on top of the buildings. "Remember you told me once, right here, that you dream of a world where all the nations' flags could fly in the unity of peace? If I can help to make that happen, then yes, I would be very happy."

A pigeon flew up from the ground. The flutter of its wings answered him before she could. Clark turned away from her and stared out at the IJN *Idzumo* sailing upstream toward Soochow Creek.

"There is still hope, isn't there?" she asked.

This time, he didn't make her any promises. He stood, alone in his thoughts, watching the tide of the river rise as the IJN *Idzumo* approached closer and closer toward them.

———

On her way home, Eden made an extra stop to visit Isaac at his place. Her heart swelling with anticipation, she knocked on his door. She couldn't wait to tell him the good news.

She never expected him to be happy about Neil coming into her life, but Neil's offer to help him might give him some solace.

With Neil by her side, everyone's future became secure.

"Eden?" Isaac answered. A ray of happy surprise lit his face.

She entered and gave him her warmest smile.

He closed the door and scratched his head. "Could I get you some water? I wasn't expecting guests. I don't have anything else."

"I'm fine. Don't worry about it." She glanced at the leftover piece of bread on the plate next to the open medical journal on his table. "I came to talk to you about something Neil suggested."

"Your boyfriend?" he groaned.

Eden ignored that. "I know you're waiting for your parents to get their money transferred out of Germany so you can go to medical school. What if you didn't have to wait? What if you could apply now?"

"What do you mean?" He straightened his stance, his face showing interest again.

"Neil offered to put up a scholarship fund for you. He said he'll pay for your tuition so you can study to become a doctor like you always wanted."

Issac stood still. A flash of redness rose to his neck. "No."

"No?" She took a step toward him. "Isaac, this is a wonderful opportunity. You're too smart. You should be more than a physician's assistant. Let us help you."

He backed away from her. "Let us help you," he mocked. "I'm disappointed in you, Eden. I never thought you'd be a social climber."

A social climber? "What? What are you talking about?"

"I thought you were better than this. I guess even you can't resist the name Sassoon."

Eden clenched her jaws. How could he say this? How could he say such hurtful things? "I'm trying to help you."

"Thanks. I don't need your help." He straightened his back and placed his hands on his hips.

Why was he being so ungrateful? Why was he acting so rude? "You're jealous. You're insulting me and you're foolishly refusing a good opportunity because you're jealous."

"Jealous?" He laughed. "I see. That's how you think of me. A jealous, petty-minded little person. Or a pauper who would jump at an offer of charity no matter how dirty the hands it came from."

"What do you mean, dirty?" she asked, confused.

Isaac's body loosened. His mouth fell open as surprise overtook his anger. But then, he straightened his back again and crossed his arms. "No. I'm not going to stoop low and speak ill of your boyfriend, even if you think I'm that kind of person."

"Explain it to me." Eden squeezed her hands. "Why would you say it's 'dirty?'"

"No!" Isaac turned away. "I didn't mean to bring this up. Look. Regardless of what you think of me, who you socialize with is none of my business. I would never interfere with who you date or which man you choose. If there were something you really wanted to know, you'd be asking questions yourself anyway."

Eden dropped her hand. Her frown deepened. "Well, I want to

know now, and I'm asking. Why don't you just tell me what you're talking about?"

Isaac furrow his brows. "It's not my place to tell," he grumbled. "You're an investigative reporter, aren't you? The hospital. Go find out yourself." He opened his door.

The hospital? Eden dug her nails into her palm. "Fine." She swung around and stomped out.

The door behind her slammed. She turned her head around and glared. Isaac! What was wrong with him? She'd come to offer him a chance she thought he couldn't refuse. Like always, his stubborn self wouldn't open his eyes to all the good things around him.

Whose eyes aren't open? a little voice inside her asked.

Even as she wanted to stay angry, the voice of reason was forcing her fury to subside. Yes, Isaac was stubborn. No, he didn't always say the right things to ease others' feelings. But Isaac would not lie. Not to her.

What did he mean by 'dirty?' Dirty money? At the hospital?

Who could she go to if she wanted to find out more?

She knew at least one person Neil associated with at the Hospital St. Marie. The urologist, Dr. Green. But if Neil and Dr. Green were friends, Dr. Green certainly wouldn't divulge anything to her.

Someone else who knew them might though. Someone who wasn't a friend. Someone who had something to gain if offered the right price? Maybe someone on the staff?

Tomorrow morning, she intended to find out.

In the garden by the fish pond at the home of Kenji Konoe, Clark stood listening to the sparrows spreading the call of welcome to spring. If only the tranquility of this place could flow from here to the rest of the world, everything would be so much better.

Beside him, Konoe, a *Kazoku* member of the highest nobility rank from the great line of Fujiwaras, threw a handful of fish food into the water. "You're asking me to interfere with something outside the realm of my responsibilities."

"Protecting the lives of the weak is never outside of the realm of a man's responsibilities," Clark said. "Especially not those endowed with the power to protect."

A school of fish dove toward the food. One sprang out of the water, like a dancer jumping up in mid-air.

"Why did you choose to ask for my help?" asked Konoe. "You could've followed the proper channels through your office and made a formal request to our navy."

"Because I know you don't approve of what's going on in that comfort house," Clark said. It was written all over him. The wrinkling of his nose, almost undetectable, had hung there since Clark first showed him Eden's notes and photos. He also knew Konoe's disgust had little to do with morals. Rather, Konoe disdained all behaviors that debased his aspiration for purity and a higher state of existence.

Clark watched Konoe empty the rest of the fish food into the pond. "Your soldiers are degrading themselves. How can you hope for them to follow your path? This practice of using comfort women is the opposite of everything you believe about the need for men to leave behind their desires. If your soldiers are continuously tempted to feed their own lust, how will they ever achieve the elevated plane of 'no self?'"

A pleased smile cleared the nauseated look on Konoe's face. "So you've thought about what it means to reach the sphere of 'no self?'"

"I have thought about it. If you want to know, I've made some very difficult choices recently to leave behind the very things I would've wanted for myself because of it."

"Then why are you concerning yourself with helping a few *Joseon* women?"

Clark glanced sideways at him. Interesting choice of words. Konoe couldn't bring himself to describe these women as Japanese, even when his country was imposing upon the Koreans to adopt Japanese names, identities, culture, and way of life.

Konoe didn't think of these women as Japanese. To him, they would always be inferior.

"Why do you preoccupy yourself with things so mundane?" Konoe asked. "You should have bigger concerns on your mind than what lowly soldiers with no self-control are doing with women."

"Because I came to a different interpretation of 'no-self.'"

"You did?" Konoe glanced curiously at him.

"I think that to fully realize a life of 'no self,' a man has to put the greater good and the interests of his people above himself."

Konoe pondered his words. Slowly, he nodded. "Interesting thought."

"You're a member of the Japanese military. You can't separate yourself from your men as long as you're a part of it. What they're doing is a stain on you too. Your turning a blind eye won't erase it. That stain marks you."

Konoe scowled in indignation. He turned back toward the pond.

"Help these women," Clark said. "If purity of mind really means something to you, then show me."

Konoe sucked in a deep breath, then clasped his hands behind his back. "I'll see to it that this comfort house's operation will terminate at once."

"And the women?"

"They'll be sent back home from wherever they came. I don't go back on my word."

"Thank you," Clark said, feeling at last a wave of relief. Konoe did have a conscience. He might not value the same things as most people, but he had principles which he lived by.

A falling leaf dropped into the pond. A ripple of rings spread across the water surface, like circles of *"mu"* echoing their master in a state of "no-self."

"I'm agreeing to do this only because it is your request," Konoe said. "Not many people can understand my hope to rise above the ordinary. In China, I believe you are the only one. Consider it a gesture of sincere goodwill on my part." He gazed out at the bird flying off the branch of a tree. "I fear, the goals of Imperial Japan and China might come to a clash."

"Yes," Clark said. Konoe's admission of the tensions between their countries surprised him. It was a sensitive subject he himself felt uncomfortable bringing up. "The instability of the situation worries me."

"Your friendship is something I value. You can rest assured, within these walls of my home, nothing will ever affect that. But outside, my loyalty will always be with the Empire of Japan."

"As mine will always be with China," Clark said with the same tone of regret. If the conflicts between their countries did come to a head, Konoe's friendship would be his loss too.

20

DOUBLE-CROSSED

TUCKED AWAY in a private back dining room at the restaurant Taoyuan, Ekaterina opened the menu and gushed, "Wow!"

Clark waited for the waitress to finish pouring the tea, then ordered a bottle of *maotai*, a Chinese white wine of the highest grade with alcohol content up to fifty proof. "Think Lukin can handle it?" He held the bottle up to show Ekaterina.

True to her word, Ekaterina had persuaded the reclusive Fyodor Lukin, the local White Russian fascist who the KMT suspected to be colluding with Japan against the Soviets, to join them tonight.

"*Maotai* wine is as strong as any vodka if not stronger," Clark said as the waitress opened the bottle and poured half of it into a little glass jug used for serving Chinese white wine.

Ekaterina shrugged. "I'm more interested in the food. Is this true? Does this place really serve twelve-course dinners the way they used to make imperial cuisine for Chinese emperors?"

"That's what this restaurant is known for. It's why I picked it. I'm having dinner with a royal princess, aren't I?" He opened the menu himself as the waitress left the room. The real reason he chose this place, though, was privacy. Taoyuan had the best private dining rooms in Shanghai for anyone who wanted to enjoy an extended meal in a discreet, secluded setting.

"There are five different sets of courses here. Which one should we choose?" Ekaterina asked.

Clark flipped through the menu. Instead of answering her, he closed the menu and put it aside. "Do you think he'll believe me?"

"Why wouldn't he?"

"I've never done anything like this before. I mean, we've been pretending we're having an affair, but I haven't had to actively lie to anyone like a spy."

Ekaterina laid down the menu. "You'll do fine. We've gone over this. Lukin wants Japan to bring a fight to Russia. You want Japan to bring war elsewhere and not China. You two have a common ground. Exploit that. Ask him what the Imperial Japanese Army is doing to help him."

"He's deluded if he thinks Japan will wage war against the Soviets."

"Feed his delusion then," she said. "All you need to do is to get information from him on what he's doing with the IJA to plot against the Kremlin. Then the KMT wouldn't have to make up things to feed to Sokolov."

Ekaterina made it sound so easy. Clark wished he could say the same for himself. How did she talk him into this anyway? It was never his intent to get this deep into espionage work.

The waitress brought in a man in a dark brown suit.

"Fyodor," Ekaterina greeted him after the waitress closed the door.

Fyodor Lukin removed his hat, although his thick mustache and beard still concealed half of his face.

"Mr. Lukin." Clark stood up and offered his hand. "I've been looking forward to meeting you."

Lukin shook his hand and sat down. "Her Serene Highness assured me I can trust you."

"I hope we can trust each other." Clark picked up the glass jug filled with *maotai* and poured it for both Lukin and himself. He offered it to Ekaterina, but she refused with a soft wave of her hand. "To begin, you can trust me this is the best bottle of *maotai* money can get."

Lukin let slip a smile and picked up the little white cup of *maotai*. He downed it in one shot. Clark did the same as he kept his eye on the man. Lukin licked his lips and set down the cup. "Vodka is a lot smoother, but this is not bad."

Clark poured him another shot. "I hear the IJA is interested in training Russian emigrants to help take the land at the Russian border across Manchuria." When Japan signed the Anti-Comintern Pact with Germany last November, it seemed they were baiting Stalin to go to war.

Keeping his guard, Lukin threw Ekaterina a quick glance. Ekaterina nodded and Lukin said, "Your information is correct."

Lowering his voice, Clark asked, "Can you tell me about it?"

Lukin still hesitated.

Clark leaned forward toward him. "If it's true that Japan and Germany are joining forces to attack the Soviets on two fronts, then I want to help you. My government wants Japan to divert its army to the Soviet border. You want to take your country back from the Bolsheviks. Japan at war with Stalin will give the KMT time to build up our army and our regime. We're on the same side."

Lukin's face twitched. Seeing his reservations start to give way, Clark pressed on. "We can work together. We have an opportunity right now. My government has access to the Soviets. I can give you crucial information about them to pass on to the IJA. We can even get you German support. Germany's our ally. Katia told me you are a supporter of Hitler. I think Germany would want to deal with a friendlier regime than the Bolsheviks."

"Stalin's your country's ally too, isn't he?" Lukin asked. "Why would you want to take a risk with us?"

"He's our ally, to a point," Clark said, turning his wine cup. "He's also a communist. You can't trust the communists."

"No." Lukin relaxed and drank his shot. "You can never trust the communists. Those bastards!"

At that, Clark knew he'd gotten Lukin on his side. He refilled their wine cups with more *maotai* from the glass jug. "It's no secret Chiang Kai-shek wants to focus on wipe out Mao Ze Dong and the Reds. As long as Japan is not a threat, the KMT couldn't care less if the Kremlin regime fails." He looked intently at Lukin. "Let us help. What can you tell me?"

Lukin finally nodded. "We've formed a unit of Russians under the IJA's Kwantung Army command."

"The Kwantung?" That garrison was the IJA's largest and most prestigious command.

"Yes," Lukin said. "Our unit is called the Asano Detachment. It operates up in Manchukuo. The detachment is all Russian."

"Really?"

"I'm in talks with the IJA to form another Russian unit in Shanghai."

"And the IJA agrees?"

Lukin shifted his eyes. "We have a high level of support from the Russian community here. The Union of Russian Veterans, the Cossacks' Union, even the Russian Orthodox Church. They're all ready to fight if we can form an army unit."

His sidestepping of the question didn't escape Clark. "How many Russians altogether are you talking about? It would take a sizable army to fight the Soviet Army."

Before he could answer, Ekaterina interrupted, "I have to visit the ladies' room." She tossed her hair and picked up her purse. "Excuse me." She got up and left the room.

Lukin resumed after she closed the door. "What we don't have in numbers, we can more than make up for in fervor. Do you know what I was before I left my country?"

"No."

"I was a chemist. I was a pioneer in scientific research. If it weren't for the Bolsheviks, I would've done a lot of important things to advance the field in Russia. The Bolsheviks don't want people to think. They pit the lower classes against anyone who is educated. They call us enemy of the proletariats. I wanted so much to raise the scientific standard for my people. They wanted to crush us instead. They're afraid of the truth. You see, when people are uneducated and ignorant, they're easy to control."

Clark's heart softened. Those were Lukin's lost dreams. If the KMT failed, he would have the same kind of lost dreams too.

"A government that is anti-intellectual will never move its people forward." Lukin clenched his fist. "The Bolshevik regime has no pride for the country. All they want to do is suppress. Suppress our culture, suppress our heritage, suppress anyone who objects to their power." He pounded his fist on the table. "Contrast that to Germany. Look at what Hitler has done. He brought pride back to his people."

"Hitler?" Clark asked. He was with Lukin up to that point. "I'm not sure I agree. Hitler's version of pride for his people goes beyond culture and heritage. He's racist, and he's dangerous." He probably shouldn't have said that. Now was not a good time to contradict Lukin, but he couldn't help himself.

Where was Ekaterina? He wasn't a trained spy. She should be here to help if his tongue slipped.

"Dangerous, you say?" Lukin asked. "Let's talk about danger then. You work for the KMT. You're against Mao Ze Dong and his Red Army, am I correct?"

"Yes."

"Wouldn't you agree then that communist ideologies are dangerous, with the way they incite class warfare?"

"They do worry me," Clark said, guarding himself without saying more.

Lukin looked him in the eye. "They should. Your country hasn't seen anything like the Red Terror. Not yet anyway. But if Stalin ever decides to back Mao—"

The door opened. Clark expected Ekaterina to walk in. Instead, the waitress entered with her two big men. She held the door open. "Mr. Yuan, your other guests have arrived."

"My other guests?" What was she talking about?

"Thank you," said one of the men. He spoke with a thick Russian accent. Clark didn't recognize him. He'd never seen the man before.

The waitress bowed and left the room. The man closed the door, then sat down next to Lukin. His companion took the seat on Lukin's other side.

The man who sat down first grinned. "Fyodor. It's been a long while."

Clark glanced at Lukin. A bead of sweat dropped from Lukin's temple.

"Dur . . . Durchenko," Lukin stuttered.

Durchenko swung his thick arm over Lukin's shoulder. "I've been looking all over for you." He pulled out a handgun and stuck the muzzle into Lukin's side. "I'm sure dinner here is good, but Commissar Sokolov has a much better meal he wants to serve you."

"Wait!" Clark said. "What's going on?"

"It's okay, Counselor Yuan," Durchenko said. "We'll take it from here. We appreciate your help." He jammed his gun against Lukin. "Get up."

Shaking, Lukin rose. He turned his frightened eyes to Clark. "You tricked me."

Clark tried to answer, but he never got the chance. Durchenko pulled Lukin away from the table while his companion opened the door.

"Thank you again, Counselor," said Durchenko. "The Commissar wishes you the best." With his gun still held against Lukin and his arm locked around his body, he forced his captive out of the room. The other Russian nodded at Clark—a cold, cordial nod, then closed the door.

Those were Sokolov's men? How did they know he was meeting Lukin here?

Ekaterina. Why wasn't she back yet? Was she okay? He bolted up from his seat, but the door reopened. Her hair swaying, Ekaterina sauntered back to the table. Her face brightened by a fresh coat of lipstick.

Clark sank back down in his seat. Ekaterina. She set this whole thing up.

"Have we ordered yet?" She picked up the menu.

His chest heaving, he watched her turn the pages.

"Where's Lukin?" She looked to her left, then her right.

"You set me up," Clark said, trying to contain the anger in his voice.

Ekaterina lowered her stare. Her shiny red lips curled into a small, calm smile.

Clark glared at her. "You double-crossed me."

"I did not."

"You deny it?"

Ekaterina tilted her head. Exasperated, she rolled her eyes. "You and the KMT hired me to gain Sokolov's trust. I just gave Sokolov something to eliminate every last bit of doubt he has about me."

"Why didn't you tell me first?"

"Tell you? If I'd told you, you might have blown our cover. Even you said so yourself earlier, you've never done anything like this before."

"You're supposed to introduce Lukin to me so I can make use of him. What good is he to me now? You handed him to Sokolov?"

"Lukin's information is useless to you." Ekaterina tossed down the menu. "Listen to him," she snickered. "He's going to raise an army to fight the Bolsheviks? He's living in a fantasy!" She picked up the bottle of *maotai* and poured herself a cup, then drank it in one shot.

The little cup Lukin had drunk from lay on its side, knocked over on the table. Fantasy or not, this man wanted to do something to help his country rise. Clark could understand that. Lukin had wise words of warning about the dangers of the communists.

His throat still constricted, Clark asked, "What will happen to him now?"

Ekaterina didn't answer for a long while. "It's probably best if you don't know."

Clark squinted at her. "What kind of person are you? You signed his death sentence. How can you be so cold?"

"I'm not cold." She glared back at him. "You don't know Lukin like I do. Lukin, Sokolov, they're the cold ones. Lukin's a fascist. He isn't worth a tear from you or me. You haven't seen him and his men parade around in their black shirts and Nazi armbands. He worships Hitler, the same man who would kill the woman you love without a blink of an eye."

Eden? The thought of Eden being killed jolted him. "Don't you say that. Don't you make light of Eden or her life."

"You don't think that could happen?" Ekaterina asked. "You haven't seen human depravity like I have. You can't even imagine the things men would do when they single out groups of people as their political enemies. Mark my words, Clark. The Nazis will kill. When they do, their methods will be brutal. You just wait and see. A day's going to come when you'll thank me for putting away human garbage like Lukin."

Clark didn't want to believe her. But that lifeless, old look in her eyes returned. What had this woman seen? What had ever happened to put that look of death in her eyes?

"I've lost my appetite." She pushed the menu away on the table. "When you have thought this through, we'll talk again." She stood up, grabbed her purse, and left without looking back.

Clark pushed back his chair. He stared at the *maotai*, then grabbed it and took three gulps straight from the bottle. The burn of the alcohol was the only thing left he could trust.

21

UNCLEAN HANDS

THE MILD SPRING air of April breezed past Eden as she walked toward the Chinese nurse from the Hospital St. Marie who was sitting on the bench. On the fields of the Public Gardens, children and their amahs had returned to play, and the elderly had resumed their tai chi exercises under the greening trees.

"Miss Bai?" Eden asked as she approached the bench.

"Miss Levine?" The woman on the bench asked and wiped her fingers across her lips.

Eden ignored the pile of peanut shells scattered by Bai's feet and sat down beside her. "Thank you for meeting me."

"Sure! No problem," Bai said and offered Eden the open paper bag in her hands. "Would you like some fresh roasted peanuts. They're really good."

"No, thank you." Eden placed her purse on her lap. "You've worked with Dr. Green for five years?"

"Yes."

"And you're willing to tell me information about him I want to know?"

Bai wiggled her brows and grinned.

"Ah! Of course." Eden opened her purse and took out an

envelope of cash. The nurse reached out her hand, but Eden snatched it back. "You do have proof, do you?"

"I wouldn't be here if I didn't." Bai opened her palms. "They're all here." She pulled a packet from her bag and held it out to Eden. Eden took it and handed the cash over in exchange.

Bai snatched the money and stuffed it into her bag. "I'm glad someone is finally looking into all his shady businesses. That Dr. Green is not a good man." She scrunched her nose and bobbed her head.

"Why do you say that?" Eden took out her pencil and notepad.

Bai huddled closer. "You didn't hear this from me, but his specialty isn't urology. I mean, urology is what he officially practices, but his real specialty is extortion. A lot of the money our biggest donor Neil Sassoon contributes to the St. Marie doesn't go to the hospital. It goes to Dr. Green and some of the other doctors working under him. They sell their patients' medical records to Mr. Sassoon."

Eden tensed when Bai raised Neil's name. She kept her outward appearance calm so Bai wouldn't notice. Good thing the Chinese didn't pay much attention to the Westerners' society gossips. Bai had no idea Eden was in any way associated with Neil. That was obvious when Eden had first approached the nurse and identified herself as a reporter. "Why would Sassoon want the patients' medical records?"

"From what I understand, these patients are Neil Sassoon's business rivals. And these aren't medical records of ordinary illnesses. Do you know what Dr. Green is best known for as a urologist?"

"No."

Bai raised her hand to the side of her mouth and whispered, "Venereal diseases."

"Ugh." Eden pulled back.

"Yes. Dr. Green passes on confidential medical records to Mr.

Sassoon. After getting those records, Mr. Sassoon can use them to force his competitors to make deals with him. He'd threaten to expose his competitors' secrets and ruin their reputations and families if they don't give him the terms he wants. That's also how he forces his competitors out of business."

Eden's heart sank. Was Neil really doing all these things Bai alleged? This didn't sound like the Neil Sassoon she knew at all, but the nurse had no reason to lie. "Why don't the patients complain? How can Dr. Green get away with this?"

"Easy!" Bai rolled her head. "Of course, the patients wouldn't know what they'd be in for when they first come to see Dr. Green. By the time they're threatened, it's already too late. They'd either have to do what Mr. Sassoon wants, or their secrets would be out. Imagine how embarrassing it would be if their illnesses become public. Anyway, they can't really be sure it was Dr. Green who divulged the information. The Hospital St. Marie is big. Anybody could've taken their records and released it."

That was true. Isaac, too, had said the hospital wasn't well-managed. He said the different departments often didn't know what the others were doing. "One thing I don't understand, how does Dr. Green come across enough of Neil Sassoon's business competitors to make this scheme worthwhile? It sounds to me the odds of catching a business competitor with an embarrassing illness would be very low. There must be better ways to go after a competitor."

"You're underestimating how easily wealthy men can be tempted, Miss Levine." Bai waved her finger. "My guess is, Mr. Sassoon or Dr. Green must have somehow set up honey traps for these competitors to catch diseases. Although if this is true, then it all happened outside of the hospital, and I have no proof of it. But I have to tell you, there sure are an awful lot of coincidences of Mr. Sassoon's competitors showing up to see Dr. Green." She narrowed her eyes.

Bai's suggestion hit Eden like a waft of cold wind. What kind of man was Neil? Not only did he threaten his competitors, but he actively caused them to become ill too?

She didn't want to believe it. "Let's say what you said is true. Why do these men come to see Dr. Green? Why don't they go see other doctors? It seems so unlikely to me that Neil Sassoon could set up this kind of traps and then assume they would go to a doctor who's colluding with him."

"How do you know Mr. Sassoon isn't working with other doctors?" Bai asked her back. "Maybe he's bought every doctor in the city who treats venereal diseases. You don't know."

Eden's mouth fell open. How big was this scheme?

"Anyway, it wouldn't be hard for Mr. Sassoon to buy everyone off," Bai said. "There are only a few hospitals in Shanghai with English-speaking doctors who can cater to Westerners. Besides, Dr. Green really is one of the best doctors here who knows how to treat syphilis and other diseases like that. If the patient's symptoms get bad enough, Dr. Green is the best one they can go to for help."

"This is so terrible." Eden dropped her hands on her notebook.

"Yeah. There's more."

"More?"

"Mm-hmm. Dr. Green doesn't only sell the records of patients with venereal diseases. He sells some of his patients narcotics. They get addicted and they have to keep coming back to him to buy more."

Eden bit her lip. "Is Neil Sassoon involved with that too?"

"Not as far as I know. I think Dr. Green sells drugs on the side on his own to make extra money. But there were a few times when he sold Mr. Sassoon information about mistresses of men who came to the hospital for abortions."

"My gosh." Eden didn't want to hear anymore.

"Like I told you, Dr. Green is a bad man. He's lousy to the nurses and the staff too. He's always yelling at us, calling us names in front of the patients and working us like slaves. If you ever want to write an article about how badly he treats the employees, I'd be glad to tell you all about that too."

Eden stared at the packet Bai had given her.

"Those are copies of the records of Mr. Sassoon's donations to the hospital for the last three years." Bai opened her bag of peanuts again. She crunched open a shell with her fingers, extracted the nuts, and popped them into her mouth. "You'll see that every time Mr. Sassoon makes a donation, the hospital would allocate a big chunk of the money to Dr. Green five days later."

"The hospital condones this?" Eden asked.

"The hospital likes getting money. All they're doing is following Mr. Sassoon's instructions to give portions of his contributions to Dr. Green. The hospital doesn't ask any questions after that. Too bad none of that money ever comes down to the staff. There's also a list of names of the patients whose records Dr. Green had sold to Mr. Sassoon. You can try contacting them, but I doubt they'll talk to you. They won't want their dirty secrets exposed to the public. But you can probably find information about their business dealings with Mr. Sassoon. Maybe you'll find something to verify what I told you."

Her mind now a web of confusion, Eden couldn't reconcile everything Bai had told her about Neil with the man she thought she knew. "Thank you, Miss Bai. I appreciate your help."

"Anytime." Bai patted the side of her bag where she'd placed the cash Eden had given her. "I can't wait to read your article." She stood up. "Goodbye!" She waved and went on her way.

Alone on the bench, Eden took in several deep breaths, trying to gather her thoughts. Before she wrote anything, she had to confront Neil. Maybe the nurse Bai was wrong. Maybe there was another reason why Neil was paying Dr. Green. If so, Neil deserved a chance to explain.

She clutched the packet, hoping to hold on to this little sliver of hope.

At Neil's penthouse apartment at the Hamilton House, Eden watched the streetlights from the floor to ceiling window while Neil finished his call on the phone. Outside on the streets below, cars came and went, flushing the roads with their headlights. Did their lights carry hope to her, or did they carry her hope away?

"Yes, yes." Neil's voice repeated in the background. "I'm pleased to hear that!" He laughed. "I would never give you a bad deal . . . Thank you, thank you . . . Great. Talk to you later." He hung up the phone. With a bright smile, he came over to Eden. "Sorry to keep you waiting. I just closed another deal. Wait till I tell Uncle Victor. Now I can show him I've got a knack for real estate."

Eden turned around from the window. Whatever he won tonight, it wasn't about to make up for what Sir Victor would find out when she published her article on his extortion activities at the Hospital St. Marie—if those activities were true.

"Come on. Let's have some dinner. I told my chef to make us a special filet mignon. I've got a great bottle of Krug too. Let's open it and celebrate." He put his arm around her and started to lead her to the dining room.

"Neil, wait." Eden pushed lightly against him. "We need to talk."

He lifted his brows, but said, "Sure. Let me get us a drink. What would you like? Rosé? Bordeaux?" He walked over to his bar.

"Nothing, thank you."

"Okay." He opened his crystal decanter to pour himself a glass of McClelland. "What's on your mind?"

Eden wetted her lips. "I want you to be honest with me. What is the nature of your dealings with Dr. Green?"

Neil stopped. The whiskey had only filled half his glass. "Dr. Green at the Hospital St. Marie?"

"Yes." Eden laced her fingers.

"We're friends." He put down the decanter. "I'm on the hospital's advisory board. I donate money to them from time to time. That's how we met."

"What's the money used for?"

Neil laughed. "What do you mean? It's used to treat patients who can't afford healthcare, I guess. Or to buy supplies and equipment."

"The money doesn't go to Dr. Green?"

"It might." Neil shrugged. "Maybe some of it goes to paying the staff's salaries."

"Only his salary? Nothing more?"

He laughed again. "Why are you asking all these questions?"

"Why don't you answer me?" She walked closer. "Your donations would only go to pay his regular salary if he receives any part of it? Nothing else?"

"Yes!" He raised his glass.

Eden's heart sank. This part, she knew, wasn't true. She'd seen the accounting records Miss Bai had given her. The nurse had marked all the large and irregular payments the hospital paid to Dr. Green out of the contributions given by Neil.

It would've been better if Neil simply didn't lie to her. "What about the name George Abrams? And Reginald Goodwin? Do you know these people? What about the company Langley Real Estate Enterprises?"

Neil's smile vanished. He leaned back against the bar. "I have business dealings with these men. Langley's a well-known company in Shanghai. Of course I've heard of them. Everyone has."

"Is that all?"

"Why? What have you heard differently?"

Her frown deepened. Why didn't he just own up to it? She could've kept a modicum of respect for him if he did. "George Abrams bid against you for the distributorship for the Sam Foster sunglasses. Dr. Green got him hooked on heroin and you used that information to force him to back away from his bid."

Neil clutched his glass. He remained silent as he stood still by the bar.

"Reginald Goodwin is the president of Langley. Dr. Green treated him for syphilis. He then told you about it and you threatened Goodwin with his secret. You blackmailed him into selling you the plot of land near the race club for an exorbitantly low price. You threatened to expose him and destroy him if he didn't."

Nodding and pressing his lips together, Neil swirled the whiskey in his glass. "Who told you all this?"

"It doesn't matter. Is it true?"

Neil took a gulp of his whiskey. "None of this is as bad as it seems. This is how business is done in Shanghai."

"No. What you did went too far, even for Shanghai."

"Hardly!" Neil laughed. "There are tons of people doing things ten times worse than what you're accusing me of doing. You ought to know. Nobody does business in this city without getting their hands dirty."

"Your Uncle Victor does. He's built an empire without resorting to these tactics."

"My uncle," Neil grunted. "My uncle is the reason why I did these things in the first place. Ever since I came to Shanghai, all I've done is try to show him I have what it takes to run a business. He could put me on the board of his company, or make me a director of one of his subsidiaries. He won't even give me a chance." He took another gulp of his drink. "I'm not a bad person, Eden. You know that. I only want to show Uncle Victor I'm capable of starting and running businesses." He put down his glass and came over to her. "The Sam Foster glasses are going to be all the rage once they come into this market." He put his hands gently on her shoulders. "As for Langley, I've already gathered a group of investors. We're going to build a spectacular hotel with a new dancehall right by the race track. I'll prove to Uncle Victor he can trust me, and I won't have to use Dr. Green anymore."

Eden shook her head. "I can't keep a secret like this."

"What do you mean?" His voice tensed.

"I'm a reporter. I think I've stumbled onto a story."

"Eden." Neil looked at her in disbelief. "Don't. Please."

"I have to. My conscience won't allow me to keep it a secret. Not when there's a corrupt doctor misusing patient information, or worse, secretly feeding people drugs and turning them into addicts so you or someone else can blackmail them. I have to let the public know what kind of man Dr. Green is and what he's doing."

"Okay, okay." Neil nodded in defeat. "Can you at least keep my name out of it?"

"That would make me biased, wouldn't it?" Eden asked. "Besides, Dr. Green isn't likely to stay silent after your girlfriend exposes him for what he did."

Neil closed and raised his hand, then dropped it. "Eden, I beg you. Don't do this. How about this? Let me pay him a sum of money and ask him to resign. We'll send him away. This way, he won't harm anyone anymore. And I won't do anything like this again. I promise! We can forget about this."

Like it never happened? She watched his twisted face. "No. That's not good enough."

"Eden . . ."

"It's just not good enough." She picked up her purse and headed toward the door. If he had owned up to his mistakes, she might have forgiven him. But he had asked her to hide the truth, and that, she could not do.

She opened the door. "Goodbye, Neil." She looked at him one more time. He returned her gaze, his eyes beseeching her to change her mind.

This wasn't the way she had wanted things to end either. But part of her almost felt relieved, like she'd been wanting a good reason to extract herself from him, and no such reason existed to justify her choice until now.

Silently, she closed the door. Her heart alternately falling and rising as she walked ahead and out of the building.

2 2

RED TERROR

She didn't contact him. Two weeks had passed since their fallout after Sokolov's henchmen abducted Fyodor Lukin, and Ekaterina hadn't contacted him at all. She really wasn't going to apologize.

Grudgingly, Clark arrived at the Metropole Hotel where she lived. Maybe a proper apology was too much to expect from a spy for hire. Maybe to her, this whole plot was nothing more than an adventure to add some excitement to her life. But while she could abandon what they started and walk away, he still had to answer to his authorities. However reluctant he felt, he had to come and sort things out. This time, he didn't check in with the concierge, and he didn't bring any flowers.

Anyway, he didn't trust her enough to continue working with her anymore, and he detested having to pretend to be someone he wasn't. If she wanted to quit, then frankly, he would be more than happy to accommodate.

Coming upon her suite, he knocked on her door.

"Who is it?" Ekaterina's voice called from the other side.

"It's Clark. You and I need to talk."

No answer. He knocked again. "Ekaterina?"

"I don't want to talk right now."

He threw up his hands. She was the one in the wrong. Was she going to make him apologize instead? No. He wouldn't do it. "I have to see you. I have to report back to Sītu. If you don't want to talk now, then when can you talk?"

"I don't know. Come back later."

Rolling his eyes to the ceiling, Clark placed his hands on his hips and sighed. "Later when? You need to give me a date."

No answer again.

"Ekaterina?" He knocked again, really making noise this time. "Answer me. I'm not leaving until you do."

The knob turned and the door opened a crack. Annoyed, Clark pushed it and entered. Inside, Ekaterina limped toward a room service delivery cart piled with plates of leftover sandwiches and poured herself a cup of tea, her hair disheveled and her sloppily tied bathrobe hanging lopsided on her body.

It was past eight o'clock in the evening. Had she gotten out of bed at all today?

Clark came up behind her. "I'm sorry to disturb you, but if you're no longer planning to work with us, you ought to at least tell us."

"I needed some time." She put down her cup and turned her head. A black and blue bruise covered half of her face. Her bloodshot left eye, all swollen, could barely open.

"Katia!" Clark gasped. "Are you okay?" He grabbed her arm. The sudden movement made her wince and she held her arm to her waist.

"I'm sorry." He yanked back his hand.

"I'm all right." She bent over and sucked in several deep breaths.

"What happened to you?" He reached out, trying to help her stand. "Why didn't you call me?"

"It's nothing." Ekaterina put down her tea. "Sokolov's wife found out about me, that's all. She hired a couple of thugs to send me a message." She went over to the sitting area and eased herself down on the couch.

"Sokolov's wife?" Clark frowned. "Why would she . . ." He glanced at Ekaterina.

Ekaterina smiled. Her smile looked twisted beneath the ghastly bruise on her face.

Clark sat down beside her. His earlier anger now all but vanished. "I thought you'd gained his full trust after giving him Lukin. Why are you still sleeping with him? We've never asked you to do that."

"I know," she mumbled. She rounded her shoulders like a small injured animal.

Clark softened his voice. "Then why? What are you really trying to do? You couldn't be doing all this for the KMT. We don't pay you enough."

Ekaterina bent her head. A tear dropped down from each of her eyes. "My real name is Elizaveta Khovanskaya. I was born in a city called Ekaterinodar. It's not called that anymore. The Bolsheviks renamed it to Krasnodar after the October Revolution."

She brushed her hair behind her ear. Clark pulled his handkerchief out of his pocket and gave it to her.

"Thank you." She took his handkerchief. She always looked so steely and in control. It pained him to see her like this.

She dabbed the handkerchief against her cheeks. "I left my city in 1919. I was only five years old. A man who worked with my father was walking me to my father's shop. His name was Mikhail Komarov. I remember my mother saying goodbye to us at our house. I remember him holding my hand, and I was taking big steps to try to keep up with his pace. He laughed when he saw what I was doing and slowed down." A tiny smile crept up her face. "We were just coming upon the town square when the Cheka arrived."

"The Cheka. The Soviet secret police?"

"Yes." Ekaterina nodded. "They came to arrest the enemy of the people, and that included anyone who owned private property. As soon as Mikhail saw what was happening, he picked me up and ran. But I turned around to look, and that was when I saw my father and grandfather. The Cheka hauled them onto the street, pushed them down, and shot them."

"My God," Clark whispered. How awful for a five-year-old child to witness her family being killed.

"You'd think a child wouldn't remember so many details, but I can still see so vividly everything that happened that day. I saw the man who shot them. I'll never forget his face." She pulled up her legs and hugged them against her chest. "Mikhail never brought me home. Everything that happened after that is hazy in my memories. We ran away. We left Ekaterinodar. Somehow, he got us onto a train and we began our long journey to Harbin. He told everyone I was his daughter. There were people throughout the way who hid us in their homes until we reached the train."

"You said they hid you in their homes?"

"Yes. There must have been an underground network helping the escapees. I can't remember who they were or how Mikhail found them. We'd hide in their houses during the day. At night, we'd walk for many hours through cold, muddy fields. Sometimes, I would ask Mikhail where my mama was. He told me not to worry and she'd be coming soon. After a while, I knew he was lying and I stopped asking. I never saw my mother again."

"I'm so sorry," Clark said. Sorry didn't feel enough to console her for all her losses.

"I heard a lot of things when we were in hiding. The adults didn't know I was listening. I was so little. They'd leave me to play by myself and forget I was there. Sometimes, I'd pretend to be asleep so I could listen to what they had to say. They said the Cheka tortured people. Looking back, my father and grandfather might have had it easy. They died a quick death. Many of the others weren't so lucky.

The Cheka hung them, impaled them, crucified them, drowned them, flayed, scalped, and skinned them. They put them into tanks of boiling water or tar. They stripped them naked and poured water on them, then left them out in the cold until they froze into a block of ice. I remember seeing corpses outside sometimes when we were on the run. The Cheka left them there. They wanted everyone to know what they were doing to the *kulaks* and the rich. They called them bloodsuckers. The enemy of the people."

A tight lump formed in Clark's throat and he swallowed.

"I've heard even worse stories later from people who'd made it to Harbin like us. The Cheka was very creative in the different ways they beat people and made them suffer."

Clark stroked her back. "I'm glad you made it out." He wondered what the Cheka would have done to a five-year-old child and he didn't ask. He didn't want to know.

"Mikhail was a good man." Ekaterina sniffled. "I don't even know if he had any family back in Ekaterinodar. I tried to ask him but he'd never talk about it. He wouldn't talk to me at all about what happened back home. Anyway, we eventually crossed the border to Manchuria and went down to Harbin. In Harbin, Mikhail found work wherever he could. Mostly manual labor like construction, delivery, that sort of thing. He took odd jobs too like washing dishes and cleaning public bathrooms in restaurants. When I turned fourteen, I stopped going to school to help out. It was my choice. I became a seamstress for a tailor. I was very happy I was old enough to work because, by then, Mikhail's health was failing. All the hard work over the years wore him down. But even so, I wasn't able to do much for him. He died when I was sixteen. He caught pneumonia."

"You've been on your own since then?" Clark asked.

"For a little while," she said. "The tailor had a customer. A man. He took a liking to me. His name was Maxim Ulanov. I didn't see much in my future as a seamstress. He had money. I became his mistress. At least I could live a little easier that way, or so I thought."

Clark grimaced. Another sad story of someone who this harsh world had thrown into the bitter sea and forgotten. "What happened then? How did you come to be in Shanghai?"

"I moved into his home. It turned out, Ulanov was a valet of Grand Duke Michael Alexandrovich in Petrograd before the Grand Duke was arrested and sent to Perm, where he was last seen. In Petrograd, the Duke had left behind some assets he'd hidden, including a hundred and fifty gold bars. He was planning to take all of his assets and move with his wife Natalia and their eight-year-old son, Count George Brasov, to Finland. When the Duke was arrested, Ulanov stole the gold bars and left the country."

"That's terrible." Ulanov might have left the duke's wife and son destitute.

"He was a terrible man. I won't tell you the things he made me do in the three years I lived with him. Even animals shouldn't be humiliated and degraded the way I was. He got himself into trouble with a lot of people outside too. He was a fraud. He was always running some kind of scheme. He must've pushed it too far because shortly after I moved in with him, he made us pack and move to Peking."

"Peking? That must've been tough for you," Clark said. At least in Harbin, she was among Russians. "How did you manage?"

"It wasn't as bad as you'd expect, actually. Living with Ulanov was difficult, but he was also out a lot, doing whatever it was that he did. I had a lot of time to myself. I started learning English so I could get around, at least among the foreigners. I took classes too. Art, painting, to fill the time. I even took classes on manners and etiquette. Ulanov didn't mind indulging me that way. It made him feel like he had class and taste to have a mistress who liked the finer things in life."

"He wasn't worried you'd run away?"

"Run away?" Ekaterina laughed. "How? Where to? I had no money, and I had nowhere to go. In Peking, Ulanov rented a very luxurious apartment. At least, he wasn't stingy. We even had maids. I had a comfortable home."

Clark creased his forehead. She was right. Life had left her very few choices how to survive.

"The crowd Ulanov ran with in Peking all had dubious reputations. I met a number of them. They were all frauds, including several self-proclaimed counts and countesses."

"This was how you got the idea to present yourself as a princess?"

"Yes. But not immediately. For a while, I really thought I could do no better than being someone's mistress. It was either Ulanov or someone else. But one night, Ulanov came home with a knife in his chest. It might've happened just before he arrived. He was able to open the door and let himself in. He told me to get him a doctor, and I almost did that. But then, something made me stop. I thought, if the situation was reversed, he wouldn't try to save me. So I stood there. I watched him wave his arm on the floor, yelling at me to call a doctor. Yelling at me like I was a dog. When he finally died, I wasn't sorry."

Clark peered at her. How could anyone fault her? He couldn't. After all she'd been through, who was he or anyone to judge? "At least that chapter of your life was over."

"Yes." Ekaterina loosened her arms around her legs. "After he died, I decided I had to get away. I didn't know what he did in Peking or who he offended, but I didn't feel safe staying in that apartment. By then, I was the only one who knew he had those gold bars. I took them and got on the first train to Shanghai the next morning. I also knew I had to change my identity."

"And you decided to present yourself as the Grand Duke's daughter."

"Yes." She tossed back her head. "There are so many princes, princesses, counts, and countesses from fallen royal houses passing through China anyway. Why not me? With those gold bars, I could live quite comfortably for a very long time. And I certainly have more credibility given how much Ulanov told me about Grand Duke Michael's history and family."

"That's true," Clark said. From time to time, one could still run into taxi girls claiming to be princesses from the Qing Imperial Court.

"I named myself Ekaterina after my home city. I heard that the Cheka killed more than three thousand people there by the time they were through. I didn't want to forget where I came from."

Three thousand. Clark shuddered at the thought.

"That would've been the end of my story if I hadn't seen him," Ekaterina said. Her eye that wasn't bruised glared out with the look of the dead.

"Who's him?"

"Sokolov. I was shocked when I saw him during a ballet performance. It'd been years but, oh, I remember his face so clearly. He's aged a little, but he hadn't changed much. He was the man who shot my father and grandfather."

"No! Really?"

"Yes. I couldn't believe it myself, so I went about finding out who he was to make sure I was right, even though I knew from my memory I was correct. That was how I got into the business of selling information. To get information, I had to give information. My identity as the Grand Duke's daughter came in very handy. It helped me tap into the local White Russian community. It's amazing how far people will go to believe a lie to keep their dream alive."

"Give yourself some credit," Clark said. "You carry off the role very well."

"Thank you." She smiled. "Anyway, I did confirm Sokolov was a Cheka officer, and he was part of the unit that raided Ekaterinodar. I've been looking for a chance to get close to him ever since. The KMT's offer was just what I needed. I'm going to bring that sonofabitch down."

"Bring him down?" Clark pulled away. His hand on her back tensed. "What are you planning to do?"

"I don't know yet. I can murder the bastard myself, but that would be too lenient. He deserves something worse."

"No." Clark shook his head. He couldn't let her risk herself like this, and he couldn't let her run rogue on the KMT. "Katia, please. Whatever you're planning, stop."

"I can't. I finally understand why I was spared that day eighteen years ago when the Cheka came and killed all those people in my city. My life finally has a purpose. I will make Sokolov pay for what he did."

"No." Clark grabbed her shoulder. "You'll jeopardize my government's plans. I can't let you do that."

"Don't you dare try to stop me, or I will disclose all your plots to Sokolov. You try and stop me and I'll bring us all down."

Clark tightened his grip. The fierceness in her voice! He knew she would do it too.

"Please." Ekaterina softened her voice and put her own hand over his. "Trust me. I won't jeopardize your plans. When the time comes for me to make my move, I'll make sure I won't leave your government in a bind. You know why?"

"Why?"

"Because I trust you. I trust you will keep everything I'd told you a secret. I trust you won't get in my way. We can still work together, because you're the only friend I have."

Clark's arm went limp. "Is there anything I can do?"

"Hold me."

"What?"

"You asked me what you can do. I want you to hold me. I don't want to feel so alone."

He sighed and pulled her into his embrace. It was useless. Nothing he could say would stop her. The flat, lifeless look of the dead in her eyes said as much. This woman's soul had died long ago. Only her living corpse remained to finish the one last task she had come to do.

She closed her eyes and fell against his body. In his arms, she felt so fragile. As much as he knew he couldn't stop her, he still wished he could save her.

If only he could. She might feel vulnerable now, but he knew her. When she woke up tomorrow, none of what happened tonight would mean anything to her. For him, the only way forward would be to slowly extract the KMT from dealing with her.

Maybe he couldn't stop her, but he could withdraw. It might be the only way to save her and everyone else.

23

STOLEN DREAMS

Some people were born with all the luck. Neil Sassoon was one of them. The universe seemed to align to favor them even when they ran themselves into a bind.

When Eden sent her article to print, it more than broke her heart. She couldn't say she loved Neil yet, but she was growing fond of him. All the attention he'd given her was flattering. He'd shown such kindness to her family too. She'd nearly convinced herself she could grow to love him.

But after everything he had done for her, she was paying him back with an article that exposed his worst secrets. Even though she was doing the right thing, it felt wrong. When the article came out, all of Shanghai society would be talking about it. Sir Victor would be furious. Neil's reputation would be ruined.

Except the Shanghai society wasn't talking about it. The spectacular explosion of the German airship *Hindenburg* at Lakehurst, New Jersey knocked every other news report off the front page. The photographic and newsreel coverage mesmerized everyone around the world. "Oh, the humanity!" Herbert Morrison's voice resounded on every radio. Eden's article had the luck of being sent to the press on May 6, the same day when the disaster happened. With so many victims burned to death, the scandal of strong-arm tactics used by a local business tycoon was reduced to an afterthought. When the horror subsided, the endless speculations began as to what caused the blimp to burst. Was it sabotage? An electrical spark? Maybe it was leaking hydrogen, or a puncture in the zeppelin's fabric covering. No. It had to be sabotage. Maybe there was an anti-Nazi communist on board. Maybe Hitler ordered the airship destroyed himself!

Before the furor of the disaster subsided, news reports of King George VI's upcoming coronation in England took center stage. His brother, Edward VIII, had abdicated the throne last year for love for the American divorcée Wallis Simpson. In the International Settlement, a series of public festivities had been planned. At night, the entire Bund would be lit up. Who wanted to think about evil doctors and unscrupulous businessmen when they could celebrate and party?

At her office, Eden closed the copy of the newspaper in which her article was buried. By the time everything returned to normal, no one would even remember the name Dr. Green. She had hoped her exposé would force the Hospital St. Marie to take corrective actions. Now, it was doubtful. Neil's reputation, of course, would remain intact.

The clock on the wall struck five. Eden turned off her desk lamp and picked up her purse. "Good night, Dottie. I'll see you tomorrow." She got up and headed for the elevator.

"Goodnight, Eden," the hardworking secretary said without looking up from the typewriter.

Taking her usual route, Eden hopped on the tram. She wondered how Sir Victor had reacted to the news about Neil's misconduct. Whatever else was happening in the world, Sir Victor must have seen the article, and he wouldn't simply overlook it.

The truth was, she risked tainting her own name too when she wrote that article. No doubt, there were vultures waiting to pounce on the chance to call her vicious and ungrateful. Vultures like those who were seeking to curry favor with the Sassoons, and the women hoping to take her place by Neil's side. In the end, she, too, benefited from the fact that her article received little attention.

Maybe she should be happy about that, she thought sarcastically to herself.

The tram arrived at her stop. She wiggled through the passengers to get off. At the entrance of her building, she came upon something she hadn't expected to see. "Neil?"

"Hello." He approached her with a timid glance and a bouquet of roses in his hands.

"What are you doing?"

"I'm waiting for you."

She stared at the flowers. Waiting for her? After what she'd written about him?

"I've thought everything through. I did some things that I never should have done. I'm not proud of it, but I can't undo what I already did. What I can do is try to do right going forward, and one thing I can do right is to ask you to come back into my life." He held up the roses. "Can we start over?"

"Neil . . ."

"Give me a chance. Let me prove to you I can be the man who deserves you."

Eden gazed at the flowers. She couldn't believe he wanted to continue on with her. She didn't think he would ever talk to her again.

She raised her eyes. His chest heaving, he waited for her answer. It couldn't be easy for him to admit he was wrong, not to mention overlooking the fact that she exposed his dirty dealings to the public.

"Dr. Green's been let go," Neil said. "The hospital terminated him."

"Did you pay him off?" She pulled her arms into her sides and glanced at him.

"No. I swear. He asked me to defend him to the hospital administration, but I told him I couldn't help him. He'll be leaving Shanghai, that's all I know."

Eden nodded. At least one good thing came out of this and all her efforts weren't wasted.

"If it pleases you to know, Uncle Victor was furious with me. I might've permanently ruined any chance I have to become his heir."

"That wasn't my intention." And she was speaking the truth. While the exposé would impact Neil's relationship with his uncle, that was never her goal. She reported the story because that was her job, and she wanted to stop Dr. Green from harming more people.

"It doesn't matter," Neil said. "If that's the case, it was my own fault. I was too impatient. I wanted so much to impress my uncle, and I was willing to do anything to show him results. But what I ended up showing was a sham, and he certainly isn't impressed in the least now. He said the only way he'll forgive me is if you decide to take me back." He chuckled.

Eden didn't find that funny. "Are you here then because your uncle wanted you to come?"

"Gosh, Eden, of course not!" Neil cried. "I'm here because I can't bear to be without you. I . . . I love you."

He loved her? She shifted her weight away from him.

"Eden, please, give us another chance?" Neil held the bouquet toward her.

Her heart softened, she took it. The roses were only beginning to blossom. They needed more days and tending to come into full bloom. Could she throw something so beautiful away?

Was he not at least worthy of another chance?

"Eden? Neil?" Mrs. Levine's voice interrupted them. She came toward them holding two bags of groceries.

"Mother." Eden turned toward her voice.

"Mrs. Levine," Neil greeted her, his voice sounding unsure.

How awkward. Eden took a step away from him. How should she explain all this?

Mrs. Levine looked at both of them, then at the bouquet. She eyed at Eden for her daughter's reaction. When Eden hesitated, she softened her face. "I can make some tea if you two would like to come upstairs."

Eagerly, Neil looked at Eden.

"Sure." Eden relented. It was only tea. "Come on up."

Neil's face lit up. Mrs. Levine switched the grocery bag in her right hand to her left to open the door. Neil rushed forward. "Let me help you." He took the bags from her and held open the door.

Following behind them, Eden sniffed the fragrance of the flowers. Neil had gone out of his way to make amends. Maybe he would change and become more conscientious? There was something to be said for a person willing to own up to the past and correct his mistakes.

At their apartment, Eden was surprised to see her father home with Isaac. Her father didn't usually get home this early. She was about to greet them when she saw Isaac bent over in his seat, distraught, with his head in his palms.

"Is everything okay?" Mrs. Levine put down her purse and went over to them.

"No," Dr. Levine said. The last time he looked so grave was the night when he gathered the family to tell them he wanted them all to move to China. "Remember Isaac's neighbor back in Munich, Hans Müller? He offered to help Yosef and Hadassah get their money out of Germany into Switzerland and deposit it into a bank there?"

Isaac gritted his teeth and pulled on his hair. Neil exchanged a glance with Eden and quietly put down the grocery bags.

"Isaac just got a letter from home. Müller disappeared."

"What?" Eden rushed over and sat down with them. Neil followed and stood by her side.

"He took the last deposit of the money to Switzerland and he never came back."

"Did something happen to him?" Mrs. Levine asked.

"That's one possibility," Dr. Levine said. "But his house next door is emptied out. The furniture is still there, but most of the personal belongings are gone. Yosef found this out when a couple showed up and told him they were the house's new owners."

"My goodness," Mrs. Levine said.

Eden mustered her nerves and asked the unthinkable, "Did he run away?"

No one spoke a word at first. Finally, Dr. Levine said, "It would seem like it."

"Oh, Isaac." Mrs. Levine put her arm around him.

"He's been our neighbor for more than twenty-five years." The bitter words spurted from his mouth. "I can't believe he would do this to us?"

Eden turned her gaze away. She couldn't bear to see his hurt face. It reminded her how vulnerable they were as Jews in Germany. Even people they thought they could trust were turning a blind eye to their plight, or worse, taking advantage of them.

Without thinking, she reached up and held Neil's hand.

"Do you know what bank in Switzerland he deposited the money into?" Neil asked. "If it's a bank where we have contacts, I might be able to get in touch with someone."

Isaac pulled up his head. Hope seized his eyes. "The Raiffeisen."

"I believe I do know someone who can help." He gave him an encouraging look. "Let's not panic yet. If the money is in that bank, I'll see if there's any way to recover it."

Eden held her breath. It was a long shot, but there was hope. Isaac wouldn't be stubborn enough to refuse Neil's help, would he?

Isaac let out a deep sigh. "Thank you. I'd appreciate that."

"And regardless of the situation with the bank, I'll help you get your parents here. If money's the only issue, they don't have to worry about that."

Isaac scrunched his face. She could see how hard he was holding his tears back. "Thank you."

Thank goodness. Eden exhaled. Neil held on to her hand, and all she could think now was how glad she was that he was here. His steady grip reassured her. Like a drifting log in the ocean, it gave her something to hold on to, in this world where nothing was stable and no one could be trusted.

24

INCIDENT AT THE MARCO POLO
BRIDGE

THE EARLY MORNING street seemed usual as Huang Shifu weaved the Cadillac through the pedestrians and the disorganized lanes of cars. Through the passenger window, Clark watched the beginning of another day. Vendors selling breakfasts of buns, scallion pancakes, and soy milk from their carts. Clerks and secretaries hurrying to their offices and pushing past the elderly folks taking morning walks. Merchants opening their shops and laborers hauling and delivering goods. The only thing absent were school children. The summer month of July had arrived and school was out. Children of foreign expats often returned to their home countries this time of year until the next school year began in the fall.

If they would return at all, Clark thought as he watched everyone obliviously going about their day. People had no idea yet how rapidly the situation in Peking was deteriorating. Two days ago, another skirmish had broken out between the Chinese and the Japanese troops in the town of Wanping near the Marco Polo Bridge sixteen kilometers southwest of Peking. The tension had been rising for months. The Japanese buildup of troops up north had increased to a ridiculous fifteen thousand men, almost all of them along the railway. Why? It was obvious. If war did break out, whoever controlled the railroad would have the advantage to win.

And why fight at the Marco Polo Bridge? Because the bridge was the only link between the North and the KMT government in Nanking. If they could seize hold of the bridge, the Japanese could cut off communication and transport between the Chinese central government and its people in the North.

In the backseat, Clark closed his eyes and took a deep breath before opening them again. He dared not speak about what he knew to anyone outside of work for fear of driving them into a panic.

The car arrived. Clark clutched the handle of his briefcase and got out. The nervous tension permeating every floor of the Foreign Affairs Bureau did nothing to ease his fears.

When he entered the reception area, he did not expect to see Eden waiting for him.

"Good morning," he greeted her. "What are you doing here?"

Eden stood up. "Sorry I came unannounced. Charlie Keaton sent me here." She showed him the paper from yesterday dated July 8 and the brief article on what was happening at Marco Polo Bridge. "He's hearing conflicting stories from his contacts up in Peking. He wants to know if you can tell us what's really happening there and whether there's anything specific you want us to print."

Clark passed his eyes over the photo of the Japanese Kwantung troops and the Chinese 29th Route Army soldiers shooting at each other from opposite ends of the bridge. He folded the paper and said, "Come with me."

He brought her to his office. At his desk, his secretary had left him a bundle of messages from people wanting him to call, including several from Ekaterina. He pushed them aside and put down his briefcase while she took a seat. "I have thirty minutes before my next meeting."

Eden nodded. "You look worried. Is everything all right?"

What should he tell her? He didn't want to scare her, but she was a reporter. Sooner or later, she would find out. Better she heard the story from him than anybody else.

He clasped his hands on his desk. "Off the record, we think a war's going to break out."

She looked intently at him, waiting to hear more.

"Up north, the Japanese have been building up their troops. We're talking an estimate of fifteen thousand men, all of them along the railroad line."

Eden frowned. She curled her fingers on her lap.

"They're using a loophole in our law for allowing foreign militaries on our land. The law was passed a long time ago, right after the fall of the Qing Dynasty. The Western countries demanded it so they could place troops here to protect their people and their assets. Japan is using that law as an excuse to deploy and mobilize their army here. It's making people very nervous."

"Yes. I've seen Japanese soldiers training in a park in Hongkew. They looked very serious."

"Up north, it's worse. They run a lot of simulation exercises in civilian areas. We think they do it on purpose to intimidate the locals. Two nights ago, a Japanese unit ran a nighttime training in Wanping. They were supposed to give the local residents advance notice when they train. This time, they didn't."

"So the Japanese soldiers were running around in residential areas training in the middle of the night?" Eden asked.

"Yes. What I heard was, the Japanese soldiers got too close to an infantry unit of Chinese soldiers. Some argument broke out and they exchanged fire."

Eden shook her head.

"That's how a lot of these skirmishes usually begin," Clark said. "Anyway, while this was going on, a Japanese soldier went missing. The Japanese command accused the Chinese of capturing him. They demanded to search the town. The local officials wouldn't let them. While they were negotiating, the fight between the soldiers escalated, even though the Japanese soldier wasn't missing. He'd returned to his unit on his own, but the armies on both sides started mobilizing. They've been fighting since then."

"Oh no." Eden bent forward. In a low voice, she asked, "What do you think is going to happen?"

Clark stared at his hands. "I don't know. Usually, the people in charge on both sides would come to a halt and stop the fighting. What's different this time is that the order to attack came from the Japanese army command."

Eden rounded her shoulders. "Are we safe?"

He pressed his lips. "I don't think the Japanese would threaten areas occupied by Western countries." It was the most reassuring answer he could think of.

A clerk knocked on his door. Clark answered, "Yes?"

"Counselor," the clerk said, "your meeting is about to start."

"I'm coming."

The clerk closed the door and Clark turned his attention back to Eden. "I have to go."

"I know." Eden nodded. "What do you want me to tell Charlie?"

"Nothing yet. My meeting now is a briefing on the situation in Wanping. Let me find out more. I don't want to cause a panic. I'll call you later."

Eden stood up. She put her purse strap over her shoulder. Clark got up from his seat to open the door. "Eden."

"Yes?"

"I want China to be a safe place for you. There's nothing I wouldn't do to make that happen." He clutched his hand around the doorknob. "I'm sorry I can't guarantee you anything."

"Clark." Eden looked at him, surprised. "Don't apologize. You can't control what the armies will do."

No, he thought. He couldn't. How powerless he was. His country, the third largest country in the world, couldn't guarantee the safety of its people against a country made up of little islands. He couldn't protect the woman he loved. "I feel like we've let you down."

"Don't say that." She touched him on the arm.

He glanced at her hand. If he could, he would take her hand and tell her why he wanted so much to keep her safe.

"You've been such a good friend," she said. "You've done enough already. Speaking of which, I want to thank you for helping with that comfort house. I went by there last week. It looks like it's no longer in operation."

"No need to thank me," he said. He wished he could do more about that too. For all they knew, the Japanese might have simply moved the comfort women to another location. Although, he did believe the women in that building had been released. Konoe wouldn't renege on his word.

"Right now, you have more important things to worry about."

He watched her drop her hand off his arm. The clerk approached them again. "Counselor?"

"I'm coming." Clark tossed his head.

"You better go," Eden said. "I'll wait to hear from you."

Clark watched her depart, then hurried toward the back of the floor to Sītu's office.

"Sorry to keep you waiting." Clark came into Sītu's office and took a seat next to Tang Wei.

Sītu dismissed his apology with a wave of his hand. The scowl on his forehead hadn't left since this latest incident began. "General Qin of the 219 Regiment in Wanping came to an agreement with the Japanese forces yesterday. The terms were not at all favorable but we almost had a ceasefire. But it was futile. The communist resistance fighters ignored their talk and continued to push back and the shooting never stopped. As of this morning, the Japanese have started bombing the town again."

Tang Wei threw Clark a look, a "What did I say?" look showing he had been expecting this outcome all along.

Clark ignored him. Since the time when he discovered Tang Wei had been self-dealing and selling arms to the Silver Shadow, his view of Tang Wei had changed. His respect for him had dropped tenfold. "Can we still negotiate a truce?" he asked Sītu.

"We're prepared to do that, but the Japanese Garrison Army isn't responding to our calls for retreat. The Party believes we've come to a breaking point."

"A breaking point?"

"Yes. We don't think we can contain the tensions between the two sides any longer. It's obvious, the incident in Wanping was planned. The Japanese were tempting war. When this conflict broke out, it was pouring rain in Wanping. What were they doing insisting on training in such muddy conditions if not to incite trouble? They want to frighten all the town folks and let them hear their gunshots. Then they made that preposterous request to run their exercise through the town? Of course, the authorities in Wanping said no."

"Exactly!" Tang Wei held up his cigarette. "Their missing soldier had already returned, and still they demanded we let their troops come into the town to finish their training? In the middle of the night? And when the people in Wanping said no, they encircled the town and shot cannons at four in the morning? It's outrageous. I've been supporting peace all along, but this is an intentional act of war."

All along? Clark flashed him a look, but didn't call him out. Anyway, Tang was right. Even before this incident, there had been reports that Japanese soldiers were dressing up pretending to be communists and picking fights with their own soldiers to incite the people in Wanping to protest against Japan. When that scheme didn't work, they pressed the tension further with their feeble excuses of "military exercises." The Japanese's actions made him seethe too.

"Our soldiers are ready to fight," Sītu said. "Yesterday, General Song Zhe-Yuan of the 29th Route Army sent a telegram to Generalissimo Chiang. He said he and his troops are ready to fight till death. We can't watch the Japanese shorties bully their way in anymore."

"What happens now?" Clark asked.

"We'll see how this plays out. This time, the Party has decided to stand our ground. Whether we can maintain peace is now up to Japan. Yuan Guo-Hui, talk to Joseph Whitman. The American Secretary of State Hull issued a statement yesterday calling for Japan to exercise self-restraint. That's not enough. Can you try to persuade them to take a stronger stand?"

"I'll try." Clark shifted in his seat. "I'm not hopeful. They haven't shown any inclination to become involved at all."

"I'm not optimistic either," Sītu concurred, "but try anyway. A war can ruin their businesses and they've got their people here to protect. It might be enough to force them to come to our defense."

"What about the Russians?" Clark asked, remembering the messages from Ekaterina on his desk which he hadn't yet read.

"We're consulting with the Kremlin at the highest level. Stalin's sending us more tanks and ammunition to help us mobilize. Don't concern yourself with that for now. Focus on dealing with the Americans." Sītu balled his fists. "Tang Wei, start putting together statements to clarify our position on peace. Use strong words to denounce the Japanese aggression. We need the public opinion behind us."

"Understood." Tang Wei took a long drag, then stubbed out his cigarette.

Sītu's phone rang. He gestured for Clark and Tang Wei to leave and picked up the receiver.

Outside of Sītu's office, Clark said to Tang, "Are you glad now? We're at war for real."

"Don't take your frustrations out on me," Tang said. "Japan would wage a war here sooner or later. Don't tell me you can't see that. At least now, I've got some money to protect myself." He put his hands on his hips. "I want whatever's best for the country too, but I'm also realistic. We can dream when we have the luxury to dream. When circumstances change, we adapt to reality. Don't say I didn't warn you. Look out for yourself. Who knows what the people at the top will do? They might talk big and then sell us out."

Clark hmphed and walked away. He wouldn't admit it, but what Tang said was right.

It was time for everyone to look out for themselves.

25

SHANGHAI UNDER SIEGE

IN THE OFFICE of Joseph Whitman, Clark handed him a copy of the KMT's official statement to the United States. Whitman read it over, then put it down with a deep sigh. "It's not in anyone's interest for a full-fledged war to break out."

"No it's not," Clark said. "But if an enemy country intrudes upon American soil, takes over Boston, then mobilizes their army from there on down to New York, what would you do?"

Whitman folded his hands on his desk. Since the conflict in Wanping had deteriorated into a full-scale fight, Japan had dropped all pretenses of peace. The fight had escalated into a bloody battle. And now, four weeks later, the Chinese Army was in retreat. Japan had now pushed their way down to Peiping and Tientsin, taking over the railways up to the border of Shanghai.

"If another country attacked America and their troops were surrounding New York, would your President agree to withdraw all your troops from New York as a condition to a ceasefire?" Clark asked. He'd never spoken so curtly to his American friend.

"No. I suppose not." Avoiding Clark's gaze, Whitman fiddled with his hands.

"And yet, that's what Japan is asking us to do," Clark said.

"That's what you all are asking us to do. How can you ask us to withdraw our troops from Shanghai under the circumstances?"

Whitman turned his head. Yesterday, the international community in Shanghai had called an emergency conference. When Britain, France, the United States, and Italy proposed a ceasefire, Japan demanded China withdraw all of its troops from Shanghai.

What Japan was asking was outrageous. Yu Hung-Chun, who was Shanghai's mayor and the Chinese representative at the conference, rejected the demand. The copy of the letter Clark gave to Whitman just now officially confirmed Generalissimo Chiang's stance to decline Japan's demand.

"We continue to support pacification. There hasn't been a formal declaration of war by either side. Until someone declares a war, it would be an aggressive action by us if we step in. We have an intense desire to maintain peace everywhere. Secretary of State Hull would be glad to continue informal talks with both sides to resolve this."

"Joseph, you know talks won't solve anything anymore. What difference does it make if they formally declared war or not? Look at what the Japanese are doing. They might not have declared war in words, but their actions are proof. Look at the massive number of troops they've deployed here in the last four weeks."

Whitman gazed out the window. By now, Japan had stationed more than one hundred eighty thousand men in the Peiping-Tientsin area alone. Their superior navy—something China didn't have—and their access to the sea, enabled them to bring in reinforcements. China had no navy and could not stop them.

"From our conversations with Japan, they are willing to halt their advancement." Whitman unfolded his hands. "The IJA doesn't want to divert their troops to the South. It would weaken their offensive in Manchuria and leave them vulnerable to the Soviets."

"We are past the point of conciliation," Clark said. Chiang

Kai-shek had finally come to the conclusion that they had reached their last resort. He'd said this repeatedly in his edict to the Chinese Army two weeks ago after the loss of Peiping. In his edict, he wrote with heartfelt words and pleaded,

At this irrevocable last juncture, of course we must sacrifice. Our position is to defend war, not to seek war. Defending war is only because we have no other choice . . . Obviously, we are a weak country, but we can't not protect the lives of our people. We can't not bear the responsibilities bestowed upon us by our ancestors and our history. Therefore, when we are pushed to the edge, we can't not defend war. As we are a weak country with no possibility of an agreement, if we forego even an inch of our land or our sovereignty, we will be guilty to our nation for thousands of years hence . . .

Whether the incident at Marco-Polo Bridge will escalate to a war between China and Japan depends entirely on the position of Japan. The key to peace is entirely up to the actions of the IJA. To the very last second before all hopes of peace are extinguished, our hope is still for peace.

"My government maintains that Japan has breached the Kellogg-Briand Pact's requirement to refrain from initiating war," Clark said. "Therefore, we cannot accept the current proposed terms for a ceasefire. I'm here to deliver that confirmation."

Whitman sank back in his seat. His face awash in regret. "I can't tell you how sorry I am. You know if it were up to me, I would do more."

"I know." Clark understood, more than Whitman would know. After all, what could one man do alone? He himself had given everything he could, and still, he could do nothing that would salvage anything.

"I understand this is your government's position." Whitman picked up the letter Clark had given him. "But between you and me, what are your thoughts about all this?"

Clark stared at his hands. What were his thoughts?

Grief.

Bitter, heart-wrenching grief.

"I never wanted war," he said. "There's so much I want to do for my country and our people. When I came back to Shanghai from America last year, I had so much hope. My country can do great things, and we were only beginning. But we keep getting obstructed. We want to move ahead, but we have Mao Ze Dong pulling us back with his backward ways of thinking. We can advance and modernize, but he wants to turn us into a nation of uneducated farmers. Then there's Japan. They've taken our territories. They keep inching their way in. In Wanping, they demanded we place our troops and security forces under their military command. Every time we try to negotiate peace, they asked for something outrageous. And when we reasonably refused, they used that as an excuse to attack us." He gritted his teeth and swallowed. "We lost so many people. The deputy commander of our 29th Route Army took a bullet in his head. Our 132 Division chief got ambushed and died and six hundred soldiers perished. Half of the cavalry division of our 9th Army were killed. Are we to stand back and let them die for nothing?" He drew in a deep breath. The air flowed in, trapped in his tensed chest.

Whitman listened. His face sad and helpless.

"So now, you all want us to concede to Japan's demand for our troops to withdraw from Shanghai. Are we supposed to let their soldiers enter our land with no restrictions whatsoever, while our own soldiers can't move about freely within our own country? If our enemy points their guns at us, we can't return fire? Tell me, what country in the world would accept this?"

"None. You're right," Whitman said with a deep sigh. "I will pass this message on." He folded the letter and held it in front of him. "God help us all."

Clark let out a helpless smile. God help them all.

Leaving Joseph Whitman's office, Clark told Huang Shifu to take him home. As a precaution, his father had arranged for his mother and Mei Mei to leave for Hong Kong. With negotiations for peace coming to an impasse yesterday, the family had decided they should depart on the five o'clock ship today. Clark had cleared his schedule for the afternoon to go home to see them off.

In the garden of the Yuan family villa, Chinese asters bloomed in varied shades of red, lavender, pink, and white as they always did in early August. How unfortunate that men could not step back from their proclivity to destroy, when nature's reminder of beauty lay everywhere.

In the house, Clark found his mother and Mei Mei in the living room making last minute preparations.

"Xiaochun," Madam Yuan called out for the maid. "Can you check if we've packed the wet towels? I want to have wet towels if our hands get sticky from eating fruits and snacks on the ship."

"Yes, Madam." Xiaochun grabbed the leather tote bag. Clark watched his mother. Her oblivion to the gravity of the situation both saddened him and warmed his heart. He wished his mother's mind would always stay innocent this way.

"Mei Mei, don't forget to bring your scarf," Madam Yuan called out to her daughter.

"It's August, Ma," Mei Mei replied. "It's hot."

"You could catch a cold from the evening wind on the outside deck."

Clark chuckled and walked over to them. "Is this everything?" He tossed his head at the pile of bags and suitcases.

"Eh! Guo-Hui, you've returned." Madam Yuan fanned herself. "Yes. We're almost ready." A pained expression overtook her face. "I'm so worried about you all. I really want you, your Ba, and Wen-Ying to come with us."

"Don't worry, Ma." He patted her shoulder. "We'll come if the situation gets worse, I promise. I can't leave right now. My work needs me. Ba has to stay to watch our businesses. As for Wen-Ying . . ." He frowned. His hard-headed sister. "I'll talk to her again. I'll try to convince her to leave."

"Yes. Talk to her," said Madam Yuan. Her eyes flitted to Xiaochun pulling on a stuck zipper. "Xiaochun! Be careful with that. You'll break it." She rushed over to the maid.

Clark and Mei Mei exchanged a glance. Clark shook his head, then said to his sister, "Take good care of Ma."

"I will." She nodded.

"I'll go check on Ba," Clark said and went to the study.

In the study at his desk, Master Yuan spoke into the telephone receiver, "Yes. Yes. Hurry. The sooner the better." He jotted the terms of his conversation in a notebook. Clark stepped in and waited. Master Yuan glanced up from behind his glasses. "Thank you. We'll talk soon." He finished scribbling and hung up. "Guo-Hui?"

"Ba."

Master Yuan dropped his pen on his desk. "I just closed a deal with the Do Kow Cotton Mill. They have a factory building and warehouse next to their mill at the northwest side of the International Settlement. I bought it. I want to move our battery factory there, just in case."

"Good idea." The Japanese wouldn't be as bold dealing with Western countries and the foreign-controlled districts.

"The question is, how do we protect our workers? Even if all the equipment and materials are moved, we still need workers." Master Yuan took off his glasses and sighed. "Never mind work. I'm more worried for our people and their families. If the Japanese come to attack, who cares about businesses." He picked up his cup of tea and took a sip. "I want to reserve a section of the warehouse and make it into a dormitory. The workers with children and elderly family members can move in there temporarily. The place will be cramped and not very comfortable, but safety is the first priority."

"I agree," Clark said. "I'll help."

"Help." Master Yuan laughed. "Forget it. You have more important things to do right now. We'll talk when you and your group of government officials can figure out something to stop the Japanese."

Easier said than done. "Ba, after you move the factory, maybe you should go to Hong Kong too and keep away for a while. I have to stay here anyway. Uncle Six can watch over the business. If there's any problem, he can come to me."

"You stay here, or I stay here, what difference does it make? We're all ants in a wok." Master Yuan threw up his hand. "Besides, how can I leave our band of workers and employees like I'm abandoning them? Almost half of them have worked for us for decades. Maybe if this whole city blows up and everyone including the foreigners have to run, then I'll run too."

Clark swayed back and dropped his head. He hoped it wouldn't come to that.

Wen-Ying entered the room. "Ba." She gave Clark a quick glance.

"Yes?" Master Yuan asked.

"Ma and Mei Mei are leaving soon."

"I'm coming. You two go on out. Let me finish up." He waved them away.

Clark left the room with his sister. In the corridor, he stopped her. "Wen-Ying."

"What?"

"Why don't you go to Hong Kong with Ma and Mei Mei?" he asked as they passed the grandfather clock in the hallway. It was only quarter till three. The ship to Hong Kong wouldn't leave until six. "You still have time. Shanghai is not stable."

Wen-Ying stopped. She pulled a copper pendant engraved with

a triangular symbol out from underneath her blouse. "I'm a sworn member of the Heaven and Earth Society. I'm not running." She tugged the pendant back in her collar and walked away. Her firm eyes told him there was no persuading her to change her mind.

"Wen-Ying . . ." He followed after her. Before he reached her, Uncle Six shouted from the front entrance. "Oh no! Oh no! Oh no!"

Clark exchanged a puzzled look with Wen-Ying. Immediately, they hurried into the living room.

"Oh no! The Japanese attack! It's here! It's here!" Uncle Six stumbled in.

"They're bombing Chapei!" Huang Shifu shouted behind him. Chapei was the working-class district north of the International Settlement and next to Hongkew. It housed numerous factories and mills that powered Shanghai's well-oiled economy.

Madam Yuan raised her head from checking the suitcases, looking confused. Mei Mei gasped and slapped both hands across her heart.

Clark came up to Uncle Six. "What are you talking about?"

"The Japanese attack started! They're dropping bombs over in Chapei!" Uncle Six swung his arm at the front door.

"So soon?" Clark asked. Hollow fear spread through his veins. He looked at his mother and sisters, and everyone else in the room. Everyone froze in shock. His father came rushing in. "What? What's happening?"

Clark swallowed and tried to think of what to do. "Huang Shifu, take me to my office." Still stunned, the driver nodded. Clark took a deep breath, trying to steady his voice. "You all stay put," he said to everybody. "I'll go find out what's going on."

"Guo-Hui!" Madam Yuan came after him. Her face doused with worry.

"I'll be fine. We're in a foreign-occupied district." He did his best to appear calm, even though inside, the news had knocked the wind out of him. "I'll call home as soon as I find out what's happening. Huang Shifu," he said to the driver, "let's go."

"Yes, yes, Young Master." Huang Shifu nodded frantically, like he'd found a lifesaver.

Clark turned around and left for the door. He wasn't anyone's lifesaver. The quicker he left, the less they would see his fears. And he didn't want them to fear yet. Not until he knew for sure what was going on.

In the passenger seat, Clark looked at the direction of Chapei where the Japanese planes were flying overhead. From burning buildings, thick coils of black smoke whirled up to the sky. Huang Shifu zipped their car through the traffic, driving as fast as he could. As soon as they arrived, Clark jumped out, not caring at all to wait for his driver to open the door. He rushed into his office building. On his floor, ringing phones screamed on every desk. Voices of the staff overlapped as they rushed to answer the calls. Ignoring them all, Clark headed straight to Sītu's office. Tang Wei and two other top-level agents had already gathered.

"What's happening?" he asked. "Did we know they were going to attack?"

"No." Sītu signaled him to take a seat. "But we expected they would sooner or later. Our army's ready."

Warily, Clark slid into a chair and exchanged a glance with Tang Wei. Tang's face twisted in alarm. All traces of his bravado about fighting the Japanese had disappeared.

Sītu, however, sat with dignified resolve. "Generalissimo Chiang has mobilized the German-trained 87th and 88th Divisions to defend Shanghai. The Western powers will now have front-row seats to see what our best troops can do. We'll show the world we are the victims and we're worth their support."

If only so. Remembering his conversation with Joseph

Whitman this morning, Clark didn't think the foreign powers would step in even if China fell to ashes.

"I have here a message from the Generalissimo." Sītu pulled out a piece of paper from the stack of letters on his desk. "He said, the Japanese will want to expand southward and take over the entire coast. We won't let them succeed. If this battle doesn't end quickly in our favor, the Generalissimo's plan is to draw them inland. His plan is to change their path and make them fight from East to West. Trade space for time. China is a vast country. We'll win by forcing them into a slow war of attrition deep into our heartland. We'll exhaust their armies and resources. What we lack in tools and machines, we'll make up with land and numbers."

Clark sat still and listened. The war that everyone said would come was finally here. Deaths, doom, and destructions lay ahead, and all they had to fight with were bare hands, outmoded equipment, and flesh and blood.

Sītu glanced up and winced. "Those Japanese robbers took our land in Peiping and Tientsin by foul play and lies. They slaughtered our fellow countrymen. We will fight those dwarfs to their death."

The heat of injustice rising inside him, Clark closed his fist. Like Chiang said, their country was weak. But its seed of splendor was growing. Even the infestation of crimes and corruption had not stopped the flourishing of its sprout. Through the web of challenges his society faced, he could see the bright lining on the horizon. Their people were just getting started. If only they were given time! Time to reach the greatness of what they could become. Instead, they must now trade time for space. They must accept the inevitable destruction to their land, and the death toll and blood that were still to come. Why? Why did Japan have to ruin them before they were even given a chance?

"Now that the time has come, our country must unite," Sītu said. "The Generalissimo's words are clear." He read from the letter, "'We must be determined to sacrifice, and we must have conviction that we will win. Our hearts must be aligned. We will do all we can for our country and drive out the Japanese thieves. We will bring prosperity back to our people.'"

"He's right." Clark sat up and raised his head. "It's all up to us. We'll have to do all we can to unite our people's hearts." He turned to Tang Wei. "We can still beat back Japan. Our people need to hear that. We need to raise their morale."

"Yes," Tang said with a firm nod. "We can rally our people."

Clark glanced back at Sītu. "We'll call for support any way we can. If no one outside will help us, we'll help ourselves."

Sītu nodded. "Good. The Generalissimo will be glad to hear we're united and determined. Our military strength has always been concentrated in the North. Japan has taken down our best generals in Xian and Peking. They'll think they can march into Shanghai with ease, but they'll be in for a shock. We've got our best troops here. If the Japanese want to fight, we'll battle with them head on till they die and we live. Now get to work."

Along with Tang and the other agents, Clark stood up. The world he had hoped to build had collapsed. Conviction that they would win the war was all he had now. He'd hold on to that to the very end.

26

A CITY ON FIRE

WITHOUT WARNING, the bombs began to drop. No sirens to alarm the defenseless civilians. No official declaration of war to alert the world. In the Chapei district next to Hongkew, the bombs exploded in the middle of the populated streets on top of blocks of buildings. Houses and shops came tumbling down, their debris bursting into dust clouds and evaporating in the air.

Stunned, Eden stopped. Along with the pedestrians around her, she gaped at the horrific scene. Earlier today, Charlie had asked her to come to Hongkew to observe the Japanese-occupied district. Throughout the week, troop after troop of Japanese marines had descended into Shanghai. No one thought the outbreak in Peking would spread this far south. Yesterday, local leaders of the foreign countries held a conference with both China and Japan to attempt to bring forth a ceasefire. In the end, the Western nations threw up their hands. The nuisance of a dispute between these two sets of inferior people was beyond their help. Not worth them stepping in and risking their own armies to impose peace.

How events would unfold then was anybody's guess.

As she gazed at the smoke-filled sky, an Asian man in a dark suit and silk tie asked her, "Are you a tourist?"

Eden creased her forehead. What an odd question. Did he not see that planes were bombing the city?

"Do you speak English?" he asked.

"Yes," she answered, utterly confused.

"You want to see what's happening?"

"Yes."

"Come with me. You can get a better view on the roof of the Japanese Club." He pointed to the top of the building behind them.

Dazed, she followed the man inside. Groups of people in the lavishly furnished lobby rushed past them, exiting to the streets to see what was causing the noises outside. The man led her to an elevator. The elevator conductor recognized him right away. While riding up, the man and the conductor engaged in an animated exchange in Japanese. The conductor's face widened into a grin. Puzzled, Eden shifted her eyes from one man to the other. Were they talking about the bombing? Their planes attacked a part of the city. Why did they look so thrilled?

The elevator door opened at the top of the building on the tenth floor. The man waved at Eden. "This way."

She followed him out to an outdoor rooftop restaurant. About a hundred people had gathered here in the open. They stood behind the enclosure and watched the attack in awe. Their voices buzzed in excitement, like spectators at the start of a sporting event. Walking behind the man who had invited her, she came to a spot where they could see the whole expanse of Chapei to the outstretched land beyond.

Above her, the rumble of engines buzzed in the gray sky. Her heart thumped faster and faster with the sound. A Japanese warplane swished down and dropped a light over the district at Jukong Road. The surrounding area glowed, giving the pilots a clear view of their targets. Two more planes glided in, dumping another two loads of bombs onto the unwitting souls below.

"*Banzai!*" The men next to her threw their arms up in victory when the bombs hit. More cheers of *Banzai!* followed. The men hugged each other and a round of applause broke out. Eden widened her eyes in disbelief. She couldn't imagine herself reacting this way even if bombs had killed German Nazis.

She turned her focus back to the attack. How many people did the fallen buildings crush?

Before the raging booms died down, another squadron of planes flew in. Again, the first one set off a flare. Six more planes followed and swarmed above the Commercial Press, the country's newest print factory for universities and schools. Like a horrible parody of clouds, the planes rained their bombs from above. Soon, the plant exploded in fire.

Another roar of cheers and applause broke out around her. Dear God! These people were celebrating the horror!

"It's their fault," said the man who brought her here. "Our marines needed to get through Chapei this morning. The Chinese police wouldn't let them pass through. They shot at our soldiers." The man hmphed. His nose twitched to one side. "We show them who's superior now."

Eden took an involuntary step back from the man. What cruel, inhuman heart could say such a thing? Women and children were burning below.

Up above, several planes changed direction mid-air and dived toward the North Station. Eden moved closer to the side of the roof facing that spot. The train station was where the Chinese 19th Route Army had barricaded themselves. A labyrinth of locomotives and rail tracks ran between warehouses and factories and converged there. It was the pulse of the country's bloodline connecting the North and the South.

Like a wolf pack surrounding their prey, the Japanese planes circled above the station. One dived down toward the roofs of the station buildings and dropped its bombs. Eden gasped and squeezed shut her eyes, then opened them again. How terrible! The pilot had flew low to make sure his bombs would not miss.

A load of bombs followed, smashing to pieces the tracks, trains, and buildings. From behind the explosions, gunshots rang out. The Chinese soldiers returned fire with their rifles. Eden held her fist to her mouth. Gunshots popped between booms. Her heart broke watching the rifle fire. Their bullets pelted against the heads of the planes like stones from David's sling. But the Japanese Air Force didn't fall like Goliath. The harder the Chinese fought, the angrier the exploding bombs roared. A few more blasts later and the station, too, went up in flames.

Trembling, Eden raised her hands and covered the sides of her head. She'd never seen such terror in her entire life. Her whole body shook. All of Chapei was flooding in a sea of fire. The blaze spread from rows and rows of houses and buildings to the next, carried forward by wind.

The Japanese men around her continued to cheer. Amidst their barks and laughter, she inched to the edge of the roof. Over the enclosure, she gazed down farther to the distant streets in Chapei below. Mobs of people were screaming, crying, running for their lives. They had grabbed whatever belongings they could. One man ran with a mattress on his back, another with a birdcage swinging from his hand. All were pushing their ways toward the Garden Bridge to the International Settlement. Their numbers mushroomed by the minutes. How many were there? Thousands? Ten thousand? Twenty thousand?

An alarming thought jumped to her mind. She better get back before the mob reached the bridge. She hated thinking this when so many people below were trying to escape. But if she didn't get there before the masses, she'd never be able to get through the thick crowd to get home.

Quickly, she left for the elevator.

Outside, the trickles of refugees began to swell. Cries of the injured and shouts of the confused mixed with earsplitting cracks of guns and thundering of bombs. Eden hurried toward the bridge and crossed to the other side. At the end of the bridge, the Shanghai Volunteer Corps, a band of multinational weekend warriors who served as the International Settlement's own militia units, stood guard. They huddled in their positions, their mouths hung open as refugees began to spill in from every lane, street, and alley toward the Hongkew side's entrance to the bridge.

Eden checked the tram stop and the traffic. Should she return to the *China Press* office? Or should she stay to watch?

Remaining here would not be safe. The swarm of people coming this way could end in a stampede. But how could she go back? She was a reporter, and she was an eyewitness to this brutal attack!

This attack was wrong. Everything about it was wrong. She couldn't run and hide. She had to report about this. She had to let everyone in the world know the horror the Japanese were inflicting onto the thousands who were dead or trying to flee.

The border separating Chapei and the International Settlement on the west side of Soochow Creek should be a safer vantage point. She hailed a taxi and directed it to take her where she wanted to go. Along the way, units of the Shanghai Volunteer Corps, a mix of Americans, Portuguese, Scots, Italians, as well as real ex-army Russians, Filipinos, and Chinese hired by the Britons, kept watch at multiple lookout spots. The British and American soldiers and sailors, the Dutch Marines, and the Italian Savoyard grenadiers were all out on guard too. Since yesterday, their governments had commanded them to patrol their district's border after the international attempt to bring a ceasefire failed. The security forces increased in the Frenchtown too. A detachment of colonial Vietnamese troop had arrived to their sector, all dressed and ready to commence defense as the Chinese and Japanese intensified the mobilization of their troops.

And yet, none of these guardians of peace looked the least bit concerned. Like the civilians around them, they gawked as the Japanese warplanes hurled bombs at the Chinese. Their shock soon turned to awe. Their amazement no different than when they saw the luminous fireworks on the Bund three months ago when George VI was crowned King.

Was she the only person appalled by the disaster unfolding before them?

The taxi dropped her off at North Szechuan Road near a troop of American Marines. Eden hopped out of the car and traversed her way toward the piles of sandbags behind the barbwire fences. The foreign governments had installed these barricades last week at every intersection to protect the perimeters of their Shanghai territories. Already, a curious band of expats had come to the area to watch the show. Clusters of foreigners milled about on the sidewalks, building terraces, and rooftops. At the tables in the outdoor seating areas of the restaurants nearby, foreign men in three-piece suits and ladies in summer dresses sipped gin cocktails and champagne while they watched the garrisons of Chinese and Japanese soldiers exchange shots just yards away.

"This is just like last time when the Japanese raided the city," an older woman behind Eden told her friend. "Five years ago, they did the same thing. That time, they almost razed Chapei to the ground, and I stood in this very same spot and watched it all happen." She held her binoculars up to her eyes. "I wonder how bad it'll get this time."

The woman's companion stretched her neck to get a better view. "Are we safe here?"

"Oh, yes," the woman said. "We're in our own territory. They wouldn't come over here. They didn't last time."

"It looks pretty bad. Shouldn't our troops do something?"

"What can we do?" the woman answered. "Those yellow people won't listen to us." She peered into the binoculars lenses again. "My! There are so many of them. Want to see?" She offered her friend the binoculars.

Scowling, Eden walked away. She couldn't listen anymore to the woman's tone of voice. This wasn't a game. Real people were dying.

The crackle of gunfire surged and ebbed. In an interval when the noise of battle subsided, a U.S. Marine said to another, "Maybe we should go over and see if there's anything to report back."

"Sure. We'll go take a look." The other Marine adjusted the strap of his gun on his shoulder.

Before she could think it through, Eden called out to them. "Excuse me!"

The Marines turned around.

"May I please come with you? I'm a reporter for the *China Press*." She unzipped her purse and dug out her press pass.

The Marines shrugged at each other. One of them said, "Come on."

"Thank you." Eden followed them to the opening of the fence. On the other side in Chapei, heaps of smoking bricks, stones, and wood had piled up on the sidewalks. Blistering fumes of gunpowder and fire seared her nose. The IJA's aerial bombs didn't attack this part of the city, but cannons and gunfire had shattered the buildings' windows and walls. Car engines exploded and vehicles were burning in a blaze. In one day, this vibrant community had fallen to ruins.

Oddly, the soldiers on both sides held their fire when the American Marines passed. The Americans could saunter around without being afraid of even a stray bullet. Eden moved closer behind them.

The Marines came up to the Chinese soldiers behind a blockade of sandbags. One of them asked, "Who's in charge here?"

The Chinese shouted their replies. All of them spoke at once in Chinese.

"Can anyone speak English?" the other Marine asked.

The Chinese soldiers tried to answer again, gesticulating wildly and pointing at the Japanese as they spoke.

Unable to find anyone who could communicate with them, the Marines gave up and proceeded to the Japanese side. There, a naval lieutenant assured them they would keep the fighting outside of the International Settlement's border.

With nothing further they could do, the Marines returned to their post. Eden followed until they were back within their own bubble of a safety zone.

It was a bubble, wasn't it? The world around them had crashed into hell. But inside the barricade of sandbags and barbwire fence, life continued, untouched by the sweep of atrocities that had wiped out everything that had once flourished.

But even the foreign shelter felt the effect after all. When she boarded a tram back to her office, the traffic gave way to the masses of refugees pouring in. They carried on their backs sacks of belongings, chickens, babies, the old, and the sick. They came in wheelbarrows, handcarts, bicycles, and on foot.

And there were those who were injured by shell fire. They plodded forward like waifs, with blood dripping down their tarred skin and clothes. The refugees flowed through every road and lane, settling into whatever doorway, patch of grass, bench, or ledge they could find. All of them now homeless.

What would happen to them?

The tram came to her stop. As she climbed off, a woman trudged past, carrying the limp body of a boy. His shirt and pants covered in dirt and footprints.

Eden watched the woman and her boy disappear into the swarm, then continued to the *China Press* building. Her own senses had numbed. Her mind had gone blank. Mechanically, she let her legs take her back to her office where she found Charlie at his desk. "I saw the attack," she told him. "I saw everything."

Charlie glanced up from his desk.

"I'll go write up my report about it." Her eyes glazed, she went to her desk.

In front of the typewriter, she tried to begin. For a long time, she sat. No word would come out. She squeezed her forehead and tried to type.

The

The what? How could she describe the terrifying moment when the warplanes' bombs exploded on top of hundreds of people?

They

They who? The Japanese pilots? The Chinese soldiers retaliating at the North Station? The Japanese spectators cheering on their troops? The lolling foreign troops or the ambivalent expats standing by on the side?

Or the refugees with their battered bodies and shocked eyes? Or the woman carrying the limp body of her boy trampled under the weight of thousands of escaping feet?

All at once, tears rushed down from her eyes. She propped her elbow on her desk and dropped her face into her palm, brushing away her tears as she tried to muffle her cries. All those people. How would they recover? How would they survive?

"Eden." Dottie, the secretary, came toward her desk.

"Yes." Eden sniffled and wiped away her tears.

"This gentleman is looking for you."

Eden glanced at the man behind Dottie. It was Neil's chauffeur. "Carson?"

"Good evening, Miss Levine," Carson said, holding his hat to his chest. "Mr. Sassoon told me to come. He wants me to drive you home if you're still at work."

Neil. She breathed a sigh of relief. The thoughtful gesture comforted her so much. She had no idea how badly she needed it. "Thank you, Carson. But I'm still working."

"It's all right. I can wait in my car. It's parked downstairs."

Eden put her hands back on her typewriter.

"Eden. Go home." Charlie came over.

"I . . ."

"You've been sitting there for an hour. Go home and get some rest."

An hour already? The paper in her typewriter was still blank. "I can't. I need to report on what I saw."

"You need time to process what you saw," Charlie said. "Why don't you get a good night's sleep and come in early tomorrow? Do a write-up about what you saw in Hongkew. That was what you were sent to report on today, remember? I'm putting out a special evening edition tomorrow when we have more confirmed facts and details. We can get your article in then."

Eden glanced at her hopelessly blank page. Maybe Charlie was right. Her mind wasn't functioning well right now anyhow. "Okay." She grabbed her purse and belongings.

"I'll see you tomorrow." Charlie waved goodbye and headed back to his office.

Eden picked up the phone. "Can you please give me a minute?" she asked Carson.

"Of course. I'll be waiting out front." Carson bowed his head and went back to the reception area.

Quickly, Eden dialed home. She should've called earlier. Was everyone okay? Her parents must be worried sick. What was the matter with her? She'd forgotten how to function.

"Mother?" she said when Mrs. Levine answered.

"Eden! Where have you been? I left you so many messages."

Messages? Eden shifted her eyes to her desk. Dottie had left a stack of messages for her. She didn't even remember to look.

"Dottie said you went out on an assignment. I'm so glad you're okay."

"I'm fine. How are you and Papa? Are you okay? Is Joshua?"

"Yes, we're all fine. Your father went to the Red Cross Hospital to see if they need help. I picked Joshua up from school after the bombing started. All the other parents went and brought their kids home too. Those Japanese planes were flying over us all day. What's happening?"

What's happening? We're at war, she wanted to say. But she stopped herself. She didn't want to scare her mother.

Actually, they weren't at war. China and Japan were at war. The international bubble was not.

"I'll tell you more when I get home," Eden said. "Neil sent his driver to get me."

"Did he? Thank goodness. It's madness outside. So many escapees. It's terrible!"

"Yes, it is." She ran her fingers through her hair behind her ear. "I'll be back soon." She said goodbye to her mother and hung up.

On her way out with Carson, he said, "Mr. Sassoon wants me to drive you to and from work from now on until things calm down."

"Oh?" She almost refused, but then thought better of it. So many refugees had come in and clogged the streets. Who knew how the attack might impact the tram and bus lines.

Besides, having Carson drive her would give her parents more peace of mind. "Thank you then."

"My pleasure."

They came to the car and he opened the door to let her in. As he drove onto the road, Eden remembered. Neil! Where was he? How thoughtless of her. Neil had sent her his driver, and she didn't even think to check on him.

"Where is Mr. Sassoon right now?" she asked.

"He's home. He left the office when the warplanes started dropping bombs."

She checked her watch. Not too late yet. "Carson, can you please take me to Mr. Sassoon's first?"

"Yes, ma'am." Carson steered the wheel toward Neil's home. In the backseat, Eden clutched her hands. She wanted to see Neil. She wanted to see him so much. She felt like the world was crumbling, and she wanted a rock to hold on to.

Outside, the sky had turned dark, but the refugees were still wandering, looking for shelter for the night.

Entering Neil's apartment, Eden could hear his voice on the phone all the way from his study. She thanked his Chinese maid and went toward him. When he saw her leaning against the door frame waiting for him, he smiled and waved. She crossed her arms and smiled back.

"Well, tell them we'll pay double," he said into the receiver. "We have to get at least the first shipment in! Our flagship shop is set to open on September 1st. We have an opening event on the calendar and all the press will be there. What am I going to do without inventory?" He tapped his fingers impatiently on his desk as the person on the other line spoke. "I don't care. It's your job. I'm holding you accountable. Do something!" He plunked the receiver down and came over to her. "Eden! Boy, am I glad to see you." He gave her a light kiss on her forehead. "Crazy day today, wasn't it?"

"Yes." Crazy didn't begin to describe it. "Is something wrong?" She tossed her head toward the phone.

"Yeah." He held his waist and scratched the back of his head. "It's the sunglasses. My first delivery of inventory is due to arrive tomorrow. The shipping company just called and said they're not sending their ship to Shanghai until the Japanese stop sparring with the Chinese. It's ridiculous!"

Sparring? Eden frowned. "The inventory can't wait?"

"No!" He paced away. "I've got a huge gala planned to launch these glasses to the market. They won't even tell me when the products would get here."

Eden glanced away and hugged her arms closer. "I saw new

warships pulling into the Bund. All the commercial ships have halted."

"It's all temporary. Those Japanese warships shouldn't be an issue. I don't even know why the non-Chinese commercial ships have to stop running."

"Neil!" Eden glared. "Did you see what happened today?"

He dropped his shoulders and looked at her, his mouth agape.

"Did you see what the Japanese did?"

"No." His voice wavered. "I know they dropped bombs in Chapei. I saw a lot of people filling the streets from my office window. I didn't want to be caught in traffic, so I came home. When I got back, my staff at the office told me on the phone the Chinese and the Japanese were still shooting and bombing each other. I didn't want you to have to take the tram in this chaos and I told Carson to go pick you up from work."

Eden laughed in disbelief. "Neil, a lot of people died today. Thousands. The Japanese planes dropped bombs in the middle of the city." Tears rushed to her eyes again. "All those people you saw filling the streets are now homeless. Two hours ago, I saw a boy. He was trampled to death. And all you worry about are your sunglasses? What's wrong with you? What's wrong with all of you?" She covered her face and sobbed.

"Eden . . . I'm sorry. My God, I'm so sorry." He came over and put his arms around her. "I wasn't thinking."

"No, you weren't," she scolded him and wrested herself away from him. "What you ought to be thinking now is how we can help all those poor people!"

"You're right. You're absolutely right." He tried to console her. "I'm an idiot. Let me make up for it. Tell you what, I'll set up a relief fund for the refugees. Whatever I can do to help."

Heaving her chest, Eden wiped her tears with the back of her hand. Maybe she was being too harsh. Neil didn't see everything she saw. Charlie was right. She should get a good night's sleep. When her mind was clearer, she could write about what happened today so everyone including Neil would know. "I'm going home."

"You sure?" Neil asked. He looked sincerely sorry. "Don't leave yet. Stay for a while. Have dinner here with me."

"No." She sighed. Her eyes had dried. Exhaustion was weighing her down. "It's been a long day. I want to see my parents and Joshua."

"All right," he said, his voice full of regret. "Carson can drive you back."

"Thank you." Eden turned to leave.

"Wait!" Neil called her back.

"Yes?"

"If the commercial ships aren't coming, what about Isaac's parents?"

The Weissmans? They were so far away from what happened today, Eden hadn't even thought of them. True to his word, Neil had used his contacts and discovered that the Swiss bank account Isaac's neighbor had used to hide and deposit the Weissman's money was closed. Isaac and his parents were devastated when they found out. Once they learned what happened, Neil immediately offered to pay the Weissmans' way out of Germany. The only obstacle now was to find two spaces on a ship. More and more Jews were trying to leave, and every ocean liner that could carry them had a long waiting list.

"I still haven't been able to find passage for them," Neil said.

"What should we do?" Eden clasped and pulled her purse strap. "Should they even come to Shanghai?"

"Let's not panic yet," Neil said. "The Chinese and Japanese have always been at each other's throats. This might all blow over in a few days. Let's wait and see what happens. One way or another, we'll get his parents out of Germany. I promise."

Eden dropped her arm to the side. She hoped Neil was right. Not only because she desperately wanted to help Isaac and his parents, but also because of the frightening thought tucked in the back of her mind.

If China plunged deep into war and even the International Settlement fell, where would she and her family go?

She turned around and pushed that thought away.

27

BLOODY SATURDAY

IN HIS OFFICE, Clark hung up the phone and sat back in his seat. He needed a moment before making his next call. Since yesterday when the Japanese began demolishing Chapei, he had been on the phone non-stop. War had begun, and their army needed cash. A lot of cash. His most urgent task now was to raise as much funds as he could from everyone he knew who had the means. And for once, the country's heart was united. Patriotism, fury against Japan, and the pain of seeing the flow of Chinese blood prompted an outpour of support. Local tycoons he knew answered the call for help, no questions asked. Some even called him on their own. Beyond Shanghai, locals in Hong Kong and Singapore were rushing to set up relief funds to help the injured and homeless refugees. The passion of his own people to stand together gave him just the ray of hope to believe that they could defeat their enemy.

That hope came with a burden. As offers of help flooded in, so did the desperate cries from those who had lost homes, families, and businesses. To those who suffered losses, he had no good answer when they pleaded for help.

In his seat, he stared out at the violent rain splashing against the window. Under the angry gray clouds, flags and signs fluttered and flapped in the wind. As though Japan's aerial attack wasn't enough, a typhoon sweeping the coast of China had now come to Shanghai. Was it Heaven's wish that his country should fall, or was it Heaven's howl of torment to see his country stricken in ruins?

Was there no mercy for the thousands of refugees? Must they suffer the battering of the storm when they already lost everything they owned?

The minute hand of the clock on the wall struck five. Last night, he'd worked until well past eleven. With barely six hours of sleep that offered no rest, he returned here to his desk early in the morning. The office had stayed open all night. Staff members unaffected by the attack worked in shifts around the clock, doing whatever they could until weariness forced them to leave. Friday merged into Saturday but no one noticed the passing of the night.

At home, his mother and Mei Mei never made it onto the ship out of Shanghai. The sudden attack disrupted the entire city and all commercial vessels had canceled their journeys until further notice.

He picked up the phone, ready to call on the director of Kiangnan Paper Mill, but stopped. Should he give Ekaterina a call first? They hadn't spoken in weeks. Not since the fight broke out at Marco Polo Bridge. The conflict with Japan had sidelined him from everything else. He started dialing her number, but terminated the call. No. He wanted to call Eden first to make sure she and her family were okay. The shellfire must be terrifying to them.

"Counselor! Counselor!" A clerk barged into his office. "Something horrible just happened."

"What?" Clark asked.

"Our planes tried to bomb the *Idzumo* half an hour ago."

The *Idzumo*? The Imperial Japanese Navy's flagship that moored like a menace at the Whangpoo River?

"Our pilots missed! The bombs landed on Nanking Road. They struck the Cathay Hotel on the Bund! A lot of people on the street got hit."

"What were they doing?" Clark groaned. Their own pilots! How now would he and his government answer to that? China's own planes just killed its own people and brought casualties to the international district, including one of its most prestigious landmarks. In no time, this event would be all over the international news. Would it elicit sympathy from the world, or sneers at their military's incompetence?

Even worse, how many hundreds or thousands were killed?

"Understood," he told the clerk and tried to keep hold of his thoughts. His phone began ringing again. He reached out to pick it up. His secretary came running in and interrupted him.

"Counselor!"

"Yes?" He stopped and let the phone ring unanswered.

"Not good!" the secretary cried. "Another one of our planes just dropped a load of bombs on the Great World Amusement Center."

"Heavens!" he cried out. His body collapsed in his seat. Only one block away from the race course, the Great World at the corner of Avenue Edward VII was a giant complex filled with restaurants, food stalls, pubs and lounges, casinos, and theaters where Chinese and foreigners alike frequented for dining, drinks, and fun. To their credit, the Shanghailanders had stepped up overnight and made it into a refugee camp. Thousands of people who fled Chapei had found refuge there after they swarmed into the International Settlement.

Why? Why would the Chinese plane drop its bombs there?

"I need to talk to Sītu." He got up to try to get some answers.

In his office, Sītu sat at his desk, surrounded by the highest ranked members of their Bureau. With his eyes lowered, Sītu spoke on the phone. He made one phone call after another, sometimes getting through, sometimes not. "So this was the case," he muttered every so often while listening to whoever he was talking to on the other line. "Who do we talk to?" he asked. "When will we hear?" he demanded to know.

Forcing himself to be patient, Clark stood with the others, anxious to hear what caused the pilots to make such grave mistakes.

Finally, after what felt like an interminable wait, Sītu hung up. "It seems that the typhoon affected the pilots of our 5th Flying Group when they tried to bomb the *Idzumo*. They miscalculated the distance. In this weather, they needed to adjust the bombsights from a lower altitude before they struck."

The staff groaned.

"As for the Great World Amusement Center, the pilot's plane got damaged. He needed to unload the bombs to gain speed to escape."

"How could he!" one of the staff members cried. "There are thousands of people at the Great World! He dropped bombs there so he alone could escape?"

Others, too, cried out in outrage.

"That mixed-egg!"

"Dumber than a rice bucket. This kind of pilot, we'll obliterate ourselves without the Japanese."

"He should've flown away and let himself die."

Clark watched them condemn the pilot. The news stunted their spirits just when they felt a slight hint of hope. What was more, it blew open the weakness of the Chinese Air Force for all to see. Their poorly trained pilots couldn't handle the weather or the pressure.

"Enough, enough." Sītu slapped the top of his desk to get everyone's attention. "There is some good news. A squad under Gao Zhi-Hang's command shot down six Japanese planes. They returned with no casualties. This is the news we need to get out to the public."

No one cheered. The minor victory felt hollow compared to the horrific loss.

"As for the errant bombs on Nanking Road," Sītu continued, "we'll explain it was caused by turbulent winds. In regards to the Great World, we've been instructed to explain that Japanese anti-aircraft missiles had damaged our plane's bomb rack. Our pilot was injured and was unable to fly the plane away before the bombs dislodged."

The agents acquiesced with mumbles of yeses. As awful as the situation was, they still had to convince the public to stay on their side.

One by one, they returned to their offices. Their plodding footsteps as heavy as their hearts. On the main floor, Huang Shifu came running toward Clark with the receptionist behind him. "Young Master! Young Master! Something terrible happened!" he shouted. "You have to come home right away!"

"What's the matter?" Clark asked. He'd never seen his driver look so haunted.

"It's Master. He . . .he . . ."

"He what?" Clark grabbed the driver's arm. His co-workers crowded around him.

"He . . . He and Uncle Six were at the Bund. They went to look for our workers who were camping there. They heard some of the ones who got bombed out of Chapei had gone there."

At the Bund? That was all Clark heard. He didn't hear the rest. The world began to whirl behind him. His breaths shortened. His body felt paralyzed. His chest choked with horror. "Where on the Bund? On Nanking Road?"

"No. But they were near there. The bombs dropped and Master suffered a heart attack. Uncle Six tried to take him to the hospital but the streets are in chaos. So many people were injured. They were all trying to get to the hospitals. Uncle Six had no choice. He brought Master home. Madam sent me here to find you. She doesn't know what to do."

Clark's heart plunged. How could this be possible? With one disaster rolling in after another, how could Heaven seize his father too? "Take me home!" he said to Huang Shifu.

His mouth still open in fright, Huang Shifu bobbed his head and hurried toward the elevators. Clark followed. Things couldn't get this worse, he told himself. It couldn't. It was impossible. When he got home, he'd find out this was nothing but one big scare.

He repeated these thoughts over and over in his mind as Huang tried to speed up past the crowds of refugees that had overtaken the streets.

———

As soon as the car stopped in front of his house, Clark ran inside. The corridor and living room, normally full of life with servants carrying out their daily tasks, was empty. His heart sank further when he heard his mother's wails. Immediately, he ran upstairs. In his parents' bedroom, his mother knelt on the floor, her body collapsed over his father lying under the blanket on the bed with his eyes closed. Mei Mei and Wen-Ying huddled next to her, both with tears washing down their faces. Their servants and maids stood in the room, all sad and some crying.

"Young Master," Uncle Six came up to Clark. He wiped his wet eyes with the long, wide sleeve of his *tangzhuan* shirt. "Heaven has no eyes!" he cried. "Heaven has no eyes!"

"Ba? How is he?" Clark swung toward him. Uncle Six's face dropped and he shook his head.

"Ba!" Clark flung himself toward the bed. He grabbed his father's leg and tried to rock him awake. "Ba!"

Wen-Ying put her hand on his back. "Ba couldn't go on anymore," she whispered.

Clark stumbled back. How could this be? Just this morning, his father was eating breakfast with them. He talked at length about his plans for relocating their employees from Chapei into the make-shift dormitory in the new warehouse they bought next to the Do Kow Cotton Mill.

His mother gripped his father's arm. "Ren-Qiu! How can you leave us behind like this?" She cried out in pain. "I always told you to watch your health. You never listen to me. When you leave this way, what are we going to do now?"

"The bombs shocked him," Uncle Six said to Clark. "At first, the bombs were exploding only in the river. The planes were shooting at the Japanese ships, and we avoided the water. We were heading toward the crowd on Nanking Road to take a look when the bombs hit the ground. Then we turned around to run away. Master suddenly bent over and fainted. I dragged him to the car and we tried to rush him to the hospital. But so many ambulances were going there too. Master stopped breathing before we reached it. When we got there, a doctor said he must've had a heart attack and it was too late."

Tears welled in Clark's own eyes. Madam Yuan bawled, "Ren Qiu! Ren Qiu! Come back! Come back . . ." Mei Mei put her arms around her mother and sobbed.

Dazed and in shock, Clark raised his head and looked at everyone in the room. All strength and energy had gone out of his body. As he tried to make sense of what was happening, warplanes vroomed and reeled through the sky above, passing the International Settlement airspace on their way to deliver their blows of death.

At the *China Press* office, Eden gathered with the editorial staff to review their reports since the attack broke out in Chapei. Her sleep last night didn't bring peace to her mind, it gave her nightmares instead. But it did clear her mind enough for her to return to work this morning, and she was able to transpose the horrors she'd witnessed into words.

As for the *China Press*, Charlie Keaton's instructions were clear. They would not stand for Japan's aggression and their continual encroachment on the Chinese.

His position didn't surprise Eden. After all, the real owners of the *China Press* were Chinese. The pro-China slant did not bother her, not after what she saw yesterday. The Imperial Japanese Air Force slaughtered thousands of civilians. Civilians! The act was unforgivable. This morning, she drafted her article and told the world exactly what she saw. The headline: "Baby Killers: Japanese Army attacked Civilians." She wrote it with no regret. The article would appear in tonight's special evening edition. She hoped everyone would read it and see this horror for what it was.

At the table in the conference room, Charlie scribbled in his notepad. "Modern Warfare." He held up his notepad to show them the words. "This will be our theme tomorrow. The unimaginable destruction and consequences of war fought with modern technologies and machines. That will grab the attention of the world when the international press runs our syndicated articles. They'll be horrified when they see our pictures." He pointed his pen at the stack of photos showing the ravaged streets and injured bodies of civilians. Their staff photographers had taken yesterday.

Emmet picked up a picture of the razed buildings and shook his head.

"What else?" Charlie asked the team. "I want side stories. Something more focused on the human experience besides military actions and politics of the war."

"We can interview the refugees," Emmet said.

"What about the international community's efforts to assist the refugees?" Eden asked. "The Great World Amusement Center is now a refugee camp. The Jesuit Seminary is organizing volunteers to distribute clothing and food. My friend Miriam told me this morning she was going there today to help."

"Charlie! Charlie!" Dottie slammed open the door. "Oh my God!"

"What?" Charlie looked up.

"A bomb just dropped on the Cathay Hotel. The Chinese planes misfired their bombs onto Nanking Road. It made a direct hit on the street between the Cathay Hotel and the Palace Hotel."

"The Cathay Hotel?" Eden cried out. That was Sir Victor Sassoon's property. The prized jewel of his real estate holdings in Shanghai.

"There's more. One of the planes flew away from the Bund and dropped its bombs on the Great World."

"Jesus Christ!" Charlie cried out.

The staff around the table gasped and groaned in shock.

Eden immediately thought of Miriam. "Charlie, I need to go there. My friend Miriam is there. I have to go find her."

"It'll be chaos there," Emmet said. "You won't be able to find anybody."

"I don't care," Eden said. "I want to go." She pleaded to Charlie. "If you're sending us to the scenes, send me there."

Charlie glanced at her. "All right." He pointed his pen at Eden and two other reporters, plus two photographers sitting on her side of the table. "You, you, you, you too. Go and see what's happening at the Great World." He then pointed at Emmet and the reporters and photographers on the left side. "The rest of you, get yourselves to the Cathay Hotel and Nanking Road. Looks like we'll be working all night."

Eden jolted up from her seat and hurried to her desk. She stuffed a notepad and pencils into her purse. Without waiting for the others, she rushed off and hailed the first taxi she could find. On the way, she hunched in the seat, whispering prayers for her friend to be alive.

The taxi took Eden as far as it could up to the roadblocks set up by emergency rescuers. Unable to go any further by car, Eden got out and walked against the flow of traffic toward the Great World. The magnitude of the destruction revealed itself as she came nearer to the palatial amusement complex spanning the block. A bomb had hit the center of the building. It ripped the building open into a giant crater more than three meters long. Another bomb had torn away the building's facade on one side, exposing the interior from the fourth floor down to the ground. The explosions left behind a wreckage beyond any words she could use to describe the scene.

Stepping over shell fragments, hinges, electrical cables and cords strewn over broken rickshaws, doors, tires, fallen lamp posts, and pieces of walls, she tried to decide which direction to go. Sirens howling from fire trucks and ambulances split her ears. To avoid the noise, she walked left past the cries of the survivors and shouts of the police. As she came closer to the tram abandoned in the middle of its track, a frightening realization dawned on her. She was no longer a bystander observing from the outside. The lethal bombs had blasted away the protective bubble shielding the international community. Gravel, shattered glass, splintered wood, and stones crackled beneath her feet with each step she took.

But nothing could match the horror of human carnage before her. Corpses lay everywhere, some face down, some on their backs. Others lay mangled and twisted on their sides. A wave of nausea brimmed in her gut as she took in the sight of dismembered arms, headless torsos, and crushed legs scattered all over in pools of blood mixed with intermittent rain. Horrified, she closed her eyes. Gusts of typhoon wind blew in, spreading the billowing smoke and carrying with it the stench of burned human flesh.

Covering her nose and mouth, Eden turned her head to avoid the smell, only to be met with the sight of charred skeletons inside a car still searing in flames.

Where was Miriam? Did she escape? How could she find anyone in these ruins?

Two medics carrying a wounded man on a bamboo mat walked past her. Their shirts and pants reeked of blood. A truck pulled up to the sidewalk. Rescue workers jumped out and began lifting the dead bodies away. "Bring them over here if they're Chinese," one of them said. "If they're not, put them in that truck over there." He covered his nose with a handkerchief to ward off the stench and pointed across the street at another truck, where rescuers were hauling dead bodies into a pack of open coffins.

Warily, Eden walked toward the other truck. She'd take a quick look, that was all. Just to check and make sure.

Her breath quickened as she approached. The chance of her finding her friend there was nil, Eden told herself. Miriam could've escaped. Or maybe she was injured and was on her way to the hospital. Even if the unthinkable had happened, what were the odds of her happening upon Miriam's body in a random truck? Her whole run here was as good as a wild goose chase.

With quivering lips, she tried to laugh off her fears. She didn't really expect to find anyone. Not at all.

Reaching the other side of the street, she peeked at the open back of the truck. In a coffin, a man's body lay. His glassy blue eyes dead but wide open, still staring in shock at the unexpected catastrophe that had taken away his life. In the coffin next to him, a young man, his clothes blown away by the force of the blast. His naked body now nothing but the remains of a future that would never come to be. What would happen when his mother received the news? Eden's heart ached for her.

Gazing beyond the lad, she stopped her eyes at the woman in the coffin behind. At first, she didn't want to believe. And yet, reality struck. There she was. Her friend. A large piece of shrapnel had cut into her skull.

"Miriam!" Eden cried. "No! No!"

The rescuers came up beside her. They didn't catch her in time. She stumbled back and nearly fell. "Miriam!"

But her friend was gone. The wrath of war had come to destroy. It would spare no one caught in its way, not even the foreigners.

28

BURDEN OF THE FIRST-BORN SON

AT THE FUNERAL HOME, Clark knelt with his sobbing mother and sisters next to the coffin as the guests streamed in throughout the day to pay their respects. Behind him, a large framed portrait of his father sat on the altar. Every time he looked at it, his heart wrenched. This was all that was left of his father? A photograph of him smiling, with the smoke of burning incense blurring the view of his face and flowers blossoming uselessly next to his favorite dishes which he could no longer taste?

A year ago, when Clark came back to Shanghai from America, he'd thought he would work with his father for many, many years to come. Together, they would grow their family name into something even bigger. How did it happen that he was now wearing the white hemp cloth of mourning?

Outside on the steps in front of the entrance, a monk chanted continuously as he burned offerings of joss papers, the currency of the dead, which his father could use on the other side. If an afterlife did exist, would the amount of cash for the dead they were burning be enough? Clark had wanted to burn a lot more. But so many people were killed in the city last week, the city had sold out of things needed for wakes and funerals. In fact, if it weren't for the help of Xu Hong-Lie, Uncle Six's nephew who had joined the Yuan Enterprises eight months ago, they might have even missed out on getting a coffin. The foreign and local governments had to bury thousands of corpses last week without coffins in mass graves. The funeral homes were overwhelmed. They couldn't handle services for so many deaths all at once. His mother suffered another blow when she learned that they weren't able to buy a paper car and driver to burn for the funeral offerings. The funeral homes had run out of stock.

His poor mother. It might sound trivial, but Clark understood how much she needed to feel she was still doing everything she could for her husband.

Luckily, Hong-Lie was able to find a paper house with servants and a paper outfit of a suit with a gold watch. Clark didn't even ask how much those items cost. If there really was an afterlife, he hoped his father would understand that they were trying to give him everything they could.

What must the king of hell be thinking now when the masses of spirits were suddenly arriving at his gate to receive his judgment? Was it anything like seeing the scores of refugees now filling the city? Would he mark in his ledger all those who were to blame for this tragedy so that he could hold them accountable when their final days came?

Gao Zhen, director of the Shanghai Commercial and Savings Bank and a longtime family friend, arrived with his wife. Clark, as the eldest son, bowed and greeted them when they came up to him. They had already come once to pay their respect during the seven-day wake before the funeral. Seeing the Gaos gave Clark another layer of guilt on top of his grief. Gao was among the wealthy in Shanghai who Clark had pressured into funneling cash to the KMT. The big-hearted man nonetheless had come today to share their grief.

The Gaos walked up to the altar, and they each offered three sticks of burning incense to the deceased. While they bowed,

Madam Yuan broke out crying again. "Ren-Qiu! What a horrible way you died!" She wailed and pounded the floor, then fainted and collapsed. Quickly, Wen-Ying rushed to pull her to the back row of empty seats on the side. Their maid, Xiaochun, went over with a wet towel and menthol oil for her head.

Gao Zhen finished the offering ritual and came back to Clark while his wife spoke to Mei Mei. Gao gave Madam Yuan a side glance and put his hand on Clark's elbow. "Your family depends on you from now on. Going forward, you'll have to take more caution in your actions. Beware not to let anyone sway you to do wrong."

"I know." Clark nodded. He felt so ashamed.

"If there's anything I can do to help, come find me."

"Thank you."

After the Gaos left, Clark wiped a tear with his sleeve. With his father gone, his entire family and everyone who depended on them were now looking to him. How would he shoulder this burden alone when grief was tearing him apart inside and a war was waging outside?

At the entrance, Uncle Six and Xu Hong-Lie greeted Eden and her family at the reception table. Hong-Lie offered them each a piece of candy to lighten the bitterness of death and a red envelope with a coin for good luck to take with them when they left. As Eden walked toward the altar, Clark felt a comforting warmth spreading in his chest. It was the first good feeling he'd experienced since the war broke out.

The Levines came to the altar and a servant offered them each three sticks of incense. Eden exchanged a look with Clark. Even without words, he knew she understood his pain.

When they finished, Eden came over to him. "How are you?"

He tried to answer, but instead had to swallow the lump in his throat.

"I'm so sorry about what happened. My father's been volunteering nonstop at the Red Cross Hospital trying to help. I can't believe this. So many people . . ." Her voice trailed off and she wiped the tears from her eyes. "My friend Miriam died too. She was at the Great World when the bombs hit. She was my first friend in Shanghai."

"That's terrible. I'm sorry to hear that."

Eden sniffled and put on an upbeat smile. "Your father was such a good man. He was so welcoming when we first came to China. I remember him giving us maps of the city, recommending restaurants for the best Chinese food. That was all before you came back to Shanghai."

Clark eased his face. "Thank you for saying that." Hearing Eden's voice gave him a gush of strength.

Eden looked around them. "How's Ekaterina?"

"Ekaterina?" Clark didn't know. He hadn't heard from her. And with the outbreak of war and his father's death, he hadn't had a chance to think about her at all. He should send her a message after the funeral.

For now, he tried to think of something to say in response. "She . . ." A sudden urge came over him. He wanted to tell Eden the whole affair with Ekaterina was a lie. What did it all matter now anyhow? He wanted to tell Eden the truth.

"Clark," Dr. Levine said, interrupting his thoughts. He and Mrs. Levine had finished talking to Mei Mei. "Our condolences. We're so, so sorry."

"Thank you." Clark bowed his head.

"Let us know if there's anything we can do." Mrs. Levine said and put her arm around Joshua's shoulders.

"I will." Clark flashed his eyes back at Eden. The words he wanted to say stuck at his throat and he had no way of getting them through to her with her parents and brother around.

"I still have your father to thank for sending so many Chinese patients to me," Dr. Levine said. "I might've lost my whole practice last year if it weren't for my Chinese patients."

Clark nodded. "We owed it to you for helping my father get

well. I only regret this city is now so dangerous. All the bombings and attacks must be so unnerving to you."

"We can handle it," Dr. Levine said. "This country gave us a place to land when we needed one. Now it's our turn to stand behind it. Besides, we're not the victims here. I've been volunteering at the Red Cross Hospital, doing what little I can. It's heartbreaking seeing all the people injured and dying. Thankfully, Eden's friend, Neil, set up a relief fund. That's been a godsend."

Neil Sassoon? Clark glanced over at Eden. Eden averted her eyes.

"He's been giving us the use of his driver too," Mrs. Levine added. "It makes moving about in the city so much easier. The buses and trams are no longer running outside of the foreign districts. They're always crowded now. The ladies from our synagogue and I have been bringing food to people in refugee camps. We wouldn't be able to do that without the car and the driver."

"That's very kind of you all to help." Clark lowered his gaze. Of course Neil Sassoon would be there for them. How rash of him to have nearly told Eden the truth about him and Ekaterina. Eden probably didn't care one way or the other.

"Take good care." Dr. Levine patted him on the arm. Mrs. Levine and Joshua both said goodbye. Eden gave him a sympathetic smile and followed her family out. From behind, Clark watched her silhouette disappear, taking away the last remnant of what might have been the joy and hope of his life in a world plagued by the misery of war.

29

FLAG OF THE RISING SUN

ON HIS WAY to the Shanghai mayor's press conference, Clark gazed out the car window at the Old City in the southern part of Shanghai still under Chinese control. "Control" was an overstatement. The traffic lights ahead, if still intact, no longer blinked. On the sidewalks, rubble and garbage piled up, sometimes next to corpses. Across the road, a mob of people crowded in front of a store, jostling to buy rice. This sector might as well be a battered man breathing its last breath.

How could Heaven let this bright city fall so fast to ruins? Did the soldiers of the 9th Army Group not show enough of its worth? For eight weeks, these German-trained troops fought back, rifles and bayonets against cannons hurling from the sea. Without a navy of its own, China could only watch as the Japanese navy fired their missiles and demolished buildings and people. It could not stop the endless waves of Japanese troops arriving by water to replace the ones the Chinese soldiers had taken out on land.

In vain, the Chinese Air Force tried to sink the *Idzumo,* the naval destroyer that was Japan's symbol of pride. But in the sky too, Hirohito's warplanes reigned. The typhoon that had swept the city when the siege began eventually petered out, but the IJA continued the storm with its own rain of death. The Chinese's anemic fleet of Curtiss Hawks could not drive the enemy planes away.

Still, the Chinese soldiers held on. Forty thousand lives already lost, and still, they would not surrender. No one thought they would last this long. No one expected these poorly equipped and thinly supported men to show such valor. Could Heaven not grant the city they were trying to protect a veil of mercy for all they had done?

Apparently not. Relentless shelling had leveled the northern parts of Shanghai from Chapei, Putoong, to Nanshi. In late August, the Sincere Department Store fell to aerial bombs. After that, the South Train Station. In one raid, thousands of refugees who were waiting for trains to escape to the southern cities were mutilated and killed.

Within the sandbagged fortress of the International Settlement, Clark watched his city's demise. Their casualties kept mounting. The black armband he wore on his sleeve felt like a mark of mourning not only for his father, but also for the death of Shanghai itself.

For two months, life in the Old City south of the Frenchtown went on. For a while, geography kept the terror contained in the north. But five days ago, when the Japanese took advantage of their dominance at sea and deployed their troops at Hangzhou Bay, the Chinese troops finally had to retreat inland. On the Whangpoo River, the *Idzumo* sailed, a blatant declaration of Japan's victory.

What would happen now?

In the passenger seat beside him, Xu Hong-Lie, the nephew of Uncle Six, wondered out loud, "The mayor will probably surrender."

Clark pulled his eyes back from the window. "It's possible," he said. He had not heard anything definitive yet from the city's officials. Then again, nothing was definitive anymore. Without their army, the Nationalist government in Shanghai would soon crumble. No direction had been given by the central government. Everybody was now on his own. Among those working for the KMT, no one knew what anybody else would do.

It wouldn't make any difference to him anyhow. Since his father passed away, his priority was to look after his family, the business his father left behind, and all the people they employed. He'd tried to divide his time between his home and his work with the KMT, but the events of the war outpaced him and he could not keep up.

Thanks to his father's foresight, they had already moved the manufacturing equipment of their battery plant into the International Settlement. While Clark was preoccupied with helping the Party fend off Japan during the summer months, his father had transferred most of their properties and companies into foreign sectors. The factory was their last major concern when war broke out. Over the last eight weeks, they had brought as many workers as they could into the make-shift dormitory in their new plant. That cautious act in the end saved hundreds of lives.

When his father died and all the burden of continuing the work fell onto Clark, it was Xu Hong-Lie who'd stood by him. Hong-Lie made sure that every division of the Yuan Enterprises would continue to run and all the processes Clark's father had implemented were put into place. Clark couldn't have handled it all without him. Uncle Six, his father's right-hand man, was besotted by grief. Hong-Lie, who was closer to Clark's age and not nearly as emotionally tied to Clark's father, stepped into his uncle's place and gave Clark all the information and help he needed to help him take over control.

Looking at the ruin that was Shanghai now, Clark could not deny feeling regret for his decision to delay joining his family business. In the end, did his work for the KMT make any difference? He could've spent his last year working with his father. He would've cherished that experience, and he wouldn't have had to scramble to pick up the pieces as he was doing now.

The car arrived at the Shanghai municipal government building, where a scatter of journalists stood to listen to the mayor of Shanghai speak. Yu Hung-Chun, nominally still the head of the city, took to the microphone. Clark walked closer to the front, with Hong-Lie following behind him. He didn't have high hopes for Mayor Yu to deliver any news that could save them from doom. He only came to find out if the city government—or what remained of it—had any final plan to evacuate this sector. He also wanted to see how the people would react.

The mayor stood at the podium and gazed out at the audience. "Thank you for coming," he said. His demeanor still defiant and resolute.

The reporters mumbled in response. Clark stood to the side against the wall and crossed his arms.

"Hmm-mm." Mayor Yu cleared his throat. "Let me begin by saying that we're not yet ready to give up. We cannot accept Japan's blatant aggression. Japan disrespected our rights as a sovereign nation. They created the incidents to draw us into war. They obstructed all efforts by the international community to bring a truce . . ."

Clark stared at the ground. What good was this rhetoric? In Shanghai at least, grandstanding now would only waste time. Was Yu speaking at the direction of the central government? How did he think he could still use words to save face?

"Our city's direction will not change under any circumstances." Mayor Yu shook his finger in the air. "Our soldiers will defend us. Our people's hearts are of one mind. I am here, standing on your side. Together, we will unite our heart and strength, and fight Japan until death."

The audience responded with another doubtful buzz of

mumbles. The mayor's fervent speech failed to elicit passion or applause. Clark looked over his shoulder to Hong-Lie. "Let's go."

Hong-Lie smirked. He stepped aside to let Clark walk ahead of him and they returned to their car. As they drove back to the International Settlement, Clark directed Huang Shifu to take him to the KMT Foreign Affairs Bureau. Earlier in the morning, Sītu had called and asked him to stop by.

While in traffic, Clark asked Hong-Lie, "Did you see all those people pushing and shoving to buy rice when we were driving to the press conference?"

"How could I have missed that?" Hong-Lie said. "I feel sorry for them, but it makes me nervous too."

"I agree. If this war continues, the city will have a food shortage. You go ahead back to our main office first. Huang Shifu can come back to pick me up. I want you to start making calls and find out how we can stockpile a reserve of food. We should figure out a place to securely store it too. I don't know how bad things will get. It'll be good to have enough reserved for our employees."

Hong-Lie looked at him with a light grin. "How much is enough?"

Clark paused, not quite understanding the question.

"How much would be enough for you?" Hong-Lie asked.

This time, Clark loosened and chuckled. At least Hong-Lie could still joke. Of course, they couldn't possibly buy enough. The war had no end in sight.

The car pulled up to the front of the Foreign Affairs Bureau. Huang Shifu got out to open the door.

"Relax a little," Hong-Lie said to Clark, more like a confidant than someone talking to a superior. "You take too many worries onto yourself. You alone can't solve every problem. If you collapse too, it'll be a disaster for everyone. If you need help, my uncle and I are here. We'll do our best to support you."

"Thank you." Clark nodded, then got out of the car. How

fortunate for him that Hong-Lie was here at this difficult time. He should take it as a sign. In Heaven, there is no road to a dead end. He should not let himself fall into despair yet.

———

It had been more than a week since Clark last came to the Foreign Affairs Bureau. The floor now was all but deserted. The phones had stopped ringing. The clatters of typewriters had ceased. All the lower and mid-level staff were gone. Many who had lived outside of the foreign-occupied sectors had deserted their posts to seek refuge. Others had lost faith in the Party and had left to find ways to cope and survive.

Who could blame them? The Party's central regime in Nanking itself had fled the city and gone inland, leaving few instructions on what should happen next.

Most of the senior aides, too, were nowhere in sight. Only a few remained, rushing to destroy records and documents at the last minute. Tang Wei's desk was empty. Had he fled too? Clark wondered.

In his office, Sītu gathered his belongings and put them into his briefcase. Clark interrupted him and knocked on his door. "Deputy Secretary."

"Yuan Guo-Hui?"

Clark glanced at his briefcase.

Shamefaced, Sītu put away the last of his documents. "Our situation now, you can see for yourself."

"Our soldiers put up a good fight."

"They did," Sītu said. "It's a shame we lost our best fighters here. The Generalissimo is moving the capitol to Chungking. He's redeploying the troops to Kunshan and Wufu." He tucked in his chin and muttered, "If they're not already too exhausted to make it there."

Another heart wrench. After the bloodbath, their army didn't even have the support to bring their soldiers to safety. The poor men had to try to get there themselves on foot.

"There will be a plane leaving for Chungking tomorrow. It'll be taking key officials from Shanghai. The Party will help us regroup when we arrive."

Clark smiled at the irony. "Just now, Mayor Yu told everyone at the press conference we'd fight till death. He said our direction hadn't changed."

"Mayor Yu will be on the plane. I'm certain about that," Sītu said.

So, Yu outright lied. With leaders like him, no wonder their country could not stand. When the news articles came out tomorrow, everyone would find out he'd abandoned them here.

"If you want, you can come with us." Sītu shut his briefcase. "We can still use someone like you. Perhaps even more so now than ever."

"Thank you for the offer," Clark said. "But right now, my family needs me."

Sītu nodded. "I thought you'd say that."

"If I can still be of help in Shanghai, you can contact me."

"That would be good, especially if you can maintain your connections with the foreign governments. Maybe one day, our regime will return."

Clark straightened his stand. "Take care."

"You too."

Sītu picked up his briefcase and exited his office. After he left, Clark looked out the window. There lay the future, uncertain, shrouded in gray clouds. Nonetheless, he'd made the choice to remain behind, for better or for worse.

If Mayor Yu's escape after his passionate speech had dealt the last blow to the city's morale, then the Japanese' victory parade on the same day was a slap in a dead man's face. Emboldened by their win, Japan demanded to march through the International Settlement north to south from the Chapei to the Old City. The Shanghai Volunteer Corp., all teeth and no bite, gave in.

From the window of Joseph Whitman's office at the American consulate, Clark watched the Japanese troops flaunt their triumph. The arrogant way they strode through the streets in front of all the Western foreigners, unopposed and unrestrained, ate him up inside. Civilian Japanese crowded the street, waving their flags, shouting *"Banzai"* in celebration of the ruins their soldiers had created. If his mind could kill, he would blast that red orb of rising sun to nothing.

"Clark?" Joseph returned to his office. A dark-haired gentleman followed behind him.

"Yes." Clark turned around.

"Sorry to keep you waiting." Whitman invited him and the gentleman to take a seat. "Clark, allow me to introduce. This is Cornell Franklin, Chairman of the Shanghai Municipal Council."

"We've met before." Clark extended his hand. "You were at the Chamber of Commerce Ball."

"Yes, I remember." Franklin shook his hand. His firm grip and straight smile gave Clark a jolt in the spirits.

"Cornell's from Mississippi originally," Joseph said. "He practiced law in Hawaii. He served as a judge in the First Circuit before he came to join the U.S. Court for China in Shanghai."

Politely, Clark listened as he observed the judge.

"We want you to know you still have friends in this city," Franklin said to him.

"Thank you," Clark said. It was kind of them to still remember him.

"We value your friendship too. The reason we've asked you to come today is, we want you to consider taking your father's seat on the Council."

"Me?" Clark asked. Joining the Shanghai Municipal Council was the last thing on his mind.

"Yuan Enterprises has escaped the Japanese attack relatively intact. With so many Chinese companies destroyed, we'd like to work with you. Your company's fuel and energy business is vital to the International Settlement. We can work together. Having you on board on the SMC will be beneficial to both of us."

Clark stared at the two men. "I don't know what to say. I'm flattered. I honestly haven't thought about it."

"Understandable," said Franklin. "You've had a lot to deal with recently."

"The situation's a win-win," Whitman chimed in. "The KMT government might no longer be here, but we still have a large Chinese population to contend with. We also have to care for the flood of refugees. We can really use a Chinese member like you who can directly liaise with the local people."

"Joe's right," Franklin said. "Your family is well-respected in Shanghai. Having you on the Council will help keep peace in our sector. Wouldn't you want peace too? Peace for you to continue your family's business, and peace for your countrymen to recover and return to a more stable society? They've lost so much already."

"Yes," Clark said. He looked at Whitman. From Whitman's smile, he realized this was Whitman's way to try to help him out. Their offer was the first good thing that had come his way since the war broke out in Shanghai.

This was what Whitman meant when he told him they were links in a chain that towed the world forward.

"Thank you," Clark said. "Thank you so much. I'd be happy to accept. I'll be glad to do for this city what my father would've done had he been here."

"Excellent." Whitman exhaled a deep breath. Franklin leaned forward and offered Clark his hand. People said one could tell a lot about a man by his handshake. Clark hoped that was true. Franklin's handshake felt warm and reliable. Without his father or his government now, he needed to build new columns he could rely on if he and those who depended on him were to survive.

30

THE COLLABORATORS' TURN

LIKE A TERRIBLE STORM that had finally passed, the blasts, whistles, pops, and clatters that had terrorized the city eventually came to an end. With Shanghai now under enemy occupation, the still-raging war had moved South.

Needless to say, Japan's destructive force continued.

At the office that used to be his father's, Clark put away the newspaper filled with articles on the latest reports and news about the war. He picked up the smiling Buddha figurine on the desk. What made his father buy this little ornament? Was it a token for good luck? Or was it a gift from a client or a friend?

Clark returned the figurine to its place and ran his hands over the desk surface. His father used to sit here every day. Being here, he could still feel his father's presence. That feeling, real or not, brought him a gentle wave of comfort.

His father would be pleased to know their business had returned to full operations. For their employees who had lost homes or family during the battle, he had given them money and other forms of help. His father's soul in Heaven could rest in peace if he were looking down.

More correctly, he would rest in peace, as long as he didn't look over to the former Chinese sectors. Japan had taken those as their occupied zones. He dreaded to guess what life was like for those who had not escaped.

Gathering his thoughts, Clark picked up the phone and dialed the Metropole Hotel. He still had one unfinished piece of business related to the KMT.

The receptionist's answer took him by surprise. "I'm sorry, sir, but Princess Ekaterina had moved out."

"Moved out? When?"

"Let me check . . . Two weeks ago."

Two weeks? Did she receive his messages? Why didn't she call him back?

Could she have left the country along with all the foreign women and children who fled the city when the Japanese bombing began? That would be the most likely explanation.

This woman. He actually worried about her. In return, she didn't even say goodbye.

"Is there anything else I can help you with, sir?" the hotel receptionist asked.

"No. Thank you very much." Clark hung up the phone. At least that chapter was finally over. A lot of good it had done.

A knock came on his door. "Director Yuan?" his secretary asked on the other side.

"Yes, come in." Clark put away a file on his desk.

The girl came in with Tang Wei. "This gentleman wants to see you. He said he and you are old friends."

Surprised, Clark stood up.

"Yuan Guo-Hui, how are you?" Tang Wei smiled.

"How is it you're still here?" Clark asked.

Tang took a seat across from his desk, as though nothing had passed between them and nothing had changed.

Slowly, Clark sat down. "I thought you had already left the city."

"Leave the city?" Tang laughed. "I almost did, but thought

better of it." He ran his eyes around at the room. "Nice office. Much better than our old office at the Foreign Affairs Bureau."

The secretary returned with a pot of tea and a cup for the guest. Clark motioned for her to close the door on her way out.

"Didn't Sītu or someone from the KMT invite you to go with them to Nanking?" he asked.

"He did." Tang pulled out a pack of cigarettes and lit one up. Clark pushed the ashtray on the desk toward him. Tang nodded thanks and took a deep drag. "I declined." He blew out a cloud of smoke.

"You declined? Why?"

"Look at how the Japanese ravaged this country from north to south these last four months. The Party has no hope to fight back and win. I don't want to bet on the wrong horse anymore. Why follow Chiang Kai-shek to rule a bunch of bumpkins inland only to watch them fail."

"So what do you plan to do now?" Clark asked.

Tang took the butt of the cigarette out of his lips. "I've thought it through. Rather than fight against the tide, I've decided to make peace with the inevitable. The Japanese need help putting this city back in order. I'm going to help them."

"You're working with the Japanese?" Clark balked. He never expected this from Tang Wei.

"I didn't come to this decision lightly," Tang said. "Think about it. Those shorties have this city now, whether we like it or not. We can leave it to them to try to run this place their way, or people like me can step in and smooth the relations between the conqueror and the occupied. Our people can only benefit from having at least some Chinese in charge. It'll be better for them in the end."

"You're justifying!"

"And you're letting your emotions do the talking. In truth, this is the best solution."

"I don't want to listen to this anymore." Clark threw up his hand. "Why did you come to tell me all this?"

"I came to ask if you want to join me." Tang Wei spread his elbows on the armrests. "I thought it'd be a chance for you too. If you want, I can put you in touch with the right people."

"Join you to collaborate with the Japanese? Never!" He couldn't even believe Tang asked.

"Being patriotic won't do you any good." Tang Wei took another drag. "I tell you, you have a lot more at stake than me. The shorties would love to do business with you. They desperately need fuel, batteries, and energy. If you use your head, you'd realize it's in your own interest to work with them. You never listened to me when I warned you to look out for yourself. This time, you really should."

Clark bolted up from his seat. "Get out." He pointed at the door. "You are a thief who'd sell out your own country. I don't have friends like you."

Tang Wei's mouth dropped open. But quickly, he regained his composure. "You idiot." He stubbed out his cigarette. "There's treasure on the ground and you don't even know how to pick it up. Let's watch you run your father's business to ruins."

"Get out!" Clark pointed to the door again. "From now on, don't ever return."

Tang stood up. At the door, he gave Clark one last look of disdain, then left and swung closed the door.

Alone in the room, Clark's fury broke and he swiped the papers and pen on his desk to the side. How could Tang Wei go down that road? How could he collaborate with the enemy after seeing them slaughter thousands of their own people and obliterate their cities? And then he had the gall to come and ask him to do the same? To see Tang betraying their own . . . it was no less than a knife stabbing at his heart.

He took a deep breath, then fixed the mess he'd made. What Tang Wei chose to do was his own choice. A lot would be changing in the coming days. He needed to keep his mind clear and confront every situation as it came.

Another knock came on the door. "What is it?" Clark called out.

Xu Hong-Lie entered. "We have a problem."

"What problem?"

"We went back to our old factory this morning to retrieve the supply of materials we hadn't moved yet to the new plant . . ."

"Yes?" Clark knew that. During the early weeks of the Japanese invasion in Shanghai, they'd moved all the battery plant's equipment to the new location in the International Settlement. The owner of Do Kow Cotton Mill who sold them the new plant had gone above and beyond to let them enter the new factory premises before the property sale even closed. The only thing they hadn't gotten out in time were the battery production materials.

The Yuans' old go down was near Jessfield Park and close to the Jessfield railway station. Since it was located in the western suburbs, it'd been spared from major damages from the shelling. Hong-Lie had gone back to retrieve the materials so they could resume production at the new plant.

"What happened?" Clark asked.

"Someone stopped us."

"Who? The Japanese soldiers?"

"Liu Kun. He said he's now the new district director in that area."

"Seriously?" Clark asked. Liu Kun was the member of the SMC who Soong Mei-Ling forced out when Clark bargained with her to give his father a seat on the Council. "Is this a joke? How can he be the new district director?"

"He had Japanese soldiers with him," Hong-Lie said.

That meant Liu Kun had turned and become an enemy collaborator too. Just like that, their own people had folded one by one at the feet of the short emperor.

Hong-Lie came closer to the desk. "He said we have to apply for a license to move our properties. He also said our factory ownership is under review. He claims the Provisional Government of the Republic of China is examining all the real property ownership in the occupied areas for prospective requisitions."

Clark shook his head. Like that old saying, a June debt called for a quick settlement. His demand knocked Liu Kun down, now it was Liu Kun's turn to return the blow.

And let them not forget his former fiancée Shen Yi was Liu Kun's new bride. Surely, she was having the last laugh now.

Provisional Government of the ROC. Clark smirked. Why not just outright call it the Imperial Government of Showa?

"What should we do?" Hong-Lie asked. "The materials that are still in there are worth a lot. We'd take a big loss if we don't get them back. Worse yet, we can't start production. It'll be a while before we can get new orders of supplies. The commercial shipping lines are still trying to return to normal operation."

Clark sat down and folded his hands on his desk. "Let me think about this. I'm not sure there's much we can do." He couldn't see Liu Kun giving him any leeway.

"All right." Hong-Lie backed away.

A light knock sounded on the open door. Wen-Ying poked in her head. "Ge?"

"*Daxiaojie,*" Hong-Lie greeted her. Wen-Ying nodded and acknowledged him.

"What brought you here?" Clark asked her.

"I want to talk to you." She entered the room.

"I'll get back to work." Hong-Lie excused himself, then left and closed the door.

"Have a seat," Clark said. "What do you want to talk about? It can't wait till I come home?"

"I don't want to talk about this at home in case Ma hears us."

She opened her purse on her lap, then shocked him by pulling out a handgun. She placed it on his desk.

Clark frowned. He sat up. "What's this for?"

"For you. You should carry it on you from now on as a precaution." She warned him in a low voice. "The Japanese army is all around us. For Chinese locals with power, they'll want to force them to collaborate. They'll want to eliminate those who won't. They already started. Tian Di Hui got wind."

Tian Di Hui. The reminder of the Heaven and Earth Society added another layer of stress he didn't need. Was Wen-Ying safe being a part in their underground resistance movement?

"We're targets. Especially you."

The thought made him shiver.

"I already arranged for bodyguards to accompany Ma and Mei Mei around the clock. I'd do the same for you too, but I didn't think you'd like that."

Clark nodded. Wen-Ying, who was as bright as ice and snow. Always smart and capable. In these uncertain times, she had thought of what he didn't. "I wish Ma would go to Hong Kong and take cover until we know how everything will turn out," he said.

"Me too," Wen-Ying agreed. The commercial passenger ships were running again now. The foreigners had been sending their wives, girlfriends, and children away in droves, but their mother wouldn't leave because their father died. She insisted she wouldn't leave him behind. Nothing he and Wen-Ying said could change her mind, and Mei Mei wouldn't leave if no one else from the family would leave. She said she would live and die together with all of them.

"What about you?" Clark asked.

Wen-Ying shrugged. "Don't worry about me. I'm a Tian Di Hui member. I know how to protect myself."

That didn't stop him from worrying. "What is Tian Di Hui

331

plotting to do? What are you doing for them now? Are you in danger?"

"I can't tell you," Wen-Ying said and got up. "Be careful," she warned him again and took off.

Clark stared at the handgun on his desk. He picked it up and turned it over. The world he lived in just grew another shade darker.

31

SEIZING THE MOMENT

AT THE OLD CITY just south of the Frenchtown border, Eden followed Father Jacquinot de Besange through the Nanshi Refugee Zone. The tall, one-armed Jesuit priest had set up this special demilitarized zone to house thousands of Chinese refugees whose homes had been destroyed during the eight weeks of battle between the China and Japan. Wherever they walked, crowds of Chinese would wave at him, welcoming the approaching sight of him with his round-rimmed glasses and his short but thick square mat of gray beard. Every so often, he would raise and tip his fedora to the delight of the Chinese ladies sheltered at the camp. How remarkable it was to see him bring a smile to these poor women huddling in a swamp of misery, their future unknown.

But what Father de Besange had done was so much more. Miraculously, the man had negotiated an agreement with the French concession government and the war authorities on both the Chinese and Japanese sides to allow for this space to keep the civilian refugees safe. Unbelievably, every side so far had respected the agreement too.

"You can see here, we've been giving out steamed buns and

333

bread to the people every day." The priest pointed his wooden arm at the table set up at a storefront where volunteers were passing out food. Eden jotted down the details of the scene in her notebook. Two Chinese kids about twelve or thirteen jostled each other, trying to get into the line of people waiting hungrily for their share. Accidentally, the kids bumped into a Japanese soldier passing by. The soldier glared and shouted at them. The kids' eyes widened in terror, and they stood frozen in place. Father de Besange frowned and walked over to them.

"Go on, move on along." He knocked his wooden arm on the soldier's head. "Don't you have to get back to your unit?"

Startled, the soldier took a step back. He stared at the priest, who was a full head taller than him, then grumbled and walked away.

Eden, dumbfounded, stopped writing.

Father de Besange paid no more attention to the Japanese. He raised his wooden arm at the building on the block next to the food relief tables. "I'm planning to convert that building into a school." He watched the clusters of refugees and shook his head. "I can't see how these people will be able to go back to where they used to live. Their homes are gone. Besides, it won't be safe for them to go back. What we'll have to do is help them build a new life here within this safety zone. Here, I've got the officials to allow me to have a Chinese police force to maintain protection and order." He led Eden down the block. "So we'll have a school there. Getting children back into classes is a priority. We'll set up a hospital too. That's a necessity. And then, maybe we'll have a community center to help everyone find jobs and help them transition to a new phase of life."

"This is incredible, Father." Eden scribbled her last note. "God only knows what would've happened to these poor people without you."

"Eh." The priest dismissed her praise with a wave of his hand. "I'm only doing what any person should do when they see fellow humans suffer. I'm looking forward to reading your write-up, Miss Levine. You be sure to include the information I gave you about donations. We have a lot of people in need here. We have thousands of mouths to feed every day until they get back on their feet. And it's November. The weather's getting cold so we'll need clothes and blankets."

"Of course, Father. I'll do anything I can to help," Eden said as she put her pencil and notepad back into her purse. "Thank you for your time."

The gentle priest said goodbye and went back to his flock of refugees huddled on the sidewalk. A group of small children ran up and caught the bottom of his swaying coat. Watching them, Eden felt almost moved to tears.

A car honked behind her and Eden turned around. Neil waved from the passenger side window. She waved back and went toward him. Carson opened the door and she climbed in. "Thank you for coming to get me."

"Don't mention it," Neil said as Carson got back inside and drove them away. "I want you to be safe."

Grateful, she moved closer to him. The drive back to the Frenchtown was normally easy, but with all the barbwire and sandbags still surrounding the foreign-occupied sectors, they had to drive all the way around the border to the entrance where they could get across.

"Do you have to go back to the office for anything?" Neil asked.

"No." Eden checked her watch. Five thirty. It'd be another hour before they could get back and the office would be closed except for the printing staff. "I'm calling it a night."

"Good. I have something special planned for us."

"Oh? What's that?"

"Later. It's a surprise."

Eden wrapped her arm around his. The car slowed down to turn a corner and she watched a riot break out on the side of the street they passed. These riots happened very often now. People were fighting over the diminishing supply of food in the areas the Japanese had conquered. How ugly would things get if normal city operations didn't begin again soon in these places? Were the residents inside Frenchtown and the International Settlement safe? What if the rioters tore down the barricades and broke through en masse because they were hungry?

The car entered the International Settlement, passing a woman holding her toddler while gazing across the barbwire. Eden stared at her empty face. No sadness, no fright. She just looked weary and empty. She had never seen an expression of such total loss of hope.

Nearby, a group of Ta Tao policemen—the newly formed police corp under the command of the Japanese for the invaded areas—held up a hand grenade at the members of the Shanghai Volunteer Corp standing guard at the border. "Come closer," they shouted to the SVC guards. "We dare you to come closer."

The SVC guards didn't answer. They didn't even dare to look the Ta Tao police in the eye. They moved further back when their harassers lobbed the grenade across. Thankfully, it was only a scare and the grenade did not explode.

In their car, neither Neil nor Eden said anything. All they could do was lower their heads and look the other way.

They arrived at the Park Hotel on Bubbling Well Road and Neil brought her up to the swanky dining room on the top floor. The host seated them at a candlelit table next to the spacious glass facade.

"I didn't expect this." Eden sat down and smoothed her skirt. "What's the occasion? I feel underdressed."

The sommelier came over and poured them each a glass of champagne. She raised the glass, ready to take a sip, but Neil stopped her with his hand. "Wait."

A waiter came and gave her a single rose, then bowed and walked away.

Eden pushed aside the menu and picked up the flower. "What's this?"

"I've been thinking . . ." Neil reached into the inner pocket of his jacket and pulled out a little square jewelry box. "We've known each other for almost a year. In all my life, I've never met anyone like you."

"Neil . . ." Eden shifted her eyes around. This sounded like . . . no . . . he wasn't doing this, was he?

"I see no reason anymore why I should wait to tell you this." He got up, knelt down on the floor, and opened the jewelry box to show her a sparkling diamond ring. "Eden Levine, I love you with all my heart. I want to spend the rest of my life with you. Dear Eden, will you marry me?"

Eden threw her hands up to her face. This was all too sudden. She wasn't mentally prepared.

"So? What do you say?" Neil asked.

"I . . ." She wetted her lips. "It doesn't feel right."

"Why?"

"The city just came out of a war. It's a disaster all around us." She remembered the rioting people she saw when they were riding in the car, and the homeless woman holding her child. "I don't know if I can be happy for myself right now. So many people are suffering." She thought of all the dead bodies at the Great World. "My friend Miriam just passed away. It feels wrong to jump into something festive so soon."

"I disagree. I think we should try to find happiness now for the very same reasons." He held the ring up higher toward her. "All that fighting and bombing these past weeks reminded me how precious life is. We ought to seize the moment whenever we can. If we don't, we might come to regret it."

Eden turned her head. By now, the other diners in the room were taking notice. Smiling, they all watched, waiting for her to answer.

"I don't like what's happening in Shanghai either," Neil said.

"If this war between the Chinese and the Japanese doesn't end soon, I want to take you back to England with me." He lowered his head, then raised it again. "I can't bear to think that something bad might happen to you. I want you to be my wife so I can honor you and protect you. I don't want to see you drifting in this world, stateless, with no place to call home. No matter what happens from now on, I'll take care of you. You and your family."

"Neil . . ." Eden softened her grasp. The diamond of the ring sparkled as Neil slightly turned his hand. She thought of the carnage she had seen these last two months. She thought of Isaac's parents, helpless and still trapped in Hitler's den. If China was no longer safe, what would she and her family do? A sudden panic spiked in her heart.

She looked into Neil's gaze. Could she not fall in love with a man who wanted to care for her and protect her? She stroked the side of his head.

"Is that a yes?" Neil moved closer to her. "Would you say yes?"

"Yes." She closed her lips and nodded. God had blessed her. Neil had wealth, power, and respect of the community. In this treacherous, unstable world, he had the means to protect her and her family. Wasn't this why she and her family fled Munich? For their safety? What more could she ask for? How ungrateful she would be if she didn't appreciate such an abundance of blessings before her feet?

The dining room broke out in applause. Neil, ecstatic, put the ring on her finger. Everything whirled by, with Eden herself feeling like she was watching from the outside. Her eyes welled up and she wiped a tear away with her finger. Was that a tear of joy? Of course it was. What else could it be? But then why did she feel sad? Why did she feel an inexplicable pang wrapping itself around her heart when this should be one of the happiest moments of her life?

Neil sat back in his seat and raised his glass of champagne. Following his lead, she raised her glass and clinked it against his. The restaurant manager came to their table and offered his congratulations. A photographer, pre-arranged by Neil, came and snapped a shot. The moment of their engagement, memorialized forever.

3 2

YOUR DEATH OR MINE

IN A PRIVATE DINING room at the restaurant Maple Forest Pavilion, Kenji Konoe poured a shot of Yamazaki whiskey into the glasses. When he raised his glass, Clark did not return in invitation to cheer. Clark sat at the table, blank-faced and unmoved by the barely touched dishes of fine cuisine on the table. The fact that he even showed up here tonight was due respect enough. If it were anyone Japanese other than Konoe, he would've said no, even if it might have brought risk to himself. He wasn't about to toast to his own city's demise.

Konoe shrugged it off. *"Kanpai,"* he said and downed the shot. "Have you ever tried Japanese whiskey? Suntory only began producing whiskey in 1924. The first bottle wasn't even sold until 1929. But quality-wise, this is amazing. It has a more subtle, refined taste than Scottish ones. Try it."

Clark ignored the whiskey. "Why did you invite me here tonight?"

Konoe smacked his lips. "I worry you might be displeased with how everything has turned out between our countries."

Displeased? "My being displeased doesn't change the outcome of what Japan has done to us."

341

"I'm sorry it has to be this way," Konoe said. His face showing sympathy, but no regret. "I would hate for the conflict between our countries to ruin our friendship. Look, we're here tonight, in a Chinese restaurant, drinking Japanese whiskey. A fusion of our two cultures. Can't we celebrate that?"

Clark smirked. He swirled the whiskey in his glass on the table.

"I am sincere about what I said." Konoe refilled his own drink. "If it's any consolation, I took the liberty of clearing away one of your problems."

"What problem?"

"The problem of a man named Liu Kun."

Clark stopped his hand.

"There will be no more nuisance and petty complaints from anyone to stop you from managing your assets in your factory from now on," Konoe said. "Better yet, I hope you will move your plant back to its old place, where it belongs. My people—" he smiled and stopped short, "I mean, the incoming regime would like very much to do business with you. Energy, fuel, and batteries are all products we would want to procure."

Of course they would, Clark thought. But Konoe was out of his mind if he thought Yuan Enterprises would supply the fuel to help the Japanese army kill more Chinese.

Choosing his words carefully, Clark sidestepped the subject. "We just finished putting everything in place at our new plant. My people are eager to resume work. There's no sense in more delays." He made it a point to add, "Besides, the infrastructure in the old area is completely broken."

"That's true." Konoe drew back and took a sip of his whiskey. "What if I ask you to work with us? Of course you already know, the KMT's former Minister of Finance of Shanghai is now heading up the new Provisional Government. There are many opportunities in the new regime. You could be on our side."

Clark tensed. Wen-Ying had warned him about this, only he

hadn't expected it to come from Konoe. "I'm surprised, Kenji. I thought you were above running around doing political biddings. Shouldn't you be meditating on the higher purpose of life in your garden?"

Konoe chuckled. "I'm glad you feel at ease enough with me to make fun of me. You're right. Soliciting on behalf of my government isn't something I normally do. Too often, it requires dealing with imbeciles like Liu Kun." He spread his elbows out on the table. "I'm not here on behalf of my government. I'm asking you as a friend. A true friend. If we join forces, we can do more and achieve more." He held up his glass. "You'll be safer on our side than on your own."

"You worry about my safety? If I say no, will I be in danger?"

Konoe looked him in the eye. "I hope you don't really think I'm so dishonorable a friend."

"It's hard for me to think friendship is anything of consequences considering how many of my people have been slaughtered."

"Very well." Konoe lifted his head. "Then let me make it clear. No. You're free to decline, and no one will retaliate if you do. Like I said, I value our friendship, and I don't operate that way. I don't need to." He drank the remainder of his whiskey. "As for the casualties, you and I both know that neither of us has the power to stop it. If you can't blame yourself, why do you blame me?"

Clark looked away. His face and chest remained tense. He couldn't dispute Konoe on that point.

Konoe put down his glass. "Anyway, like I told you before, the casualties are unfortunate, but inconsequential. People like you and I should be using our minds for something bigger. We can create a glorious sphere of Greater Asia. That glory is what will last through the end of time, not the fleeting moment in time that any individual person spends on this earth. If we devote our minds purely and singularly to transforming the world, that will be the mark of greatness we can leave behind."

"And like I told you before," Clark said, "I don't see things your way. As to your invitation, I'm afraid I'll have to say no. It's not my plan to collaborate with the Japanese government. I'm taking up a position as a member of the Shanghai Municipal Council. Collaborating with you would be a conflict of interest."

"The SMC?" Konoe asked. "I see they got to you first." He leaned in closer. "You can disregard the conflict of interest. No one in this city ever takes that seriously anyway."

No one? "I do. I take my role seriously. And if I double deal, you wouldn't deem me worthy of being your friend anymore, isn't that right? You and I aren't men with anything shameful to hide. What we do, we do openly."

Konoe pulled back. His casual attitude replaced by an air of nobility.

"I'm sure the Japanese members on the Council will adequately represent your country's interests without me." Clark raised his glass and drank all his whiskey in one gulp.

"Okay. My loss." Konoe refilled their glasses. "Allow me then to wish you good luck in your new post." He raised his glass. This time, Clark returned the toast. In his heart, he toasted to himself, and to his father and his own people. He'd said no to Japan. It was a small victory, but an act of defiance nonetheless.

Konoe summoned the waiter and signed the bill. When they stepped outside to wait for their cars, Konoe said to Clark one more time, "It's never too late for you to reconsider. If you change your mind, I'd be happy to hear from you."

Clark put his hands into the pockets of his trench coat. "That's very—" Before he could finish speaking, a man in a black fedora and black *tangzhuan* robe coming off the sidewalk across the street caught his eye. The man pulled out a gun and pointed it in their direction. Immediately, Clark thought the man wanted to kill him, but the man's gun was not pointing at him. It was directed at Konoe.

Without thinking, he pushed Konoe away and lunged out of

the line of fire himself. The man's gun went off four times. A car sped up the road and screeched to a halt. The assassin raised his arm, threw something onto the ground, and jumped into the car. The vehicle's engine roared and whisked him away.

Konoe, who had fallen, pushed himself back up. Clark went to the spot where the assassin had stood. On the ground, he found a large copper coin engraved with the sign of a triangle. He'd seen this triangle before. It was the same as the one on Wen-Ying's necklace. The assassin belonged to underground resistance group Tian Di Hui. This coin was their declaration of war.

Did Wen-Ying have a hand in this? Clark clasped his fist around the coin and put it into his pocket.

Still catching his breath, Konoe came up beside him. "You saved my life. Thank you."

Clark gazed out at the direction in which the assassin had disappeared. Did he do the right thing saving Konoe? He stepped back from the Japanese captain. "You should be more careful," he said to him, then walked away to his own car, where Huang Shifu was already waiting.

Back home, a maid opened the front door and greeted Clark. Inside, the heavy air of mourning still hung. The joyous chatter and voices that usually filled the living room had been gone ever since his father passed away. Quietly, Clark gave the maid his coat and went to Wen-Ying's room. Her door was open ajar. At her desk, she pored over a set of papers. Standing at the door, Clark knocked.

Wen-Ying turned around in her seat. "Ge?" She shuffled the papers into a stack and put them into a drawer. Clark didn't ask her what she was doing.

"How was dinner?" she asked.

"You tell me." He pulled the coin out of his pocket and dropped it onto her desk.

Wen-Ying glanced at the coin. "Our attempt failed," she said. She didn't sound surprised or concerned.

"Konoe doesn't deserve to die."

"And our people do?" Wen-Ying stood up. "What about the thousands of people who were bombed? Which one of them deserved to die?"

"Killing Konoe won't stop anything. His role in the army is nominal. I guarantee you, he's not the one waging war. That's not his way," Clark said. He traced a circle on her desk with his finger.

"Killing him will make a statement," Wen-Ying said. "It'll send a message to the shorties we're not done yet. The spirit of the resistance lives. As long as we're still here, they better be looking behind their backs." She picked up the coin. "Are you defending him?"

"I don't know." Clark shook his head. "Taking his life feels too extreme. I'm not ready to blindly kill everyone without considering their accountability."

"Then leave it up to us." She dropped the coin into a drawer. "You're affected by your friendship with him. Maybe instead of killing him, you can use your *guanxi* with him to our advantage in some way?" She peered at him.

Clark didn't answer her. He turned around and left the room. Maybe Wen-Ying was right. He was letting his friendship with Konoe cloud his judgment. But Konoe trusted him. He'd helped him and got Liu Kun out of the way. It didn't feel right to abuse that trust.

Perhaps he was a fool to think that. But with the world having fallen into chaos, and men acting like beasts with no bound of moral decency, he wanted to hold on to what was left of justice.

Didn't it still mean something? To be moral and just?

33

THE ENGAGEMENT PARTY

When Victor Sassoon told Eden he wanted to throw her and Neil an engagement party, she had specifically asked him to keep the celebration small. Every day, photos and newsreels were broadcasting casualties of the "Yellow War." When she walked on the ragged streets of Shanghai and saw all the homeless refugees, going to a party was the last thing she wanted, let alone a party for herself.

As it turned out, she and Sir Victor had a very different idea of small. The party took place at the beautiful Seville dining room at the Cathay Hotel, which the Baron's people had efficiently returned to full operation within two days after it was bombed. The hotel suffered damages to its seventh floor and its arcade, but otherwise, its services had returned to normal.

Tonight, as many as two hundred close friends and relatives of the Sassoons and her family had gathered here for their "small" party. Eden dreaded to think how big the wedding would be when they added their more distant family and acquaintances to the list of guests.

Unlike her, Neil was overjoyed. Nothing he had done in business had impressed Sir Victor as much as his having convinced Eden to marry him. The Baron even donated a hundred thousand dollars for refugee relief in their name.

Marrying into the Sassoon family had its drawbacks though. Immediately after their engagement was announced, Neil assigned two burly Russian bodyguards to accompany Eden wherever she went.

"I don't want two men following me all the time," she'd told him.

"I know it's an imposition, but this is a safety measure we can't avoid. With a war going on, all the criminal elements are running around without control. You're my fiancée. I don't want you to be kidnapped for ransom."

Reluctantly, she gave her consent. With all the Sassoons' wealth and power, they should have more freedom. Instead, she felt trapped. Like this party now. This whole night, she'd been going around greeting and thanking everyone for coming to celebrate the most special event of her life, and she didn't even know half of the people.

Such necessary obligations were small inconveniences when compared to all the blessings though, weren't they? Her parents couldn't have been happier than when she and Neil announced the news. It made Hanukkah last week all the more meaningful. After everything they'd witnessed these last two months, the happy news came to them like a light shining onto their lives.

The sumptuous feast began with appetizers of caviar and salmon canapés. At the long table in the center of the dining room, Eden picked up her fork and rested the tines on her plate. Food riots were breaking out across the city. Was it callous of her to indulge in such fine delicacies, or was it worse for her to not eat and waste food when so many were hungry?

"Everybody." Sir Victor stood up at the head of the table. "I would like to propose a toast to my nephew, Neil, and his fiancée, Miss Eden Levine."

All the guests stopped eating and raised their glasses.

Sir Victor glanced at the engaged couple. "Neil, I can finally stop worrying about you." A round of laughter broke out. "I was kind of worried there for a while. We already have one fool of a Sassoon who doesn't know how to change his bachelor ways who keeps falling for the wrong kinds of women. We don't need a second one. Thank God." The guests laughed again. Eden looked over at Neil with a polite smile. "Neil, you're a very lucky man, and I know it's luck because the men in my family are spoiled. We're like children. But for luck, a smart woman wouldn't put up with our tomfoolery through the long haul. After all, look at me. Why else am I still not married?" The Baron grinned and waited for more laughter to subside. "So, Neil, you're one lucky man. Eden, you're strong, gracious, and smart, and beautiful. We're blessed to have you join our family. The Sassoon household in Shanghai needs a woman's touch. Your addition to our family is just what we need. Congratulations, to both of you."

The guests cheered with a round of applause. Eden smiled and nodded at those sitting at her table to acknowledge their good wishes. They returned her smile, but who were these people? She barely knew any of them, except for her parents, Joshua, and Isaac.

But even Isaac now looked unfamiliar. Sitting beside Joshua, he applauded with the others. A mask of resignation and acceptance veiled his face. When their eyes met, she almost wished he would jump out of his seat and take her away. But he didn't. He gave her a warm smile like everyone else. His smile disappointed her. If she was making the wrong choice, Isaac would not be the one to save her from it.

The dinner resumed and the waiters began clearing away the appetizer plates. Vera, the woman sitting across the table—Eden believed her name was Vera, although she couldn't be sure—said to her companion, "Christmas and New Year's will be drab this year. I was planning to have a little Christmas celebration. Nothing fancy, just a dinner party at my home. But half the ladies

I know are gone, so I had to cancel." She took a sip of her wine. "I hope New Year's Eve will be better."

"New Year's Eve will be fine!" said her companion. "Stewart always hosts a good party. He's rented the entire ballroom at the Palace Hotel. People will be looking for an outlet to shake off their stress after all that bombing."

Eden dipped her chin. If they needed release from their stress, what about all the homeless refugees? Where would they go to shake off their fear and despair?

The waiter laid a plate of salad in front of her. She picked up her fork and pushed the leaves around.

Vera—if that was her name—put down her glass. "I wish Sally and Margaret were here. Things aren't the same without them."

"My dear, fewer women in Shanghai means more men will be looking at you," her companion teased. "Maybe this Yellow War will cool down by then." He sighed and shook his head. "That's just terrible what the Japanese are doing. Who knows? Maybe the KMT could fight its way back up here. If that's the case, Sally and Margaret can come back."

An older gentleman sitting next to Vera—Eden couldn't remember his name—dabbed his mouth with his napkin. "If you ask me, the Japanese taking over isn't such a bad thing."

Eden stopped poking at her salad and raised her head.

"The way the Chinese run things is a mess. You always have to bribe everyone to get anything done. And you can't rely on them when you do business with them. They lie. They tell you one thing and behind your back, they're doing something else. Maybe Japan coming here is exactly what they need. The Japanese can clean up this place."

Eden clapped down her fork. "How can you say that?" The guests around her looked up, startled. "Wherever you're from, how would you like it if the Japanese come to your country, bomb and kill thousands of you, and take over your country? You callous ignoramus." She pushed back her chair and stomped out. Neil quickly dropped his napkin on the table and ran after her.

Breathing hard, Eden fled through the corridor and down the stairs. She did not know where she wanted to go, only that she wanted to get away. Behind her, Neil called out, "Eden! Eden!"

At the bottom of the staircase, she stopped.

"Eden!" Neil caught up to her. "What's the matter? Are you okay?"

"No. No, I'm not okay. I can't listen to that kind of talk."

"Aw, Milton? Don't listen to him. He's a twit. He's an old man. He spouts nonsense."

"It's more than nonsense. Japan? Clean up this place? Like how Hitler and the Nazis want to clean up Germany? Clean it up from the Jews?"

"That's not what he meant, I'm sure of that."

She opened her mouth to say more, but couldn't. So many emotions were whirling inside her, she couldn't find the right words to explain how she felt. Her chest tightened as she tried to breathe. Her body trembling, she squeezed her fists.

"Eden, sweetheart, come here." Neil put his arms around her. "It's all right. It's all going to be fine." He stroked her back and tried to soothe her. "I know everything you've seen lately upsets you, but it's not the first time China and Japan had gone to war to sort things out. It'll all pass. Everything will go back to normal. Even if it doesn't, we'll find a way to move on. Everything will be fine. Trust me."

In his embrace, Eden closed her eyes. She wished she could close them and open them again to find that all the atrocities in the world had gone away like a bad dream.

34

NANKING MASSACRE

THE COLD DECEMBER wind blew a leaflet on the road toward his feet as Clark approached his car to head home from work. The leaflet flipped over, revealing yet another laughable lie propagated by the Japanese. "Reformed Government will improve Chinese lives," it said. "Unite for greater prosperity of Asia." Clark halted his steps and watched the wind sweep it away.

Lies. All these bizarre lies from Japan, casting itself in a positive light when its army was marching south, killing more people and overtaking more land that did not belong to them. Who did they think they were fooling?

In his car, he said to Huang Shifu, "I want to plan a big dinner for Uncle Six."

"Is that right?" Huang Shifu glanced at the rearview mirror. "He'd appreciate that. He's worked with us for so long."

Yes, he had. For as long as Clark could remember, the loyal, old servant had been by his late father's side, tending to his family's needs both at their home and at work. He had given his resignation earlier today. The fall of the city and the death of Master Yuan had hit him hard. At his age, he didn't have the fire to rebound anymore. He wanted to retire.

"What about a twelve-course banquet dinner at the Tang Court?" Clark asked. "We'll invite all his best buddies at our company."

"The Tang Court?" Huang Shifu turned the steering wheel left. "That's his favorite restaurant. He'd be delighted."

"We'll do that then," Clark said. A dinner for Uncle Six and an expensive going-away gift would be a good way to honor him. It would be a good excuse to force his mother to get out and do something to brighten her mood too. Since his father passed away, she had lost all interest in doing anything. All she could do to cope was to remain in mourning in her bedroom.

When he arrived home, the maid opened the door. "Young Master!" She patted her heart and her face eased in relief like she'd seen a savior. "Oh, good thing you're back."

"Why?" Clark gave her his coat. With a worried face, she pointed at the living room. Wen-Ying, Mei Mei, and his mother had all gathered there. Wen-Ying had her arms around a teenage boy dressed in a Western-style suit. A man he'd never met before was sitting with them.

Clark went into the living room. He recognized the boy right away. He was Peng Amah's grandson Peng Ji-Rong. Peng Amah had worked for the Yuan family since before Clark was born. She retired last year to join her son and his family in Nanking. Her son, Peng Ah-Hai, was a chef. He owned a hot-pot restaurant.

"Ge!" Wen-Ying looked up from her seat.

Clark glanced at her, then at the stranger. "What's happening?" he asked. Why was Ji-Rong here? Why was he bawling? Why were his mother and Mei Mei crying?

"Guo-Hui Ge!" Ji-Rong cried harder when he saw Clark.

"Ge." Wen-Ying tossed her head at the stranger. "This is my friend Fan Yong-Hao." She tugged her necklace and flashed her pendant with the triangle symbol at Clark.

Clark gave her a quick, subtle nod to let her know he understood.

"Fan Yong-Hao has friends with war relief groups helping civilians. They brought Ji-Rong to him," she said.

"Yuan *xiong*," Fan greeted Clark, addressing him as a brother.

"How do you do?" Clark greeted him, then sat down next to Ji-Rong. The boy appearance here alone didn't bode well. "How did you get here? Where's Peng Amah? And your family?"

Ji-Rong broke out crying. "They . . . they're all dead."

All dead? A chill ran up Clark's spine and brought goosebumps to his arms. "How did this happen?" he asked, even though he could already guess.

"They were killed when the Japanese attacked Nanking two weeks ago," Fan said.

Ji-Rong wiped his sleeve across his eyes. "They came into the city in groups. Some of them in ten, some in twenty. They stormed in and barged into every house. We'd heard the Japanese were coming. That day, Ba and Ma had gone out to try to find out how we could escape before the troops arrive. I was hiding at home with Grandma and Jie." Ji-Rong's jie. Clark remembered the girl, the seventeen-year-old sister Shanshan. She had come with their family to Shanghai last year to bring Peng Amah to Nanking. "A group of them slammed open our door. They shouted but I didn't understand them. They grabbed me, then Grandma and Jie. They searched our house. And then . . . and then . . ." He sucked in breaths, hyperventilating with terror-strickened eyes. "They stuffed a cloth into my mouth and held me still, then they tore the clothes off Grandma and Jie and they raped them."

Raped them? Peng Amah too? She was fifty-six years old!

Clark listened in horror. The goosebumps spread from his arms to his back. His entire body shivered.

Ji-Rong blew his nose. "I screamed but my mouth muffled. I wanted to hit those Japanese dogs and save them, but they were holding me down, making me watch. Grandma and Jie screamed again and again. Those Japanese dogs slapped them. They wouldn't stop. They were laughing."

"Despicable," Clark spit out the word through gritted teeth. He looked at Wen-Ying and Fan. "Beasts."

"In the end, they shot Jie in the head. They stabbed Grandma. I can still hear her scream in pain. They kept stabbing her. Their faces looked like devils. They were enjoying it. They stabbed her with knives and bayonets. Finally, they staked a bayonet into her heart and she stopped screaming."

Madam Yuan and Mei Mei cried again. Clark clenched his fists. This was beyond war. This was pure evil. "What happened then?" He asked Ji-Rong, forcing out the words through his throat. "How did you get away?"

"I thought they would kill me too. After they killed Grandma, they turned to me. That was when Mr. Rabe came in."

"Mr. Rabe?"

"Yes. John Rabe. He's a German businessman. He works for the big German company Siemens. He comes to our hot-pot restaurant once a week to eat. He and Ba became very good friends." Ji-Rong sniffled. "He marched into our home just when the Japanese dogs were about to come at me. He saw Grandma and Jie's dead bodies, then came over to me and pulled the cloth out of my mouth. The shorties who were holding my arms let go. Mr. Rabe grabbed my hand. He yelled something at them in German and took me out of the house. I don't know if the shorties understood what he said, but they saw his Nazi armband and they became unsure. They looked a bit frightened of him. But I think Mr. Rabe was a bit afraid of them too, even though he didn't show it. When he led me out by my hand, his hand was trembling."

His heart twisting in pain, Clark stroked the boy's head. He'd read in the Chinese newspaper *Shen Bo* that Japan invaded Nanking, but the articles didn't say the Japanese soldiers were ravaging civilians. Then again, how could any Chinese reporter go into that city, which was now overrun by Japanese troops?

"Mr. Rabe took me away," Ji-Rong continued. "On the streets, I saw masses of dead bodies. So many dead bodies. All the women had their clothes and pants torn off. The Japanese soldiers were still murdering people around us like they had gone mad. They looted every house and building, even the ones owned by Westerners. Mr. Rabe gripped my hand very hard. He was walking very fast and I had a hard time keeping up with him. The soldiers were shooting at everyone who was trying to flee. Bullets were flying from every direction."

Clark exchanged a glance with Wen-Ying and Fan. Their faces looked as bitter as he felt.

"Mr. Rabe took me to the refugee safety zone he'd set up. After I arrived, one of Mr. Rabe's servants told me my father had come earlier to try to get help. But by the time he reached the zone, he'd already been struck by bullets. His last words were that the Japanese soldiers had captured my mother and we were still hiding out at home. That was when Mr. Rabe decided to come and try to rescue us."

Clark let out a long, shaky breath. He thought what the Japanese army did in Shanghai was abominable. But what they did in Nanking was a hundred times worse. These beasts. These inhuman beasts!

"The refugee safety zone was packed. Many people crammed themselves in one of the two dugouts in the garden. There was no more room and Mr. Rabe couldn't let any more people in. they tried to climb in anyway from over the wall. Outside, there were men, women, and children crying for help. Even Chinese soldiers tried to climb in when Mr. Rabe's people told them the Japanese would only let him bring civilians into the zone. At the gate, the Japanese soldiers kept banging on the door. They said they wanted to search the zone to make sure there weren't any Chinese soldiers hiding inside. Mr. Rabe wouldn't let them."

Clark tried to imagine the scene. Once, at a temple, he saw a painting of hell. It depicted what happened to a deceased person at each level of hell. At the eighteenth level, the last and deepest, it showed a mass of people drowning in a lake of fire. Their bulging eyes as big as their screaming mouths. They held up their arms, shrieking for help. The Japanese army had turned Nanking into the eighteenth level of hell.

"How did you get here?" Clark asked. The attack on Nanking was still happening. It wasn't over yet.

"That night, Mr. Rabe asked me through his servants if I have any family left," Ji-Rong said. "I told him about *gong gong, po po*, and uncle." He meant his grandparents and uncle on his mother's side. "They lived in Nanking too. Mr. Rabe asked me who else. I guess *gong gong's* family must be dead too. I have no one left. I told him about you all. Grandma always said your family treat her like one of your own. Mr. Rabe then told me his safety zone couldn't accommodate everyone, and there was one last chance for me to escape that night if I were brave enough. I didn't want to be difficult. He already saved my life. I told him I wanted to escape. When the massacre slowed down in the evening, he told me to change into this suit and sent me off with a white couple who were among the last to flee. The couple claimed I was their adopted son and they brought me here to Shanghai by train. I was terrified the whole way. When we got here, the couple said they were planning to leave Shanghai by ship, but they couldn't take me because I don't have a visa to enter England with them. Even in Shanghai, the Japanese guards didn't want to let me through. They demanded to see my British passport. The man who brought me then made a phone call. After his call, a man named Masao Takeda came and spoke to the guards. Only then was I allowed to enter the city. The British couple told me to go with Takeda. At first, I didn't want to. He was Japanese. I want to kill all the Japanese to avenge my family. But Takeda spoke Chinese.

He said he would bring me to your family. I really didn't believe him until I saw *Daxiaojie*." He raised his teary eye to Wen-Ying.

By now, Madam Yuan was sobbing beyond control. Wen-Ying stroked Ji-Rong's back and said to Mei Mei, "Ji-Rong's journey must've been very hard. Why don't you get him something to eat and let him wash up so he can get some rest?"

Mei Mei wiped her tears. She coaxed Ji-Rong to follow her to the dining room. After they left, Madam Yuan cried, "Ay! Heaven has no eyes! Peng Amah's whole family died so terribly. I don't even know what to do. I have to go light incense to the gods. I'll beg the gods to protect them in Heaven. I'll beg the gods to protect us and no tragedy will come our way anymore." She rose from her seat and went out to the altars for the gods and ancestors.

Clark pounded his fist after she left. "Japan. Really too despicable!"

"Ji-Rong was very lucky," Wen-Ying said. "The British man who brought him here is a SIS agent. He had contacts with Tian Di Hui in Nanking. He called us. Takeda is one of us. He's a mixed-blood Chinese-Japanese. He's our covert agent working for the Japanese military."

Clark nodded. "We have to take good care of Ji-Rong," he said through gritted teeth.

"That's a matter of course. Aside from that, we have a message for you."

"A message for me?"

"Somebody wants to speak to you." Fan Yong-Hao pulled a small piece of paper from his shirt pocket and gave it to Clark. The paper showed an address on a side street off Yates Road. "He asks you to go to this place tomorrow at two o'clock."

"Who?" Clark held on to the paper. "Is it someone from Tian Di Hui?"

"We're not at liberty to say," Fan said. "In the current climate, the less said out loud, the less is heard. It's safer for everyone this way."

Clark read the address again.

Wen-Ying grabbed him by the hand. "Ge, trust us. You'll find out when you get there. When you arrive, give them your name and show them this." She gave him a bronze turtle figurine with the Tian Di Hui triangle symbol camouflaged in the carving on its shell.

Clark frowned and turned the figurine between his fingers. "All right. I'll do as you say." He put the paper and the figurine into his pocket. Around him, the grave, dark atmosphere thickened. It was trapping them all, and there was no hope for escape.

3 5

JUNTONG

The next day, Clark went to the place at the address shown on the note he got from Wen-Ying and Fan Yong-Hao. The place turned out to be a private medical clinic on the first floor of a lane house. Puzzled, he entered. The clinic was empty except for the nurse at the reception desk. He gave the nurse his name and showed her the turtle figurine. She looked him once over, then got up. "Come with me. Dr. Wu will see you now."

Clark put the figurine back in his pocket and followed her into an examination room. The nurse went to the bookcase beside the desk and pushed it open to reveal the entrance concealed behind. She tipped her head toward the entrance.

Hesitant, Clark went into the secret gateway. The nurse pointed at a room at the end of the corridor on the right side.

He thought of the common saying—since you've arrived, you might as well proceed with calm. He walked toward the room and the nurse closed the entrance behind him.

In the room, a man in a crisp black *tangzhuan* stood waiting with his back toward the door. When Clark entered, the man turned around. It was Dai Li, the head of *Juntong*, the Chinese secret police. Clark had met him once before. Last year, when the workers of his ex-fiancée's father Master Shen went on strike and Master Shen pleaded to Clark for help, Dai Li had approached Clark and offered to snuff out the labor unrest. Under duress, Clark had reluctantly agreed.

But Dai Li did more than that. When the strike ended, several of the communist student leaders who had protested with the workers were raped or beaten. The ringleader was killed. The notorious *Juntong* leader had hinted to Clark that he would punish the students, but Clark could not confirm whether Dai Li was indeed the one who had harmed the students.

"Yuan Guo-Hui." Dai Li gave Clark a welcoming but cold smile.

"Director Dai," Clark said. "I couldn't have guessed it was you." He thought all the major KMT leaders had left the city.

"Shanghai's too important for us to abandon entirely," Dai Li said with his arms behind his back. "Shanghai has become a Japanese stronghold. I depend on my people here to gather intelligence on the enemy's next moves. They keep me informed on everything happening in this city."

"Your people include Tian Di Hui?" Clark asked. He didn't much like the idea of Wen-Ying working for Dai Li. Dai Li was not known for being merciful to his own followers, although his followers were known to be fiercely loyal to him.

"No," Dai Li softened his voice. "Tian Di Hui and *Juntong* are two separate entities. But our interests are aligned. My priority is intelligence. Tian Di Hui's mission is resistance. We work together when the need arises."

Still guarded, Clark watched him. "If you didn't ask me to come here today to discuss Tian Di Hui, then what do you want to speak to me about?"

"Don't mind me opening the door and seeing the mountain then. The Party needs your help."

"What kind of help?"

"Your companies and your battery plant are up and running

again. Inland, our army needs supplies, petrol, and raw materials. You can help us establish a transportation channel under the guise of commerce. You can help us receive supplies from overseas at the ports of Shanghai, then reroute them to us as commercial deliveries and get the shipments past Japanese inspections."

"You want me to use my business transactions as a cover."

"Yes."

"Did Wen-Ying agree to this? This would put our company at risk."

"Your sister is one of China's hot-blooded sons and daughters. She knows why I'm speaking to you today. The final decision is up to you."

Clark stared at the floor. Since his father passed away, he'd sworn he would hold on to Yuan Enterprises to the end. Using it to covertly support the KMT's war against the Japanese would bring enormous risk.

"The Japanese won't stop. You know what happened to your family's old maid and her family. The atrocities are still being committed in Nanking. Are you going to stand by and watch while more people suffer?"

Poor Peng Amah. Clark wrenched his hands. Indescribable pain stabbed through his heart. The pain was soon supplanted by anger.

No. He could not remain here, sheltering himself while his people bled and cried. At worst, they would all perish together. "I'll help." He raised his head. "Tell me how you want to proceed."

Dai Li smiled. A cold, unflinching smile, like he had known he would get what he wanted all along.

ALEXA KANG

On his way back to the office from his meeting with Dai Li, Clark began to think through the details of how he could divert cargos of military supplies inland without raising the suspicions of the Japanese. This wasn't a plot he could carry out alone. In his company, who could he trust?

Xu Hong-Lie was the first to come to his mind.

This would be a grave request. Everyone who helped him would expose themselves to risks. If they were ever caught, the Japanese would target them all to be killed.

The car arrived at his office and he got out. When he stepped up to the building entrance, a woman approached him. He couldn't see who she was behind her sunglasses, hat, and the large scarf wrapped over the lower half of her face.

"Clark."

He knew the voice. "Ekaterina."

He grabbed her elbow. She stood before him in an old gray coat. In her tattered hat and scarf with faded colors, one could've easily mistaken her for a White Russian hairdresser or milliner. "Where have you been?"

She checked to make sure no one was near them. "I need your help."

36

A MARRIAGE OF CONVENIENCE

"Oooh, I like this one!" Ava cooed at the photo of the apricot chiffon wedding gown with scooped neckline and a plunging V-cut back. "If I had to do it all over again, this is the dress I'd choose."

Eden picked up the photo but extended her arm to hold it further away. "Mmmm, it's a little too revealing for me." She couldn't see herself under the chuppah in front of five hundred guests, all watching her bare back. The sheer skirt, practically see-through, wouldn't elicit the right kind of admiration either.

"Here are some more." The girl at the bridal shop laid down another batch of photos, magazines, and sketches.

"Thank you." Ava smiled at the girl while Eden spread the photos and sketches out on the table. "Mr. Bernard! Don't touch that!" Ava yelled as her pet monkey tried to pull on a gown displayed on the mannequin. Mr. Bernard squeaked and returned to climb up next to her.

"What about that one?" Ava showed her the picture with the high-neck, long-sleeved gown with a dotted Swiss lace bodice. "You'd be all covered up in this."

Eden pulled the picture closer. Yes, she would be covered up indeed. So covered up in fact, she could feel it choking her, restricting her at every turn even without putting it on. "No. Too stifling." She tossed it back onto the table. In fact, this whole wedding felt stifling.

She scanned the rest of the pictures. Long ones, short ones. Embroidered ones, sleek ones. None of them fit her in her mind. None of them felt right on her.

What was wrong with her? She was never one to be so picky about what she wore. The girl who had brought the pictures had been so patient already. Why was she making such a fuss? It was only a dress. "Maybe I'm not suited to be married."

"I certainly am not." Ava lit a cigarette in her cigarette holder. "That didn't stop me from going through with getting married though."

Eden laughed. "Why did you do it? Were you in love?"

"More like I caught a momentary bout of insanity." Ava put Mr. Bernard onto her lap. "Old Bernard did sweep me off my feet, I'll admit that. He could be a real charmer when he wanted. Plus, all the weddings I went to at the time were getting so stale. People didn't know how to throw a good party. I was bored. I had some fantastic ideas how to spice things up. I wanted to throw the biggest bash anyone had ever seen in Boston." She took a sip of cucumber juice from her tall glass. "Bing Crosby sang at my wedding. No one since has ever topped that. But I think your wedding will finally give mine a run for the money. With Victor Sassoon running the show, your wedding's going to be nothing short of spectacular."

"If that's the case, it won't be because I wanted it that way," Eden said. "I can't even say Neil ever swept me off my feet." She felt guilty as soon as she said that. "I do like many things about him." She bit her lips. "Do you think that's enough to make a strong marriage?"

"You're asking the wrong person." Ava blew out a cloud of smoke. "I'll say this, if Victor Sassoon would throw me a party, I might consider getting married again just for that. If things turn sour later on, just get a divorce."

"Ava!" Eden laughed. "How can you take marriage so lightly?"

Ava inhaled another drag. "We're women. Everyone expects us to get married. We'd have to do it at least once, or else we'll be labeled as a spinster. And trust me, you don't want anyone to ever call you that. No man would pay attention to spinsters, but a divorcée? A divorcée is always attractive for an affair, especially if she is loaded with money. So I'd say, any way you look at it, marrying Neil Sassoon is a good decision. If it turns out marriage is not for you, you can divorce him. Your alimony alone will be enough to last you five lifetimes." She inhaled another drag.

"I can't do that." Eden lowered the sketch she was holding. "I wouldn't want to take advantage of Neil that way."

"I'm sorry," Ava apologized. "I get carried away sometimes when I talk. Of course you wouldn't be flippant about marriage like I am. I can't help it. By the end of my marriage, Bernard and I were ready to strangle each other. Right? Mr. Bernard?" She asked the monkey and Eden laughed. "I do hope you and Neil will be happy together," said Ava. "It's why I'm still in Shanghai. I want to be here for your big day and wish you a happy marriage in person. I'm going to really miss you when I leave. But my father's worried about me being in China. He wants me back in the States. I don't blame him. What's happening here . . ." She sighed and shook her head. "Who knows? Japan, China, Europe. The whole world seems to be going crazy. Even I am starting to worry about traveling abroad."

The reminder of war and brewing unrest pulled Eden back to reality. She glanced at the pictures of the wedding gowns on the table. Whichever one she chose to wear, her parents and Joshua would no doubt watch her take her vows with the happiest smiles on their faces. Seeing them happy and smiling, always, was the thing that really mattered. She would do anything to keep them that way.

"Are you having doubts?" Ava peered at her.

Eden shook her head. "Just nerves. I'm sure every bride feels it. It's all so overwhelming." She gathered the photos and sketches, and looked at them again in earnest. They weren't so bad. In fact, they were all beautiful. Any one of these dresses would make her the most dazzling bride in the world. She asked the girl who was helping her to come over.

"Yes, Miss Levine?"

"May I see the fabric of this one?" She pointed at the photo of the dress with the high neck and long sleeves.

"Of course." The girl left to fetch the material.

Eden sagged into her seat. A voice inside her whispered. She took a big gulp of her cucumber juice and silenced that voice.

Just nerves, she told herself. Just nerves.

37

A PRINCESS ON THE RUN

Ekaterina's reappearance took Clark by surprise. Quickly, he looked around to make sure no one on the street was watching them, then hustled her over to his car, where Huang Shifu usually sat waiting.

"Where have you been?" Clark demanded as soon as Huang Shifu closed the car door. "I've tried to contact you so many times."

"It's a long story," Ekaterina said. "Can you come with me back to my place? I'll tell you all about it."

Clark ran his eyes over her again. She had done a good job disguising herself. Quite an extraordinary, in fact, the way she had made herself look like nothing more than a poor worker. "Where's your place?"

"Rue Eugene Bard by Rue Galle."

"That's right on the border of Old City!" Clark said. "It's swarming with refugees and so close to the Japanese troops. What are you doing there?"

"Hiding. It's chaos there. It's harder for anyone to find me. I can get lost in a crowd."

Clark sighed and shook his head, then directed Huang Shifu

to take them there. When they came within eight blocks of the place, Ekaterina asked them to stop the car. "We should walk from here. Your Cadillac will draw too much attention."

Clark told the driver to stop. On the street, he followed Ekaterina, who kept her head down as she moved along in short, quick steps. Even Clark, himself a young man in good shape, almost had to run to keep pace with her. Along the way, refugees who had become beggars trailed him, pleading for help and cash. The streets, once bursting with commerce and activity, were now a purgatory strewn with litter and misery. Over on the other side of the sandbags and barbwire fence, Japanese guards stalked.

They came to a walk-up building where a woman in a dirt-smeared blouse and pants was huddling at the entrance with her two kids. Ekaterina sidestepped around her, unlocked the door, and led Clark in. She took him past the dim hallway and up three flights to a unit with an iron front door gate, and invited him inside.

The interior of the flat, at least, looked comfortable. It had a matching set of table, sofa, bookcase, chairs, and lamps. Art deco design, no less. A reproduction of George Barbier's *Farewell at Night* hung on the wall as the living room's centerpiece. The only thing it lacked was natural sunlight. The unit had but two small windows, and Ekaterina had left both curtains down. Given the fact that she was in hiding, it made sense.

"A French writer lived here," Ekaterina said as she took off her hat and gloves. "He fled when the bombings started. He sold this place to me for a quarter of what it's worth. Furniture included." She flopped on to the couch. Her playful smile, which he recognized, returned. "Have a seat."

"Whatever you're doing, it's no laughing matter," Clark chided her and sat down.

"You're right." Ekaterina dropped her smile.

"Tell me, why am I here?"

Ekaterina glanced up at him. Her emotionless eyes as empty as ever. "I did it. I took my revenge on Sokolov."

"What?"

"When the Japanese began attacking China up north and driving the KMT army into retreat, I decided the KMT wasn't going to be useful to me anymore. Luckily, Sokolov captured Fyodor Lukin before all that happened. It saved Sokolov from the worst of the Great Purge last year. He came to trust me entirely after that. I owe you a big thank you."

"Yeah, don't mention it." Clark rolled his eyes. He still couldn't believe she'd tricked him. "Why not just let Sokolov die? You could've let Stalin deal with him as an 'anti-Soviet element.'"

"An easy death is too good for him. A lot of the people Stalin killed during the purge were victims. Sokolov was not a victim. Not in any sense of the word. I needed to make him pay."

"So what did you do?" Clark asked.

"He came to believe I really fell in love with him," she said and held up her chin. "I told him I couldn't bear being a Chinese man's mistress any longer just for the sake of keeping myself from destitution. I told him I was in fear for my life if the Japanese attacked Shanghai and you abandoned me."

Clark laughed and rubbed his forehead. "All right. Then what?"

"I guess he felt bad his wife almost made mincemeat out of me too. It also helped when the Japanese really started dropping bombs in Shanghai. He took me in and put me up in his private apartment, the one that his wife didn't know about. After that, I waited. I wanted to know everything he was doing for the Soviets. I wanted to know everything he knew. I knew it'd only be a matter of time before he became careless. People always become careless around the ones they trust. I was biding my time."

"That was when you moved out of Metropole Hotel?"

"Yes. Sokolov kept a lot of secret information in his private place. He always locked it away. He didn't know I was watching for where he kept the keys. Sometimes, when he was asleep, I'd steal the key to see what documents he was hiding."

"I can't believe you did that," Clark said. Even listening to her now put him on an edge. "What if he woke up?"

"I had to take my chances. I was careful."

Clark gulped. She was lucky.

"Sometimes I'd listen to him talk on the phone too. He didn't know I was listening. I played dumb as best as I could. Soon enough, he took down his guard. He didn't think I was anyone he needed to guard against, and I'd convinced him I was absolutely loyal to him. Even if not, he thought my life depended on him." She paused. "I found out the Kremlin is in talks with the Americans. The Soviets plan to make an offer to Cordell Hull to make a pact to counter the Nazis."

Clark uncrossed his legs. "Go on."

"They're going to tell the Americans they'll defend Czechoslovakia if Hitler decides to attack."

"What did you do with the information?"

"I gave it to the Germans."

"You what?"

"I stole the copies of his records and took them to someone I know at the German Embassy, with documented proof of Sokolov as the recipient."

"You're joking!"

"I sure am not. I also gave them the record of military units stationed at the Ukrainian and Belarussian borders."

"You're out of your mind," Clark said. He had to admire her though. What gall!

"Sokolov is a dead man when Stalin finds out," Ekaterina said. "But so am I." She stared at the floor. "Sokolov's men are out for my head." She twiddled her fingers. For the first time, fear entered her voice. "I'm hiding here for now, but I have to leave this city. I can't stay in China. I don't know where to go." She half-raised her eyes to Clark. Her voice softened to a whisper. "I have no one else to go to."

Clark frowned and asked, "Was it worth it? All this?"

"Yes. Even if I must die, it is worth it." She sprung up from her seat. "I'm not asking for your approval. I'm not asking you to judge me." She paced the room. "I'm asking you to help me. Is there any way you can help me leave this country?"

Clark dug his mind for a solution. "It's not so easy anymore. I'm no longer working for the government."

Ekaterina turned toward him. Her eyes desperate.

"There might be a way . . ." He thought of Joseph Whitman.

A spark of hope lit up her face.

"I can't guarantee it, but my old liaison at the American consulate's office in Shanghai may be able to help. If you have confidential information about the Soviets, the Americans may give you safe harbor in exchange for what you know."

"Thank you!" Ekaterina blew out a breath and covered her heart.

"Don't thank me yet," Clark said. "Whether the Americans will agree is out of my hands." He didn't want to raise her hope just in case, but Whitman did say he would personally help if Clark needed him.

"Wait to hear from me." Clark stood up. "In the meantime, lay low and stay out of sight. If you need anything, you can call me. I can send my men to help."

Ekaterina came to him and gave him a hug. "You're a good man, Clark. A good friend."

Perhaps. It really didn't matter what kind of man or friend he was. From what he knew of her, Ekaterina had been through enough in life. If he could lend a hand so she could finally live in peace, why hesitate? The world could use more mercy. Especially now.

He raised one arm and hugged her back. When she finally released him, he walked toward the door.

Before he left, he paused. "Take care of yourself."

"I will." She thanked him again and locked the door.

He went down the dim stairwell. He had a feeling, Whitman would find a way.

Why? Because they were the links in the chain of hope.

NEIL'S SECRET

ARRIVING HOME, the first thing Eden noticed was the huge bouquet of red roses on the credenza. Seeing the blossom of flowers, she inhaled a deep breath. This morning, her father had told her in secret he would send her mother flowers to surprise her for their thirtieth anniversary.

"Mother!" She called out while she took off her shoes. "I'm home."

Mrs. Levine came out of her room, patting her hair which she had neatly tied up in a bun. "Eden. Good. Would you help me with the back buttons? I can't quite reach them."

"Sure!" Eden came over to her mother. For once, her mother had put on something more daring and extravagant. The silk crepe dress trimmed with sequins looked splendid on her. "You really should dress up more, Mother. You look beautiful."

"Stop flattering me." Mrs. Levine waved her hand. "I'm too old."

"No, you're not. Papa will be so proud when he takes you out tonight." Her parents had a reservation at the Vienna Garden Ballroom. The weather had turned warmer with the change of season and their open-air pavilion was in use again. The orchestra would be playing outside.

"I'm still not comfortable with the idea of going out while leaving you and Joshua behind."

"Oh, Mother, Joshua and I will be fine." Eden turned on the electric fan. "I'm an adult, and Joshua's old enough to take care of himself."

"I know. But your wedding is in three days. I feel like I should be here for you." She glanced at the trunks stacked against the wall. "It'll very different after you move out."

"Mother, it's not like I'm going away." Eden closed the last button on her mother's dress. "I'll come home a lot, and you can visit me and Neil anytime you like. We'll only be across town."

"Come home a lot," Mrs. Levine laughed at her. "You'll have a new home, a new life. You'll be busy. But sure, this will always be your home too." She led Eden to the sofa and sat down. "You've grown up so much. I'm very proud of you."

Eden wetted her lips. She'd rather change the subject. "Tell me, Mother, what's the secret to a long, happy marriage?"

"Oh, I don't know." Mrs. Levine looked up at the ceiling. A joyful smile spread across her face. "I suppose I could come up with a slew of advice about being understanding and considerate, making compromises and all that. But truthfully, it's just a feeling of loving someone."

"The feeling of loving someone?" Eden tilted her head.

"Yes. The feeling changes over time. At first, it was a lot of excitement. You wonder about the other person all the time. You get a tingly heart and sweaty palms when you see them. It's all very silly, but it's the truth. When I first met your father, I was giddy like a schoolgirl every time I saw him."

Eden's smile receded. Somewhere in the back of her mind, a thought was tapping at her. She couldn't remember ever feeling this way about Neil. She had, however, felt something somewhat like this about someone else.

"But your father did have all his hair back then." Mrs. Levine clasped her hands and stretched them out over her knees. She almost sounded like a giddy young girl now. "You might not believe this, but he was quite an attractive man, if I don't say so myself. All my girlfriends were jealous." She laughed and Eden laughed along. Her father did always look handsome in his old photos.

"Those nervous feelings will fade," Mrs. Levine said. "The excitement eventually ebbs, but something stronger will come into its place. You feel a bond. A deep bond. You develop a connection between you and the person you love, and you'll never want that connection to be broken. If your love is strong enough, it'll never be either. It'll only grow deeper. Every morning when I wake up, I feel blessed and happy that your father is in my life."

"What about the fact that Papa was a doctor?" Eden asked. "Maybe it sounds too pragmatic, but it was something you considered, wasn't it?" She felt uneasy asking, but she really wanted to know. "When we choose to spend our life with a man, shouldn't we take into account whether he can protect us and give us a comfortable life?"

Mrs. Levine turned to Eden and studied her face. "Of course your father's work made him a good prospect, but it wasn't the reason I chose to marry him. I suppose I wouldn't have married a man who didn't have a good job or ambitions, but I never had to deal with that situation. I do know one thing, I would've fallen in love with your father regardless. And looking back now, I can't imagine not being with him, no matter who he was or what he'd chosen to do with his life." She put her hand on Eden's. "I know Neil has a lot to offer. But I hope you've agreed to marry him because you love him. Materialistic things can offer a lot of comfort, but they'll never give someone true happiness."

"No, Mother." Eden shook her head. "I'm not marrying Neil for his money. Not at all."

"I didn't think so." Mrs. Levine smiled and pulled back her hand. "I'd like to think I've brought up my daughter to have better values."

Eden smoothed her skirt over her knees. Values were important. But still, Neil could offer them protection, in ways that went beyond money and financial security. How could she tell her mother that without alarming her? The recent bombings around Shanghai were horrifying enough. The news coming out of Germany about how the Nazis were treating the Jews didn't sound good either. If she had a chance to make sure her family was safe, she didn't want her parents to urge her to give it up.

"You do love Neil, don't you?" Mrs. Levine peered at her daughter.

"Of course," Eden said. "Yes. I love him. I wouldn't marry him otherwise. I really do love him." And she did. Maybe not the way her mother loved her father, but there were many things she did love about Neil. He was always so kind, and so gentle with her. He was wealthy, but wasn't pompous. Moreover, he loved her. He treated her like she was the center of his world.

As for a deep bond, surely that would develop over time, if she tried hard enough. Anything could happen, as long as she put her mind to it, right?

"If you're sure," Mrs. Levine said. "I wouldn't want you to put yourself into anything if you have even the slightest bit of doubt."

"No," Eden said, her voice squeaking. "I have no doubt at all. Why would you think that?" She shifted in her seat. "Say, that's a beautiful bouquet of roses Papa gave you."

"Oh," Mrs. Levine laughed. "That's not for me. Mine is in my bedroom. He gave me peonies. The roses are for you. They're from Neil." She stood up. "Speaking of your father, I better finish getting ready. He'll be home soon. He's getting off work early today. We're going to have a drink at the top of the Park Hotel and watch the sunset before we go to dinner."

Eden watched her mother return to the bedroom, then got up

to look at the bouquet. She flipped open the small greeting card accompanying the flowers, then frowned.

My Dearest Collette,

I haven't forgotten you. I know this week will be hard for you, but please know I'm thinking of you.

Love,
    Neil

What was this? Who was Collette? Who was Neil writing to?

She checked the envelope of the card. 214 Rue Bourgeat. The florist had delivered the flowers to the wrong address. Could this be a mistake? Was it sent by someone else whose name was also Neil? That was the only possible explanation.

Or was it? Somehow, it gave her a bad feeling.

Well, easy enough to find out. The florist's name and address were on the card. She put her shoes back on, picked up the bouquet and her purse, and walked out the door.

———

Carrying the bouquet, Eden came to the China Flower Shop on Yu Yuen Road. The Chinese lady owner at the counter saw her walk in and lowered her glasses. "Hello, Miss. May I help you?"

"Yes." Eden walked up to her. "This bouquet was delivered to my home today."

"Is something wrong?" The lady narrowed her eyes and pursed her lips.

"It seems there's been a mistake. It's supposed to go to someone named Collette Lavasseur at Rue Bourgeat."

"Oh." The lady frowned and read the greeting card tied to the bouquet. She called out to one of her staff. "Ah Qun! Ah Qun!"

A thin-faced man rushed over. "Yes, yes," he said in Chinese.

The lady babbled a torrent of words in Chinese at him. The man examined the card and spoke back, bobbing his head.

"I'm so sorry," the lady said to Eden. Her whole face scrunched. "He made a mistake. It's all a mix-up. I do apologize."

"A mix-up?" Eden picked up the flowers. An idea sprung to her mind. "Collette is my cousin. Today's her birthday. I asked my fiancé to send her an arrangement of flowers on behalf of both of us. My fiancé's name is Neil Sassoon. Do you know if these flowers are from him?"

"Neil Sassoon . . ." The lady flicked her eyes up and tapped her finger on her chin. "Ah! Yes! Mr. Sassoon is a very important customer. Let me check my book." She hurried back to her counter. "Yes, indeed. We had an order today from Mr. Sassoon to Miss Collette Lavasseur."

Involuntarily, Eden squeezed the bouquet. A thorn poked through her finger, piercing her with a twinge of pain.

"I can't believe we made such a mistake." The lady fanned herself with her hand. "Oh dear. Please forgive us. We'll deliver the flowers to Miss Lavasseur right away."

"It's okay." Eden held the bouquet closer to her chest. "I'm about to go visit her anyway. Why don't I just take the flowers to her?"

"Will you do that?" The lady clapped her hands together. "I'm so, so sorry. It won't happen again." Her face widened with a grin. "I can give you a twenty percent credit on your next order."

"That won't be necessary," Eden said. "Thank you very much." She turned around and left. As soon as she stepped outside, her smile vanished. She walked around the corner, pulled the small greeting card off the clip, and dumped the flowers into a rubbish bin. A taxi drove by and she hailed it.

The driver stopped and waited for her to climb in.

"214 Rue Bourgeat please." Eden showed the card to the driver.

The driver glanced at the card, then steered the wheel. Eden sat back. Her mind thick as a cloud as she prayed that there might still be a good reason why Neil would send a bouquet to someone named Collette and signed the word "Love."

At Rue Bourgeat, the taxi stopped in front of a row of stone houses and Eden climbed out of the car. Dragging her feet, she walked toward the building numbered 214. Did she really want to do this? Her wedding was in three days. If she walked away now, everything her marriage promised would be hers. She would be the new Mrs. Neil Sassoon, the envy of the entire city of Shanghai. She would have the wealth and power to help those in need in whatever way she wanted, be they Chinese war refugees or Jews fleeing Germany. Most importantly, she would be able to assure safety for her family, and even Isaac and his family. She would never have to be afraid again.

She paused. She could turn around now. Then she wouldn't have to find out anything.

Or maybe there was nothing to find out. Maybe there was a perfectly good explanation for those flowers. If so, shouldn't she go and make sure that she was only imagining things? If she was being unfairly suspicious and acting like a silly jealous bride, then she ought to go ahead. This way, she would know that the fault was hers and she should trust Neil instead of doubting him.

Yes. That was what she should do. She should find out the fault was hers, not his. She fiddled with the greeting card with the address and continued her steps until she reached the house numbered 214.

What a pretty stone house. She could clearly see the Beaux-Arts influence from the symmetrical, cream-colored stone balconies on the facade. The dainty pots of yellow, purple, and pink flowers set on top of the balcony enclosures in front of each window added just the right touch of color. From outside, the entire building looked like a delicious French dessert.

Beautiful architecture aside, there was one little problem. The building obviously housed more than one unit. How would she know which unit belonged to Collette Lavasseur?

Maybe this was a sign. Maybe she wasn't meant to come here.

She took a step back and gazed up at the building from the first floor to the third. She almost walked away, but a woman walking up the street was staring at her. The woman stopped and stood there with her baby stroller. They locked eyes for a moment. Still holding the small greeting card, Eden pulled her hand against her body.

The woman broke their gaze. She pushed the stroller up to the entrance of the house, forcing Eden to step aside. "I didn't expect you'd come here today," the woman said with a noticeable French accent.

"You know me?" Eden asked.

"Of course I know you. I've been wondering when you'd eventually show up." The woman turned the key and opened the main door. Eden took a quick glance at the stroller. The toddler inside waggled his arms and grinned at her.

"Are you Collette Lavasseur?"

"I am. If you've come to kill me, can you wait until I get the baby back into the apartment and put him to bed first?" Collette grabbed the stroller's bar and pulled it backward up the step through the door. Eden scooted and picked up the stroller's other end to give it a slight push inside.

"Thank you." Collette turned the stroller around, then called out to Eden. "Are you going to come in?"

Eden sucked in a deep breath, then followed her inside. Collette brought the stroller into a flat on the first floor. She waited until Eden entered, then closed and locked the door.

Inside, bright sunlight poured in through the window. Eden ran her eyes once over and surveyed the unit. Such a comfortable place. Expensively decorated too. The spacious living room was furnished with a plush sofa and art deco–style pieces with exotic-looking wood and shiny metal trim.

Turning away from the abstract painting on the wall, which was no doubt an original piece and not a reproduction, Eden took a good look at Collette. She appeared to be about the same age as Eden herself. Twenty-two, perhaps twenty-three? Her golden hair gave the impression that she was a natural beauty, except for the slightly hard jaw line. It didn't detract much from her face though.

Without waiting for Eden to speak, Collette picked up the child and took him into his bedroom. Unsure what to do, Eden followed them. "Is that your child?"

Collette turned her head and rolled her eyes. "Sure. He's mine."

"What's his name?" Eden asked. She couldn't speak harshly in front of a little child, even though Collette's attitude wasn't exactly welcoming. Besides, she still didn't know who Collette really was.

Collette's answer clarified that point. "Harold Sassoon. We call him Harry."

Eden's heart sank.

"I guess Neil hasn't told you about us." Collette put the child into the crib. "Go on, you go to sleep now," she said to the child. The toddler rattled the crib's bars and laughed.

"How old is he?" Eden walked a little closer.

"Thirteen months." Collette straightened the little pillow. The baby bounced his bottom on the bed. He had no idea the mess of the life he was born into.

Collette tucked him in and left the room. "Would you like a cup of tea?" she asked as she walked to the kitchen. "You need to come out of there. He needs his afternoon nap."

Eden had no choice but to follow her.

"Do you want some tea?" Collette asked again, sounding almost annoyed as she put the water on the stove.

"Yes, thank you," Eden answered without giving it any thought. She couldn't care less about the tea, and she wasn't interested in dwelling on the subject.

When the water boiled, Collette made a pot of Darjeeling and put it on the kitchen table with two cups. "Have a seat," she said to Eden.

Her body all tensed, Eden pulled out a chair and sat down.

Collette poured the tea into their cups. "Why'd you come here?"

Eden grasped her purse on her lap. She didn't know. She didn't even know what to expect until just now. She asked the biggest question on her mind. "I want to know what is your relationship with Neil?"

"It's obvious, isn't it? I'm his lover."

His lover. That meant he and Collette had been together since before Eden herself had met him. Their son had been born longer than Eden and Neil had known each other. "How did you know about me?"

"Neil told me. After you met his uncle, he told me he was pursuing you with the intent to marry you."

"And you were okay with that?"

Collette shrugged. "Sooner or later, he's going to marry somebody. It was never going to be me. I'm not Jewish, and I didn't come from a wealthy or distinguished family. His uncle would never make him an heir if he doesn't marry a Jewish girl."

The words struck Eden like a blow. Was Neil lying to her this whole time? Did he court her and ask her to marry him only because she was Jewish? "Why did you stay with him if you know he would never marry you?"

Collette's lips curved up on one side. "What else should I do? I'm an unmarried woman with a child."

Eden lowered her head and wrapped her hands around her cup.

"I met Neil when I was nineteen," Collette said. "My best friend's father came to China when his company sent him here to take up a post. I came to visit her one summer. She told me how exciting and exotic Shanghai was. While I was staying with her, I met Neil. We met at a party. We fell madly in love. When the summer ended, he asked me not to leave. I didn't want to be away from him either. He was upfront. He told me he could never marry me. But I was naive and in love. I didn't believe him. I thought I could change his mind in time," she said with a self-deprecating chuckle. "Then I got pregnant. I thought that might finally turn things around, but it didn't."

"How could he leave you in this predicament?" Eden asked. Who was the wronged woman here? Her or Collette?

"He takes good care of us, as you can see." Collette raised her hand at the room. "Unless you plan to change that." She tensed her shoulders, her demeanor now guarded.

Taken aback, Eden said, "No. That's not my intent at all."

"Then why are you here, if not to get rid of me? Your wedding's in three days."

"I don't know. I didn't even know who you were until just now."

Collette's face loosened. "You never suspected?"

"No." Eden shook her head. She could see now, she was very naive herself.

"What made you come here today?"

"Neil sent you a bouquet of flowers. The florist delivered it to my home by mistake."

Collette let out an ironic laugh. "That's funny. He sent you flowers too. The florist delivered them to me." She glanced over to the pot of orchid on the kitchen counter. "I was going to keep it. It's beautiful."

Yes, it was. The dozen roses Neil sent to Collette were opulent, but the orchid was more elegant and refined, and certainly more expensive. Obviously, Neil had put more thought into what he wanted to send her than to Collette.

She didn't tell that to Collette.

"Look," Collette said, her voice all businesslike, "if you could have a little mercy, for my boy if not for me, I promise I won't ever get in your way. You won't even know I exist."

Eden swallowed hard. What was Collette proposing?

"It's what women in upper-class society do, isn't it? They just have to turn a blind eye." Collette ran her finger along the surface of the table. "We can coexist."

Coexist? Eden bit her lip. Was that a joke? Sharing her man with another woman? What kind of marriage would she have? "Excuse me, I have to go." She gripped her purse and rose from her seat. "Sorry I bothered you." She started toward the door.

Collette followed and opened the door for her. "Do we have a deal then?"

Eden stared at her. Without saying another word, she turned and left.

Outside, she sucked in the air. Summer was coming and the air had become humid and stifling again. She felt like she couldn't breathe.

She stumbled off the pavement and hailed a taxi. She had to speak to Neil. This was unacceptable. How could he have led her on all this time? He'd made her believe he really loved her. How could he keep Collette and his own son a secret? She had to hear it from his own mouth.

TO STOP THE ENEMY

IN HIS OFFICE, Clark opened the Chinese Engineering and Mining Company's commercial brochure to the page with photos of the Kailan mines in Hebei Province near Peking. Across from his desk, Xu Hong-Lie pulled the brochure closer and scanned the pictures and the accompanying English text. The company had published the brochure for its shareholders back in London. Through a joint venture with the Chinese government, the CEMC managed China's largest coal-mining enterprise, the Kailan Mining Administration, also known as the KMA.

"The KMA produces six million tons of coal a year. Two million tons are transported to Shanghai for power and industrial uses," Clark said while Hong-Lie flipped the pages. "Most of the rest is imported to Japan. They're the largest single supplier of coal to Japan."

"I'm surprised Japan hasn't taken it over yet." Hong-Lie stopped at a page with a picture of the KMA's chief manager, Edward Jonah Nathan. The picture showed Nathan with a group of British and Chinese men in suits in front of the KMA office headquarters in Tientsin. "They already control that entire area.

The British openly condemned Japan for initiating war against China."

"Condemn, yes. But they're nothing more than a paper tiger. I've had several discussions with Edward Nathan since I joined the Shanghai Municipal Council. Nathan's based in Shanghai. He has telegrammed the British government for instructions but they haven't given him any answer. He's got financial interests to protect, and he promised the Japanese he would continue to cooperate with them and serve as their business adviser."

Hong-Lie dropped the brochure onto the desk and sneered.

"Having access to the coal supply in Kailan is vital to Japan. Without it, they'll lose half of their iron production. It would damage their steel production too. If the Kailan mines are destroyed, it would cripple their army. It'll stop the bloodshed. It'll be at least six months before they can resume their operations. In that time, our army may be able to drive them back."

"It'll deprive this city of energy too."

"A small price to pay," Clark said. "Dai Li and his people up north are ready to give the plan a try." He paused and clasped his hands on his lap. "I intend to help him."

His elbow propped on the chair arm, Hong-Lie dropped his chin on his fist. "I've never done anything like this."

"Me neither. Neither you nor I ever thought we'd be doing anything more than running a business. If you refuse to participate, I'll understand. But the welfare of the entire country depends on us. This operation can save so many lives. Right now, besides my family, I trust you more than anyone else. I hope you will consider it. Also, your abstention would bring doubt to the rest of the workers we've brought in to join our activities. That would jeopardize our support for the resistance."

Hong-Lie thinned his lips and tapped his fingers against his cheek. He furrowed his forehead, then blew out a deep breath. "What do we have to do?"

Clark sank into his seat in relief. Secretly shipping supplies to the KMT, which they'd been doing in the last three months, was child's play compared to the plot to destroy the Kailan mines. It made him nervous too when Dai Li first approached him about it. So much was at stake, and so much could go wrong. Errors in execution of the plot, accidental breach of confidentiality. The risk would be even higher if he had to depend on anyone not as capable, reliable, and loyal to him as Hong-Lie.

"This is the plan." Clark turned to a page in the brochure which showed the areas of the mines. "See the areas marked in red? Those are the deep pit mines in the low-lying grounds near the Hai River. Dai Li wants to blow up the surrounding areas, flood those mines, and make them inoperable."

"Mmm." Hong-Lie nodded.

"Here's the mines' central power plant." Clark pointed his pen at the spot marked with a hand-drawn star. "The resistance fighters will blow this up. If this plan succeeds, the mining operation will be completely disabled." He glanced up at Hong-Lie. "On May 12th, Dai Li will be delivering a cargo at the port on the Bund. The cargo will be crates labeled as pottery, but they will contain dynamite. He'll be sending dynamite from different routes to the members of the resistance group. We're responsible for the route coming in from the International Settlement. Our job is to transport the dynamite to the north by train as shipments of batteries. Dai Li wants us to personally oversee this mission. We will ride the same train as passengers. I will head up north as far as possible under the guise of a business trip. You will come as my assistant. When we reach the station at the Hai River, an agent of Dai Li who works there will switch the cargo to a local freight train headed to the Kailan mines. I will continue on to Peking. You will transfer onto the freight train and bring the cargo across the canal to the next stop toward the mines. Dai Li's operatives will be waiting to receive you. Once the cargo is unloaded, you can return home."

"Okay. I understand."

"Are you sure?" Clark asked. "I need your help, but I don't want to understate the risks. We're taking dynamite into the occupied territory. The Japanese army is entrenched in the north. If they catch us shipping explosives, we will be put to death. If the plan is discovered, or if the plan succeeds and they find out we're involved, they will kill us. I want you to understand the gravity of what we're asked to do."

"Trust me," Hong-Lie said. "I know the risks. I'm not afraid."

Clark relaxed. At least, their job was only to be carriers. Who were those brave people risking their lives to carry out the explosions? He worried for them, but the thought of them comforted him too. There were still those who answered the patriotic call to defend their country. As long as these people would keep up the fight, China still had hope.

4 0

A WEAK MAN

EDEN ARRIVED at Neil's apartment, her face hard as stone. He didn't notice her mood when she walked in.

"Eden! Darling!" He put his arm around her and kissed her on the cheek. "I wasn't expecting you. Weren't you planning to have dinner with your friend Ava tonight? I thought you wanted to have one last evening to enjoy yourself before the wedding festivities start." He tried to kiss her again.

Leaning away, Eden stiffened. "We need to talk."

"Okay." Neil backed away. "What's wrong?"

"I met Collette Lavasseur."

Neil's smile vanished.

"I met your son too. Harry. He's a beautiful boy."

Turning away, Neil dropped his head.

"Why didn't you tell me?" Eden asked.

Neil looked up. His eyes full of guilt and regret. "I didn't think you'd ever have to know."

"You were going to keep this a secret from me? Forever?" She stepped closer. "I'm about to become your wife."

"I didn't want to hurt you," he said. She could hear the pain in his voice.

"Hurt me? What about Collette? What about your son? Aren't you hurting them?"

"I'm doing the best I can for them. They'll be well cared for."

Eden pulled back and took a close look at him. Who was this man in front of her? How could the person she thought she knew be doing something like this? "Why are you marrying me? Is it because I'm Jewish? Are you marrying me to please your uncle?"

"No!" Neil swung around. "I mean, yes, I wouldn't marry anyone who's not Jewish, but that isn't the reason why I want to marry you. I'm marrying you because I love you."

"You love me?" Eden curled her fingers. "What about Collette? Do you love her?"

"I . . . I . . ."

"Do you?"

"Not as much as I love you."

Eden let out a silent laugh. This was a farce. The whole situation was a farce. What happened? How did she become part of this drama?

"I love you more than anybody else, I swear!" Neil threw his arms around her. "Please, Eden. You have to believe me. I can't live without you. I'll do anything you ask. Anything!" He tightened his arms and hugged her closer. "If you don't want me to see Collette again, I won't. Give me a chance, please."

Would that be enough? If he never saw Collette again? Eden dug her nails into her palms. Was that what she wanted? What about his son, Harry? How would the boy fit in this picture?

"Our wedding's in three days," Neil said. "We can't turn back now."

Couldn't they? Eden's thoughts swayed. Five hundred guests. Their wedding would be the biggest social event in town. How would she face the world if she didn't go through with it?

If things turn sour, just get a divorce. She thought of Ava, laughing as she held up her cigarette holder and a glass of wine.

No. Eden shook her head. This wasn't how she wanted her marriage to be.

"Don't let this get in our way," Neil pleaded. "We can get through this. If you stay with me, we can get through this together."

Could they? What did that even mean?

"I know I've disappointed you. I'm so sorry. I really am," Neil sobbed. "I'm a weak man." He loosened his arms. Still holding her, he fell onto his knees. "I have so many flaws. Everyone thinks I have it all, but they don't know the pressure. Everyone's always judging me and what I do. My mother, my father, Uncle Victor, my older brother, my mother's family in England. Even my aunts and uncles and cousins living in Arabic countries who I've never even met. They all think I'll never measure up. I felt like a nobody until I met you." Still sobbing, he pressed his face against her. "You're strong. I need you. You're the only one who believes in me. Even when I made a big mistake, you forgave me and gave me a chance. You can make me a better man. Please. Don't go away. You can save me. If you stay, I'll become everything you want me to be. Please."

Eden stared at him. She should be angry at him, but she felt sorry for him.

She didn't feel strong. She felt entirely lost.

"Tell me you won't leave me." Shaking her lightly, he hung on to her. He looked so sad, so broken. She put her hand on his back.

All this time, she thought she was holding onto him as her pillar.

If he needed her to hold onto instead, then who would she turn to when she needed help?

She gazed out of his windows. Night had fallen. In the dark, she could see no answer.

41

HER LAST GOODBYE

AFTER HIS SECRET meeting with Xu Hong-Lie, Clark left the office and went to the small apartment where Ekaterina had been hiding out for the last few months. Of all the things that had happened since he came back to Shanghai, Ekaterina was one which would at least have a good ending. And even though she had betrayed him once, he was glad to be able to help her in the end. Perhaps, when she reached America, she would finally find peace, and live a life in which she would never have to rely on deceit to find her way again.

When he arrived at her building, she was already waiting at the entrance. Huang Shifu stopped the car by the sidewalk and opened the passenger door. Clark got out of his car and greeted her. She looked radiant in her peach-pink straw hat and matching floral summer dress. Her face, without the red rouge and lipstick, looked younger and brighter. He could even see a trace of innocence seeping its way back.

"This is it?" He pointed at her single suitcase. "This is all you're bringing on a cross-continent journey?"

"This is it!" She lifted her suitcase, then put it back down. It didn't look very heavy either. "I'm leaving all the burden behind. I'm giving myself a fresh start."

"That's good." Clark grinned. "That's very good." He softened his voice. "The Chase Bank has converted your gold and transferred your money to Washington, D.C. When you arrive, there will be an account waiting for you in your new name."

"My new name," Ekaterina said, ready to break into a smile. "Elisa Saichenko."

"Elisa Saichenko." Clark couldn't help feeling happy for her. Was that a spark of life in her eyes he just saw? "Someone from Washington will come to pick you up when you arrive in San Francisco. My liaison, Joseph Whitman, made all the arrangements. His colleagues will be able to help you get settled once you arrive."

"Thank you." Ekaterina gave him a look of deep gratitude.

Clark nodded. "The State Department and the War Department will want to talk to you."

"I know." She pulled her purse to the front. Her exchange of information of everything she knew about the Soviets in return was the real reason why the U.S. Government agreed to let her enter and remain in their country. "I'll be fine. I can handle them. They can't be any trickier to deal with than anyone I've already had to deal with here, except you."

"True, true." Clark smiled again and leaned back with his hands in his pockets.

A taxi stopped at an empty space across the street. The driver got out and came up to them. "You Miss Elisa Saichenko?" he asked with a heavy Chinese accent.

"Yes," Ekaterina answered and winked at Clark.

"I take you to harbor."

"Thank you," she said to the man, then turned back to Clark. "Thank you for arranging my ride."

"My driver could've driven you." Clark glanced at the taxi. His Cadillac was so much more comfortable.

"It's okay. Your fancy car draws too much attention. I just want to get on the ship. The fewer people notice me, the better."

She was right, of course. But he would've liked to indulge a good friend one more time. "Take care of yourself."

"I will. You too." She dipped her head. "Goodbye. If you ever come to America again, look me up."

"I will." Clark shifted his feet. "I definitely will."

She gave her suitcase to the driver and followed him across the street to the taxi. As they walked, she turned around and waved. Clark waved back and watched her climb into the backseat. The driver closed the door, then went to put the suitcase into the trunk.

Another taxi pulled up and double-parked next to the line of cars parked on Clark's side. The driver hurried out and came to the entrance. He squinted and looked around. "Excuse me," he said to Clark. "Are you Yuan Guo-Hui?"

"Yes," Clark answered. How did this man know his name?

"You called for a taxi this morning to pick up Elisa Saichenko?"

"Yes." Clark's heart did a summersault. What was going on?

"Sorry I'm late. I had such bad luck today. Someone slashed my tires. I had to change them and I got delayed. I drove here as fast as I could."

His heart dropping, Clark looked across the street. The driver who'd taken Ekaterina slammed shut the trunk and walked away from the car. Immediately, he ran toward her. "Ekaterina!"

Before he even got off the pavement, the taxi carrying her exploded with a loud boom. The sudden sound propelled Clark to duck down between the cars parked on his side. A rain of glass and metal blasted into the air. The dust and debris blew all the way to where he hid, assailing his nostrils along with the burning smell of fuel mixed with roasted flesh.

"Ekaterina!" Clark bolted up and ran toward the flame. From the broken passenger window, he could see her lifeless body fallen sideway in the back seat. Blood dripped down from the top of her head. He came within five feet of the car, but the heatwave from the fire and clinks of falling shards kept him away.

Behind him, the real taxi driver screamed, "Help! Help!" Pedestrians stopped in shock and circled around the scene.

Huang Shifu ran toward Clark. "Young Master! Young Master! Are you all right?"

Clark clenched his fist. Sokolov did this. It was the only explanation. Somehow, the cold-blooded Commissar and his people had found out where Ekaterina was hiding. This was revenge. If he went down, then he wasn't going to let her get away either.

"Are you all right?" Huang Shifu asked him again.

Heaving his chest, Clark shook his head. "I don't know. I don't know."

Down the street, police sirens wailed. The fire continued to burn. Helpless, Clark watched it grow. The blaze of injustice enveloped the now dead princess, consuming her and refusing to let her go.

Entering his house, all Clark felt was exhaustion. An exhaustion unlike anything he had ever known. He ignored the maid who opened the door, and dragged his weary body to his room.

"Young Master? Young Master? Do you want tea? Shall I bring you a glass of water?" the maid called out and followed a few steps after him.

He barely heard her. With heavy steps, he trudged up the stairs. Once inside his bedroom, he closed the door and sagged onto his bed.

Why? Why couldn't fate spare Ekaterina? How much more destructions did people have to suffer before Heaven would finally say enough?

When the fire trucks arrived and put out the flames, her charred body had become completely unrecognizable. So much beauty, all drifted away with the smoke.

Life. How fragile it was. How powerless he was in the face of the god of death. Everything a mortal soul like him had tried to plan—her false identity, her escape via the Dollar Line, the contact with the agents at the U.S. Department of State—their importance all lost in one stroke.

He hunched his back and stared at his hands. All that was left for him to do now was to say a prayer. Rest in peace, princess. If the world had shown her nothing but cruelty, may she enter Heaven, and finally know peace and joy.

He loosened his tie. On his nightstand, Eden's wedding invitation lay at the base of the lamp. Seeing her name, a sharp stab of pain speared through him, adding to the dull heavy pain already tearing him apart. At one time, he could've told her everything in his heart. He could've pursued her, however difficult it might have been for them to face the world together. Instead, he chose duty. And for what? Look at all the losses around him. What difference did it make?

And why couldn't he tell her everything now?

Yes, it was too late. She had found the man she loved, but her wedding wouldn't take place until the day after tomorrow. At long last, he could finally tell her the truth. To let her know how he'd always felt about her.

Would it be so wrong if he did that? What was right or wrong anyway? In this upside-down world where humanity itself hung on the edge, he couldn't tell right from wrong, or wrong from right anymore.

All he wanted was for her to know why he made his choice. If tomorrow, his own life went up in flames, this might be the last chance he had to say to her what he'd buried deep in his heart. He owed it to her—to himself, to let her know that she was the one he'd always loved, even when forces greater than himself had compelled him to walk the other way. He didn't want to die without her knowing this.

After that, he would wish her well. He would wish for her a long happy life with Neil Sassoon by her side.

He picked up the wedding invitation and went downstairs to the study. At the desk, he began to write.

Dear Eden,

I don't know if it is right of me to write to you now with all the things I'm about to say. If not, I hope you will forgive me, and grant me this one chance to tell you what I have always wanted you to know . . .

42

SHATTERED DREAMS

In the grand suite of the Cathay Hotel, Eden sat still while the beautician touched up her makeup. In two hours, she would be standing beside Neil. Under the chuppah, she'd be wearing the wedding gown hanging on the mannequin body by the wall, taking her vows.

In the end, after the night she'd confronted Neil about Collette, she couldn't go through with calling off the wedding. He'd pleaded. He pleaded so hard. He promised he would end things with Collette. He would support their child, Harry, and give them financial support, but he swore he would never be unfaithful to her after they were married. He knelt before her, a broken man. She didn't have the heart to hurt him.

What was more, she didn't have the heart to break everyone's dreams. Her parents, Joshua, Sir Victor. Everyone would be so disappointed.

As long as Neil kept to his promises and was a good husband, what point would there be for her to throw everything away?

Over at the table, her bridesmaids snacked on hors d'oeuvres of lox, fruits, and cheese. Ruth Kadoorie, Celine Bloom, and

Dorothea Meyer. Women of the highest status in Shanghai, all ready to welcome her into their fold.

"I love your wedding dress, Eden," Ruth said and popped a grape into her mouth. "All the guests will be stunned when you walk down the aisle."

"Thank you," Eden said, trying not to move her face while the beautician smoothed out the rouge. After fussing through dozens of pictures and sketches, she had chosen the floor-length, high-neck, long-sleeved gown with the bodice of dotted Swiss lace. She thought it was a good choice, sufficiently conservative. Definitely appropriate for the occasion and proper for the new Mrs. Neil Sassoon in front of their five hundred guests.

Ava, who'd be among the guests, didn't like it much though. "You'll look like mummy once you put that on," she joked.

"There!" The beautician pulled back the brush. "You look gorgeous, my dear."

The bridesmaids let out a collective, "Aww." They came over to Eden.

"Are we ready for the dress?" the beautician asked.

"Yes!" Celine shouted. Dorothea clapped her hands. Ruth squeaked in delight.

"Wait," Eden said. "Let me get my brooch." Yesterday, her mother had given her a pink topaz and diamond brooch. It was a family heirloom passed down from her grandmother. Sir Victor's jeweler had given her the most lavish set of necklace and bracelets to wear for today and for this evening, but the brooch meant more to her than anything she could buy.

She went into the bedroom of the suite and retrieved her black beaded purse from the drawer of the nightstand. The purse was what she was using to keep her most important personal items during her stay here. Her brooch, her keys, her wallet, and . . . Clark's letter.

The letter came to her home yesterday, hand-delivered by a courier. She still hadn't gotten over the shock. She didn't want to leave it behind in case anyone saw it while she was gone, so she took it with her.

Leaving the sounds of voices and laughter of the women in the sitting area of the suite outside, Eden opened the clasp of her purse. She meant to take out the brooch, but took out the letter instead.

Hesitantly, she unfolded the letter.

Dear Eden,

I don't know if it is right of me to write to you now with all the things I'm about to say. If not, I hope you will forgive me, and grant me this one chance to tell you what I have always wanted you to know. Since the first day I met you, I've been in love with you. For so many reasons, I could never honestly tell you how I feel. At first, I didn't think I could give you the best life you deserve. You're a Western foreigner. I'm Chinese. Society is cruel. People don't look kindly upon a woman if she entangles herself with a man outside of her race. My own family was an obstacle. I was bound to an engagement I never wanted. I didn't think it was possible to break the chains of traditions. I didn't think I had the liberty to pursue free love.

My mind changed when I watched you stand up for what you believed, against all the obstacles in your way and the disapproval of your entire community. You inspired me to break free. You showed me you had the strength and courage to stand up against the world. I had hoped then I could overcome whatever obstacles that stood in the way and give you my love, if you had felt the same way and wanted to give us a chance. Although I could be wrong, I believe you would have wanted that too.

But some obstacles are too big to ignore. There are things in this world beyond our own control. Even though my heart was going one way, the weight of duty and the threat of war pulled me onto another path. After Chiang Kai-shek's abduction, my government was in desperate need of Soviet support. To help Ekaterina Brasova infiltrate the Kremlin in

Shanghai and introduce her to a key person through whom we could try to influence Stalin, I was asked to pose as her lover. It broke my heart to walk away from you, but at the time, I felt it was the only right choice. I had the safety of my whole country to consider.

Maybe it was all for the best. I will take solace in knowing that you're to become the wife of the nephew of the most prominent man in Shanghai. I won't say that I'm happy. How can I be, when the woman I love will be forever out of my reach? But I will wish you well from the bottom of my heart. I will always want the best for you.

But I want you to know this: Ekaterina and I were never lovers. It was an act, a cover-up.

Why am I telling you this now? I guess it is because I've learned that life is very fragile. For all that I've given up, my government was unable to stop the forces of Japan. In this city, thousands have died, including my father. I watched the Japanese level our buildings to the ground. In Nanking, thousands were massacred. What happened to my family's longtime maid and her family there, I can't even talk about it. I'd known Peng Amah since birth. To know what the Japanese troops did to her, I can never explain what the pain is like. I'm a living being, but my soul feels like it's dying. Earlier today, I watched Ekaterina die with my own eyes. Her enemies planted a car bomb and blew her up.

Right now, I sit alone, thinking of all the losses. I remember the day two years ago when you and I walked along the Bund, watching the flags of the nations. I had so many dreams back then. Dreams of helping my country advance and modernize. Dreams of making life better for the poor. Dreams of working with my father to expand my family's business and make my parents proud. All those dreams are gone now. Around me, there are only deaths.

Forgive me for sounding so morbid. Your wedding day is coming up. It is extremely discourteous of me to write you this depressing letter just before the happiest day of your life. I fear though that I won't have another chance. I couldn't very well write this letter to another man's wife. So please forgive my imprudence. But as I said, life is fragile. If something should happen and I am no longer here tomorrow, I want you to know that

I love you. I've always loved you. When I look at all the devastation that has shattered my dreams, the one dream I will always lament losing is a chance to fall in love with you.

I will not be attending your wedding. I do not wish to bring bad luck to you at the start of your new life. Furthermore, I wouldn't be a sincere guest. If I see you walk up the aisle, I would be wishing you were coming to me instead of another man.

Instead, at the moment when you say your wedding vows, I will be at the Bund, by the steps of the statue of the Angel of Peace where I can watch the flags. There, I will make a wish. For you, for your happiness, and for all of life's blessings to be upon you. I will wish for the world to be at peace, and for it to become one where no law or human divide will ever stop two people from falling in love again.

Always,
   Clark

Reading the last words, Eden held the letter against her heart. Why didn't he tell her sooner? She would've understood. She would've waited, for however long it would take until they could have their chance.

"Eden!" the beautician called out to her. "Did you find your brooch? It's almost time. We'll have to leave soon."

"Coming!" Eden gripped the letter, then folded it and put it back into the purse. She took out the brooch and went back into the sitting room.

"All right! Here comes the bride!" The beautician held up the wedding dress. All smiling, the bridesmaids rushed up behind her.

Slowly, Eden walked closer to the dress. Her breaths shortened. That high neck. The long sleeves. The tight bodice. The constriction in her throat tightened. That Swiss dotted lace, so beautiful. Why did it look like a net? Why didn't she notice that before today?

What was she doing?

"I'm sorry. I have to talk to Neil." She turned around. Without waiting for them to respond, she hurried out of the room. Neil was on the floor below her, in the Riverside Suite.

She followed the stairs to his floor and came to his room. "Neil!" She knocked on the door. "Neil, we have to talk." She knocked again.

Neil opened the door. "Eden?" His eyes widened in surprise. "What are you doing here?"

"Please, I have to talk to you." She glanced at his groomsmen standing behind him. "Alone."

"All right." Neil furrowed his brows. "Fellas, would you give us a moment?"

The men mumbled yeses. Eden stepped aside to let them out.

"Come on in," Neil said to her after they left. She entered and he closed the door.

"We're not supposed to see each other before the wedding." He tried to lighten the air.

Eden ignored his joke. "This is not right. We can't go through with this."

"What do you mean?" Neil asked, his voice shook. "Is it because of Collette? Are you still upset with me?"

"No, I'm not upset. And yes, it is about Collette. You promised me you would end your relationship with her. You asked me to forgive you. You said I can save you, that I can make you a better man. But you see, I can't. Only you can make yourself a better man, and the way you can do that is to do right by her. She's the mother of your son. If you have any feelings left for her, you should go to her. She needs you. And more importantly, your son needs you."

"But . . ." Neil's face fell. "But I told you already. I'll take care of them. They won't want for anything."

"No. You're leaving them without a name, when you should be their guardian and protector. And for what? So you can inherit your uncle's fortune? That's not what an honorable man would do."

"Eden," Neil whimpered. "What are you saying? Are you leaving me? You don't love me?"

"I do," she said. Bittersweet tears brimmed in her eyes. "I do love you, just not enough. And not the right kind of love. You're a very sweet man. You indulge me in countless ways I don't deserve. You offered me a world I'd never dreamt of ever being a part. I don't want to take advantage of what you give me anymore. I don't deserve it. I'm not entirely blameless either. When I accepted your proposal, the main reason I said yes was because I thought you can save me and my family and get us out to someplace safe if the war gets worse. Maybe to England or another country. I wanted a safety route, and it's not fair to you."

Neil dropped onto the sofa and covered his face with his hands.

Eden came closer to him and touched him on the shoulder. "You should be with Collette and your son. You can still make things right. Forget your uncle. Stop trying so hard to become his heir. You're chasing the wrong dreams."

Neil lowered his hands. "We have five hundred guests waiting."

Eden laughed. "They'll live." She took her engagement ring off her finger. "Maybe now's a good chance for you to introduce Harry to them? There's still enough time for your driver to fetch him."

Neil frowned.

"Goodbye, Neil."

"Where are you going?"

"The place where I should've been all along." She put the ring in his hand, and left the room. From the hallway, she took the elevator to the ground floor. At the main entrance, the groomsmen and a group of guests had gathered. Keeping her head low, she darted to the side entrance. Once outside, she made her way past the crowd toward the riverfront. The monument of the Angel of Peace was only a short walk away. Clark. Would he really be there?

THE ANGEL OF PEACE

ON THE BUND looking out the river, Clark rolled up his shirt sleeves and rested his arms on the balustrade surrounding the statue of the Angel of Peace. Behind him to his left, the flags of the nations continued to fly at the top of the buildings, asserting the illusion of their might in the view of the fleet of Japanese warships moored near Soochow Creek.

He glanced at his watch. Two o'clock. What was Eden doing now? Was she walking down the aisle? Soon, she would be saying her vows. Along with her words under the chuppah, so would go the last of his dreams.

"It's still a magnificent view, isn't it?" Her voice whispered behind him like a warm breeze, soothing his mind.

Wait. How could that be?

He turned around. Was she an illusion, or was she a dream?

"Why are you here?" he asked. "Aren't you supposed to be getting married?"

"No." She shook her head. "I think I'm supposed to be right here, with you."

Clark's mouth fell open. Did he really hear what he just heard? Did she leave her own wedding? For him?

Eden stepped up to the balustrade next to him. "I wish you had told me about Ekaterina from the start."

"I couldn't. What we were doing was too dangerous. It was better you didn't know. And I didn't know how long the assignment would last. It could've been years. I couldn't burden you and ask you to wait for me."

"You should've given me the choice to decide that myself."

"I wanted to protect you."

"I know."

"What about Neil? Did you really leave him? Are you sure you know what you're doing?"

"Neil will be fine. It would've been a mistake if I hadn't walked away from him."

Clark watched the wind blow the strands of her hair over her shoulder. "I'll never be able to offer you what he can. My family's business is big, but it's nothing compared to the Sassoons. And with the war, I don't know how well I'll be able to hold on to everything."

"You think I care about all that?" Eden laughed.

"No." He gazed up with a shy grin and slid his feet on the ground. "But in all seriousness, the political situation in my country is precarious. I won't have any way to save you if the Japanese push us any further."

"You keep saying your country. What if I tell you this is my country too? I don't have any other place I can call home." She rested her arms on the balustrade and let the soothing wind from the river blow past her face. Clark joined her as the fishermen unloaded their catch from their sampans onto the dock and the beggars on the Bund shook their bowls at the passersby.

She turned and looked him in the eye. "This is the world we live in. Don't leave me out of it. If it's your world, then I want to be a part of it."

"Eden."

"We can keep the dream of us alive, can't we?"

Clark nodded. This dream hadn't died. She had come to him and brought it back to life.

"So what happens now?" She cocked her head and smiled.

A sea of emotions running through him, he took her hand. "My work isn't done yet."

"What do you mean?"

"I'm no longer with the KMT, but there are things I'm doing to help our country fight back. I'm working with people who are part of a resistance movement. What they do could be a matter of life and death, for me as well. If you're with me, you'll be opening yourself up to risks. Are you sure you can accept that?"

"I'm not afraid," she said. "If what you're doing will help China rise again, I'll stand by you. We'll face what's ahead together."

Her words filled him with hope. He laced his fingers with hers and pulled her close to his side. Under the statue of the Angel of Peace, his own angel had come to restore his dream.

THE MINES OF KAILAN

IN THE DINING compartment on the train, Clark sipped his cup of lukewarm tea while he waited for Hong-Lie to make his next move. Since he was a kid, Clark had always excelled in the Chinese chess game *xiang qi*. It was something he sorely missed during the six years he lived in America. For him, Western chess could not compare. Even now, back in Shanghai, he rarely came across another player who could challenge him.

Hong-Lie came close. The game kept them occupied and relieved their boredom through the days and hours on their way north. Most importantly, it diverted their minds from all the dangers of what they had really come to do—to bring a crucial shipment of dynamite to the guerrillas planning to blow up the Kailan mines.

Clark held his breath as Hong-Lie stalled. The poor guy had almost no choice left. Of all the pieces he could use to protect the General, which was the piece he must keep alive to not lose the game, the cannon and elephant were the only ones left. Plus one useless little soldier. Clark himself still had a chariot, but he didn't think he'd need to use it. If Hong-Lie made the wrong move as Clark expected, Clark could strike his General with the horse and take the game.

And Hong-Lie did exactly that. He moved the elephant to shield his General from Clark's chariot, forgetting that Clark had a horse that could sneak right in.

"General!" Clark called out—the Chinese equivalent to "checkmate"—and pushed his horse into place.

"Ayah!" Hong-Lie groaned. "I lost again. That's eighteen wins for you and ten for me. I give up."

"You can't give up," Clark said. "You can only get better if you keep playing. Come on. I'll get us some food so we can take a break. We'll arrive at the Hai River station in two hours. It's almost dinner time anyway. You should eat something. The local train might not serve food. We should have time for one more game after that."

"All right." Hong-Lie put the pieces and the gameboard back into the box.

Clark left him and went to the counter to buy them each a rice box and another thermos of tea. When he returned to their table, he found Hong-Lie holding a black and white photo of himself and a young woman. He asked his friend, "Who's that?"

"My lover." Hong-Lie grinned. "Sun Xiu-Qing."

"Can I see?" Clark put the rice boxes and thermos on the table and sat down.

"Sure." Hong-Lie gave him the photo.

"She's very good looking," Clark gave her a customary compliment. The fair-looking young woman was in fact more than that. In the photo, she exuded an air of clear calmness, like a white lily. Together with Hong-Lie, they made a striking match, although it wouldn't be appropriate for Clark to comment on these observations. "How'd you meet her?"

"At school. We've been together for quite a while. Before we can develop our relationship further, her father wants to see me show some accomplishments in my career. I think . . . it's about time." He broke into a smile. "Before I left for this trip, she told me her father actually asked when I would marry her. When I get back, we'll begin to make plans."

"Oh?" Clark exclaimed. "Congratulations then! I'll be waiting to drink your celebratory wine."

Hong-Lie laughed. He took the photo back and put it into his shirt pocket.

"Come on, hurry up and eat." Clark pushed a rice box and chopsticks toward him. "The food's getting cold." He opened his own box and poured more tea into their cups from the thermos.

Hong-Lie flipped open the rice box, then stared out the window. "I only wish for things to be better. Life is basically all the same. One just wishes to pass the days in peace. Raise a few children and hope they too will grow up well. When one gets old, there would be children and grandchildren around us. Only with the Japanese here, what would the future be like? I don't worry about myself. I'm just one rotten life." He shrugged. "But I do want to take good care of Xiu-Qing. In the future, when we have children, I want them to grow up in a good, peaceful world. Will they have that if the Japanese are here?"

Clark pushed his chopsticks into the rice. How could he answer that? "Nothing is final yet. Take it one step at a time."

"You're right." Hong-Lie took a bite of the pickled vegetable. Clark knew he only said that because Hong-Lie never expected Clark to have an answer either.

They finished their food and tried to play another game, but gave up halfway. As the train approached their next stop, Clark's mind wandered to what would happen when they arrived, and his heart grew heavier. His enthusiasm for the game waned. Hong-Lie must have felt the same way too because he happily conceded the game.

The conductor clacked open the door to the car and shouted, "Hai River!" He stalked down the aisle, stopping briefly to signal Clark with his eye and a nod. The man was a *Juntong* operative.

Dai Li had alerted Clark to watch for the conductor's signal back in Shanghai.

Clark and Hong-Lie returned to their cabin to get their duffle bags. The train pulled into the station and stopped. When they got off, Clark could see the station workers connecting several freight cars to the local train, including the freight cars carrying their dynamite. Everything was moving on as planned.

"Smooth wind all the way," Clark said to Hong-Lie, the words for wishing him a safe journey.

"See you later." Hong-Lie proceeded to the other side of the platform toward the local train.

"Be careful." Clark could not help warning him again.

"You too." Hong-Lie turned his head. He waved goodbye and walked on. Clark watched him board the car, then search for a bench to rest. The next train to Peking wouldn't arrive yet for another hour. He took out his copy of Agatha Christie's latest, *Death on the Nile*. It'd been a while since he dug into a good English book. Taking his mind away to Egypt definitely helped him sleep better last night.

Night was approaching and the sky darkened. Behind him, the local train's engine powered up. The clacks on the track grew louder as it pulled away from the station and the small town toward the rural plain. Clark looked up and watched it rattle off into the sunset, then returned to his book.

As he finished the chapter and turned to the next, a distant boom interrupted him. He gazed up. Another blast echoed around the town. This one boomed even louder. More explosions followed. A ball of fire shot up into the air from the direction where the local train had gone. Twisters of black smoke rose and coiled around the fire.

For a few seconds, Clark stared at the flare. Was that the train? Did something just happen to the train?

His heart nearly stopped. His hands loosened. Did their dynamite blow up?

Xu Hong-Lie! Clark dropped his book and sprung up from the bench.

The passengers at the station cried out in shock. Whistles of station agents screeched as the men rushed toward the end of the platform to try to get a better look. The station master ran inside the depot.

Amidst the chaos, Clark stood alone, his heart now pounding like a giant hammer.

Snapshots of thoughts fired into his mind. The train. The dynamite. Their mission to blow up the mines. Hong-Lie.

No . . .

He took a step toward the scene of the rising smoke. He could go no further. His legs had lost their strength. Terror had blown his center of gravity away.

What should he do?

The people at the station and areas nearby had now gathered on the platform for the local trains. All were trying to find out what catastrophe had struck. Wresting his mind away from their buzzing voices, Clark searched within for answers. None came forth. Soon, the rural sky turned pitch black, and the traces of smoke could not be seen anymore.

— *To Be Continued*

AFTERWORD

In the *Shanghai Story* trilogy, we have now come to the point in time when WWII has officially begun in the East. There are historians who argue that WWII actually began in 1937 with the outbreak of the second Sino-Japanese War.

Looking at where the story has gone so far, one aspect I find most difficult to write about is racism. My goal for writing fiction has always been to entertain. I chose to write historical fiction because going back in time through fiction is a form of escapism, and the WWII era is rich and fascinating. The problem is, I do not enjoy writing about racism in fiction. Of course, I have my own opinions on this issue, but I have no interest in asserting my opinions on social issues in my stories.

Nonetheless, racism was such a big part of the war and how people viewed each other during that time, it was impossible to not include it somehow when my characters interacted with each other and with the world. My challenge then, as a fiction writer, was to decide how I would approach this issue.

When writing stories about the European theater, the narrative of our history is very clear about who were the heroes and who were the villains. In the Pacific, things are not so clear.

In *Shanghai Story* Book One, I struggled with having to portray Western racism. In the West, the Allied countries have always been portrayed as the "good guys." They rescued the Jews and fought against the German Nazis. But in the East, white foreigners from the Allied countries were themselves racist colonial lords. I did not enjoy having to show that the Allied countries' attitudes toward people of other races weren't exemplary either.

In *Shanghai Story*, I felt especially uncomfortable having to write about the racism of the British people. My grandmother had lived through the WWII era and escaped to Hong Kong before the communist cultural revolution. But for years, she had kept a little framed photo of Chris Patten on the top of her television. Patten was the British-appointed governor of Hong Kong from 1992 to 1997, when that region was returned to China. My grandmother, who was not a political person, felt a special affection for Patten. She thought he was a good leader who had done good things for the Hong Kong people. She kept that photo on the TV until she passed away. I myself had traveled to London once, and had a marvelous time. Basically, I have nothing against the British people, and I felt very uncomfortable having to write them in an ugly light.

In *Shanghai Dreams*, I had to dive even deeper into the issue of racial conflicts. This time, my struggle was about how to portray the Japanese. Personally, I am very fond of Japan. I grew up watching anime and reading manga. Consequently, I developed a deep love for the Japanese culture. In college, Japanese was one of my majors. I have traveled to Japan many times, and I would recommend it as one of my top three countries to visit. Moreover, my sister-in-law is Japanese-American. It was painful for me to write a story which brings to attention the ugliest part of Japanese history.

It was equally painful to write about the victims. The subject of comfort women still evokes a lot of pain and anger today.

Memories of Japan's attempt to erase Korea's culture and identity, and the horrors it committed in China and other Asian countries during the war, are still a source of tension between Japan and other Asian people in the Pacific region. When I wrote the chapter "Massacre in Nanking," I had to stop in the middle and take a break. It was horrific to try to put into words what had happened, and my scene barely touched on the atrocities the Japanese troops committed.

As always, I strive to be objective when writing my stories, without injecting my own opinions. I am not a historian or a social commentator. As a fiction writer, I want to show the world in the past as realistically as possible, without letting my own views or other outside factors influence how I would write each scene.

This was easier said than done, especially in today's political climate. Our PC culture has caused many writers to hesitate in how they write about certain subjects, or whether they should write about something at all. Big publishing houses are now hiring sensitivity editors to comb through manuscripts before publication to ensure the books would not offend readers. On college campuses and elsewhere, there are demands to obscure historical figures because their past views or actions do not meet the standards of our time.

In *Shanghai Dreams*, I had written instances when Chinese characters used racial slurs in their speech when they referenced the Japanese. My editor flagged those parts, warning me that the use of such words, when said by characters who are not clearly villains, might upset some readers. She advised me to consider the risks. But I had already thought about these risks when I drafted the derogatory terms into the story. I decided that the inclusion of these words, rather than excluding them to avoid backlash, was the correct choice.

How so? You might ask. To begin, I didn't include racial slurs as gratuitous insults to Japanese people today. I didn't even include them just to show that these slurs were said by Chinese people back then. When I wrote this book, I had placed myself into the world of 1930s Shanghai. I tried to see the issue of race through the lenses of the people who had lived during that time. In that place, I felt it would be utterly unrealistic to write my story any differently.

In the 1930s, Japan had been encroaching on Chinese territories in the north. The threat of war was very real. Racial tensions between the Chinese and the Japanese had been festering for many years. By the time the war broke out in 1937, the tensions had reached a breaking point. Japan's actions during this time had provoked a very deep resentment among the Chinese. And yet, China was a weak country. It didn't have the technology or resource to defend itself against Japan, which the Meiji government had taken steps to modernize in the mid-1800s. For many Chinese people, speech was the only way they could retaliate. In this context, the situation was not one where the Japanese were a minority group of people being slighted, harmed, and marginalized. It was a case where speech was a form of resistance against an enemy state already taking over China.

In *Shanghai Dreams*, Clark, the protagonist, never used racial slurs himself. My editor suggested that if Clark reacted more negatively when he heard such slurs being used, it might help to cue readers that I am not supporting the use of racist speech. She also thought it might be problematic to readers that Clark did not show negative reactions upon hearing such slurs. I disagreed on that point. In the pre-war era, tolerance for racism was much higher than it is today, even for people who were being discriminated against. Racial slurs were part of everyday speech, and people generally accepted it. Clark was a man of his time. It didn't feel authentic to me that he would have the sensitivities of people in today's world.

But does that mean I had to bring the history of tolerance into my story, when social injustice has become a lightning rod for controversies today? Couldn't I have left this part of history out of my story to avoid upsetting readers? Couldn't I ignore it rather than draw attention to it?

When I took into account the historical context behind the story, I became convinced that avoiding the issue would, in fact, be injecting an opinion by omission. When researching for this story, I had read letters that Chiang Kai-shek wrote to his troops. Chiang himself referred to the Japanese many times as the "short army," or variations as such. When the head of state and commander-in-chief was speaking this way, it felt disingenuous to pretend that his followers did not do the same. It also made little sense in my mind that Clark, who should be very familiar with Chiang's attitudes and how he spoke, would frown upon other military or government officials such as Sītu, when they spoke in the same manner as Chiang.

I also took into account the emotions of the characters. The Japanese were brutal in how they invaded China in 1937. By the time they got to Shanghai, thousands of Chinese had been killed. For the Chinese, their cities had toppled. Their country was falling into enemy hands. When Sītu gave a speech to rally up morale, it made no sense to me that he would refrain from using a derogatory term. His speech would not be as emotional without it, and would not be honest and genuine. As for Clark, I think he would be very cold and heartless if, at this point, his thoughts and concerns were about slandering the Japanese, when he knew how horrifically his own people were being killed and treated.

Going a step further, I think it would actually be more offensive if I had avoided racial slurs in my book. In the pre-war era, racist attitudes existed among Asian peoples. I didn't want to write a simple-minded story where the Chinese were portrayed as enlightened because they were the victims, and misrepresent the Japanese as the only ones who held prejudicial views. It was true that during the war era, the Japanese saw themselves as superior to other Asian people. But it is also true that even victims of racism are not necessarily above having prejudicial and racist views and attitudes themselves. In this book, I felt it was authentic to show that during this time period, the Chinese, too, held unenlightened views just like everybody else. Omitting this would be asserting that the Chinese somehow knew better than the others when it came to the issue of race.

My struggle in this book did not end with speech. For months, I debated in my head whether I should incorporate John Rabe into the chapter "Massacre in Nanking", or whether I should just write a fictional missionary priest. John Rabe was a German Nazi who openly supported the Nazi regime and ideologies. In today's political climate, positive portrayal of a Nazi can be manipulated by neo-Nazis to gain sympathy for themselves. Therefore, in spite of the historical truth, I did not take my decision lightly.

In the end, the image of Rabe walking the besieged streets of Nanking unarmed to save the victims, shielded by nothing but his Nazi armband, was so strong and vivid in my mind, I could not leave it out. What he did during the Nanking invasion was an act of incredible courage and compassion, and he deserves recognition for it. He should not be substituted by a fictional priest just because he had submitted to views and supported people who we, in hindsight, would not condone. Today, with social media firmly entrenched in our everyday life, people are too often being defined by a single action, or a single comment or tweet. A snapshot of a person's action in one moment in time can define him or her for life. Today, we seem to have forgotten that people are complicated beings with many sides, or that a person can mature and evolve. We value condemnation over forgiveness when someone makes a single mistake. We demand apologies, but we no longer expect true acts of redemption, nor do we allow for a chance for redemption. In today's world of sound bites, short attention span, and instant gratification, perhaps all these are inevitable. But in my little corner, John Rabe reminds me that even someone who had committed a grave wrong, can be something more.

So I leave it up to you, my readers, to see for yourself these various pieces of history through my story. No matter what choices I make, some will no doubt disagree. What I can say, though, is that I did my best to present the story according to the experience of the people of that time. As long as I can accurately show you what the world was like in the past, I leave it up to you to judge where we had gone right or wrong in our history, and what you think would be the best way for us to move forward.

In spite of how difficult it is for us to face our past, I think past wrongs is something we should remember. Hiding it would not change the past, nor would it truly make up for past wrongs. Rather than looking at past wrongs as something too offensive to acknowledge, we can instead look back at history and see how far we have come. We are still a long way off from resolving all the injustices in our world, but we can only measure our progress if we can see how bad things were in our past. When we try to revise history to fit our own model of how things should be, we lose the lessons we can learn from the past.

My next novella, *The Moon Chaser*, which will be released as part of *The Darkest Hour* anthology, explores the theme of race on a different level. *The Moon Chaser* is a spinoff story from the *Shanghai Story* trilogy. It is a story about Yuan Wen-Ying, Clark's sister. In *Shanghai Story*, Wen-Ying was the character with the most rigid view about race. Her position on this issue would lead to exclusion rather than inclusion. Her views weren't unusual for someone of her time. Such views still manifest itself in our society today from left to right. I wanted to see what someone like her would do if she is thrown into a situation where her mind tells her one thing, but her heart tells her another. What would happen if she falls in love with a man who is Japanese? (Ok, half Japanese, but the challenge is there.)

The Darkest Hour is currently available for pre-order and is due to release on January 22, 2019. (That's the anniversary of D-Day of the Allies' landing on Anzio Beach, for those of you who have read the *Rose of Anzio*.) The character Masao Takeda was introduced in the chapter "Massacre in Nanking." You can find out what happens to him and Wen-Ying in *The Darkest Hour*.

The final installment of this story, *Shanghai Yesterday*, will be released next year. Be sure to sign up for my newsletter if you wish to receive updates on news and release dates.

Alexa Kang
November 2018
www.alexakang.com

AFTERWORD UPDATE

Shanghai Yesterday, the final book of the *Shanghai Story* trilogy, was released on March 20, 2020.

The Darkest Hour anthology was published on January 22, 2019, and became a *USA Today* bestseller. This anthology is now out of print. The novella, *The Moon Chaser*, has been re-released as a standalone, and can be purchased on Amazon.

Shanghai Yesterday
Book Three of the *Shanghai Story* Trilogy

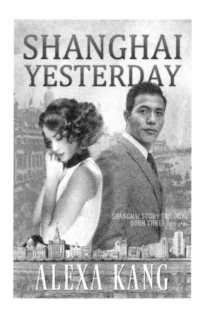

When the twilight dims and the Jewel of the Orient fades, will truth and justice rise again? Will the dreams of yesteryear return to restore all that was withered and lost?

Get your copy now on Amazon

Subscribe for a free story

On his last night in New York, a young grifter sets out to turn the table on those who shorted him before he leaves for the draft. Will he win or lose?

Sign up for my mailing list and receive a free copy of the WWII story **Christmas Eve in the City of Dreams**, plus news on book releases, free stories, and more.

http://alexakang.com/newsletter-2/

About the Author

Alexa is a WWII and 20th century historical fiction author. Her works include the novel series, *Rose of Anzio*, a love story saga that begins in 1940 Chicago and continues on to the historic Battle of Anzio in Italy. Her second series, *Shanghai Story*, chronicles the events in Shanghai leading up to WWII and the history of Jews and Jewish refugees in China. Her other works include the WWII/1980s time-travel love story *Eternal Flame* (a tribute to John Hughes), as well as short stories in the fiction anthologies *Pearl Harbor and More: Stories of December 1942*, *Christmas in Love*, and the USA Today Bestseller *The Darkest Hour*.

I would love to hear from you.
Contact me or follow me at:

www.alexakang.com
alexa@alexakang.com

You can also find me on Facebook and BookBub.

Also by Alexa Kang

The Rose of Anzio Series

*A sweeping saga of love and war, **Rose of Anzio** takes you from 1940s Chicago to the WWII Battle of Anzio in Italy and beyond.*

Book One ~ Moonlight

Book Two ~ Jalousie

Book Three ~ Desire

Book Four ~ Remembrance

New Release

Nisei War Series Book One

Last Night with Tokyo Rose

Official Release Date: January 22, 2021

Get your copy now on Amazon

Read free on Kindle Unlimited